# the Impaler's Wife

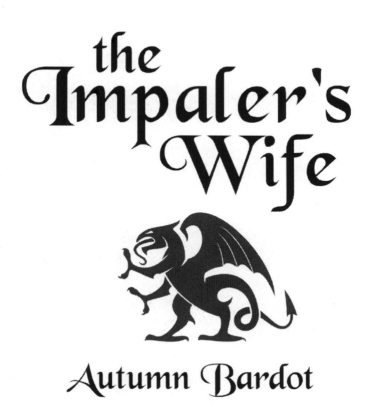

## Autumn Bardot

Flores Publishing

D1546353

# THE IMPALER'S WIFE

AUTUMN BARDOT

FLORES PUBLISHING

**Forest in Hungary**

Seven men in gray robes circled the fire near a frost-covered riverbank. Their chants rose above leafless ice-glazed trees into a frigid starry sky. One man threw back his head and howled. From a distant hill, a lone wolf answered. A second man howled. This time the wolf pack joined, men and beasts united, their wail a bestial invocation.

Nearby, a mist thickened over the river and gathered into a half-formed specter. The breeze shifted. The murky apparition crept forward, advancing like a lynx stalking its prey until it enfolded the men in a vaporous blanket. It swallowed their chants. Devoured their howls.

The phantasmic fog stretched its ether arms into the forest, curled around trees like an embracing lover before it thinned, faded, and dissolved.

The men were gone. Not so much as a footprint remained.

From behind a dense thicket not far away, a man watched the ancient ritual. He pulled a worn book from his cloak, ran his hand over the familiar cracked leather cover with reverence, and opened to the page marked with a red silk ribbon. He read one passage three times.

"I *will* discover your secrets." Vlad Dracula closed the book and pressed it tight to his chest.

## Ilona

**Spring 1464**
**Székesfehérvár, Hungary**

"That's my future husband." My sister Margit jabs me with her elbow. "Prince Vlad."

Stunned by her announcement, I scoot forward on the bench and crane my neck. The cathedral is packed with dignitaries for cousin Matthias's coronation. Getting a clear view of Prince Vlad seated with all the other nobles across the aisle proves difficult. I lean forward but it's futile, a stout nobleman blocks the way. Another inch forward...my bottom teeters at the edge of the pew.

Vlad Dracula is a mystery. Courtiers debate his virtues and evils. Even Aunt Orsulya and Aunt Erzsébet argue over the truth of his fierce reputation. Is he really as ruthless as people claim? His nickname, the Impaler Prince, certainly suggests as much.

"Ilona, stop staring." Aunt Orsulya turns her hawk-like eyes on me.

I love my aunt, but her diligent guardianship of my earthly behavior and eternal soul is rather excessive. She takes deathbed promises seriously, especially since it was my dying mother's wish that her daughters obey every royal rule and Catholic creed. "Why is Prince Vlad here? Since when does cousin Matthias–"

"King Matthias."

I roll my eyes. "Since when does King Matthias allow political detainees to attend coronations?"

"I don't know and don't care. Prince Vlad is of no consequence, his imprisonment is nothing but a diplomatic problem."

"Father spoke highly of him," I remind her.

Aunt Orsulya creases her brow. "Unless the diplomatic winds shift Vlad Dracula will remain little more than a condemned potentate with a notorious past." She digs her bony elbow into my side. "Do not catch his eye. He wants to solidify his ties with Hungary by marrying into the Hunyadi family."

My younger sister married before me? And to a prince?! Why am I not considered first? I look down to find my nails digging into my palms, a myriad of questions simmering in the pit of my belly. I sneak a peek at Vlad Dracula seated among members of the Diet. Aunt Orsulya is mistaken about Prince Vlad's insignificance if King Matthias sits him with such distinguished nobles.

Another peek later and the stout noble blocking my view settles back in the pew affording a good long look at Prince Vlad.

He is handsome, although not classically so, his face being much too intense. He wears a plumed cap and mink *baveri*—very rakish—and yet his straight mustache, almond eyes, and long thin nose give him a stern air. He turns to speak to the nobleman next to him, and the severe set of his mouth vanishes as his lips curl upward. His smile is wide and slightly lopsided, all grimness vanishing. I suck in my breath. Smiling Prince Vlad is very handsome and roguishly elegant.

Not only that, he is certain to be far more interesting than all those simpering and dull courtiers who stride like peacocks about the palace.

Aunt Orsulya tugs on my sleeve. "Stop gawking and watch the ceremony."

I give my aunt an innocent smile before pretending to be impressed by the dignitaries in the chancel.

Aunt Orsulya narrows her eyes, frowns, then resumes watching the coronation.

She sees through me but because false smiles are more a courtly grace than a sin I do not worry for my soul. I used to worry about the state of my soul but after listening to the archbishop discuss Eternity and Grace and Penitence the more I think those notions are a way for ecclesiasts to control unschooled farmers and guildsmen. The conniving courtiers and scheming diplomats I know practice a much different creed. One of duplicity, ambition, lust, and cruelty. But of this I must remain silent and hide my understanding of highborn hypocrisy under courtly manners and layers of silk.

Aunt Orsulya pats my arm and leans close, her lips hovering over my ear. "People are watching. At least pretend to be interested."

I am interested in the coronation, just not with the details of every little ritual. The stout noble once again blocks my view of Prince Vlad, and I shift my attention to the ceremonial pageantry.

Dressed in a brocade dalmatic robe and gilded mitre, the Archbishop of Esztergom passes the Holy Crown to the Count Palatine. "Do you accept Matthias Corvinus as King of Hungary?" He lifts the glittering gold crown high in the air for all to see.

"Agreed. So be it. Long live the King!" A chorus of voices rises in the basilica's vaulted nave.

Cousin Matthias's voice booms with confidence as he

promises to protect the Holy Faith, Holy Catholic Church, and the kingdom of Hungary.

Archbishop Dénes Szécsi lowers his head and bestows an exceedingly lengthy blessing. After listening to too many 'exalted this' and "heavenly that" my gaze drifts past the ceremonial-robed nobles to cousin Matthias, Hungary's twenty-one-year-old sovereign. He holds the keys to the kingdom. He alone will decide my destiny and fortune. I ought to be nicer to him.

The verbose prayer ended, I snap back to attention when Matthias prostrates himself at the altar as the choir lifts their voices with the "Litany of Saints."

I do not remain statue-still for long. My feet tap with impatience under my dress, my meandering thoughts like a huchen fish jumping from the Danube. Every noble of any importance is here. In all likelihood my future bridegroom is in this cathedral. My feet stop tapping as prickles of anxiety skitter up my spine. Is my future husband sitting across the aisle? In the pews behind? Who will Matthias choose? A wrinkled old count or a handsome young duke? What treaty will my marriage guarantee? What alliance will it forge? Though the cathedral is heated by hundreds of guests the chill of reality runs through me. I will have no say in Matthias's decision. None at all.

And then I see Aunt Erzsébet, Matthias's mother, sitting two pews ahead. She wields more political influence than any woman I know. Maidservants tremble in her presence. Her ladies-in-waiting bow to her every whim. Even her son the king respects her ideas. Though she's fearsome, I admire her.

Boisterous hurrahs interrupt my grand ambitions, and I join the others in joyful whoops as Matthias brandishes his sword three times.

Margit squeezes my fingers. "Do you think my crown will have diamonds, rubies, sapphires, and emeralds?"

I wiggle my fingers from her too-hard grip. Margit

wearing a crown! A knot of envy gathers in the pit of my stomach. "The crown of Wallachia?"

Margit's brows shoot to her forehead as her head bobs eagerly. "He wants a wedded union with our family."

"He's Matthias's prisoner. Prisoners cannot wed." Can they?

"They do not attend dinners with visiting kings and sultans either, but *he* does. What kind of prisoner is that? Matthias will not detain him forever." Margit flutters long dark eyelashes. "Won't I make a pretty princess? Aunt Erzsébet thinks so."

My foot flinches beneath the voluminous folds of my velvet brocade dress. How foolish of me not to suspect Aunt Erzsébet had a hand in this. "Pretty yes, but beauty has nothing to do with making a strategic marriage."

Margit's finger wraps a blonde tendril that had escaped from her tall hennin. "Aunt Erzsébet thinks Prince Vlad and I are well suited."

I swallow my surprise. "Why is that?"

Margit leans into my shoulder. "Don't make me repeat what everyone thinks."

I roll my eyes but her comment burrows into my gut. Everyone thinks Margit is the prettier sister. With her milk-colored skin, flaxen hair, doe-shaped blue eyes, generous bosom, and high forehead she is the picture of coquettish beauty.

I do not take after the fair side of the family. My looks are inherited from the Báthory clan on my mother's side. I have hair the color of a raven, ash-hued eyes, and fist-sized breasts. I like to think my features convey wit and intelligence. My name, however, suggests altogether different traits. Ilona means 'torch.' Aunt Orsulya claims I must surely harbor the twin sins of lust and rage deep within me, which is another reason she remains diligent about protecting my immortal soul. I disagree. I am neither immodest nor prone to anger.

7

I steal a look at Margit. She is uncommonly pretty but I think she prefers flattery and allure over instinct and intellect. Pretty only gets a woman so far in court. Aunt Erzsébet is proof. And while Margit has never shown any ambitions until today, I find myself thinking more and more of Aunt Erzsébet's influence.

"Don't believe everything Aunt Erzsébet tells you," I say. "We are just pawns in Matthias's chess game."

Margit lays her pale hand to her breast. "Call yourself a pawn but I plan on nights with a prince."

"Only if you don't spread the entrance gate to your rook."

Margit's cornflower blue eyes narrow into slits. "I am a virgin and will remain so until the archbishop bestows the marriage sacrament."

I give Margit's forearm a squeeze. "Your witty repartee is improving."

"Oh, you're teasing me." The tightness in her mouth melts. "Mmm, I must respond to 'rook' then." She taps her finger on her lips. "I would never lower my drawbridge before the nuptials." Her lips press together in a triumphant smile.

We giggle until Aunt Orsulya throws us a stern look and directs our attention to the chancel where King Matthias rides his horse up a small earthen mound of soil collected from all across Hungary—impressive since he's doing this while balancing the crown on his head and holding an orb— points his sword in all four directions and vows to protect his land and people.

Coronation now concluded with spectacle and pomp, I am impatient to leap to my feet and stretch my legs. Aunt Orsulya stays me with an outstretched hand.

"Piety becomes a maiden better than eagerness to depart," she says between lips that don't move.

Margit and I exchange an exasperated look. Fortunately,

we are rescued by Aunt Erzsébet, who breaks free from the throng of well-wishers to pause at our pew and scowl at us.

"Why are they dawdling?" She aims her caustic tongue at Aunt Orsulya before returning her irritated gaze on Margit and me. "Go to the palace and pay homage to my son the king." As Margit and I exit the pew, Aunt Erzsébet sidles next to Aunt Orsulya. "The pretense of piety does not benefit our unmarried cousins unless they become brides of Christ, which will never happen while I draw breath." Her velvet-clad arm snakes out and latches onto Margit as she passes. "I need to speak to you at the palace."

Margit gives me a smug smile the moment Aunt Erzsébet rejoins her doting entourage of ladies-in-waiting and flatterers. "Told you."

Envy and frustration congeal in the pit of my belly. I am next to marry. Not Margit. Have Margit and Aunt Erzsébet grown that close they now conspire in secret? What else does Margit keep from me? I look at my younger sister with fresh eyes and wonder if her innocence is a ruse. Perhaps, she is not as innocent as she appears, and takes lessons in scheming from Aunt Erzsébet.

"Have you and Prince Vlad been introduced?" My voice drips honey, my question sweetly harmless.

"Not formally." Margit leans in. "I was passing through the small chambers when I came upon him admiring Father's portrait. After introducing myself as Mihály Szilágy's youngest daughter we exchanged a few pleasantries. He even confessed to being struck by my beauty."

"I heard he's very courtly." My voice is tight with envy.

Margit looks down her nose. "I heard he has an eye for beauty." Her mouth presses into a superior smirk before stepping into our garland-festooned royal litter.

I climb in after her and take a seat by the open window.

Aunt Orsulya, sitting opposite, presses a handkerchief to her forehead. "A magnificent day." She peeks through the curtained window at the long line of litters in the courtyard. "It will be a tediously slow ride up the hill."

"Should we walk?" I smooth my dress.

"Walk?" Aunt Orsulya's nose wrinkles as though she smells rotten food. "Among the rabble? You are a saucy girl, Ilona." Aunt Orsulya flutters her gilded fan in front of her flushed face. "Pull back the curtains. It's much too hot in here."

I peer out the window. A warm breeze caresses my cheek. The streets are alive with music, a thousand merry celebrants singing my cares away. The basilica bells peal, the tuneful clanging rising over the boisterous crowd. Street musicians play. Common folk dance jigs in the street. Merchants hawk trinkets. Peddlers tout their wares. Fresh figs! Roasted pork! Honeyed pastries! My heart squeezes tight with longing. I would rather be among the common people sharing their honest merriment than ensconced in this festooned carriage.

"Look at all the people." Margit nudges me sideways to look out the window. "Every Hungarian in the land must be celebrating Matthias's coronation."

"Maybe it's because Matthias promised free food, ale, and entertainment for everyone," I say.

Margit wrinkles her nose. "Do you have to be so cynical?"

I flinch. "I'm just stating the obvious."

Suddenly, an old hag's face fills the window. "Princess!" Her withered hand clutches the casement as she flashes a toothless grin. "Do not seek the book."

## 3

I recoil from the carriage window, away from the garlic-laced voice, away from the dirt-ragged nails, away from the filth and stench of poverty. "I am not a princess."

"You will be." Dun-hued eyes glazed with madness, the hag cackles, and thumps her fist on the carriage before disappearing into the throng.

Aunt Orsulya dabs at the sweat beading above her lip with an embroidered linen handkerchief. "A gypsy." She waves her hand across her nose as though dispelling the odor of the poor. "I wonder how she eluded the royal guards?"

"I want to meet a gypsy." Margit unfurls her fingers and stares at her palm. "A courtier told me they predict the future by reading the lines in your hand."

"They're more likely to snatch off your rings." Aunt Orsulya sniffs with disapproval.

Margit tilts her head into mine, and whispers, "The gypsy is prophesying to the wrong sister. I will be a princess, not you."

"Pagans and infidels," continues Aunt Orsulya. "Doomed to wander the world for seven years for crimes against the Christian faith."

"Aunt Orsulya, you must not condemn an entire group of people." My voice tightens in my throat. "Anyway, if that were true then the gypsies' seven-year debt would have been paid hundreds of years ago."

Aunt Orsulya squints at me. "I do not appreciate your insolence, Ilona. Be mindful, excessive intellect in a maiden is not appealing to a man."

I cross my arms and look away.

"I don't care if gypsies are heathens," says Margit. "I want one to tell my future, my royal future."

"Only God knows your fate." Aunt Orsulya wipes away the sweat trickling from her heavy headpiece.

From my window seat I watch the troupe of acrobats bounding by, their joyful leaping and tumbling like a salve to Aunt Orsulya's hurtful comment.

The townsfolk stop to watch, blocking the street and waylaying the long line of royal litters, including ours. The acrobats take advantage of their captive noble audience. One colorfully dressed troupe member bows low. The second leaps on his back. A third, a nimble slight youth, springs onto his shoulders, shakes his head, jingling the bells on his striped hat.

"Long live King Matthias!" He shouts.

"Bravo." Margit laughs and stretches her coin-filled hand through the window.

But it is not one of the acrobats who takes it.

A young wench in a dirty shawl plucks the coin from Margit's hand. "Pain will be your pleasure, princess."

Margit jerks back, her hand clutching mine.

"Pay no attention to the wench." I give Margit's fingers a sympathetic squeeze.

"Not you, golden locks." The wench, flashing a crooked brown-toothed grin, aims her stony black eyes at me. "The dark-haired one."

The carriage lurches forward, the wench left behind. I

scratch my palm while my heart hammers against my chest. Two mysterious and ominous prophecies in one day!

Do not seek the book. What book? Pain will be my pleasure? How horrible!

"I hate gypsies." Margit fluffs her skirt. "Such repulsive people."

"They do not have the benefit of our privileges," I remind her. "They do what they must to earn money. Anyway, she did not have the dark features of a gypsy." I smile despite the worry knotting in my belly. "I think she was just a mean-spirited wench bent on having fun at our expense."

"Commoners should take a different road to the castle." Margit sniffs with superiority.

My mouth drops open. "Commoners are the lifeblood of Hungary. They are Hungary. Without them who would Matthias rule?" I turn to Aunt Orsulya in hopes she will scold Margit for her snobbishness.

Instead Aunt Orsulya presses her hand to her flower-embroidered bodice. "This is all most vexing, Ilona. You had two dreadful prophecies today." She takes several deep breaths. "It is a sign from God. I will say an extra rosary tonight. So should you."

My hand slips into my dress pocket, my fingers curling around the smooth amber beads that Aunt Orsulya insists we keep on our person at all times. They never provide me the reassurance they give my aunt. "Maybe the prophecies were done in jest." I gesture to the window. "Look how happy everyone is."

"Two prophesies done in jest? I think not." Aunt Orsulya adjusts her hennin. "And even if they were, that type of fun is the work of Satan."

"I thought you said it was a sign from God." I puff out my frustration, shake my head, and try another tact. "How could that old woman—so feeble and bent her wits are gone— discern a princess from a gentlewoman? All her blurry eyes

13

see is a grand carriage taking well-dressed ladies to the castle. To her ilk we are all princesses." I pat the space beside me. "If Margit had been sitting here, she would have received the prophecy."

"And the warning about the book?" Aunt Orsulya pushes her hennin further back on her forehead. "What witty explanation do you have for that?"

I flitter my fingers across my knuckles while thinking. "It's a pagan's warning against the Bible."

Margit crosses her arms, dimples punctuating her smug grin. "What of the wench's prophesy just now about enjoying pain? That prophecy was for you, not me."

"Mmm…" I brush my fingertips across my knuckles again, back and forth, back and forth. "She spoke the truth."

Aunt Orsulya clutches the gold cross at her neck and squeezes her eyes shut. "*In nōmine Patris et Fīliī et Spīritūs Sānctī.*"

I gesture to Aunt Orsulya's new hennin, a towering beaded headpiece adorned with a waist length veil. "What's wrong with your new hennin?"

Aunt Orsulya opens her eyes and shifts the headdress back, which leaves a rosy indent in her forehead. "This style is heavy and pinches my skin."

I nod my head in sympathy. "It's painful and yet you get pleasure from its craftsmanship and elegance."

Margit claps her hands. "I receive pleasure from pain too. These sleeves," she lifts one arm, the silk cuffs dragging to her knees, "are bothersome."

"We all derive pleasure from pain." The knot of worry in my stomach begins unraveling as I untangle the cleverly worded prophecies.

Aunt Orsulya and Margit exchange unconvinced glances.

"Lent is another example," I say.

Aunt Orsulya's eyes flick upward at the slated wood ceiling as though God is listening. "Mind your tongue."

I don't. "Isn't Lent a time when we are supposed to experience spiritual delight from the pain of foregoing some physical pleasure?"

Aunt Orsulya reaches for the crucifix hanging from the blue silk cord around her neck. "I suppose."

"Don't you see?" I splay my hands. "It was wordplay meant to confound us, nothing more. Had that wench been a lady from Matthias's court we would have praised her mischievous wit."

Aunt Orsulya narrows her eyes and lifts the crucifix to her lips. "Finding a husband for you will be difficult if you insist on flaunting your intellect."

I tap my chin pretending contemplation. "Then you and Aunt Erzsébet must find me a very intelligent man."

"Or else a very stupid one," giggles Margit.

"The Hungarian court has no shortage of fools." Aunt Orsulya bursts into laughter.

Ensconced in our litter and free from prying eyes, we laugh loud and long. Aunt Orsulya wipes away merry tears and I puzzle—not for the first time—over her misfortunes. Widowed before she conceived a child, Aunt Orsulya always behaves with proper courtesies and shows a zealous devotion to God. In private, another side emerges, her disdain for men revealed through quips and criticism.

The litter stops and our heads swivel to the window. A boisterous and jolly crowd is amassed outside the castle gate where celebrations are already begun. Troubadours play lute, fiddle, vielle, and tambourine. Castle servants set large platters of bread, meat, and casks of wine and ale on long rough-hewn tables. A troupe of thespians struts across a raised platform with bows and curtsies mimicking lewd acts.

"King Matthias spared no expense." Aunt Orsulya picks off a bit of lint from her sleeve.

The liveried guards wave us through the entrance gate and into a courtyard bustling with servants, gentry, and even more entertainers. Jugglers leap through hoops and toss plates. A tiny monkey wearing a top hat rides a large hound. A jester on stilts walks a man on a leash.

I step down from the litter and rush into the welcoming arms of relatives, some who traveled great distances to attend the coronation. Pausing only to hug nephews, kiss nieces, and embrace friends, I wend my way through the crowd intent on reaching my oldest sister Jusztina—married and living far away—when Aunt Erzsébet, her face pinched with disapproval, blocks my path.

"Pay homage to King Matthias first." Aunt Erzsébet's voice is a clipped whisper. "Together." She nudges Margit, also conscripted into this most urgent duty.

I flash sister Jusztina waiting nearby an exasperated look. She rolls her eyes.

"I suppose as a pair we are more impressive than either of us individually," I say to Margit as we join all the other sumptuously dressed and decadently jeweled well-wishers in line.

Ahead of us and dabbing her neck with a handkerchief, Aunt Orsulya waits with her good friend, Lady Zsazsa. I like the woman, she is funny and honest, but her dresses do tend to be scandalous. Today is no exception. Her cleavage-baring brightly colored frock is better suited for a young unmarried maiden, not a middle-aged widow. The prude and the voluptuary: their friendship defies my understanding.

Margit squeezes my elbow. "He's coming this way."

Returning from his audience with King Matthias, Prince Vlad works his way down the receiving line, pausing to greet nobles and diplomats. His swaggering stride is equal parts warrior and prince. My heart races as he draws near, his arrogant manner both intimidating and enticing. Dressed in green velvet with a floor-length robe draping from his broad shoulders, he turns his head as though he feels he is being watched.

I am caught! My face blooms with heat and I drop my gaze to the floor.

I hear Margit's quick inhalation and the air crackles with expectancy as we wait for his approach.

"Lady Margit." Prince Vlad bows low. "It is an honor to see you on this joyous occasion."

Margit smiles wide, all dimples and doe-eyed beauty. Prince Vlad's own smile is composed and tight, the slight curve of his lips visible beneath his straight chestnut-haired mustache.

Margit curtsies. "I cannot recall a more celebrated day in my life, but then I am only sixteen years." She bats her eyes. "Have you met my sister Ilona?"

Vlad bows, I curtsy, and our eyes lock. A thousand butterflies beat against my stomach. His moss-green eyes sparkle with something beyond polite interest. His gaze, focused and intense, ensnares me. I cannot look away; his eyes keep me as pinioned as the exotic butterflies Matthias displays in his library. My body leans forward, pulled in by a man who feels like a force of nature. I swallow, my mouth filling with moisture as though a delicious supper waits. No wonder Margit is enamored.

"Delighted to meet you." Vlad Dracula's gaze travels down my neck and lingers on my bosom.

My body warms, the layers of silk feeling transparent with the prince's brazen study of my pearl-encrusted bodice. Even as my skin burns with the thrill of his attentions, I sense something beneath his emerald scrutiny that sends the chill of danger into the heated caldron in my belly. The steam it creates within me is a singular sensation, the vapor of seduction awakening both skin and soul. My breasts heave of their own accord.

"Your sister found me admiring a portrait of your father." Vlad Dracula lifts his penetratingly clear eyes to mine. "Mihály was more than my mentor, he was like a father to me." His gaze is hypnotic.

17

I can scarcely breathe and yet my pulse beats double time. "It's my favorite portrait of him."

"It looks exactly like Father." Margit's interruption breaks the spell between us.

"Really?" Prince Vlad's brow furrows. "I must confess, I do not think the artist truly captured his valor and wisdom."

"No artist would be capable of such a feat." I nod with eagerness. "Father's qualities transcend mere daub and brush."

"Well stated." Prince Vlad tilts his head to take measure of me, his studied look appearing as though he is trying to determine if I am a flatterer or a coquette.

"I think," says Margit too loudly while squaring her shoulders so her generous bosom strains against her flower-embroidered bodice, "the artist did a wonderful job, especially the mustache. His mouth is a little stern though."

Prince Vlad looks sideways at Margit with amusement—or maybe disappointment—and I realize in an instant that Margit and the warrior prince are terribly mismatched. I would be the worthier helpmate.

"Father's cruel death still haunts me." I press my hand to my heart and swallow the lump of grief that returns whenever I remember the horror that befell him. "I pray daily for his soul."

"I pray too." Margit shifts her body forward.

Prince Vlad does not acknowledge her comment, neither with glance nor words. He focuses on me, and I, him. The crowd blurs, conversations mute. I see and hear only him.

"I promise to avenge the sins of Meḥmed-*i sānī*." Prince Vlad's face is grave, his eyes hardening into stone.

"That time cannot come soon enough." I speak quickly and honestly, my blunder unrealized until the last word slips from my lips. I open my mouth to soften my mistake, to rephrase or clarify but it is too late. I see it in Prince Vlad's eyes and my body shrinks into itself.

Prince Vlad's smile stiffens, and his liquid green eyes freeze into emerald ice crystals.

Margit's eyes light up upon hearing my gaffe. "Matthias and I are very close," she lies. "I will explain that your talents best serve Hungary if you are released from your imprisonment and free to destroy Sultan Mehmed."

A shadow passes over Dracula's eyes. He smiles at Margit like a parent does to a silly young child. The folly in her words—her political ignorance and obvious flattery—exposes a charming naiveté. Which may be her intent.

Margit aims a pointed look at me, her eyes gleaming with friendly competition.

"I agree, my lady, however, I think it best if someone other than a sweet innocent cousin reminds him of my considerable talents." He looks away and down the line of well-wishers, then gives us a tight nod. "Enough of politics and vendettas, Matthias's coronation deserves nothing less than jubilant celebration and happy thoughts." Prince Vlad bows low. "I humbly beg your leave. Lady Margit and Lady Ilona, it is an honor and pleasure to make your acquaintances. I can now say with all sincerity that King Matthias's cousins are the most enchanting ladies in all of Hungary."

Margit blushes and dips in curtsy. I curtsy as well, his gaze like hot coals on my skin. At that moment I know I want him. It is a foolish thought. I have no say in the matter of a husband. But reality does not matter to my pounding heart and enraptured soul.

"He will wed me," Margit says when he is out of hearing. "Aunt Erzsébet will make certain of it." She turns to me, bright pink spots on her cheeks. "Why were you making eyes at him?"

"I was being cordial." Though the heat of Prince Vlad's gaze still warms me, I tell a cold but necessary lie. "Don't you want me to be nice to my future brother-in law?"

"Not that nice." Margit's lips pinch together.

Unable to meet her accusatory glare, I look over her shoulder to check our position in the receiving line. "Only Lord and Lady Magyar are ahead of us. Look, you can see the jewels on Matthias's crown sparkling from here."

Distracted by royal gems, Margit's pursed lips melt into a giddy smile.

Our cousin king sparkles as well in a sumptuous red brocade robe with a white ermine collar that emphasizes the flaxen hair grazing his shoulder. Sitting tall on his throne, he beams with majestic munificence despite his recent tragedies. Only a few months earlier we wept over the untimely death of his bride and newborn babe. Today, however, Matthias sits ramrod straight and content, his wife's and child's passing hidden under his royal vestments. What fortitude and control it must take to rally oneself for a public function.

"I heard Aunt Erzsébet wants Matthias to wed Emperor Frederick's daughter," I whisper as we step closer to the dais.

"What? So soon? Our aunt has no compassion," Margit whispers back. "He's still grieving."

"Political alliances come first." Like all noble maidens, Margit and I desire a lucrative marriage, dream of a love match, and worry about producing a male heir.

Mother took to childbed five times. Only three daughters survived. Mother died soaked in blood, the yearned for male heir breathing his last a day later. I often wondered if Margit and I inherited Mother's only weakness, producing daughters. It certainly is not a family trait. Aunt Erzsébet birthed two sons. The first, László, was beheaded by a vengeful Habsburg king a few years ago. Matthias is her second. And had it not been for Father's clever political maneuvering, Matthias would not be king of Hungary.

I step up to the dais with Margit.

"King Matthias." I curtsy low. "Hungary will soar to new heights under your excellent leadership."

Ignoring protocol, King Matthias holds his arms wide for

a hug. "I will accept nothing less than a kiss from my favorite cousins."

We kiss his cheek and then proceed to praise the music, commend the choir, and applaud the pageantry, extolling His Highness until he flushes with pleasure.

"Margit," says Matthias with an impish grin, "you stare at my crown like it's a fig-stuffed capon. Have you an appetite for ambition?"

"Ambition?" Margit's brows lift in surprise. "Only for a good marriage, but I dare say your crown is nothing less than a banquet of jewels."

Matthias chuckles before glancing at the Roman diplomat waiting behind us. "Will you make me a promise, sweet cousins?"

"Anything," Margit and I reply in unison.

"Promise you will dance until dawn to prove your love of sovereign and country."

We vow to have fun, curtsy, and depart. Our duty dispatched, Margit and I stroll back down the line, stopping to chat with relatives and friends.

When we reach the great hall a red-haired stranger bars our entrance.

"May the Lord bless King Matthias with a long and prosperous reign." The woman lifts her pointy chin in the air.

"Thank you for your kind words," I say. "Who do I have the pleasure of speaking to?"

"My name is not important. You have little use for it." She clasps slim pale hands in front of her and lowers her voice. "I come bearing a prophecy for you, Lady Ilona."

My breath catches and my skin prickles with fear. Three prophecies in one afternoon cannot be good. I make a quick study of the woman's credibility. She wears a simple yet artfully draped pink silk gown with a large ruby pendant against her alabaster throat. Her delicate hands are smooth and soft, unblemished from fieldwork and labor. Nothing about her elegant appearance suggests she is a guildsman's wife, gypsy, or common wench.

I take a slow calming breath and present my most polite smile. "You're not the first."

The woman's ginger eyebrows lift. "Then you will not be surprised when I tell you my prophecy concerns your future husband."

## 4

Despite my heart knocking in my chest I smile at this stranger with storm colored eyes and keep my voice steady. "I'm honored by your gift of augury."

The woman flicks her eyes right and left, making sure no others are within hearing and steps forward. "Your husband will live forever."

My anxiety vanishes and my lips twitch to suppress a giggle. Margit, however, lets out an unmaidenly chortle.

The stranger's mood changes in an instant. Coldness replaces warmth and her gray eyes harden. "Lady Ilona, mark my words." She curtsies. "Good day." She pivots on her heels, the folds of her pink skirt swaying angrily as she strides down the long corridor.

Margit touches my arm. "Is she part of the entertainment?"

"If so, she is not likely to be hired again."

"Maybe Matthias hired her to provoke conversation by creating rumor and mystery."

"That must be it. Remember when he hired four men to start a brawl a year ago?" The fake blood had splattered on the floor before the first punch was thrown. The players, unfazed, quickly traded drama for buffoonery. "Perhaps her job is to inspire a battle of witty word play." I remember the bronze statue in the front of Buda Palace memorializing the Holy Roman Emperor. "I suppose someone's deeds can make them live forever. Like King Sigismund. Or my future husband might be a scholar and write a book, and his words live forever." Bibliotheca Corviniana, the palace library, is full of manuscripts and treatises by modern and ancient philosophers.

"Or be a painter," says Margit. "His portraits passed from generation to generation."

Relieved to have found a logical excuse for the stranger's unsettling and heretical prophecy, I turn around to call her back. She is gone. Vanished. A remarkable feat considering the length of the passageway.

"I cannot wait to tell everyone that you had three prophecies today." Margit's voice has an odd lilt. "How delicious."

"Please don't tell Aunt Orsulya about this or she'll have me saying the rosary three times a day for weeks. Please." My pleading sounds pathetic but I'm worried. Three prophecies! Maybe it is a warning from God.

Margit frowns. "Oh, fine. It will be our little secret." Margit grabs my hand and tugs me into the great hall where the celebration is well under way.

The hour passes quickly, conversations about frocks, friends, and food keeping tongues wagging and ears burning until King Matthias arrives. I do not see the stranger in pink again, but I do see Prince Vlad looking my way three times.

King Matthias arrives with great pomp and signals the beginning of the feast. Squires bring silver bowls of rosewater for hand washing. Servants cover the tables with fringed tapestries, strew sweet herbs about, and place trenchers of bread and bowls of fish stew on the tables. A skinny and eager young page escorts me to the royal table. I take my seat, marveling with the others at the whimsical centerpiece, a miniature of Buda castle festooned with tulips, lilacs, peonies, daisies, and peacock feathers.

I look over my shoulder and see Prince Vlad sitting with the officers at a table nearby. Our eyes meet. His gaze ensnares me, and I cannot turn away. I should not be flirting with him, or he with me. My face flames with embarrassment and I wrench away, the heat of guilt mixing with the warmth of pleasure.

"I'm going to eat until I burst." Margit spears a hunk of veal covered in sweet fig sauce. "Men like women with an appetite."

I pick at my own trencher heaped with food, nervous excitement dulling my appetite. Prince Vlad is flirting with me! Despite Aunt Erzsébet's plans to wed him to Margit. I dare not get in Aunt Erzsébet's way. I don't want to hurt Margit but…I glance over my shoulder.

As if sensing he is being watched, Prince Vlad slowly turns his head. Like a skilled marksman he aims his gaze straight at me. I smile back, and then pink-cheeked with pleasure return to the uneaten delicacies in front of me.

Squires and pages bring the second course, and the third, and the fourth, each more extravagant than the last—roe deer, sturgeon, rabbit, capon, swan, crane, and heron—each stuffed with apples, dates, almonds, and herbs. I eat lightly, my belly aflutter as though a thousand butterflies try to escape. I press my lips to suppress a giggle as I imagine these butterflies fluttering their delicate wings around Prince Vlad.

The fifth course arrives, pastries dripping with plum preserves, mulberries in sugar, fruit jellies, custard flavored with rose water, and marzipan sculpted in Matthias's coat of arms. Nothing, however, is sweeter than Prince Vlad's attentions.

Throughout dessert, dignitaries stop by the table to toast King Matthias.

A fat drunk nobleman with crumbs in his beard and

wearing a crimson mantel and tight wide belt staggers toward the table. "To His Highness. *Egészségedre.*" He lifts his goblet.

"Who is that ridiculous man? He looks like an overstuffed sausage," I whisper to Margit.

"That's Luigi della Scala. He's the *capitano grande* of Genoa."

The *capitano grande* leers at me. I look away.

"I think he likes you." Margit smears jam on her pastry. "I wonder if Matthias needs to align himself with families from Genoa? Who knows, maybe he will be your future husband."

"Matthias would never be so cruel."

"Are you certain? What if Matthias needs to seal a diplomatic deal?" Margit wipes a jelly smudge from the corner of her mouth. "Ooh, imagine your wedding night. I wonder if you'll be able to breathe with him on top of you? His fat appendage will certainly leave you panting for more."

I wrinkle my nose. "I'll have no choice but to pray his heart stops before he deflowers me."

"Why? You'll just be wed to the next man offering political advantage." Margit shoves the pastry into her mouth. "Farmers and merchants make love matches, why can't we?"

"Because even we pawns are useful in King Matthias's chess game." I steal a glance at Prince Vlad, who is engaged in a serious-looking discussion with a count, and the weight of certainty crushes down on me. What is the point of flirting with a handsome prince when it will come to naught?

The meal ended, Margit and I join the guests in the courtyard to watch a ropedancer perform tricks from a cord strung high overhead.

Margit looks up. "I hope he falls."

"Is that so?" The deep voice is behind us.

I twist about to find Prince Vlad wearing an expansive grin.

Margit's hand flies to her bosom. "You misunderstand."

"In what way?" Dracula's eyes, reflecting the fire basket's flames, glow with mischief.

"Um..." Margit swivels toward me, her eyes begging for help.

"Margit misspeaks," I say to Prince Vlad, my voice light. "The ropedancers have a clever stunt of pretending to slip. They never fall and always snag the rope with their teeth. It makes my heart pound no matter how often I've seen their old trick."

"Ah," Vlad Dracula tilts his head, his expression inscrutable. "I thought perhaps Margit enjoyed bloody spectacles."

Margit shakes her head, her golden ringlets glinting in the firelight. "The sight of blood terrifies me."

"Ah, and rightly so." Prince Vlad nods but the quick crease in his chin suggests disappointment. He shifts his attention to me. "Do you enjoy blood sports, Lady Ilona?"

I chew my lip in thought, his question hardly surprising. Prince Vlad is a fierce warlord whose military tactics are feared and respected. Thousands of soldiers killed for him. Thousands more died because of him. His question is a trick, one designed to take measure of me. He obviously seeks a wife who understands the hard realities of royal life, but I will not pander to him. "Blood is death and life. Blood is battle and sport. Blood is heritage and destiny. I do not shirk from it."

"You possess the soul of a warrior." His eyes shine with admiration.

"You are very polite, Prince Vlad," says Margit too loudly, "to indulge my sister's gory talk."

"I find it is more about glory than gore." Vlad glances up when the crowd gasps.

The ropedancer hangs by his teeth.

Instead of watching the ropedancer's contortions back to a balanced pose, I study the curves and angles of Prince

Vlad's face. His true emotions happen below the handsome controlled surface, his genuine feelings revealed in the briefest tightening of eye, cheek, and jaw.

Sensing he is being watched, he bends his gaze to me. "I'm an apathetic spectator and prefer action."

Once again, his gaze ensnares me. I cannot look away, his eyes wolf-like with intensity. The green depths convey lust, determination, but also a hidden sorrow. My heart clenches. I want to touch his face, comfort him, understand his grief. And yet I do not move, can barely draw breath. I am captured heart, mind, and soul.

"This is boring. Shall we dance?" Margit offers her arm.

Dracula is slow to loop Margit's arm through his. But perhaps his seeming reluctance is my own wishful thinking.

As they stroll toward the dance floor, I stand rooted to the ground, controlled breaths doing little to cool my heated annoyance at Margit. Never before have I felt a connection to a man. Never before did a man look at me with such desire. Never before have Margit and I been competitors. It is a rivalry I have no practice at.

With Margit clutching his arm, Prince Vlad stops and makes a slow pivot. "Lady Ilona, will you join us?"

"Happily."

Though he waits in the shadows beyond the fire basket's radiance, I feel our connection, like a quivering string or a taut ribbon. I move forward, reeled in by a man with a dark past.

After dancing with Margit, Prince Vlad asks me to take a turn about the floor. We clap in sync with the other dancers and I circle around him, our eyes locked on one another. He makes me feel like I am the only one in the room. I blush and grin, my cheeks fevered under his gaze. Though I know every step of this dance I am unprepared for what happens next.

Prince Vlad takes my hand, his strong warm fingers enclosing mine. The jolt races up my arm and bursts like a dam through my body. My skin is washed with a sparkling sensation, skin and limbs stirred with the thrill of his touch. The next step brings us too close—kissing close—and I smell his scent. Rosemary, leather, forest, and man. Surely, he hears my heart knocking against my bodice. Prince Vlad inhales deeply and bends his head into my neck. I gasp with desire, want to feel the graze of his cheek or tickle of his moustache against my skin.

Instead he shifts about, his brazen move but a momentary disruption in the dance steps.

"Is that how they dance in Wallachia?" I ask when we next clasp hands.

"That is how I dance with a beautiful woman." His fingers warm around mine.

I blush, stammer a thank you, and wonder at the curious tightening between my legs.

That evening, Prince Vlad dances with many other court ladies. He is grace and wit, mingling among the guests with charming elegance. He acts nothing like a dangerous man kept captive against his will.

The yawning partygoers begin returning to their rooms just before dawn. I wait under the arched entrance for Margit, who stands across the great hall in a tight little circle with Prince Vlad, Aunt Erzsébet, and Aunt Orsulya. All four turn their heads my way, Margit's shoulders shaking with laughter.

They made a joke about me! I hide my balled fists in the folds of my skirt.

Margit leaves the group and crosses the marble expanse. "Aunt Orsulya bids us goodnight." She covers a yawn with her hand. "She'll probably wake us in a few hours for morning prayers in the chapel."

Early morning prayers I will tolerate. Being mocked I will not. "What was so amusing?"

Margit shakes her head and flaps her hand. "Nothing."

"If nothing makes them stare at me then I will consider myself a grand success."

"Sister, your only success today was receiving three obscure prophecies. Aunt Erzsébet said celebration days always bring out the charlatans and we all agreed." Margit pats my arm. "Don't be cross."

"You promised not to say anything," I hiss.

Margit's crooked smile is all pretend shame. "Sorry."

"You made fun of me." My belly twists, all hopes of keeping Dracula's favor vanishing like a mouse down a hole.

"Not you, the prophecies," she snaps.

I want to grab her arm and yank the truth from her, but I know her stubbornness too well. She would never admit to undermining me. The air is thick with silent anger as our skirts whisk across the stone hallway to our chambers.

Margit stops at her door. "Why are you upset? Do you think Prince Vlad's good opinion of you is diminished?"

"By mocking the prophecies, you mock me."

Margit grimaces. "Our sister bond runs too deep to quarrel over a twice-deposed and imprisoned prince."

I shake my head with feigned exasperation. "It's cousin Matthias's fault. He does not invite near enough handsome princes to parties."

"Agreed." Margit laughs, my attempt to squash the argument successful.

I ROLL over and rub eyes blurry from too little sleep and too much fun. Sunlight streams through the window, the bright swath across the floor a sign the morning meal is passed.

"Good afternoon, my lady." Bernádett brushes the dusty hem on last night's frock.

I sit up and say a silent prayer of thanks for my wonderful maidservant. It has been many years since Father saved her from poverty by bringing her here. The daughter of an obscure deceased relative, Father said Bernádett's only chance for a comfortable life came by serving our family. She was a hollowed-eyed young waif then—the result of a childhood spent in a household where fresh meat was scarce and onion-laden bread the rule.

"I brought some bread and cheese from the scullery." Bernádett points to the bedside table.

"Perfect. I'm famished." I snatch a lavender-scented roll from the plate and take a bite. "Margit expects she will be betrothed soon."

Bernádett stops brushing. "Does she now?" She sets down the brush, crosses the room, opens the door, and peers outside. Satisfied no one lurks about, she returns to my bedside. "I heard Lady Margit crying this morning. I know how a spot on her frock or pulled thread on her hennin upset her and offered my services to her maidservant Peroska."

"Very thoughtful." Knowing Bernádett's love of gossip and eavesdropping, my mouth curls into an impish grin. "What did Peroska tell you?"

"Margit is distraught over her betrothed's preference for you." She cocks a thin auburn eyebrow. "Large as a rabbit my ears grew at that bit of news. I tell Peroska that wine will soothe her mistress's broken heart and quick as a hare I run to the scullery but not before leaving the door open a wee crack."

I wag my finger. "Your eavesdropping will get you into trouble one day."

Bernádett shrugs. "Or get you out of trouble."

"I never do anything I shouldn't." I stuff the last bite of bread in my mouth. "Well? What did you hear?"

"It seems Margit's joke about a gypsy's prophecy failed. Instead of laughing at you, her betrothed declared his fondness for a maiden with a logical mind." Bernádett pushes away a lock of red hair. "She said her betrothed looks at you like a cat spying a plate of cream."

I sit up straighter. "Really? Oh Bernádett, he is a handsome prince—the perfect age. Not young enough to be immature, not old enough to be ugly. And he is not betrothed to Bernádett. Not officially."

"Do you like him?" Bernádett opens a tall cupboard.

"Very much. He and Father were friends and battled together against the Turks." I pick up a small wedge of cheese. "Anyway, he's not allowed to marry anyone because he's a political prisoner."

"Then why does Margit believe this man is her betrothed?"

"Aunt Erzsébet told her it might be a possibility." I swing my feet over the bed.

"And he prefers you?" She hangs up my dress.

"Maybe." Heat blooms on my cheeks as I recall the secret looks Prince Vlad and I shared. I long to tell Bernádett about the invisible string pulling me towards him. I want to explain how my heart pounds and body warms around him. I don't. It's not because I don't trust her—I trust her with my life—but rather that I feel silly expressing these thoughts out loud.

"My lady, guard your heart. Do not let it be stolen by a handsome face and silver tongue. Men are scoundrels."

"Not all of them."

"Most." Bernádett frowns. "What's the name of the prince causing this cat fight?"

"Vlad Dracula."

The brush clatters to the floor.

Bernádett's hands fly to her heart. "Oh, my lady, no! Surely you've heard about his horrific deeds!"

# 5

## Vlad

**Spring 1442**
**Tîrgovişte Castle, Wallachia**

Eleven-year-old Vlad grimaced as his mother fawned over his little brother. "Radu is seven-years-old, Lady Mother." Vlad swiped the heel of his leather boot back and forth across the plush Turkish rug. "How will he learn a warrior's courage if you fuss over a scratch on his cheek?"

Princess Cneajna ruffled Radu's hair. "He is a child, and you, Vlad, are far too old for your age. Have you forgotten how we doted on you after you fell off your horse?"

"I was five. The riding instructor told me to gallop bare-backed." Vlad glanced at his mother's three attendants. He rather enjoyed visiting the flower-scented ladies' chambers and the sweet-faced women with their quick smiles and milky white cleavage.

The princess waved a bejeweled hand. "Wasn't it only last month you showed us the nick on your finger from the fencing master?"

Vlad's face warmed from the memory. A milk-filled wet

nurse had thrust his head into her bosom while comforting him, the stirring that followed proving him a man.

"I'm glad Lord Father did not notice my wound." Vlad inspected the thin red line on his finger.

Princess Cneajna kissed Radu's forehead. "Vlad says we are not to make a woman of you, my sweet." She looked at her ladies. "How quickly time passes. It seems like only yesterday my sons were small. Now Mircea and Vlad show the same strength and courage as their father."

Their father was Dracul, bastard son of Mircea the Great. Dracul had scratched and clawed his way from insignificant page to respected warlord by slaying several half-brothers— legitimate heirs each one—to earn his royal place in the world. His investiture into the elite Order of the Dragon added a dragon to his shield, an unfortunate heraldry because many associated the dragon with the devil, and not the Order's oath to protect Christendom.

Princess Cneajna's eyes grew misty with pride as she looked at Vlad. Her husband's ambitions for his middle child had already born fruit. Schooling and athletic training had strengthened him. Though she had wept when her husband had taken the children outside in the sleet and snow she approved of the results. Her two oldest were robust and tough little men.

Princess Cneajna stroked Radu's golden hair. If only she could keep her youngest son innocent a few more years. Before political treachery made him suspicious. Before military leadership made him arrogant.

Radu burrowed into his mother's abundant bosom. Princess Cneajna held him tight, remembering a simpler time when fishing, jousting, archery and reading filled her sons' days. No more.

Dracul's capture of Tîrgoviște after crushing the invading Turks changed their lives. Now that Dracul was the Prince of Wallachia, he demanded his sons—his future heirs—begin their apprenticeship for knighthood. Days were busy with athletic training, their afternoons taken up with learning Italian, French, and Hungarian. Her sons' candle-lit evenings spent writing in Cyrillic, Slavonic, and Latin.

"Lady Mother." Vlad stomped his feet and pouted. "I insist you let go of Radu. We need to go somewhere important."

Princess Cneajna held Radu's pink-cheeked face between her palms, tilted his head, and kissed both tear-soaked eyes. "Never be ashamed of your tears, Radu."

Radu blinked, snot running from his nose, and pointed to Vlad. "Vlad never cries. Not even when we watched a traitor hang in the town square."

Vlad lifted his chin and squared his shoulders. "Why should I? The man deserved it. Father said his death was the perfect example of *raison d' état*—national interests reign supreme."

Princess Cneajna shuddered. To think her eleven-year-old son already understood the cruel reality of maintaining rule.

Vlad tugged on Radu's arm, and Princess Cneajna released her youngest into the care of her earnest middle child.

"Noooo," wailed Radu, his arms reaching for his mother as Vlad pulled him away.

"Thank you, Lady Mother." Vlad gave Radu's arm a yank. "Stop crying or I'll give you something to cry about."

"Vlad." Princess Cneajna's voice was sharp. "You are much too rough with him."

Vlad loosened his grip. "Lord Father says we must be tougher than everyone else."

"Why?" Radu dragged a long trail of snot across his pink-splotched cheeks.

Vlad thumped his chest. "Because warriors do not respect weakness."

Radu wiped his tears away. "I hate you."

"Radu!" Princess Cneajna admonished. "You do not hate your brother."

Vlad shrugged and looked at his mother. "Lord Father says it is better to be hated than be thought weak." He wrapped his hand around Radu's arm and steered him across the Turkish carpet toward the door. "One day you and I will fight side by side—brothers-in-arms. Will I be able to depend on you? Or will you run into the forest like a coward?"

"I'm no coward." Radu shook his head, his golden hair shining bright as a halo in the streaming sunlight that poured through the open window.

"Good. Lord Father says it will one day be our duty to keep Wallachia safe from the infidel Turks. Will you be ready?"

"Grrrr." Radu bared his teeth. "I'm a warrior."

"That's better." Vlad released his grip on Radu's arm.

"Where are we going?"

"Lord Father is meeting with important boyars," said Vlad as they turned the corner.

Radu wrinkled his nose. "That's boring."

Vlad wiped the snot smear from Radu's face with the edge of his sleeve. "How else will you learn about war and politics?"

"You'll teach me." Radu wiggled as he submitted to Vlad's impatient face cleaning.

"I'm not an expert. Yet." Vlad quickened his pace.

Radu hurried after him through several dim chambers where colorful tapestries came alive in the flickering candlelight.

A surly-looking liveried soldier guarded the thick oak door to the council chambers. When the boys approached, the guard lowered his steel-tipped pike, gave them a conspiratorial wink, and unlocked the heavy iron latch. Vlad and Radu slipped inside.

Vlad slouched against the wall as he studied the ten men

seated around the long, polished oak table. They were boyars, men of high rank, his father's most faithful advisors. They were gray-haired, paunchy, and wrinkled, their warrior days long over.

Vlad caught Mircea's eye from across the room and immediately stood taller. Vlad idolized Mircea. Wanted to be just like him. Tried to emulate his fourteen-year-old brother's good-natured, confident, and assertive manner. Thus far, he had failed. Friendliness felt phony. A show of confidence appeared to others like arrogance. Vlad found aggression far more efficient.

A boyar in a striped turban folded his arms. "The Hungarian king expected us to renew our crusade against the invading Turks."

Mircea leapt from his seat. "Lord Father had no choice but to remain neutral when the bey Şihabeddin entered Wallachia!"

"Mircea." Dracul's voice was sharp with reprimand, yet his thin quick smile revealed pride for his eldest.

Mircea sunk back into the chair and crossed his arms. Across the room, Vlad, in solidarity with his brother, crossed his as well.

A purple-robed boyar curved his neck toward Dracul. "Sultan Murad is not impressed by your halfhearted vassalage, my lord."

"They claim you are an inconsistent prince serving two masters," said a boyar with a scar from forehead to jowl. "Their trust in you is waning. The sultan's request is justified. Go to his court in Gallipoli. Appease him. Dispel his suspicions. Refusing the sultan will have grave repercussions."

Vlad gnawed on his lips at his father's dilemma and imagined a future where he would need to rely on wise counsel. Would he be as discerning as his father? Father had told him that the best advisors spoke their mind and the best rulers were not afraid to hear the truth.

Vlad inhaled the scent of ale and onions and sweat. It was the odor of debate and argument. The fragrance of powerful men making important decisions.

With wide adoring eyes, Vlad watched his father. He missed not a single detail. Not the set of his father's tight jaw. Not his hands clasped as if in prayer held against his grizzled chin. Not the quick narrowing of his eyes. Not the luminous whiteness of his perfectly tied turban. Not the glittering shine of the gem-studded clasps on his father's gown.

Vlad chewed the inside of his cheek waiting for his father's decision. Would Dracul prove his continued vassalage to the sultan by making an official visit? Or would he stand with Hungary? Dracul's precarious position required the balance of a ropedancer. Consolidating power, honoring the Order of the Dragon's vows to protect Christianity, forming alliances, squashing tenant uprisings, and fulfilling Turkish treaties were frequent topics of discussion at the dinner table.

Vlad took a silent step forward in the thick-aired room, his heart thumping with anticipation.

Dracul smacked his meaty palms on the table. "I will pay a visit to Sultan Murad."

The boyars issued a collective exhalation. Anything less might be construed as a declaration of war against the Turks.

Dracul beckoned Vlad and Radu forward. "The shadows are no place for you, my sons. Would you like to take a trip to Gallipoli to visit the sultan?"

Radu flew into his father's arms. "Can I visit a harem?"

Radu's question broke the somber mood, and the boyars burst out laughing.

"I second the request." The boyar in the striped turban hoisted his wine goblet.

Dracul's almond-shaped eyes tapered into an amused web of wrinkles. "Of all the delights in Gallipoli your only interest is a harem?" He ruffled his youngest's hair. "You are too young to enjoy its pleasures."

Vlad bit back a frown and squeezed between two rotund boyars. "Lord Father." He thrust his arm over the map spread wide across the table, and jabbed his finger marking the location of Gallipoli. "This town is on the Aegean Sea, it must be of strategic importance to the Turks."

"Indeed." Dracul beamed at Vlad. "It is a tactical strip of land. The Turks' first step into Christendom."

Vlad flushed with pleasure at his father's approval.

Dracul set his hand on Vlad's shoulder. "Always consider a town's location, evaluate its benefits and faults. Good commanders—victorious commanders—are familiar with their terrain and use it to advantage."

Vlad's head bobbed up and down. "I remember all your wisdom, Lord Father."

TWO MONTHS LATER, Vlad sat astride his horse with the others among the diplomatic entourage awaiting entry in front of Gallipoli's massive iron fortified gates.

Vlad wiped sweat from his brow as the sun blazed hot under an azure sky. He squirmed with impatience, annoyed the breeze from the Aegean did not permeate his thick embroidered cloak and elegant tunic.

Beside him, Radu tugged at the linen shirt tight around his neck. Vlad looked at his father's straight back and patient demeanor and sat taller in his saddle. He stopped fidgeting and waited while the slow-moving Turkish soldiers rolled open the gate.

The hair on Vlad's neck bristled. He swung his head from left to right, glanced over his shoulder. Something felt wrong. The horses snorting and stamping behind him, however, reassured him. Every steed bore strong guards and clever men armed with sharp swords.

On the other side of the gate stood the sultan's welcoming party, a hundred armed guards and one gray-bearded *baluchi bassi* who glared at them from under a white-plumed turban.

The nape of Vlad's neck prickled with cold as he watched his father dismount from his tasseled and velvet-tacked warhorse. After he performed the proper greetings without flaw, the sour-faced *baluchi bassi* beckoned Dracul forward.

Vlad slid off his horse the moment his father signaled his sons to join him.

The icy prickle remained as Vlad followed his father and *baluchi bassi* through the gates.

Suddenly, there was a deafening crash. Vlad whipped his head around. The gates were shut tight. Dracul's guards and entourage locked outside.

Blood pounded in Vlad's ears as the guards drew their scimitars and surrounded them.

"Lord Father?" Vlad's voice squeaked, and his cheeks colored with shame at his fear.

Dracul did not respond.

"Lord Father, what's happening?" Radu cried out as two guards wrenched him from Vlad's side.

Dracul shut his eyes and pressed his lips together as another grim-faced guard pulled Vlad's falchion from his belt.

"Father..." Vlad stared wide-eyed and agape at his powerless father.

Dracul turned away, the sight of his brave little Vlad being bound in chains felt like the weight of a mountain on his defeated shoulders.

"*Tati*," Radu sobbed while a guard tied his hands with rope.

Under a heavy brow knitted with barely controlled rage, Dracul turned his head to the smirking *baluchi bassi*. "What is the meaning of this? We come in peace. Sultan Murad is expecting us. I am Vlad Dracul, Prince of Wallachia. I am here at the sultan's request and to pay him homage."

"Indeed you will, Prince Dracul." The *baluchi bassi* folded his arms, barely giving the boys a glance as his men dragged them from Dracul.

Radu saw Vlad through a veil of tears. "What's happening?"

Vlad opened his mouth, but the thick wool hood thrust over his head muffled his reply.

## 6

## Ilona

### Summer 1464
### Visegrád Castle, Hungary

Warm winds bring the fragrance of flowers and forest to my lofty perch atop Visegrád castle. I sigh, the quiet a brief respite from the constant conversation. This year Aunt Erzsébet invited a crowd of distinguished guests to summer with King Matthias. I have already dined and danced with foreign envoys, Venetian scholars, artisans from Florence, and one obsequious Niccolò Modrussa, a papal legate from Rome.

I tuck a stray lock of hair behind my ear and peer over the low stone wall to watch a lone figure striding toward the riverbank. I recognize the slope of his shoulders, the brisk bounce, and rhythm of his gait. It is Prince Vlad.

Though a guest, he must stay in King Solomon's Tower where other political detainees are housed. I learned from an earlier conversation with Niccolò Modrussa that Prince Vlad resided in the topmost chambers, which delivers a fine prospect of the Danube and a cool river breeze. When I had asked Niccolò Modrussa if the heaven-ensconced King

Solomon finds it strange a prison tower bears his name, he replied that surely earthly concerns no longer mattered to the dead.

Gravel crunches underfoot, my happy solitude interrupted.

"Be careful, one slip and you'll fall." Margit bumps my shoulder. "Is that him?" She points to the figure at the river's edge.

"It is." I step away. Her arrival intrudes upon my shameful ogling of a man I will never have.

"Such a pity." Margit sighs loudly. "A handsome prince I will not be wedding anytime soon."

"Politics is a wind that changes directions." I spin away from the low wall when Prince Vlad turns around. Did he see me gawking? I hope not.

"That wind is not likely to change course. Matthias has no quarrel with Prince Radu." Margit's arm sways like a frantic pendulum as she tries to get Prince Vlad's attention.

"Then why is Prince Vlad summering here with us?"

Margit's head snaps around. "Us? You mean me."

I flinch at her sharp tone. "I did not realize Prince Vlad was transferred here from Buda for *you*."

"There's a lot you do not realize…or know." Margit smirks and sashays toward the vestibule. "Prince Vlad is attending the hawking party tomorrow. Did you know that?"

"Everyone knows that," I lie and wonder why I wasn't told.

At the vestibule's entrance, Margit pivots on her heel. "Did you know Prince Vlad swims naked in the river every morning?"

"You saw him?"

Margit throws back her head with laughter and disappears down the vestibule's steep circular stairwell. The echo sends a shiver down my spine.

I<small>N THE MISTY</small> gloom of dawn's half-light, our hawking party emerges from the narrow trail through the dark woodland into a glade of briars and small saplings.

"Lady Ilona," calls King Matthias from the front of the long line of riders.

I spur my horse forward, my heart leaping with surprised delight to be singled out to ride beside him. "Your Highness?"

King Matthias's gaze travels from my fashionable feathered riding hat to my sensible hawking boots. "I hear you've become quite the hawker."

I blush at his admiring smile. "I have meager skills, Your Highness." I flap my hand back and forth in respectful protest. "I am still learning my bird's temperament." Three years ago, Father gifted me a *niais*, a hawk stolen from its nest and trained by the Grand Falconer. Since then I had greatly improved my hawking skills. Practicing with a bird takes time and dedication.

"Do you hear that?" King Matthias shouts over his broad velvet-clad shoulder to the hawking party. "My sweet cousin dismisses her knack for falconry. Be wary when placing your bets, eh?"

I bite back a grin. "Wagering on skill is good practice but it's luck that causes lost ducats."

Matthias turns to me, his usual boyish good looks shifting under his skin and changing to that of a mature and worldly king. "Luck, sweet cousin, is forged by iron-willed men."

"Your excellent opinion conflicts with a passage from the *Book of Ecclesiastes,*" I say knowing Matthias enjoys clever discussion.

King Matthias arches an eyebrow. "Refresh my memory."

I grin and clear my throat. "'I returned and saw under the sun, that the race is not to the swift, nor the battle to the strong, neither bread to the wise, nor yet riches to men of understanding, nor yet favor to men of skill: but time and chance happen to them all.'"

"Ah," he chuckles. "Yes, that is a pious philosophy, indeed. Well, Lady Ilona, there is a chance your luck will soon change." King Matthias aims a pointed look at me, and then lifts his hand. "Konrad, ride with me."

My mouth falls open, a hundred questions caught in my throat. A thick cold dread wraps around my shoulders as I drop back to join the others. Did I misinterpret Matthias? His tone and expression certainly appeared weighty with meaning.

When the hawking party reaches the wide clearing at the edge of the meadow, I swallow my worry and breathe deeply, the dew-laden grass a fragrant balm to my troubled imaginings.

I dismount, tug on my hawking gloves embroidered with the Szilágy coat of arms—the demi-goat holding a pine sapling—and traipse over to the cadger to retrieve my female merlin. It is while returning to my horse that I spy Prince Vlad engaged in conversation with Niccolò Modrussa and a portraitist newly arrived from Florence. I stare with such intensity I stumble over the matted nest of a field vole.

Prince Vlad sees my clumsiness and rushes over.

"Lady Ilona, are you hurt? May I offer assistance?" Prince Vlad extends his hand.

"How careless of me." Face flaming with embarrassment, my trembling fingers rest on his arm for balance while I pull at the skirt's hem caught beneath my boot heel. My legs are shaking, the memory of dancing together at the coronation celebration as vivid as though it was yesterday. His soft eyes, warm hands, firm touch, his lips close to my neck...

"Are you sure you didn't twist your ankle? Are you able to walk without discomfort?" Prince Vlad looks especially dashing today in his olive-hued robe and green-plumed hat. He is in perfect harmony with the surroundings.

I snap my hand from his arm as though I have touched a boiling pot and take a few steps. "No injuries. Just my wounded pride."

Prince Vlad gestures to my long skirt puddling around me. "Feminine fashion is most unsuitable for hawking."

"I agree, but there are no alternatives." I look down as I navigate the uneven ground, relieved to hide my infatuation.

"Several men have placed their bets on you." He stays by my side as I remove the merlin's gold-embroidered leather hood.

"I was lucky." I dare to lift my eyes. My cheeks warm under his attentive gaze. I look away to check the fastening on the bird's tiny Milan-crafted bells.

The merlin stretches her neck and ruffles her feathers.

Prince Vlad takes the hint and scratches her head. "Lady Margit does not enjoy hawking." It is more a question than a statement.

I pluck a morsel of meat from the pouch and my merlin gulps it down. "Margit..."

Do I tell Prince Vlad that hawks frighten her, that she refuses to touch a dead animal, that she prefers gossiping to physical exertion? As much as I am attracted to him and believe we are better suited, I dare not interfere in Aunt Erzsébet's plans for Margit. I chew on my lip as I think of a gracious yet true answer.

"Silence is an eloquent reply," says Prince Vlad. "It condemns and betrays without burden of proof."

My brow furrows. "I—"

"No need to explain. I have already assessed Lady Margit's character."

"You barely know her." My voice is sharp, my astonishment slipping out before phrasing it with genteel words.

Prince Vlad lifts his eyebrows in surprise but instead of a

46

scowl he grins from ear to ear. "If you pay close attention, you'll find a person's temperaments and inclinations are revealed with falcon-like speed." Prince Vlad rocks back on his heels. "I've already deduced that Lady Margit is not a hunter. Correct me if I am wrong, but I believe Margit does not possess the courage and persistence needed for venery."

I glance over my shoulder. "How can you judge Margit's character with so little evidence?"

Despite being too far away to hear our conversation, Margit glares at us, her jealousy like claws digging into the back of my neck.

"There's plenty of evidence. Every time a falconer walks past Lady Margit recoils, and she is always in the company of the most notorious gossips. She appears to be a rather fearful and frivolous girl. Am I right?"

I swallow, my mind awhirl. Is this a test or a trick? Is Prince Vlad judging my family loyalty? I cannot possibly agree to his opinion of Margit even if it is accurate. I can't disagree either. It will show that I lack judgment. I chew the inside of my cheek. However do I get out of this moral moat without knowing if Prince Vlad values loyalty or insight?

I square my shoulders. "I am also a keen observer of people, and this is what I have discovered about you." I hold one finger. "You enjoy wordplay." I wiggle the second. "You are in need of a noble wife, preferably one with courage and wit." I drop my hand to my side. "Yet, I suspect, you are not entirely certain whether you will be happy with such a wife because women like that are not easily manipulated."

Prince Vlad grins wide, and I see his eyeteeth, which are white and slightly tapered. "A rather quick judgment. What is your evidence?"

"Your present location." I lift my chin even as my gut clenches with uncertainty at my boldness.

Prince Vlad cocks his head. "Visegrád Castle?"

"By my side." I press my lips together and give him a wide-eyed impish look.

"Ah." Prince Vlad rubs his chin and his brows knit together. "I came only to inspect the bird and handler before placing a wager."

All my cheekiness drops like a lead weight into my belly. How could I be so foolish? So presumptuous? My face burns with embarrassment yet I smile brightly. "Which hawk will you bet on?"

"I do not bet on birds. I bet on people." Prince Vlad clasps his hands behind his back and stares at me with the oddest look. Whether with amusement, surprise, or disbelief I cannot determine. Some of his expressions are most perplexing. "My ducats are on you, Lady Ilona. I will keep you no longer." Prince Vlad bows and strides away.

Not a moment passes when Margit tramps toward me, an angry spot of color on her cheeks. "What were you and my future bridegroom discussing?"

"Congratulations on your betrothal. Perhaps you ought to tell him." I lift the plumed predator between us.

Margit steps away. "We will wed. Not this year or next. But eventually. Go ahead, Ilona, capture his heart. Flirt all you want. It doesn't matter. Love plays no part in our betrothals."

"Retract your jealous claws then." I mount my horse.

Margit's brows spring to her hairline. "Jealous? Of you?"

The horn's blast cuts off my reply, and I race into the field with the other hunters.

I do not follow them, instead I head for the small stream at the field's edge. I release my merlin. With my whistle, she swoops low on wide wings toward a young hare darting in panic. My merlin disappears into the tall grass. I dismount from the horse, tromp through the meadow, and find her mantling over her prey.

"Good girl." I drop the hare into my quarry bag and feed

48

her a morsel of meat. It is a promising start to the day. The thrill and physical exertion of hunting is always a balm to life's frustrations. Like Margit's insistence that she will be betrothed to Prince Vlad.

When the second horn blares I have one hare, three quails, and a partridge. I return with the other falconers, set out my game, and hurry to breakfast.

The clearing is transformed into an outside dining area comfortable with thick pillows for lounging and low tables draped in brocade topped with artfully arranged moss. Between tall sprays of wild flowers are bowls of fruit, towers of pastries, trenchers of pork, and spun noodle nests with cooked eggs and quail-stuffed dumplings nestled inside.

"We saved you a seat." Zsazsa waves her hand. "You must be ravenous."

"Hawking does encourage the appetite." I squeeze between Aunt Orsulya and the pope's legate.

"Niccolò Modrussa was just regaling us with stories about his commission." Zsazsa passes me a plate heaped with dumplings. "Did you know the pope sent him for the express purpose of writing an account of Dracula's exploits?"

"How fascinating," I say hoping Modrussa divulges secret insight about the man who sets my heart aflutter.

"I record Prince Vlad's every word." Niccolò Modrussa plops a quail-stuffed dumpling into his mouth and chews much too thoroughly while we wait with bated breath. "This requires verifying all the details—of which there are many. His Holiness demands accuracy and that gift for discernment —which the Lord blessed me with—which permits me alone to provide a detailed yet intuitive evaluation of Prince Vlad."

"What do you make of the man?" Zsazsa licks raspberry jam off a pastry, her tongue scooping every sweet morsel from between the flakey dough.

"Er..." Niccolò Modrussa looks away, blushes, and clears

his throat. "Dracula is a man of godly principles who fancies himself a savior."

"The Son of God took an infinitely gentler route." Zsazsa nudges me.

"Prince Vlad strove to protect Christendom the only way he knew how." Niccolò Modrussa plucks a bit of roasted pork from a platter. "His ambitions were and still are noble. He wants only for his people to prosper and be free from the levies imposed by their vassalage to the sultan."

"Those are all admirable aspirations." I guzzle half the goblet of watered wine, then reach for a cooked egg dusted with saffron.

"His Holiness agrees as well, my lady." Niccolò Modrussa signals a servant to pour more wine.

Lady Magyar, sitting across the table, leans over her plate and says in a low voice, "Why then does King Matthias continue to condemn Prince Vlad's actions?"

Niccolò Modrussa dabs his prim mouth with a napkin. "I am God's humble servant and His Holiness' lowly legate, I do not pretend to understand the reasoning of kings."

"Perhaps," says Zsazsa, "the Mind of a King would make a more interesting report."

Niccolò Modrussa bobs his head in fervent agreement. "I agree, my lady, unfortunately, it is not my field of expertise. It would make for some remarkable reading though, wouldn't it?" He rubs his chin. "Which reminds me, has His Highness acquired any new manuscripts for Bibliotheca Corviniana?"

Although I enjoy hearing about my cousin's latest acquisitions, I rise from the table. "Excuse me, I do believe I must check out my competition."

Zsazsa laughs but Aunt Orsulya purses her lips in displeasure. She does not approve of my competitive nature—too unladylike.

I mosey past the game tables, each marked with a family crest.

"You are a skilled huntress," says Prince Vlad suddenly behind me.

"I was lucky and Gertrud eager." I keep my voice aloof and circle the table, his less than chivalrous comment before the hunt still gnawing at me.

Prince Vlad follows. "Gertrude means 'spear strength.' You chose an excellent name for a falcon whose claws and beak are as lethal as any spear."

I smile politely and pretend to count quarry.

"Names are a kind of prophecy, don't you agree?" Prince Vlad straightens a row of quail with precision, as though they are foot soldiers in a tactical formation.

Is this another test? A way of asking me about my name? I lift my gaze. His eyes twinkle with mischief though his mouth presses straight with indifference.

"It certainly prophesied your rule."

His lips curve up. "True, but I asked about your name."

I am a torch—supposedly I have a fire burning within. But I have yet to experience either passion's flame or anger's blaze.

My skin warms under his watchful eye. "I...well... it's ..."

"Why do you smolder, Lady Ilona?" His eyebrow quirks and his eyes dance.

The tip of my ears must be singed I burn with such embarrassment. Never before has a man dared be so forward. Or speak so provocatively. Though my cheeks burn I do not shy away from his heated gaze. The connection I felt earlier smolders with his sinful innuendo.

"I..." Tongue-tied, I shrug and shake my head. Years of practicing the art of witty conversation abandons me. The more we talk the less clearly I think!

"Your innocence is a delight, Lady Ilona." Prince Vlad gestures to the table spread with quail and hares. "Lord

Magyar may have the most, but my bet remains on you and Gertrud."

"I'm not going to win," I say relieved that topic is over. "Bet on Lord Konrad, King Matthias's friend."

"You intend to lose?" Vlad cocks an eyebrow. "You are not as courageous as I thought."

Though innocent in romantic love, I am well acquainted with genteel etiquette. "Courage often requires restraint."

"Spoken like a diplomat." Prince Vlad bows low and continues down the row of tables.

The horn trumpets the start of the next hunt. Abandoning any attempt to win, I fuss with my dress and retie my boots before mounting the horse. The other hawkers have crossed the field before I set off. Even placing will subject me to Aunt Erzsébet's sharp rebuke. 'Let the powerful nobles win,' her razor-tongued reminder rings in my ear.

In the midst of the hunt, King Matthias gallops towards me. His three red-haired Vizslas, the royal hunting dog, follow in pursuit.

"Good cousin! A word." He stops his white steed near mine. "How would you like to live in Genoa?"

No, no, no! Not the drunken *capitano grande* who leered at me during the coronation dinner. He is old and flabby and waddles when he walks. Not him!

## 7

"I am negotiating your betrothal to Luis della Scala." King Matthias chugs from his waterskin.

My stomach roils with horror. "The Genoan *capitano grande* who attended your coronation?" I had hoped to be married to a man I could respect and admire. The *capitano grande* is a rude, uncouth, flamboyant, blustering drunk.

"Yes, that's him." King Matthias wipes his mouth with the back of his hand. "His desire to wed is a bit premature. His wife is bedridden. Dying, but still alive."

"I will pray for her." May she linger for many years.

From under the golden hair grazing his eyebrows, Matthias's eyes narrow with skepticism. "Della Scalla's family ties with the Gonzaga clan make him a valuable ally. Smile, Ilona, this time next year you will be the wife of a wealthy influential man."

"I am honored. It's just that..." I twist the reins, my knuckles white as I clench the leather.

"Speak plainly, cousin."

"You and Catherine were a finely-matched couple of the same age. Della Scala is old and fat." I slide my gaze toward Matthias. Did I overstep?

Matthias bursts out laughing. "Yes, and he farts gold and belches power."

"Margit says she will be wed to Prince Vlad when—"

"Those are Mother's plans, not mine." Matthias's face darkens, his mouth tight with displeasure. "Dracula will not marry into this family. Not now. Not ever."

"I don't wish to be disrespectful, but why not?"

"He's not Catholic." King Matthias pulls a chunk of meat from his bag and feeds it to his white-plumed falcon. "Good day, cousin." Matthias races across the field, his Vizslas loping after him.

My future turns rancid in my belly. King Matthias just doomed me to a miserable marriage. He is heartless!

I swallow the bile in my throat, release my merlin, and watch her climb skyward. Oh, to have my bird's perspective. Such height offers advantage in all things. Matthias's lofty station allows him to locate his prey with ease, like this marriage contract where I am the prey, defenseless against his soaring ambition.

The final horn blast ends the day's hunting. My spine curves and my shoulders slump as I return with two doves and one quail. I dismount and plod slowly to the table, blinking away tears.

Vlad Dracula is waiting for me. "How many?"

I open my quarry bag.

He looks inside. "Your skill adds to my coffers today."

If he notices my melancholy, he is too polite to mention it.

I tug off my gloves. "How is that possible? Others bagged more than I."

"There were other wagers." Prince Vlad wears a lopsided grin and one brow is raised in amusement. Or like he has a delicious secret.

I giggle, his expression infectious, then remembering I am promised to another, drop my gaze and pluck at a loose thread on my glove with false concentration. "Did you bet on my luck or my skill?"

"Both." Prince Vlad leans close, his wine-warm breath tickling my cheek. "Luck and skill are a formidable combination. In all things. Even love."

My head snaps up. "Love?"

"Love most of all. Securing a betrothal requires skill and finding happiness in the union requires luck." Prince Vlad rubs his chin. "Or is it the opposite? An advantageous betrothal requires luck and a loving union requires skill? Which is it, do you think?"

I crush the gloves in my fist and look him square in those gorgeous green eyes. "I will love any man King Matthias chooses for me."

"You really should learn to lie more convincingly, my lady." One side of his mouth curls up, and then Prince Vlad bows and walks away.

I slam my gloves into my satchel and stomp toward the cadger with my merlin. Life is so unfair! Prince Vlad flirts with me. Not Margit. I am the better choice for his wife. But what does it matter? King Matthias promised me to the repulsive *capitano grande*, a man I will never be able to respect, let alone love. I am doomed to a miserable marriage in a far-off land. My worst fear comes true.

That evening at dinner I avoid Prince Vlad even when I feel his eyes upon me. Though my skin kindles under his gaze, I push the sparkling feeling down. What good comes of romantic gestures and amorous looks when they do nothing but remind me of what I will never have? Better to never taste love than a lifetime hungering for the impossible. Better to be content with bread than wish for meat.

I pick at the roasted hare and wave away the plum-stuffed quail. Sorrow fills my belly and yet leaves me feeling empty.

I crane my neck at the sudden screeching of chairs against the floor. A grim-faced King Matthias, his advisors, and

Prince Vlad rise from their seats and follow Matthias as he hurries from the room.

Margit tosses a bone she sucked clean onto the table. "What happened? Where are they going?"

Aunt Ursula dabs at her mouth with a linen napkin. "Sweet child, you are quite unobservant not to have noticed the messenger's arrival."

Messengers are always coming and going. I, like Margit, paid this one no attention.

"The news must be bad," I say.

It is.

Matthias tells us just how bad when he and his advisors emerge from the council chambers two sequestered days later.

"I will join our troops in Jajce, Bosnia." Matthias's voice is confident despite the dark crescents hollowing his weary eyes.

Hungary is going to war.

"THE CASTLE IS TOO quiet with all the men gone." I spread the blanket on the grassy riverbank.

"I thought you were tired of all the parties and hunting." Bernádett sets down the basket of food.

"A party every day was rather excessive." I remove my headpiece and let the cool river breeze sift through my hair. "I do not understand men. How does Matthias go from hosting parties to leading battles?"

Bernádett shrugs. "Men enjoy making war."

"Matthias did not start it," I snap in defense of my cousin. "He has no choice but to retaliate against the Turks." I glance at Solomon's Tower. "Prince Vlad must be bored. Or maybe he is angry Matthias left him behind with the old men."

"Why do you care?" Bernádett removes a small loaf of bread and a wedge of cheese.

"He is Matthias's guest." I steal a look at Solomon's tower again. Is he there now? Pacing? Writing? Reading? Since the men left, Prince Vlad kept to himself and took his meals in his room.

"Guest?" Bernádett cuts a thick slice of bread. "Is that what King Matthias calls prisoners now?"

"Why don't you like Prince Vlad?"

"He is wicked." Bernádett sets a chunk of cheese on a napkin.

I blow my annoyance through pursed lips. "Pffft. Don't believe the gossip. He did no more or less than any ruler must do to protect their country."

Bernádett palms an apple. "Some men thirst for blood— like a wolf—while others attack only when provoked—like a mother bear protecting her cubs. Prince Vlad is both creatures."

"He is a warrior prince, not a creature." I look over my shoulder to make sure no noisy noblewoman or spying servant lingers nearby. "Do not speak ill of him. You don't even know him."

"Forgive me, my lady." Bernádett angles the knife to Margit standing out of hearing by the riverbank. "Since the king departed, I have noticed that Margit sends Peroska to spy on Prince Vlad. And you."

My hand flies to my chest. "Me? Why?"

"Maybe she is spying for someone."

"Aunt Erzsébet no doubt." I roll my eyes. "She knows I steer clear of palace intrigues and never play the coquette."

"Maybe your aunt follows the king's orders." Bernádett quarters the apple.

"Well, they can spy all they want. There will be nothing to report." I cross my arms, indignant that Aunt Erzsébet thinks so little of me.

Bernádett hands me the apple wedge on a napkin. "I agree, after all, you are betrothed to della Scala."

I wrinkle my nose. "He has hair coming out of his ears." What an unpleasant man. Imaging married life with him curdles my stomach.

"It's a good match, my lady. A life with the *capitano grande* will be safe and free of the dangers that come with marrying a prince. Royalty is a heavy burden."

"One I will gladly carry." I straighten my spine and lift my chin. "Royalty assures my future children, grandchildren, and great grandchildren the titles and fortune they deserve." I smile kindly at Bernádett. A maidservant cannot understand the noble responsibility to forge dynasties and build destinies.

Bernádett tucks a strand of red hair behind her ear and juts her pointed chin toward Solomon's Tower. "Men like Prince Vlad want to be powerful, respected, and wealthy, but God requires us only to be modest, humble, and forgiving."

"Job had all of those traits." The *Book of Job*, my favorite book in the Bible, is proof of God's righteousness.

"Only after losing everything." Bernádett says softly as though I need reminding.

"It was a fair trade." My teeth crunch down on the apple.

## 8

I listen to the ladies discuss the latest Vatican tragedy while plucking at a knotted thread when a loud throat clearing interrupts the conversation.

"Lady Ilona." A white-haired nobleman leans on his cane, his eyes squinting against the hot summer sun shining down on the courtyard. "Prince Vlad commands your presence in the lower courtyard."

Aunt Orsulya's needle hangs in mid stitch. "Political detainees do not command."

With a pinched smile, Aunt Erzsébet sweeps her gaze over our little sewing circle. "My son indulges this particular guest."

"Sister." Aunt Orsulya lays her embroidery on her lap. "This is a most unusual summons."

It is more than unusual. It is scandalous. It exceeds even King Matthias's lenient standards of court etiquette.

My heart throbs in my throat, and I bite my lips to keep from smiling at Dracula's boldness.

"Prince Vlad detests impropriety of all kinds." Zsazsa looks at the nobleman. "Surely, he is not alone in the courtyard."

The elder scowls as though he feels this errand is beneath him. "There are three others."

Zsazsa pats my hand and leans close. "Go to him. Orsulya and I will squash any rumors of immodesty."

I yank the needle from the sleeve, pricking my finger in my haste, and scrape the droplet of blood with my teeth as my eyes flit from face to face. Aunt Erzsébet's lips are pursed with displeasure. Aunt Orsulya wrinkles her nose. Zsazsa's eyes sparkle with playful collusion. But Margit's face sends a shiver down my spine. Her eyes are predatory, as focused and cruel as a hungry lynx.

Like a frightened roe deer, I avert my eyes, rise, and follow the elderly noble down to the lower terrace.

Mindful of my reputation I pause at the courtyard's entrance. A royal guardsman snaps to attention. A pink-cheeked old scullery woman in a faded kerchief shucks pea pods into a basket. The third is the portraitist, who fusses with his brushes under a white canopy.

As though sensing my arrival, Vlad turns and points his thumb at the blank canvas. "This is a tedious business."

His smooth, deep voice lures me forward. I walk toward him, my disobedient feet overriding common sense. "Sitting too long without something to do does tend to dull the brain."

"My thoughts exactly." Prince Vlad sets his feathered cap atop the velvet dalmatica already draped over the chair. "Did you hear about Pope Pius's death?"

"The other ladies and I were just discussing his untimely end." I survey the pigment pots on the portraitist's table.

"It's a terrible tragedy." Prince Vlad crosses his arms. "A blow for all Christendom. Without Pope Pious's leadership his army will scatter like dried leaves in the wind. He was the driving force behind the crusade."

"Is it true he promised absolution to any man who joined?"

"He did." His brow furrows. "It's a promise I would have

liked to make to my own army." He looks past me and into the distance.

I touch the crucifix at my neck, take a deep breath, and broach a subject often discussed by the papal legate, Niccolò Modrussa. "Do you believe God called you to stop the Turks from invading?"

Prince Vlad sets his hand over his heart. "My father's oath to the Order of the Dragon became mine when he died. So, yes, I suppose you could say God called me."

I twist the cross, my fingertips squeezing the sharp-edged crossbar until my skin stings. "Should my father's quest to subdue the Turks become mine as well?" This is impossible. I am a woman with no military power.

Prince Vlad cocks his head and gives me an inscrutable look. "That's for you to decide, my lady."

"I have confidence in Hungary's military strength."

"A noble but an unfortunately naïve belief." Dracula flicks his hand at the blank canvas. "King Matthias fights my greatest enemy while I sit for a portrait." He grabs a goblet from a small velvet-draped table and hurls it against the wall.

As the red wine drips down the stone, an odd tremor runs through me. Part alarm. Part excitement. I feel his anger and resentment as if it were my own. I understand his rage. I felt the same upon learning Sultan Mehmed had tortured Father for days before sawing him in half.

Dracula fixates on the broken goblet, lost in thought. What horrors has he seen? What horrors has he endured?

He squeezes his eyes closed for a moment, shaking his head as if dispelling awful memories. "Will you soothe my vile mood by keeping me company? I always enjoy our conversations."

"If you wish." My cheeks aflame, I look away and spy his red mantle on the chair. "Are you wearing this for the portrait?"

"I suppose." He tosses it over his shoulders, sets his pearl-trimmed cap on his head, and sits down.

"Excellent." The portraitist picks up his brush. "The prince is ready to proceed."

Dracula fastens the gold button at this neck. "Am I presentable?" His eyebrows lift and he appears ill at ease.

"Not quite." With trembling fingers I adjust his cap and align the topaz broach. An awkward silence descends, our nearness tantalizingly forbidden. I should step back. Increase the distance between us. I cannot, instead my fingertips brush the ostrich plumes glittering with jewels at the top of his cap.

He looks up and grins, his eyes warm and inviting. "Better?"

I flush with pleasure, his steady gaze sweeter than honey, and tug an errant lock from his collar. "Almost." I arrange his dark smooth hair over the fur collar and inhale his enticing scent—rosemary and leather and man. "Portrait perfect."

He lets out a barely audible sigh, and with that the impossible attraction between us thickens, coils, and knots.

The portraitist breaks the spell. "My lady, may I offer a chair?" He places one at a right angle to Prince Vlad's.

"I…I…thank you." I sit; clasp my hands to keep them from shaking. "What shall we talk about?"

"Anything you like." Prince Vlad tilts his chin, his lopsided grin like someone with a delicious secret.

"Anything?" I chew on my lip. I am only an innocent young maiden. What could I possibly discuss that would interest a man of his renown? Idle chitchat will never do. Venery, weather, politics…my mind gathers and discards many possible topics until finding one that will entertain us both. "Explain why you, an Orthodox, are compelled to protect Catholic doctrines."

"Not one for trite conversation, are you?" Prince Vlad rubs his freshly shaved jaw. "Both religions share many similar beliefs. Their differences are simply philosophical."

"Aren't all religions—even Islam—a matter of different philosophies?"

Prince Vlad throws back his head and howls with laughter. "Your intellect is charming, Lady Ilona."

His unrestrained glee fills me with a kind of pride. "Aunt Orsulya says men prefer silly-minded women."

"Not all men. Certainly not me. My future princess will be clever and witty."

I shift in the chair. Do I tell him I am already betrothed? Or am I a fool to believe he is talking about me? "I expect nothing less from a man of your talents."

"Expectations are dangerous, my lady." He wags his finger. "Let's see, you asked me a theological question." He brushes a bit of lint from his mantle. "Orthodoxy believes knowledge of God resides in a person's nature. Catholics believe it is inferred by logic."

"Logic? Not faith?"

A slow grin melts across Prince Vlad's face. "It will take more than one afternoon to answer if you insist on asking the very same questions pondered by ecclesiasts and philosophers for hundreds of years."

His expansive smile is infectious, the stern-looking angles of his face stretched wide into playfulness. It is a child's honest grin and it makes me grin in return.

"I have every confidence that together we can solve all life's questions by the time your portrait is complete." My lips pucker into pretended seriousness.

The artist pokes his head around the canvas. "Should I use a smaller brush?"

"Do you have one with only three bristles?" Prince Vlad asks the portraitist but quirks an eyebrow at me.

"I shall make one for you, Prince Vlad." The portraitist lifts his thinnest brush and yanks out a few hairs.

Prince Vlad and I burst out laughing.

The hours pass with laughter and excellent conversation,

as we discuss the tenets of the Orthodox Church, debate doctrine, and examine the beliefs of other faiths.

"The good light is gone." The portraitist gestures to the sun hanging low in the western sky.

So soon?

"Thank you for a delightful afternoon." I stand, my heart suddenly banging against my bodice. I have been sitting with him much too long. I can almost hear the ladies tittering criticisms. "Our conversation was more enlightening than a day spent in Matthias's library." I glance over my shoulder as though expecting to see my aunts. "I must be going."

"Will you come again tomorrow?" Dracula regards his unfinished portrait with indifference.

My eyes sweep over the courtyard. Is the guardsman paid to spy? Why is the old woman still sitting in the corner?

I should not come back. I am betrothed. And even if I was not, Prince Vlad's Orthodox faith prevents a wedded union with our family.

"If you desire," I say despite myself.

## 9

# Vlad

**Twenty-two Years Earlier**
**Summer 1442**
**Egrigöz, Western Anatolia**

"Where are we?" Radu clung tight to Vlad's arm as he climbed out of the wagon.

Vlad inhaled the sweet-sharp scent of pine, the forest like a blanket over the hills. In the midst stood a towering stone fortress. For two weeks Vlad had charted their course. Tried to guess their location each time the guards let them out. Now he knew. And it burned like hot coals in his stomach. "Egrigöz fortress."

"*Yürü!*" A guard poked his pike into Vlad's back.

Vlad plodded forward with Radu, who clung to his sleeve, and followed the beak-nosed guard into the fortress.

Janissaries glowered at them, growled as they walked past. There were so many. Each wore a tall white hat that made them as tall as Goliath. Each wore a scimitar and dagger over a turquoise coat. Each was a master of close combat and archery. Vlad had seen their skill up close. Had watched their guard fell a deer with a single arrow from a great distance.

But not as far as the distance some of the janissaries had traveled from their homeland.

Not all their menacing faces were Turkish. Some appeared Romanian. Like the fair-haired janissary with a ruddy round face. He might be a product of the *devshirme*, the human tax levied by the Turks after capturing a Christian town, their burly farm boys the payment. Was the glaring ruddy-faced brute ripped from his family at seven-years-old, draped in a red-hooded robe, and sent to the Thracian city of Edirne to become an *askeri* warrior? Had he converted to Islam? What about the blonde-bearded janissary beside him? Would he be selected to be a *solacchi*, an expert archer responsible for guarding the sultan on his travels?

Vlad dropped his gaze to the floor when one snarled at him for staring too long.

The pointed end of the pike prodded them deeper into the fortress, across two stone courtyards, through three small chambers, and up a narrow staircase that ended at an iron-braced door.

"*Gitin.*" The janissary shoved Vlad inside.

The door slammed behind them.

Radu buried his head under Vlad's arm as the metal bolt squealed shut.

"Not too bad." Vlad tussled Radu's hair before striding across the stone cell. "At least it's clean." He pushed the rough-hewn table under the narrow window and climbed up.

"What do you see?" asked Radu.

"Just the town."

The homes looked like toys from this height.

Vlad studied the smooth stone face of the tower. Escape would be impossible.

Radu tugged on Vlad's tunic. "I'm hungry."

"They'll feed us." Vlad jumped off the table. "They need us alive."

The door squeaked open. Two servants entered with a small tub of water, a square linen cloth, two wool blankets, and a sliver of soap.

Radu stepped forward, and the man pulled out a knife and hissed.

Vlad pulled Radu back. "Don't be stupid."

"I was only—"

"Shush."

They waited until the servants left, heard the bolt grind back into place.

"You must be more careful." Vlad stripped off his foul-smelling clothes and stepped into the water. "Refreshing," he said despite its frigid temperature.

Radu sat cross-legged on the floor and watched while Vlad scrubbed his body and washed his hair.

"Your turn." Vlad shook his head, spraying water all over Radu.

Radu laughed, the first laugh in two weeks, removed his clothes, and stepped into the tub.

Vlad draped the coarse wool blanket over Radu's shivering body when he was done, then gathered the clothes and rinsed them in the gray soapy water.

"Now what?" Radu shivered as Vlad spread their clothes on the floor to dry.

Vlad wrapped the second wool blanket around his body and settled himself against the wall. "We plot our revenge."

In the thick pink glow of twilight, the same servants brought them a pottage of onions, parsnips, and cabbage with a rye roll and a hard-cooked egg. The next morning they brought barley mush. Day after day. Week after week.

Outside, the beech and oak trees changed from green to orange to red.

Vlad kept busy. He recited old lessons, told stories, and

created a physical routine of balancing, juggling, push-ups, somersaults, and handstands. He felt less helpless, more in control, when he was doing something.

"I'm tired of conjugating Latin verbs," whined Radu one afternoon.

"We must keep our minds' sharp and our bodies' agile. Our life may depend on it."

WINTER'S first snowfall floated like feathers from the sky. Vlad was watching the flakes melt in his palm when he heard the bolt screeching across the door. He withdrew his arm from the window and leapt from the table.

"*Gel.*" The guard stood in the doorway and gestured with his pike.

Both relief and fear twisted Vlad's stomach into a knot. Either they were going home or going to their death.

"Where are they taking us?" Radu's eyes widened, his face draining of color.

Vlad stuffed his fear deep inside. "Someplace better than this, I hope."

The boys descended the stairway in silence and passed through the same chambers and courtyards they had many months ago.

In the snow-dusted courtyard waited a large supply wagon.

"Get in." A pockmarked janissary, his mustache drooping past his chin, flung open the litter door. "Aren't you a pretty one." His thick fingers squeezed Radu's cheek.

"You speak Romanian." Vlad tugged Radu forward, away from the too-friendly janissary.

The janissary narrowed his eyes. "*Da.* I'm from Bistrita."

"Are we going to Adrianople to meet our father?" Vlad helped Radu into the wagon.

"*Nu*. Tokat."

"Why—"

The janissary slammed the door shut.

Radu scooted close to Vlad. "Where is Tokat?"

Vlad closed his eyes and pictured his father's council chambers. He saw the monk-drawn maps of Romania, Moldavia, Hungary, and other territories. He even saw the labeled drawings of serpentine mountain passes, villages, churches, and monasteries. He concentrated, let his mind's memory search for the right map. Found it! He leaned back against a sack and squeezed his eyes shut, willed himself not to cry.

"I don't know," he lied, his voice thick with despair.

Tokat was deep inside Turkish lands and far from Adrianople. Something had gone dreadfully wrong.

THE WAGON HIT a deep rut in the road and a basket stuffed with fabric toppled onto Vlad's head.

"Ugh." Vlad threw it off.

Radu, resting between two padlocked chests, rubbed sleep-thick eyes. "Where is Tokat anyway? The end of the world?"

"If we break any more wheels or keep getting stuck in mud it will be."

The wagon rattled to a stop.

Vlad rolled his eyes. "Not another break."

The janissary flung open the door. "*Defol.*"

Vlad scrambled out and stared awestruck at their surroundings. The mountain slopes on either side were so steep, high, and dense with evergreens they seemed to touch the sky.

The driver, a pockmarked janissary with a black mustache, let loose a yellow stream into the bushes. "What are you looking at, little prince?" He shook his penis. "Never saw one this big before?"

Radu looked away and made his own puddle.

The second janissary leaned against the wagon. "Want one?" His hand held three dried dates.

Radu snatched them and stuffed one in his mouth.

"Don't accept treats," said Vlad when they were back inside the wagon.

"Why not?" Radu plopped another in his mouth.

"Because gifts are not free."

"They know I don't have any coin."

"They don't want money," said Vlad. "They want you."

"They already have me." Radu spit out the pit.

Vlad grabbed Radu's wrist. "Do not accept any more gifts."

"Ouch, you're hurting me."

"They want to do worse."

"IT'S ENORMOUS!" Vlad pressed his head against the wagon's splintered slats.

The Tokat fortress looked like a magnificent stone crown sitting atop the barren rocky summit, its twenty-eight towers jutting high into the air. It blended well with the terrain, as if the earth itself had belched up the impregnable stronghold in proclamation of Turkish dominance.

Radu pressed his cheek against Vlad's as they stared at their new prison. "Does it have a harem?"

Vlad scowled. "Who cares? You're not allowed inside."

As the wagon rattled onward, Vlad assessed the fortress like an experienced general studying its military potential. Its main access was a steep wide strip of beaten dirt leading to a battlement-flanked barbican. The fortress portcullis was raised, a sign of supreme confidence. Who would dare attack them?

Another entrance hid in the shadows at the hill's base where the mouth of a large cave yawned wide and dark. A slow smile crept up Vlad's face. Caves meant tunnels. Tunnels for escaping, for hiding, and for trapping an enemy's army.

"Lord Father should build more tunnels," said Vlad. Tunnels going nowhere. Tunnels leading from bedchambers. Tunnels hidden in crevices. Tunnels deep enough and dark enough only the bats dare go inside.

Radu wrinkled his nose. "I don't like tunnels. And that castle is ugly. When I have a castle it will not be stuck atop some ugly rock peak. It will in the middle of town right next to Mama."

"Not mine. I want one as high as an eagle's nest and deep in the mountain forest." Vlad decided his castle would be a protecting marble angel for his people and a devouring stone beast for his enemies.

Vlad tried tamping down the dread gathering at the back of his throat but in the shadow of Tokat's soaring height he felt as insignificant as an ant on a mighty oak tree.

The wagon jostled forward until it rolled under the heavy iron portcullis.

Radu clamped his hand around Vlad's arm. "I'm not afraid."

"Good, because if our enemy smells fear they use it against us."

Radu sniffed the air.

The wagon door squeaked opened.

"*Çek git!*" The Tokat guard's scimitar flashed in the sun.

Radu ducked under the blade and scrambled out. Vlad did not. Nose in the air and shoulders squared, Vlad pushed away the steel and stepped down from the wagon with all the arrogance he could muster.

The guard drove his foot into the back of Vlad's knee. Vlad hit the ground face first.

"Get up." A half-length pike prodded Vlad's side.

Vlad swallowed his humiliation, stood, and lowered his head. With a pike tip at his back, the janissary urged Vlad into the castle.

"Vlad," whispered Radu.

"I see." Vlad's head swung back and forth in amazement, his eyes going from one vividly patterned tapestry to the next. He looked down, his ragged dirty boots marring the gleaming beauty of the marble floors.

Splendor and luxury were everywhere. Gray-bearded men in elaborate turbans sat on gold and silver chairs. Stern-faced janissaries marched by in unison. Feathered-capped pages dashed through the hallways. Tokat was no minor outpost. It was a bustling important garrison.

The boys' forced walk ended at the threshold of a sunlit rotunda. The guard pointed his pike across the expanse to a woman dressed in a face-covering headdress and a high-necked robe.

She beckoned them forward.

"Is that the harem?" Radu grabbed Vlad's sleeve as they crossed the white marble.

Vlad rolled his eyes. "Don't be stupid."

The woman led them silently through the doorway and into a large room full of small children, toys, and slaves.

"The nursery!?" Vlad stepped over a toy Trojan horse with clay wheels. "I am not a child." He stomped up to two men sitting with their arms tucked into wide sleeves. "I am a man." He thumped his chest. "I will not be treated like a child."

One man snapped at him in Turkish.

Radu tugged on Vlad's tunic. "He sounds like a woman."

"He's a eunuch," said Vlad.

"You mean they don't have..." Radu covered his crotch and grimaced.

A toothless old woman pointed to a bookcase at the far side of the room.

Frustration clawed at Vlad like a cat trapped in a basket. He kicked a ball out of the way and stamped toward the bookcase.

He pulled two books from the shelf, slumped onto a silk cushion, and opened one, then the other. "I can't read these. They're in Turkish." Vlad tossed the books aside.

The eunuchs snickered. The women, fawning over Radu, paid him no attention.

Vlad drew his knees to his chest, hid his head under his arms, and closed his eyes. This was worse than the cell at Eğrigöz. At least there he was not under constant supervision.

In the distance, a warbling croon began. Vlad lifted his head, stood, and went to the narrow window. A man chanted, his voice suffusing the sky with devotion. Vlad felt the haunting tune wash over him, seep into his veins and melt his frustration.

Vlad frowned when the singing stopped. "What was he saying?"

"Allah is Most Great." A eunuch, in flawless Romanian, pointed his finger heavenward. "I bear witness that there is none worthy of being worshiped except Allah." He gestured to the women on their knees. "The *salāt*. Prayers."

Vlad's eyes lit up. "You speak Romanian."

"*Da.*"

"Why are my brother and I in the nursery?"

The eunuch opened his mouth, but the second eunuch barked at him in Turkish.

Nostrils flaring, Vlad returned to the window. This rocky dry land with too few trees was as welcoming and interesting as this nursery prison.

"Vlad. Radu."

Vlad flinched at the thick baritone voice and spun about.

A withered old man in a multi-layered robe beckoned Vlad forward. Vlad crossed the room with quick steps, something about the man's commanding stance and steely blue gaze making him obey without question.

"Who are you?" Vlad looked up into a wizened face grooved deep with a crisscross of wrinkles.

The old man responded. In Turkish. He talked and talked. Words not understood. Words intoned with solemn cadence. Words droned through a long white beard. Finally, the man set both hands on Vlad's slim shoulders and smiled.

"What does he want?" Radu had come up behind Vlad during the old man's speech.

"I think," said Vlad, "this man is our tutor."

He was.

Their *hoca* taught them to speak and write in Turkish. He demanded perfect conjugation and pronunciation. Usually he was kind, except when he caught Radu and Vlad speaking Romanian. That earned them a stinging blow to their hands or buttocks with a switch.

"I don't like Turkish." Radu blew on the hot red lash across his hand.

Vlad poked his head outside their room, saw no one about, and closed the door. "We're learning our enemy's language. That's a huge advantage."

MONTHS PASSED. THE BOYS' Turkish improved. They were no longer escorted from room to room. By the following spring Vlad and Radu roamed the palace without supervision.

Radu gossiped with the men who lounged in the golden chairs and befriended the ambitious pages scurrying about.

Vlad looked for secret tunnels. He found one behind a

tapestry, a second beneath a wardrobe, and a third under a loose floor tile. The fourth he discovered by accident.

Still hungry after the midday meal, Vlad headed to the scullery to scrounge for food. He turned the corner, stopped, and shuffled back, his eyes fixed on the scandalous couple locked in embrace in front of the bread kiln.

"Shhh." A guard nuzzled the neck of a giggling scullery maid.

Vlad ducked into the alcove and peeked around the corner, his eyes widening as the guard fondled the maid's breasts.

"Nobody will notice we're gone." The guard lifted the maid up into the large bread kiln, smacking her ass as she crawled inside. She giggled, disappeared into the darkness, and he crawled in after her.

Vlad crept silently across the stone floor and stared into the blackened kiln. Except for a hollow scuffling from deep within there was no trace of them. Vlad glanced over his shoulder, saw no one about and, his blood pulsing with excitement, climbed in after them.

The kiln was deep and dark, a narrow shaft cut into the side. Vlad scuttled crablike around the bend. He slipped, his hand pawing the void of the vertical chute. His heart in his throat, Vlad felt for the edge, then swung his legs over and jumped into the black abyss.

He landed lightly on his feet, the drop only half a man's height. He tried to raise his arms. His fingers brushed against the rock. The tunnel was as wide as a man's shoulders. He blinked, waited for his eyes to adjust to the darkness. The faint echo of voice and movement urged him forward.

A lantern's orange glow illuminated the next turn. Vlad hesitated, cocked his ear. Clinking metal and low giggles reverberated off the cold rock walls. Vlad peered around the corner and into a grotto. And gasped.

The scullery maid was naked, her bound wrists looped

over a hook embedded in the rock ceiling. The guard parted his robe, hoisted her legs around his hips, and smacked her bare bottom.

Vlad rubbed the back of his neck. Did she need to be rescued? She moaned, her eyes heavy-lidded, her lips parted as the guard bucked against her and bit her nipple.

Vlad felt a familiar aching throb. He took his cock in his hand and stroked himself to the guard's thrusts. When the guard twirled his lover around and impaled her from behind, Vlad shuddered and caught his sticky release.

## 10

## Ilona

**Winter 1465**
**Buda Castle, Hungary**

Snowflakes flutter past the narrow window. It is a chilly reminder of time's quick pace. With icy foreboding, I contemplate the unopened letter in my hand.

Margit, sitting near the fireplace of the ladies' chamber with the others, looks up from her embroidery, her brows lifted with mean-spirited glee. "Another love letter from the *capitano grande*?"

My mouth slumps into a frown. "The second since we returned from Visegrád."

"Open it." Aunt Orsulya flutters her hand. "Maybe his wife finally died. God bless her soul."

The letter is heavy in my hand, the weight of duty pinning me into the chair. I do not want Luigi della Scala's wife to die. But it is unchristian to wish for her continued suffering.

"Fine, I'll read it." Margit snatches the letter, cracks the seal, and unfolds the vellum. "Ahem." She waits for the ladies to look up from their needlework. "'My dearest Lady

Ilona, it is with burdened heart and teary eyes I write to tell you that my devoted wife's infirmity grows worse."

The weight falls away and I exhale with relief.

"Not much of a love letter." Aunt Orsulya's pinched lips move sideways.

Zsazsa jabs her needle in the air. "At least he gets right to the point."

"Ladies, save your comments until the end." Margit waves an outward palm. "'Though her body is weak, her faith in God is strong. So strong, the selfless woman urged me to waste no time in wedding another when God calls her to His bosom. My self-sacrificing wife also extracted a promise from me to find a god-fearing woman capable of giving me an heir and lamented her failure in this great commission. As I am a faithful and loving husband, I told her King Matthias offered his cousin's hand in marriage. Oh, how virtuous is my wife! She wept with joy, laid her pale hand on mine, and wished me happiness. To satisfy her curiosity, I expounded on your beauty, youth, and noble family. I am certain you will strive to be her equal in Christian virtue. My sincerest wish is for your happiness and'—oh, by my virtue, such nonsense."

"It's not nonsense, Margit," sniffs Aunt Orsulya. "I thought it quite nice, although the emphasis he puts on his wife being self-sacrificing and selfless is a bit tiresome."

"He makes his wife to be a saint." Skepticism sharpens my voice.

"It's a stupid boring letter." Margit tosses it into my lap.

Two can play this game.

"What does your alleged betrothed write to you about?"

"Prince Vlad doesn't need to write." Margit's mouth puckers as she lifts her pointy chin. "Anyway, he's being transferred here this week."

My heart skips a beat. "Is he coming to the masquerade?" I look to my aunt for confirmation.

Aunt Orsulya draws the needle through a linen collar. "I

am not privy to King Matthias's guest list. However, Erzsébet did mention something about Matthias requiring Dracula's knowledge of Turkish. Evidently, he speaks like a native."

Margit rises from the chair. "This dull embroidery can wait another day. I have a more amusing task—designing an enchanting costume."

"A pointless undertaking," says Aunt Orsulya when Margit is gone. "I hear Dracula is more concerned with politics than flirting."

"Undoubtedly." Zsazsa tears the thread with her teeth. "Everyone's talking about Stephen of Moldavia's attack on the Chilia fortress."

"Matthias will have to walk a thinner rope than the rope-walkers he hires." Aunt Orsulya chuckles at her joke.

"The attack certainly set the political rope swinging." Zsazsa aims her needle at me. "Not interested in politics, Ilona? You look distracted."

I fold Luigi della Scala's letter and slip it into my skirt pocket. "Is Chilia important?"

"It is to Prince Vlad," says Zsazsa. "It's a Wallachian outpost."

Aunt Orsulya jabs the needle into the collar. "Battles and power, I think, are men's true loves. Not women."

A LETTER SLIDES under my door the morning of the masquerade. It has no name, the seal is marred, the sender's identity unknown, and yet my pulse quickens as I tear it open.

*Dearest Lady Ilona,*

*The memories of our conversations at Visegrád sustained me since your departure. Scarcely does a day pass that I do not picture your charming smile or imagine your sweet voice. I look forward to seeing you again at the masquerade and suspect I will find you easily—your essence drawing me like a bee to a flower. As I remain under the ever-vigilant care of your gracious cousin, I must content myself with only occasional dances and conversation, although I hope it pleases you to know my thoughts are ever by your side.*

*With admiration and friendship,*
*V*

ONCE. Twice. Three times I read his letter. With a twinge of guilt, I fold it into a fig-sized wad and conceal it in my fist. If Margit finds it—I've caught her snooping through my cupboard before—she will show it to Aunt Erzsébet and accuse me of undermining her future marriage negotiations.

I circle my chambers for a hiding spot. A velvet canopied bed. A carved table. An oak cupboard without a lock. Three upholstered chairs. Two wool carpets. There must be some place Margit won't think to look behind or under. I need a secret spot, a false plank, a concealed recess—

The mouse hole!

I am on my knees, my cheek to the floor, when someone raps on the door. Heart pounding, I shove the paper in the hole, stand, smooth my dress, and answer the door.

"Why are you opening the door?" Aunt Erzsébet sweeps inside, her eyes darting about the room. "Where is Bernádett?"

"She went to the scullery for fresh herbs." I point to the wilted bouquet on the table.

"Good. I come at a fortunate time." She sits by the fire and pats the chair beside her. "Dear child, I bring dreadful news." Her thin lips twist into a frown that is more irritated than upset.

"Is King Matthias ill?" I sit down, my mouth pressed tight with worry.

"Heavens no, nothing so frightful as that." Aunt Erzsébet casts her eyes about the room as though looking for something.

My stomach clenches. There is only one bit of dreadful news that warrants a personal visit—Luigi dell Scala's wife is dead.

"Vlad Dracula is here." Aunt Erzsébet plucks at a loose thread on my shoulder. "I do not like the man, but my son requires his expertise in Turkish battle tactics."

"Why is this—"

"Patience, niece. Prince Vlad, as you know, is a friend of the pope, who for his own unfounded reasons accuses Matthias of using crusading monies to buy the Hungarian Holy Crown."

"Ridiculous." I fix my gaze on her and not on the mouse hole.

"Indeed. The pope scandalizes my son with such accusations but who is fool enough to call the pope a liar?"

"No one," I say, wondering what this visit is really about.

"Exactly." Aunt Erzsébet twists the green vesuvianite ring on her finger. "Naturally, Matthias feels compelled to improve their relationship and has decided to answer the pope's call to defend Christianity against the Turks."

"A crusade to appease the pope? This is the dreadful news?" A note of skepticism slips out.

Aunt Erzsébet wags her finger. "Dear child, you must practice patience."

I clasp my hands together, force a smile, and do not look at the mouse hole.

"Matthias is certainly not organizing a crusade anytime soon. No, the dreadful news concerns Prince Vlad." Aunt Erzsébet's mouth droops. She narrows one eye and aims her suspicions at me. "The pope admires Dracula's rather robust defensive tactics." Aunt Erzsébet pokes her finger into my arm. "The man some people claim is Christianity's greatest warrior cannot be kept prisoner much longer. All eyes are on Dracula now. Even mine."

My courteous smile widens, and I do not look at the mouse hole. Get to the point, I want to shout.

Aunt Erzsébet tilts her head, both eyes tapered with accusation. "The dreadful news is that someone saw Dracula's servant deliver a letter to your chambers."

"My chambers?" My hand flies to my breast in mock surprise. "You've been misinformed."

Her brows knot low on her creased forehead. "You deny a letter was pushed under your door?"

"Since I know nothing about this letter, I cannot confirm its delivery." I shrug, feigning innocence, and clasp my sweaty palms. "Ask Bernádett. Perhaps the letter came while I was at breakfast."

Aunt Erzsébet's nostrils flare. "Vlad Dracula is not Catholic. He is Orthodox and a prisoner. If Matthias releases him and if he converts to Catholicism, then Margit will wed him. Not you. Margit."

I lift my chin. "You bring me old news, aunt."

Aunt Erzsébet stands, her face as red as beet soup. "Do not imagine for a single moment that Dracula's pitiful attempts at flirtation will sway me from my plans."

"You mean King Matthias's plans."

Her eyes blaze with anger and her lips curl into a snarl. "Impertinent child." Aunt Erzsébet smacks my face. "Do not cross me. And do not cross the King of Hungary. Your virtue must be above reproach. Luigi della Scala demands it. The Genoan alliance is vital."

My cheek sizzles but I am dry eyed. The burning sting sinks deep inside and courses through my body. I touch my flaming cheek and feel strength, not humiliation. "I have done nothing wrong. Nothing." Each word is purposeful, clear, and without emotion. "I submit cheerfully to His Highness's decision." I set cool lips on Aunt Erzsébet's ring-laden hand. "My respect and love for you, King Matthias, and Hungary come first. Please believe me."

My aunt lifts my chin with her cold dry hand and stares down with icy judgment. "You look innocent enough…unless you're more cunning than I give you credit for." She pats my red cheek, then points to the pile of costumes heaped on the bed. "Indulge me. Let me find you a costume for the masquerade." Aunt Erzsébet rifles through the robes, tunics, snoods, dolmens, capes, stockings, trousers, and shirts. Wearing a skewed smile, she tosses aside the beautiful, the sheer, the daring, and the elaborate. "Ah, this one will do nicely." She holds up a Turkish kaftan and wide linen pants. "If Dracula should seek you out, he will find you dressed in the garb of the people he has sworn to avenge."

All hope to appear beautifully beguiling for Prince Vlad drops like a rock in my belly. "As you wish." My voice is as smooth as polished stone.

Aunt Erzsébet walks to the door, pulls it open, and glances over her shoulder. "One of my ladies-in-waiting will help you dress."

The door bangs shut.

I sweep all the costumes to the floor and muffle my cry in a pillow. Matthias has all the power. Prince Vlad, none. Nothing can ever come of our flirtation.

"It's better this way," murmurs Bernádett while fussing with the sheer *yasmak* covering my mouth and forehead. "Your aunt is protecting you."

I steal a glance at Aunt Erzsébet's lady-in-waiting sitting in the corner. The only costume 'help' she is offering is the eavesdropping kind. "From whom?"

"Prince Vlad," Bernádett whispers. "Don't fall prey to his flirtations. I wouldn't be surprised if his idea of fun is toying with innocent maidens' hearts. I heard he flirts with—"

Margit bursts into my chambers. "Look at me!"

How can I not?

She twirls about in a skirt of peacock feathers. "I'm a woodland nymph." Her fingers dance over the bodice, a tease of web-thin material scattered with sparkling gems and cleverly placed feathers. "Look." Margit lifts her skirt to flaunt jeweled chopines.

"Your costume is stunning." Envy sticks in my throat like a dry crust of bread.

With her elevated chopines and tall-feathered mask, every guest at the party will take notice of her.

Frustration like steam heats my skin when I compare my dull costume and flat unadorned slippers. I will most certainly disappear amid the decadently attired guests. Which is Aunt Erzsébet's intent.

Margit puts her hands on her waist. "You ought to be glad Aunt Erzsébet did not insist you dress like a gypsy."

"I don't need to be noticed, I am betrothed to Luigi della Scala." I shrug, pretending indifference, but inside my enthusiasm for the masquerade molts like a goldfinch in autumn. My Turkish costume is a fabric cage but warbling about it will only expose my true feelings.

Margit tugs me forward. "Are you ready? Aunt Erzsébet insists we go together."

I can imagine the guest's twittering at our arrival: the peacock and the wren.

## 11

Greenery festoons the great hall, scattered rose petals adorn the floor, and delicious delicacies stack high on the tables. Musicians play in one corner, entertainers perform in another, and a magician confounds in the third.

"Have you ever seen anything so wonderful? I will dance until morning." Margit disappears into the crowd, her mask's tall feathers moving above the sea of heads like a dorsal fin.

Nobody notices me. I am lost in a whirl of color and noise. Invisible amid the spectacle of glittering fabric and colorful feathers. Unseen among the whimsical masks and elaborate costumes that encourage flirtation and seduction.

Then I see him.

Prince Vlad wears a tall red-patterned turban adorned with a large oval gem and a single white ostrich plume. His mask is striking, its black cruel-angled lines an intimidating bit of sculpted clay.

Prince Vlad casts his gaze my way and I move forward, my grin concealed under the *yasmak*.

He turns his back.

His obvious disgust at my costume twists like a blade in

my gut. Blinking back tears, I pivot on my heels. What is wrong with me? What does it matter what he thinks of my costume? I am betrothed. Unavailable. I square my shoulders, take a deep breath, and look for family and friends.

I join several ladies gushing over Aunt Orsulya's costume.

"It's scandalous," purrs Zsazsa as she casts an admiring eye towards the men's breeches complete with over-sized leather codpiece.

"It's wonderful." I tug on the false beard glued to Aunt Orsulya's masculine mask.

That evening, Prince Vlad avoids me. His rejection hangs like a heavy cloak from my shoulders, weighing down my feet as I dance with nobles and dignitaries. I recall Bernádett's cautionary words about Prince Vlad and his toying with young maidens' affections. Tonight I am inclined to believe her.

"Your costume is bewitching," a familiar voice says behind me. "There is nothing more alluring than lips that can only be kissed by a lover brave enough to lift the veil."

My heart leaps but I neither move nor reply.

"Have I mistaken the wearer of this costume?" Vlad Dracula circles around me, his fingers brushing my kaftan.

With burning cheeks, I lift my gaze to his, find his eyes heavy-lidded with desire. The heated thread of longing tugs at my flesh. He feels it too, because he looks at me like I am the only one in the room.

"I am betrothed to Luigi della Scala." My confession tumbles out.

"My deepest sympathies." His lips twitch as though suppressing a grin.

I scan the crowd. "Aunt Erzsébet will see us together. She's already chastised me. She knows you sent the letter."

Vlad Dracula drags a finger across his full bottom lip. "Do you think I am afraid of an old woman?"

"Of course not but—"

"Are you afraid of her?"

I square my shoulders. "I prefer avoiding her wrath."

"Dance with me." Vlad's voice is a challenge.

"You know I cannot." I scan the crowd in search of Aunt Erzsébet.

Behind the mask, his eyes glimmer with amusement. "At Visegrád you appeared a maiden of courage and intelligence."

"My aunt..." My chin drops and I shake my head.

"Then we won't dance." Prince Vlad steps close. "We will leave the castle."

My head jerks up. "What? I can't. I mustn't. It's..."

Prince Vlad whispers in my ear. "It's the perfect time. The guests are drunk or too busy flirting and dancing to notice our departure. Come with me. See Buda with new eyes."

The heavy cloak of depression slips off my shoulders, replaced by the chill of excitement. It is risky. Too risky. But every fiber of my being sings with the thrill of it. If I am caught without a chaperone my virtue is compromised. Possibly destroyed.

I lower my eyes. The tips of my slippers reach to the marble tile's edge. It's a line I dare not cross. Virtue or adventure? A few hours of fun or a lifetime of regret? The edge blurs under my indecisive stare. The two slabs become one. My slipper slides over the thin line of its own accord.

"We cannot walk out the front door," I say.

"We will leave through the tunnels."

My mouth drops open. "You know the way through the labyrinth?"

"The question, Lady Ilona, is do you?"

"It's been years." I lower my voice as a pharaoh-costumed courtier strolls much too slowly past us.

Prince Vlad studies the room as though assessing an escape route. "Change clothes. I will wait by the chapel." Vlad bows, turns on his heel, and disappears into the crowd.

Excitement gushes over me. Waves of anticipation surge through my limbs. I want to squeal, to clap, to dance. But I can only smile, glad for my mouth-covering *yasmak*.

Only one problem stands in my way.

I slink cat-like from the great hall and dart to my chambers.

"Bring me a servant's clothes," I say the moment I close my chamber door.

Bernádett, wrapped in a wool blanket, looks up from her darning. "Yes, my lady, but why do you need them?"

I fling the *yasmak* onto the bed. "I'm changing costumes. Bring a simple frock, kerchief, and shawl. Please hurry."

Face scrunched with puzzlement, Bernadette scurries from the room.

I shed the Turkish costume in haste, shivers of excitement prickling my skin. Rubbing my arms for warmth, a single cold twinge makes me reconsider my hasty decision. Will I be safe alone with Prince Vlad? He has always been a perfect gentleman. I pace back and forth, each minute an eternity.

Bernádett, a drab wool skirt, coarse linen blouse, sash, and kerchief draped over her arms, returns and shuts the door. "Is this what you want, my lady?"

I hold the rough wool to my body. "Perfect."

"Seems more like a disguise than a costume." Bernádett's brows skew in puzzled curiosity as she helps me into the blouse.

"Is there a difference?"

"I suppose not." Bernádett braids my hair, ties the ends with a red ribbon, and wraps the kerchief around my head. "Are you leaving the castle tonight?"

"What an outrageous suggestion." The lie slips like butter from my tongue. "Why do you think that?"

Bernádett's face creases with worry. "I know you are smitten by Dracula, who I have heard enjoys disguising himself as a commoner in order to mingle with his people."

"Smitten?" I laugh too loudly. "I'm changing costume. Nothing more." I lift my hawking boots from the chest and wiggle into them.

"Curious footwear for a party." Bernádett wraps the leather straps around my ankle. "Do be careful, my lady. Dracula is skilled in the art of flattery. The man—"

"The prince." I slide off my rings and drop them into her hand.

"Begging your pardon. The prince you are acquainted with is a fantasy. He's a wolf in sheep's clothing. He committed horrific acts against God. You do not know the true man."

I stand tall and look down at her slight form. "And you do?"

"No, but I know you, and the torch you carry for him is no match for the hellfire consuming his soul."

"Tonight is not the time to discuss political rumors." I flap my hand. "Do not wait up for me. I plan to dance all night."

Vlad waits in front of the chapel in a merchant's long robe, fur cap, and wolf-lined coat. His curls are brushed out and his mustache unwaxed. All noble affectations are gone, and yet his presence is not diminished. I find his rugged appearance more appealing and must stop myself from reaching out to touch his wavy hair.

Prince Vlad's mouth curves into a mischievous grin and he bows low with a gallant flourish. "I believe there is a tunnel entrance inside the chapel." He opens the carved wood door.

Inside, sconces cast flickering shadows against the chapel walls, and frankincense perfumes the air. Matthias insists the sconces remain lit as a tribute to Jesus lighting our path to goodness.

I avert my gaze from the holy relics, afraid the marble Virgin Mother, Stations of the Cross, and wooden crucified Jesus will convict me of immodesty.

"Here." Behind the altar, I tap the floorboard, which but for a tiny indentation looks like all the others. "Are you clever enough to open it?" I cross my arms and step back.

Prince Vlad chuckles, drops to one knee, and traces the edges. "Child's play." His fingernail flicks the thin mechanism hidden in the seam and the floorboard yawns open.

"You already knew!"

"Not at all." Prince Vlad lifts a lantern from off the wall hook and dangles it over the black maw. "Shall I lead the way?" He holds out his hand.

The warmth of his fingers shoots up my arm and nestles in my heart, his touch more exciting than our descent into the bowels of the palace.

"Are you frightened?" His eyes flicker gold and green in the lantern's flame.

"Does a wolf fear a sheep?"

My answer must please him because he gives a quick squeeze to my fingers.

The labyrinth beneath Buda castle is a dank vast maze of dark tunnels, rocky caves, and sealed grottos stocked with weapons, armor, and provisions.

"I haven't been down here for a long time." I pull my hand from his and stare into the black tunnel, my fingers clutching the wool skirt. "Father only showed Margit and I one way out."

Prince Vlad lifts the lantern. "Rumor has it there is an entrance under Matthias's bed."

"I don't know about that. But I do know only a few are privy to the maze's secrets." I rub my arms to ward off the chill. "Father said the Steward of the Labyrinth keeps the exit route lit. Supposedly—I've never seen him—he is very old, disfigured by fire, and missing his tongue—hacked off during battle. He knows every tunnel, grotto, cleft, and rock." I gesture to the narrow dimly lit tunnel. "Shall we?"

Prince Vlad squints into a different tunnel, one without

benefit of a single lantern. "Let's go this way. I have King Matthias's beautiful cousin all to myself. A hasty exit is not my intention."

I stare wide-eyed at Prince Vlad as icy prickles bite at the nape of the neck.

## 12

I am a fool. What compelled me to trust a man with such a violent past? I step back from the hungry-eyed prince, wrap my arms about myself, and shudder.

Vlad drapes his wolf-lined coat over my shoulders. "Better?"

"Yes, thank you." I sink into the fur, still warm from his body.

Prince Vlad's forehead furrows. "Are you quite certain the tunnels do not frighten you?"

"Szilágyi's are fearless." My voice is as brittle as thin ice.

"You certainly are your father's daughter." Prince Vlad holds the lantern aloft and strides into the tunnel.

I hurry after him, the icy shivers melting after hearing the warmth in his voice.

He holds the lantern near the wall, illuminating a crude etching in the rock. "Who drew these?"

"The wild men who lived here long ago." My fingers trace the outline of the fanciful spider-like creature. "Father said the tunnels have many such drawings."

"Is that so? How wonderful. Did you explore the tunnels as a child?"

I keep close to his side and within the circle of light. "I was only eleven-years-old when we moved into the palace. The nanny forbad us to come here. She said the tunnels led to *Alsó Világ*, the entrance to the underworld." I roll my eyes. "She also claimed *Bába* lived down here."

One eyebrow quirks. "*Bába*?"

"A withered hideous old woman with a few straw-like strands of hair coming out of her scalp."

"Reminds me of my nanny." Vlad chuckles. "This *Bába* doesn't sound very frightening."

"Oh, but she is." I laugh, Prince Vlad's easy manner dispelling my earlier fear about his intentions. "She lures children into her watery home and eats them."

"Then we have nothing to fear: We are too old to eat." He sidles next to me, our shoulders touching. "We have similar creatures in Romania. One is a demon who punishes faithless wives and wicked children." Prince Vlad stops walking, his shadow looming like a specter on the wall. "The *Martolea* rips open their victim's stomach with sharp claws, sloooowly pulls out their entrails, and loops them over a hook on a wall as a warning to others with sin on their minds."

I wiggle my fingers. "Ooooo, ghost stories."

"Are they?" Half his face is in shadow, his profile bold in the lamp's golden glow.

I want to run my fingers over the curve of his brow, slope of his nose, and the contour of his lips. I want to map his face and commit it to memory. "Those creatures are no more real than centaurs or harpies."

"You dismiss otherworldly beings too easily." Prince Vlad glances into the darkness, and then lowers his mouth to my ear. "Do not dismiss the *moroi*. These demon-inhabited corpses rise from their graves and suck the life force from the living." His leans closer, his breath warm on my neck. "Do not scorn the *strigoi* either. Those troubled souls are doomed for all eternity to walk the earth and feast on human blood."

The heat emanating from him seeps into my skin like a molten liquid warming my limbs. "How can I identify a *strigoi* if I ever meet one?"

"You can't. *Strigoi* are shapeshifters who can change into animals." Vlad Dracula circles me, his shoulder grazing mine. "Or become invisible."

His head tilts toward me, close enough I see the texture of his skin.

I adjust the coat—suddenly overheated—and stroll away. "Your talk of entrails and blood does not frighten me. We also have a blood drinker, *Táltos,* a sage with a spiritual link to God."

"Sounds heretical." Prince Vlad comes alongside me.

"Not to those clinging to pagan ways. You see, *Táltos* can travel through the three realms, the Underworld, Middle world, and Upper world."

"Like Jesus Christ?"

"Now you are the one who is heretical." I bump him with my shoulder. "Drinking the blood of a sacrificial animal gives *Táltos* the ability to climb all the way up to the top of the Tree of Life, where its boughs penetrate the Upper World. His blood drinking also gives him the power to cure illnesses and perform miracles."

"Every religion needs its miracle workers." Dracula stops to run his hand along the curves of a relief cut into the wall. "Remarkable. The deer appears to vanish into the rock." He sets my palm on the rock, covers it with his own, and guides my hand over the deer's hindquarters.

The cold rough wall. Vlad's warm strong hand. The cave's dank chill. His body heat. My own skin ignites, a thousand sensations setting my body afire. It is as though it is my buttocks he caresses and not the carved relief.

Courtiers have tried seducing me. But never this way. Not with grisly stories. Not in eerie places. Not by having me caress a stone carving.

"Primitive." There is a strange tug between my thighs.

"The most primal of urges. The act of creation." Vlad releases my hand and gives the entombed deer an affectionate pat. "Little has changed since those times. Even Christianity keeps its pagan blood-drinking rites."

"You're wrong." I drag my tingling palm against my skirt. "Catholicism abolished all pagan practices."

"*Caro enim mea mea vere cibus et sanguis meus est potu.*"

"The Holy Communion? He that eats my flesh and drinks my blood dwells in me, and I in him." I shake my head. "Jesus offers His spiritual and mystical essence. Your attempts at playing the blasphemer are futile."

"Ancient warriors consumed the flesh and blood of their enemies as a way of absorbing their power. Surely, you cannot deny the ritual's similarities."

"Are you testing my Catholic faith?" I do not know if he is teasing or serious.

"Does it need testing?" Prince Vlad's face is without emotion. "Are you content with a religion begot of blood and brutality?"

I stare at him, his face unreadable. "Don't all religions begin that way?"

"Most, but not all." The thinnest smile appears. "The origins of the Şolomonari are peaceful."

"So peaceful I have never heard of them."

Prince Vlad's laughter reverberates off the rock walls like thunder. "I enjoy your saucy wit."

I look away, my face flushing with the compliment. "Aunt Orsulya says men don't like to be bested by women."

"Only lesser men. You, Lady Ilona, will be unhappy with a man who requires only the marital pleasures of royal breeding."

I gasp, stop walking, and turn to him. "You cross a line."

"Did I?" He leans close, his cheek a mere breath from mine. "I hope to cross much more."

My legs tremble and yet my body bends toward him like a sapling in the wind. Father in Heaven protect me from falling into his arms! Luckily, the angel of virtue stiffens my spine and saves me from ruin.

I step away and wag my finger in front of his surprised face. "I shall be cross if you persist."

Prince Vlad snatches my hand. "Do you believe that the lines and creases reveal one's life?" He turns it palm side up.

"Palmistry is a heathen practice." My breath grows ragged when his fingers curl around my palm and stroke the soft flesh between thumb and forefinger.

"Not heathen, merely ancient. Aristotle believed the Heavens drew the lines for a reason, devised a skin map of sorts." Prince Vlad traces the crease from my thumb to wrist with exquisite slowness. "This is your life line. Yours is long."

We lock eyes and my mouth fills with moisture.

I once heard the ladies at court confess to being so seduced by a man's touch their thighs spread of their own accord. I did not understand then. Now I do. A pleasurable ache simmers below, a heated unfamiliar yearning.

"What else do you see?" I whisper.

"Your heart line." His fingertip sears diagonally across my palm. "The crisscross lines reveal your ambitious, flirtatious, and anxious nature. It also reveals your love of adventure and risk."

"Luigi della Scala is a fortunate man." I try to snatch back my hand, but Prince Vlad's firm grip creates a warm friction akin to removing a tight glove. I am lightheaded, my pulse racing with his torrid innuendo.

"Well then." Prince Vlad rubs his hands together as though savoring the feeling of our skin-to-skin contact.

"Which one leads to the dungeons?" He points ahead to where the tunnels divide.

His question douses my lust-fueled imaginings with cold water. "Why do you want to see torture chambers and prison cells?"

"I want to see where Matthias claims he holds me prisoner."

"Who thinks you live in a dungeon?"

"The rest of the world, Lady Ilona. Farmers, shopkeepers, merchants, guildsmen, nobles—anyone not living under Buda Palace's roof. You see, King Matthias and his councilors fabricated a frightening fiction about me."

"Why would they do that?" I doubt my cousin would stoop to spreading lies.

"They had to justify my capture and imprisonment to the world." Prince Vlad's eyes taper into disbelief. "Did you not see the pamphlet?"

"What pamphlet?" There's proof of Matthias's lies?

"Matthias ordered the chancellery to print and distribute an insulting thousand-line poem by Viennese court poet Michael Beheim called *The Story of a Bloodthirsty Madman Called Dracula of Wallachia.* It's a horribly distorted retelling of an encounter I had with a disgruntled monk many years ago and paints me as a veritable minion of Satan."

My hand flies to my mouth. "That's horrible." Surely, Matthias had been ill advised. He would never do such a thing.

"Well, it did have one unexpected yet useful result." Prince Vlad stretches out his arm. "It reminds my enemies that my reach is long and my power undiminished." He makes a fist.

"I see." And sadly, I understand. Kings, councilors, diplomats, and foreign emissaries swim in a treacherous sea. How is it possible to ride the waves of truth when the tide of lies sweeps the righteous man away?

We turn a craggy corner, and a ghoulish echo from the dark beyond makes my blood freeze mid step.

"I am not going any further." I tuck my hands into the coat. "I refuse to see prisoners caged like animals."

"A pampered life makes you weak." Prince Vlad lets loose a disappointed grunt. "A princess must not avoid the grim realities of sovereignty."

Prince Vlad may quicken my pulse and heat my loins, but I do not feel the need to appease him. "I am betrothed to the *capitano grande*. I will never be a princess." The gypsy's prophecy had proved false.

"Life is full of unexpected twists and turns." Prince Vlad rests his hand on the small of my back. "Come, Lady Ilona, look at the faces of anarchy and villainy, and see how much they resemble your friends and family."

"I will not." I back away from the entrance where moans rise from the bowels of the labyrinth like a demon's song.

"The choice is yours, of course." His tone is low and gentle, but in the lamplight his stare is wolf like.

I shift from foot to foot, look away, only to glance back. Does he hear my heart knocking against my breast? Can he smell my fear as it beads wet on my neck? Do I want to rise to this challenge? Or am I a fool for allowing him to bait me?

My fingers tighten around the lamp's clay handle. "I will humor you, my lord, but only because Father taught me courage and graciousness."

"Mihály taught you well." He holds out his hand. "My lady."

The lamp divides the darkness like a saber, each foot forward lighting our descent into hell. Ghostly groans from below seep through the rock. I sink into Vlad's fur-lined coat as though their suffering will soak into my soul.

Vlad pauses before descending the narrow rock steps leading into the labyrinth's deepest level. "Are you certain?"

His eyes glint with challenge. "A weak constitution is nothing to be ashamed of."

I lift my chin and glare with pretended insult. "I am the daughter of Michael Szilágyi and Margit Báthory. Iron courage flows in my blood." I push back my cuff and show him the blue-forked veins in my wrist. "I am as brave as Hadak Ura, our ancient pagan warlord."

"I believe you, my lady. I will not doubt again."

The clanking chains and eerie moans get louder with each step down, the noises merging into a demonic choir like that of Ördög's requiem to the Underworld. My legs shake, my neck wet with icy prickles, and my skin tightens around my chest.

I lift the lamp into hell.

The circle of light shines upon a pockmarked man stretching his arm between the bars, his fingers curled like claws. "Bless me, good sister."

In the cell next to him, a naked wretch spits onto the ground. "*Menj a fenébe!*"

"I am innocent!" A third prisoner grabs the bars and presses his wild-bearded face against the iron. "Tell His Highness there is a Turkish spy in his court. He is in danger! You must warn him!"

My head swivels toward Prince Vlad.

"There are always spies," Vlad whispers.

I walk with measured pace and let the lantern reveal each doomed prisoner. Most stare, empty-eyed; the whips, chains, skin shredders, bone crushers, and *strappado* take away all hope and spirit. Others shout obscenities. One man kneels, hands in prayer, and mutters the Hail Mary.

The weight of their misery crashes down, squeezes my heart, and crushes my breath. This place must be worse than hell's torments because these wretches yet live, have all their faculties! No one deserves this! It is inhumane! Sadistic and depraved!

My breath comes in shreds and clumps. I cover my nose with Prince Vlad's cape, the stench of rotting flesh enfolding me in its putrid embrace. My pace quickens. It is time to end this test of my courage.

"You!" A milky-eyed wretch points to Prince Vlad and begins chanting in a foreign tongue.

Prince Vlad guides me away from the cells. "You have thrice over proven your courage tonight."

"What language was that man speaking?"

"He recites from the *Corpus Hermeticum*." Dracula takes the lantern and illuminates the stairwell. "It's a pagan book of alchemy, astronomy, and metaphysics."

"It sounded like he cursed us."

"Pay no attention to a madman's rants. That particular book is nothing but Egyptian and Greek nonsense."

I tread upwards, evil's chill clinging to my limbs. At the top, I try to purge the dungeon's misery, malice, and madness with a long exhalation. Yet the horror sticks like nettles in my soul.

"This way." I move past the dark tunnel and enter the lighted one, relieved to put space and distance between the prisoners and me.

The tunnel ends at a large grotto where Prince Vlad pauses to light the ring of torches affixed to the walls. I wait on a stone bench near the baptismal fount, sighing with relief as the golden glow of the church-like arches infuses peace into my troubled soul.

Prince Vlad sits beside me. "We go from hell to heaven."

I tuck a stray lock behind my ear. "This was Father's favorite grotto. God's Buried Cathedral, he called it. His second favorite has a Titan-sized head emerging from the ground—like a god got stuck in molten rock. I was only in that grotto once. It reminded me of an insect trapped in tree sap that ages to amber—the insect forever entombed—never aging, almost alive in its resin grave."

"Do you find that horrific or beautiful?" His eyes search mine.

"Both I suppose." My shoulders move into my sigh. "Caves are dreary places."

"I rather enjoy them. Tunnels have saved my life several times." Dracula stands. "I think we are both ready for fresh air." He offers his hand, its warmth a familiar comfort.

Together we walk through the tunnel lit by small lanterns that flicker like fireflies all the way to the exit.

Prince Vlad gives the stubborn iron-crossed door a hard yank and it groans open. Outside, a sapphire dawn drapes over Buda.

"On no." My hands fly to my face. "It's so late it's early." Were we in the tunnels that long? If my aunts discover I never returned to my room...I spin about, my voice edged with panic. "I have to go back. Now."

Vlad's brows crease with concern. He tugs a handkerchief from his robe and touches it to my lips as though dabbing at a smudge. "There's something I must do first." He lays the linen over my lips and sets his mouth on mine.

Even through the thin fabric, his lips sear my own. I part my lips, feel the linen moisten with the breath of our lust. I collapse into him, my body sizzling with desire. I am about to rip away the fabric and taste his lips when he breaks the kiss.

Vlad Dracula steps back, the handkerchief between thumb and forefinger. "If you marry Luigi della Scala you will still be chaste." He drags the handkerchief across his mouth. "I will always have this."

Chaste? Prince Vlad just violated my heart and corrupted my flesh!

Back in my chambers, I touch my lips that still burn with the memory of our kiss—my first kiss—and groan. Vlad Dracula used my virtue, conceit, and fears to study the labyrinth's secrets. He took advantage of my desire for romantic adventure to learn the escape route.

## 13

# Vlad

**Spring 1443**
**Sultan's Palace in Edirne, Anatolia**

"He's a *pasha*, right?" Vlad turned to the guard after a man in a tall broad turban, silk robe, and matching shoes strolled by.

The guard grunted yes.

Vlad stood a little taller. "Is the man in the green robe an *aga*?"

"You're a quick learner."

Vlad's lips pressed into a satisfied smile. It had been less than a week since he and Radu had been transferred from the stone fortress in Egrigöz to the sultan's palace in Edirne. In that time Vlad learned to differentiate between the various kaftans and turbans. Knowing a *musti* from an *aga* from a *pasha* was not easy. The sultan's palace was a hive of activity surrounded by military headquarters, officer lodgings, and imperial residences.

"If only the sultan was as quick about bringing us to our father," Vlad mumbled under his breath.

"I heard that." The guard scowled. "You want my scimitar across your insolent little throat?"

Vlad slunk back against the wall.

On the seventh day, two guards escorted Radu and Vlad through the white marble halls and crimson-tiled rooms to a large chamber filled with boys and books.

An elegantly attired boy rose from a silk cushion. "We've been waiting for you."

Vlad bowed. "I am—"

"You are Vlad and Radu, sons of Vlad Dracul, Prince of Wallachia." The boy embraced Vlad like a brother. "I am Mehmed Celibi, future sultan and ruler of the world."

Ruler of the world…

Vlad's eyes grew wide. One day, this boy would demand a ten-thousand-ducat tribute, abduct Wallachian boys, pillage Wallachian villages, slaughter men, and rape women.

The thirteen-year-old Vlad swallowed the sourness rising in his throat. "We are honored to be your guests and look forward to seeing our father."

"He will arrive shortly." Mehmed looked down his nose with a superior smirk.

"I miss Father." Radu, speaking Romanian, huddled close to Vlad. "I want to go home."

Mehmed laid his hand on Radu's shoulder. "How old are you?"

"Eight years," he whispered and shuffled behind Vlad.

Mehmed turned his attention to Vlad. "Did you enjoy your visit to Egrigöz?"

"Very much." Vlad met Mehmed's false smile with one of his own. "We are indebted to the sultan's…hospitality."

"I like this castle better." Radu peeked around Vlad. "It's beautiful."

"All our palaces are beautiful in their own way." Mehmed spread his arms wide. "We have the finest builders, artists, craftsmen, and scholars in the world."

Radu came out from behind Vlad. "Can I see the harem?"

"You are too young to enjoy its pleasures." Mehmed stroked Radu's cheek. "But one day, oh, how the women will fawn over your sweet face."

One day? Vlad winced, unsure if he heard correctly.

Mehmed's eyes lit up. "Father!"

Vlad and Radu spun about. Their own beloved father strode into the room with Sultan Murad. Vlad Dracul, looking like a Turk in a white turban, loose gown, and robe, opened his arms.

"*Tăti!*" Radu threw himself against his father.

Vlad held back, looked for signs of torture, but saw only that his father had grown more rotund.

"Look at you. Tall and strong." Dracul clapped Vlad's shoulder. "Turkish food and climate make men of you."

A beaming Sultan Murad held out his hands, rustling the golden folds of his silk robe. "I told you your sons would thrive in my care."

Dracul smiled and nodded. He agreed. He had no choice.

Sultan Murad peered down his long narrow nose at Vlad. "How did you find Egrigöz? Pleasant?"

The sultan asked him a question! Vlad's ears and neck turned red. "M-m-my brother and I are indebted to you, Your Majesty. Your generosity will never be forgotten."

Sultan Murad's eyebrows rose in surprise and turned to Dracul. "Your son speaks our language flawlessly."

"They are intelligent and obedient boys, Your Majesty." Dracul turned his tight smile on his sons. "I have good news. Sultan Murad and I have decided you will continue enjoying his gracious hospitality for a while longer."

"Nooooo." Radu threw back his head. "I miss mother and Mircea and—and everybody."

Dracul lifted Radu's chin. "The sultan bestows a great honor on us. You will receive the finest education in the world, be tutored by the same scholars as his own son. You owe him gratitude not tears." He wiped Radu's cheek with his thumb and then gently pried himself from Radu's clutches.

Vlad caught his father's eye and felt the truth stab his heart. Their fate was sealed. Vlad and Radu must live with the enemy. It was a common arrangement. Vlad and Radu would expect kindness as long as Dracul obeyed the sultan, pledged Wallachia a vassal state, and paid yearly tributes. The consequences for disobedience—by son or father—were brutal. Death by beheading.

Vlad, finding courage not betrayal in his father's smiling face and easy manner, sent him a silent message.

I will make you proud, Father. I will learn Turkish ways so I can use their tactics against them. I will not convert to Islam. I will not be seduced by the harem's fleshy delights. I promise allegiance to you, Lord Father, and I will defend your oath to the Order of the Dragon.

If Dracul read the promise in Vlad's eyes he gave no hint.

Vlad blinked away the disgrace of subservience and bowed stiffly to the sultan. "Thank you, Your Majesty, for this great privilege. My brother and I will honor you with our scholarship."

Dracul stroked Radu's cheek. "I will give your love to Mircea and your mother."

"May we send letters?" asked Vlad.

Sultan Murad inclined his head. "Write as often as you like."

Naturally, all correspondence would be scrutinized for evidence of treachery.

Dracul gathered both sons to his breast. "Make Wallachia proud."

A vise crushed Vlad's chest and squeezed out the first drops of cold-hearted anger. Not for his father, whom he loved, but for an empire with such power it brought good Christian princes to their knees. The Turks were a plague infesting Christendom, squashing sovereigns like bugs.

MEHMED INTRODUCED Vlad and Radu to the others in the room. All were heir apparents between five and eighteen years, most already kowtowing minions. But not all.

Radu pointed to two brothers with empty scarred eyes sockets. "What happened to them?"

"The sultan burned their eyes with hot pokers when he found out they sent treasonous letters to their parents," said Vlad.

Radu paled. "I will never be disobedient."

Vlad grimaced. "There's a big difference between disobedience and treason."

LESSONS BEGAN THE NEXT DAY. Mullahs schooled them in Aristotelian logic, the principles of design, the art of rhetoric, and abstract and applied math. Ahmed Güranim—so respected even Mehmed was not exempt from his beatings—taught them philosophy.

Vlad devoured every lesson. Each morsel of knowledge fed his soul and nourished the promise to his father. Education was a weapon; a lethal tool giving Vlad the skills to command armies and rule a country.

And yet Vlad defied the mullahs. They whipped him for insolence, but the scars only made him tougher. They beat him for arrogance, but the bruises strengthened his resolve. Vlad felt purified afterward, each punishment a penance for enjoying the education provided by his enemy.

What Vlad gained in knowledge, Radu gained with friendships.

"Father would be ashamed of you." Vlad smeared a soothing balm on his red welts. "You enjoy our enemy's attentions."

"The Turks are not our enemy." Radu swept his blonde hair from his forehead. "You're jealous because they beat you and not me. You're jealous the sultan's successor is my friend. Father would be proud." He thumped his chest.

Vlad glowered. He despised the private jokes between Radu and Mehmed. Hated the seraglio women cooing over Radu's blue-green eyes. Detested the eunuch's preferential treatment. "You're as stupid as you are pretty. A friendship between a captive and his master isn't reliable. You are Mehmed's plaything, a toy for his amusement."

"Beloved toys are cherished forever."

Vlad's hands clenched into fists. One blow and Radu would run crying to Mehmed. Vlad uncurled his fingers. Perhaps Radu understood the art of diplomacy far better than he.

VLAD WAS LISTENING to the *muezzin* intone the second *ezan* of a sweltering August day when Mehmed stomped into their chambers. "Your father broke his pact."

Vlad's body went rigid. Bile climbed up his throat.

"No." Blood drained from Radu's face.

Mehmed jabbed his finger at Vlad. "Your father aided John Hunyadi's rebellion. He sent a militia led by Mircea."

Vlad pressed his lips together to suppress a proud smile. His brother led a rebellion!

His lower lip quivering, Radu rung his hands. "Now what?"

Mehmed squared his shoulders. "Father made me sultan today. He said he is too old and weary for another battle."

Vlad recoiled, stepped back, all life draining from him. "You're the sultan now?"

"I must go to war." Mehmed lifted his chin. "Radu, you are like a brother to me but when I meet Mircea and Dracul on the battlefield I will run a sword through their traitorous hearts."

Radu flung himself at Mehmed and wept in his arms.

Vlad's breath came fast and shallow as he fought the urge to pummel them both.

MONTHS PASSED. News trickled in.

Vlad buried his pride when an envoy reported that his father sent Mircea to lead four thousand cavalrymen to Hungary and Poland. He buried his despair when a messenger described how John Hunyadi, his brother, and all the soldiers fled into the forest after watching the Turks chop off the Polish king's head and jam it on a spike.

Mehmed returned gloating in his victory. Through battle-weary eyes, Sultan Mehmed peered down from his golden throne. "Your father broke his oath and now you both must suffer."

# Ilona

### Winter 1466
### Buda castle, Hungary

"You look more pleased than usual." Bernádett smiles while unlacing my bodice.

"It was an enjoyable New Year's party." My cheeks heat with the memory of dancing with Prince Vlad.

"A new year. A new husband."

"Oh…him." My grin dissolves like honey in hot water. "I hope della Scala's carriage slides off an icy bridge."

Bernádett's mouth drops open. "Don't tell your aunts that. Lady Erzsébet will be as angry as a he-goat and Lady Orsulya will make you pray the rosary until your knees bleed."

"I don't love della Scala, Bernádett. I don't want to move to Genoa. I cannot bear the thought of his sweaty body heaving on top of me."

"Then why are you smil—ah, you danced with Prince Vlad tonight, didn't you?" Bernádett shakes her head and tucks a loose strand of carrot-colored hair behind her ear.

I lift my chin. "I did."

"Dracula is promised to Margit, not you."

I puff out a grunt. "Prince Vlad is betrothed to no one."

"Does he make promises? Does he bring love tokens? Write letters?" Though her voice is gentle, her questions make me squirm.

"No." My gaze flicks to the only letter he wrote, still wedged in the mouse hole.

"My lady, did you ever think that Vlad Dracula might just be toying with your heart?" She slips the linen nightgown over my head.

"He is not that kind of man." I climb into bed and yank up the fur blanket.

Bernádett crosses the room and stokes the fire. "Did he ever try to kiss you?"

"No. Never." The lie tastes sour on my tongue.

"I didn't want to show you this but ..." With a furrowed brow, Bernádett pulls a folded bit of paper from her dress pocket. She holds it out.

I unfold the tract.

It is a gruesome drawing: A forest of naked bodies impaled through backs, bellies, and buttocks. Dismembered heads, arms, legs, feet, hands, and torsos strewn like offal before a bearded Vlad, who sits before a table laden with wine and food.

I throw it aside. "Why are you showing me this?"

"This is the real Dracula, not the charming man who seduces you." Bernádett taps the text at the bottom. "I cannot read, my lady. What does it say?"

I snatch up the paper, give it a good loud snap, and clear my throat. "This begins a tale of cruelty and evil concerning the crazy man Prince Dracula. It is a story of how he impales his own good people, skins them, roasts them, and hacks them to pieces like cabbage. He snatches babes from their mother's arms, hacks them to bits, and forces the mother to eat upon their own beloved children. These horrors are not to his enemies but are done to his own people."

Bernádett lowers her head and sighs. "This is the man you admire?"

"This…" I flick my fingers at the tract, "is slander invented by Matthias's councilors to justify Prince Vlad's imprisonment. Would Matthias give him a lavish chamber, his own squire, and servant if it were true? Would he attend royal dinners and dances? What sort of madman discusses Turkish invasions and holy crusades with diplomats?" I shake the paper at her. "Prince Vlad told me that this is how nobles deceive villagers who are fascinated by gruesome drawings and shocking stories. He said *pathos*, an appeal to emotion, is used to manipulate the uneducated."

"Pathos?" Bernádett wrinkles her nose. "Dracula woos you with foreign words."

"He was schooled by the finest scholars in the world, better than any noble in this court."

"Education is a grand thing but there are other paths to wisdom. Mine is knowing that actions, not words, reveal a person's true nature."

I am about to rip up the tract when I have an idea. "I'll keep this." I'll need Aunt Erzsébet-like confidence if I hope to succeed. "Good night."

Bernádett extinguishes the lanterns and gets in her cot at the far side of the room.

I toss and turn. Two dreams disturb my sleep. The first is the feel of Vlad's gentle kiss through the handkerchief. The second is the tract's grisly illustration. Kisses and torture. Both send shivers down my spine. I cannot reconcile the two Vlads. One is flirtatious and sensual. The other, cold and sadistic.

I WEAR the blue dress with white flowers and lace. It's perfect for the daunting task ahead of me.

"My lady."

This task is of my own making, and yet I am compelled to do it. For him.

"My lady."

Perhaps it is naïve to think I can help, but I am determined to try anyway.

"My lady."

I blink.

"You seem distracted." Bernádett weaves a shimmering strand of seed pearls into my braids.

"I'm thinking about the upcoming wedding," I lie. Again. But this time it no longer tastes sour.

"I'm glad you've had a change of heart about della Scala."

"I am resigned to a loveless marriage." I arrange the lace draping from my sleeves.

Margit pokes her head through the doorway. "Busy?" She walks in and casts an approving eye at my new dress. "Are you wearing that when you sign the wedding contract?"

I shrug. This dress has a more important function.

"It's very pretty on you." Margit cocks her head and taps her chin. "You ought to sew della Scala a shirt to show your devotion. Shall I send twenty-yards of linen to you? That might be enough to cover his belly."

"Della Scala has an older brother who also needs a wife. Shall I tell Matthias to arrange a dual ceremony?" My lips coil into a sarcastic twist.

Margit pretends to gag. "My maidenhead is already promised to Prince Vlad Dracula."

"By the time Matthias pardons Prince Vlad your maidenhead will be as old and shriveled as Aunt Orsulya's." Chin up, I stride from the room.

"I will pray for your soul." Margit's retort echoes down the hall.

Margit's taunt doesn't bother me. Well, not too much. I have another soul in need of my assistance.

I enter the royal chambers after the guards announce my presence and find my unwitting target at his desk.

"Cousin, come forward." King Matthias sets his quill in the inkpot and smiles politely.

I kneel before him. "Your Highness."

"Arise, Lady Ilona." Matthias dismisses his advisors, opens his arms, and we kiss on both cheeks. "Let me guess, is this unexpected visit about your upcoming marriage to della Scala?"

"Quite the opposite." I slip the slanderous tract about Vlad from my sleeve. "My loyal servant gave me this."

Matthias casts a quick glance over it and scowls. "What of it?"

"I am afraid for Margit."

Matthias cocks his head. "Afraid *for* Margit or *of* Margit? Because you certainly have no fear of Prince Vlad. In fact, you and he danced many times last night."

"I-I-I fear the tract's consequences." The art of scheming does not come naturally to me. My hands tremble and my voice, tight. "If everyone believes this slander then Margit's future match to Prince Vlad will be viewed unfavorably."

"I did not realize this was still in circulation." Matthias rubs his flaxen-stubbled chin and leans back in the chair. "Luigi della Scala arrives any day. Does this please you? Or did the Berserker of Wallachia steal your heart?"

"I…" I swallow, my throat dry with embarrassment.

"The time to default on the marriage agreement is long past." His rebuke is spiced with honey and vinegar.

I brave an innocent smile. "My only desire is that my family can be present at my marriage in Genoa."

"Your words are sweet to my ears, Cousin Ilona, unfortunately your eyes betray you."

I open my mouth to speak but King Matthias holds up his hand.

"Do not, sweet cousin, do anything rash between now and your wedding day. It will displease me and result in unpleasantness for Dracula."

"I would never do anything to dishonor you or Hungary." My voice is gilded with astonishment.

We hug goodbye and I depart, my heart lighter knowing my good deed is accomplished. Matthias is now aware that Dracula's reputation needs improving.

Feeling as crafty as Aunt Erzsébet, a smile swells my cheeks. What a pity I will never be a princess. I rather enjoy scheming.

Pushing Prince Vlad and our impossible love from my mind, I concentrate on more pressing matters—the ring ceremony, final fitting for my dress, and learning protocols from the Genoan envoy.

The Genoan wedding will be tedious. The contract must be signed, the ring ceremony performed, gifts exchanged, and my dowry transferred to his villa. All this must be done before I am considered lawfully wed.

"Ilona." Aunt Erzsébet waves from a cedar bench across the hallway. "I've been waiting for you." She pats the empty space beside her.

I sit, expect a discussion about wedding etiquette.

Aunt Erzsébet twists her green vesuvianite ring. "I have the most distressing news about your servant."

## 15

A unt Erzsébet lays a heavy hand on my shoulder. Its weight comes not from physical strength but from the political power she wields.

A disdainful look, an arched eyebrow, an ignored invitation, a forgotten curtsy, a whispered suggestion. These are her weapons. A woman's armaments. One slight from Erzsébet Szilágy Hunyadi—beloved mother to the king—even a perceived slight, sends the ladies at court into a panic.

A year ago she intimidated me. No longer. Now I admire her cunning. She has the king's ear, the nobles' respect, and a sage's discernment.

"Did Bernádett ruin a frock or behave improperly?" I am aglow from my diplomatic success.

A web of wrinkles gathers between Aunt Erzsébet's eyebrows. "Domestic matters do not interest me. Politics do."

"Bernádett doesn't—"

Aunt Erzsébet's jeweled hand slices the air. "When Mihály brought Bernádett to Buda he claimed she was a distant relative. Did your father ever tell you the name of this obscure relation?"

"If he did I don't remember. That was eight years ago, I was only eleven."

Aunt Erzsébet squeezes my shoulder. "My new little wren passed Bernádett in the hallway today and was struck by her resemblance to an acquaintance. She asked if they were related but Bernádett denied any knowledge of the person."

The hairs on the back of my neck lift. "Why is this a political concern?"

"My little wren's acquaintance is Romanian."

"I don't understand."

Aunt Erzsébet frowns as though frustrated by my stupidity. "I am a woman of scrupulous detail." Her knobby finger traces my shoulder seam. "Each stitch is vital to a frock. There is a kind of integrity in craftsmanship. One loose stitch compromises the others. A knotted suture, however, reinforces the seam. My desire is simply to determine the ilk of Bernádett's thread."

"Why?" Icy slivers prickle my spine.

"During her childhood in Romania many boyars disappeared, some fled to Moldova, Bulgaria, and Poland. Others —those not sympathetic to Dracula's reign—were summarily killed." She fusses with the pleated lace at my neck. "Never discount the value of knowledge, Ilona. Never underestimate the significance of family loyalty."

"I'll ask her."

"Good."

Fresh from my success with Matthias, I feel emboldened to bring up a troubling topic. "I know you prefer Margit but—"

Aunt Erzsébet's brows shoot to the top of her hairline. "Quite the contrary. Margit needs my protection and guidance. Not that she is a dim-witted girl by any means, but she lacks your cleverness. You remind me of my younger self. When my face could still betray me."

I touch my cool cheek.

"The quick crease of your smooth forehead, the briefest flare of your nostrils, a quick swallow—you must control even these tiny displays of emotion, Ilona. Especially as they pertain to disbelief or anger. Or love."

"I—"

Aunt Erzsébet sets two fingers over my lips. "You marry into a family of wealthy landholding snakes with a humanist's skin and a viper's venom. Should Luigi della Scala suspect you love Prince Vlad, the marriage contract and the king's assurance of your virtue will be jeopardized."

My heart thumps against my bodice. "I did not—"

"Do you deny Dracula seeks your company more than Margit's?"

I shake my head and lower my gaze.

"Do you deny he sent you a love letter?"

I gasp.

"As I thought." Her eyes crease into slits. "Do you deny spreading your legs for him?"

I fall on my knees. "Please believe me, aunt. I am a virgin. We indulge in only a harmless court flirtation."

"No flirtation is harmless." Aunt Erzsébet tucks a stray lock of hair under my headdress. "Know this, I will make certain your wedding ceremony—at least the civil formalities —are completed as quickly as possible. Hopefully della Scala will accomplish his part and deflower you during the trip to Genoa. In the meantime, ask Bernádett about her family."

I am dismissed with a quick cold kiss on the forehead.

I enter my chambers on wobbly legs, my promise to Aunt Erzsébet weighing me down like an old wet blanket, heavy and foul smelling.

Wanting to get it over and done with, I sniff the air. "Was someone here while I was gone?"

Bernádett looks up from the wedding trunk she packs with dresses, shifts, capes, gloves, and blouses. "A boy brought firewood. Is something missing? Besides your red satin ribbon?"

I flap my hand. "That was lost during the masquerade. No, nothing is missing. I smell my mother's perfume."

Bernádett sniffs. "I smell nothing unusual."

"You don't smell it? Are you sure someone didn't come in? One of Aunt Erzsébet's ladies-in-waiting perhaps?"

"No, my lady." Bernádett folds a blouse into the trunk.

"I swear, I smell Mother's perfume." I sink into the chair. "My mind plays tricks. Sometimes I think I hear Mother's gown swish across the floor. What do you remember about your mother?"

"It was so long ago." She shrugs. "The memories feel more like a dream."

"Do you remember what she looked like?"

"She was beautiful, an angel with raven-colored hair and eyes as blue as the Danube." Bernádett's eyes cloud with memory. "We lived in a grand house with many servants, and I remember playing with children in the nursery. Mother was happy. Always laughing. I remember leaving the big house and moving to a bigger house—a castle perhaps—and her visits to the nursery grew less and less. One day a man I never saw before—your father—came to the nursery and told me the plague took her. And then he brought me to Buda."

"Was your mother a nobleman's daughter?"

Bernádett shrugs. "I don't know."

"Do you recall your mother's name?"

"*Mami.*" The corners of her mouth fold into a wistful smile.

"You have no memory of your father?"

"None at all. Do not despair, Lady Ilona. God has blessed me with a bountiful life. I live in a castle, serve a member of the royal family. And soon, if della Scala agrees, I will accompany you to Genoa where I hope to lay your firstborn son in your arms."

I smile, relieved there is nothing to report to Aunt Erzsébet.

I STAND in front of the crackling fire yet feel only my cold fate. Moments ago, Matthias and della Scala clinked goblets together after signing the marriage contract. My fate is sealed.

Resigned to a loveless marriage, there is only one thing left to do.

I knock on Margit's door.

"Lady Margit is not in her chambers," says her servant Peroska. "She is praying in the chapel."

The chapel is deserted when I go there.

I slide into a pew, clasp my hands in prayer, and beg for forgiveness.

It's no good. The altar reminds me of exploring the labyrinth with Prince Vlad. Of his warm hands and soft eyes. His laughter. His breath on my neck. His soft heated kiss through the handkerchief.

The door creaks open.

"Margit?" I turn my head.

"It's your bridegroom." Luigi della Scala lumbers down the aisle.

I slide from the pew, clasp my hands in front—a barrier to an unwanted embrace. "Good afternoon, *gentilhuomo*."

"Ah, *gentildonna*, you have learned a bit of my language. Such devotion gladdens my heart." Della Scala offers me his arm. "Will you accompany me to supper?"

I loop my arm through his. He lunges, grips me tight, and presses his face to mine. "I am filled with lust, my beloved."

I lean away from his wine and garlic-laced breath. "Not here. Not in God's house."

"I don't care how pious you are, after the ring ceremony you will submit," he growls. "I need an heir."

"Your emissary said the marriage cannot be consummated until I move into your villa."

Della Scala guffaws. "You are mine after we exchange rings." He wags his finger. "You saucy girl, luring me here only to deny me."

"I did not lure you." I wriggle one arm free from his embrace and open the chapel door.

Three people observe our tangled exit.

A leery-eyed Prince Vlad Dracula, a smug-faced Margit, and a pleased-looking Aunt Erzsébet.

"Does the happy couple rejoice so soon?" Aunt Erzsébet looks like a cat with a mouse in its mouth.

"Thank you for sending *Signore* Luigi to join me in prayer." My lips drip honey. "Unfortunately, I fear my prayers were too brief as we shared only an amen."

Margit and Aunt Erzsébet exchange a frustrated glance.

I coil my arm around Margit's. "Sister, let us walk the castle together one last time."

"Excuse me, ladies, *signore*." Prince Vlad, his jaw shifting under his skin, appears to be suppressing a grin. "Lady Ilona's piety reminds me of my own neglect of late."

Dracula disappears into the chapel.

I LEAVE FOR GENOA TOMORROW; family, friends, home, country, traditions, and language gone with a stroke of the marriage quill.

Hot rivulets soak my cheeks and dampen the pillow. My shoulders shake under the fur blanket. I cannot sleep. My mind is a boiling cauldron; thoughts about della Scala's groping hands, his rancid breath, and my wifely duties bubbling to the surface.

I fling my feet over the bed and drape a thick wool shawl over my nightdress. I check on Bernádett. Convinced she sleeps soundly, I slip from the chambers and hurry down the hall.

I pause to take a last look at my two favorite tapestries. Even by the lantern's dim glow I see the two hawkers astride their eternally galloping steeds, their falcons forever soaring in an azure sky. The second tapestry portrays a crimson-cloaked suitor kneeling before his lady while rabbits frolic at their feet. Family. Fertility. Felicity. I want them all, however, I doubt I will find happiness with della Scala.

I continue to the west hall, my destination and reason for my midnight trek. I tread on soft feet, careful not to wake visitors staying in the guest wing.

I arrive at my favorite portrait.

"Mother," I whisper to her forever young face. "I do not know when I will see you again. Pray for—"

*CLANG!*

I spin around, my heart in my throat. Someone whimpers. I move toward the sound. The whimper grows louder. At the end of the hall, a door is partially opened, a thin sliver of light slicing across the stone floor.

The whimper becomes a moan. I creep towards the door and peer through the crack. I see only a corner of the chamber, which flickers with candlelight. Someone groans again. I press my forehead to the door, angling for a better view. The door squeaks open.

All breath leaves me.

## 16

L uigi della Scala is naked, his saggy white flesh grinding against a servant's backside. The lad, too young for a beard, bends over the bed.

"Close the door, wife." Della Scala withdraws slowly.

I am speechless, eyes fixed on the scene. My betrothed is fat and old and prefers boys!

Luigi della Scala leers, pushes back in, withdraws, enters again while the servant boy moans louder. Then della Scala shudders, withdraws, his appendage hanging like a sausage.

"Perhaps you will join us." Della Scala caresses the lad's rump. "My late wife, God bless her soul, was not so inclined. But you are not as devout as you pretend. Come, let me show you how I like to be pleasured."

My body shakes like a dry leaf in a storm. "I will tell the king." Even my voice quivers.

"I doubt he'll believe a silly girl whose heart belongs to another." He sneers. "I've heard the rumors."

I turn, race down the hallway, through the courtyard, and into the chapel where I bolt the door behind me and throw myself at the mercy of the crucified Jesus.

"Forgive me my sins. All of them. The sin of skepticism.

Of being jealous of my sister. I repent of desiring another man. Oh Lord, why do you condemn me? How may I atone for my transgressions? A hundred rosaries, alms for the poor, daily confessions, I will do anything anything anything—just numb my mind. Give me the strength to bear this marriage." I suck in the frankincense-heavy air, ready to make more bargains with God when I pause. I am not alone.

I feel a draft, inhale a whiff of pine and rosemary. "Who's here? Show yourself."

Vlad Dracula rises from behind the altar. "Is this how a bride acts before a marriage is consummated?"

I sag against the pew, relief flooding my body. "Luigi della Scala is sinful."

Prince Vlad skews his lips into a half smile. "No one is without sin, my lady."

I rub my swollen eyes. "You don't understand. He prefers boys. I saw it. He wanted me to…" A fresh sob strangles my voice.

"That's the way of some men." Vlad walks toward me. "You're a good Christian. Practice mercy, forgiveness, and humility."

"You expect me to pray for his soul?" I sniff, wipe my dripping nose.

"Not at all. I loathe the man. I'm only reminding you of your Christian duty. I am neither a Catholic nor an especially pious Christian. I ascribe to a different code. One of loyalty, courage, and justice." Prince Vlad hands me a handkerchief. It smells of forest, spice, and rosemary. Just like him. He sets a soft hand on my damp cheek. "Tomorrow you start a new life. Be strong, Lady Ilona. Have faith." He kisses my hand, his eyes devouring mine with a raw intensity that leaves me breathless.

His kiss ribbons warmth up my arm and into my body. Hot tears stream down my cheeks for what will never be, for a love I will never know.

"Farewell, Prince Vlad." I withdraw my hand and walk to the door, then turn around. "You were in the labyrinth."

"I was." His voice holds no regret.

"You left the castle. Why?"

"I have allies to appease and enemies to crush." Vlad bends low. "*Yar hamu-ka Liah.*"

"What does that mean?"

"May God have mercy on you."

MY MOUTH IS DRY, my muscles tense, my body twitchy. I dread the ride to Genoa. Six armed guards will not protect me.

Della Scala sits beside me, our bodies separated by only the fur blankets covering our legs. If only I could build a wall between us with the food baskets stacked on the other side of the carriage. I turn my head from his onions-and-sweat stench to the open window.

My heart twists, tears wrung out like washing from crying over all he made me leave behind. My family, Bernádett, my falcon, even my favorite books.

"Tears do not move me," says Luigi della Scala flatly. "Instead of weeping, think of your new future."

Sniffing, I wipe away my tears.

"Genoa is beautiful, the weather always sunny and warm." The wood creaks as he shifts on the bench. "When we arrive, we will exchange rings, give consent to the notary, and celebrate with a lavish party." He nudges my foot. "Until then we will indulge each other as husband and wife. I want a babe in your belly before we reach Genoa."

I remain mute, my voice fragile, ready to splinter into sobbing.

Luigi della Scala drones on about his house by the river,

favorite foods, horses, garden, and Venetian fashions. I reply. Brief. Polite. Detached.

When the shadows outside lengthen, della Scala sticks his face through the window. "Hurry, man! We must reach the Catholic monastery before nightfall!" He tucks his head back in and rummages for a flask. He gulps the liquid down, drags his hand across his wet mouth, and pushes the flask at me. "Drink. It will take the edge off your virgin fear."

I snatch it, start guzzling. How much do I need to drink to pass out?

Hoof beats thunder by. Guards shout. I lower the flask. The carriage lurches, slams me into the side. The flask clatters to the floor.

The white-faced Luigi della Scala peeks through the curtain. "Bandits." He latches the wood shutter closed and reaches for his scimitar. "My men will make swift work of them."

Someone pounds on the roof.

Cold with terror, I yank the fur blanket to my chin. "What's happening?"

"Shut up." Della Scala wipes sweat from his brow.

The shouts grow louder, cries mixing with shrieks. And then a blood-curdling scream outside rips all breath from my lungs. I shove my fist into my mouth, bite down on my thumb and look to della Scala for comfort. He's bloodless with fear —his scimitar shaking in his hand.

Steal clashes against steal. Long swords clang. Short blades clank and squeal.

I wedge into the corner and fold my trembling legs to my breast. Della Scala puts his finger to his lips, shakes his head.

The shouts fade into groans. Wilt into moans. Wither into bloody gurgles and punctured wheezes.

A horrible silence descends. Not so much as a footfall or horse snort. Luigi della Scala watches the door, his white knuckles clenched around his trembling scimitar.

The bandits will rob us. They will kill della Scala. I will suffer a worse fate.

The door swings wide and a masked Turk leaps in. He disarms della Scala with falcon-like swiftness.

Della Scala's blade drops. His hands fly to the crimson stain blooming across his tunic. He grunts, rasps a curse, then slumps forward.

The blood-splattered Turk, his black turban concealing everything but his emerald eyes, turns to me. He shoves della Scala's scimitar toward my feet, yanks della Scala's body onto the ground outside, and slams the door. It sounds like he drags della Scala's body across the road.

"I believe in God." I put my shaking hands together in prayer. "The Father Almighty, creator of heaven and earth, I believe in Jesus Christ, his only son, our Lord who was conceived by the Holy Spirit and born of the Virgin Mary."

*Whack! Whack! Whack!* Loud hammering stops my silent prayer. I press myself further into the corner.

"I believe in the Holy Spirit." I speak loud enough the bandits will hear. Maybe my prayer will inspire their pity. "The holy Catholic church, the communion of saints, the forgiveness of sins, the—"

A twig snaps just outside the window.

"*Remissionem peccatorum, carnis resurrectionem, vitam eternam.* Amen." A low voice finishes my prayer.

The resurrection of the body and the life everlasting.

My trembling fingers clench the cross at my neck as I stare at the door. I recite the Hail Mary. Intone the Our Father. The door never opens.

I hear men whisper, gravel crunch under their boots, reins and tack jangle, horses blow, then the clamor of hoof beats galloping away.

"Thank you, Almighty Father." Nauseous and damp with sweat, my hand closes around the scimitar's hilt as I push open the door.

The light is murky, the low orange sun veiled with clouds. The trees cast long dark shadows over the road. And yet I see it. A blood path.

I follow the red smears and splatters to horror. To crimson pools and viscera mounds.

The Genoan guards are slit from throat to groin, their bodies ooze blood and guts. The driver's head is severed, his sightless eyes gaze at the darkening sky. His body is splayed on the other side of the road.

Luigi della Scala's body is not among the dead.

I fall on my knees and retch. When nothing else comes out, I stand on shaking knees and gulp the air. And then I see him.

Luigi della Scala is nailed to a tree and carved open like a pig. His entrails hang beside him. A wad of flesh hangs from his mouth. His cock and testicles.

My legs give out and I fall to the ground. The bandits wanted this to look like the work of *Martolea,* the avenging Romanian demon.

A crow swoops down, perches on della Scala's head, and pecks at his eye.

In the distance, a wolf howl rises over the treetops.

## 17

### Sultan's Palace in Edirne, Anatolia

Dracul's betrayal changed everything.

A stained robe, an illegible Arabic character, a mispronunciation, foul breath, an arrogant glare, all these errors resulted in beatings, missed meals, and humiliating chores for Vlad and Radu.

Radu became submissive. Vlad, more callous.

One morning a janissary walked through the door. "Come with me. Today you learn the art of torture."

Radu burst into tears and ran from the room. Vlad swallowed his fear and followed the janissary to a private courtyard.

"Impalement," said the janissary, "is a punishment used since before the time of Sargon the Second. You will master its subtleties. You will learn where to place the stake for a merciful quick death or a torturous prolonged one."

Vlad reeled back, blood draining from his face. "Am I—?"

"No, not today." The janissary shoved Vlad forward.

"Today you observe. Pay attention. Look at this criminal and see your own fate, boy."

Vlad stared instead at the executioner, who was applying a substance to the pointed tip.

"A little grease ensures a smooth entry," the janissary explained as the executioner pounded the tapered shaft into the spine of the screaming victim.

Vlad swallowed the bile in his throat but still he watched. "Who is he?"

"A thief, a maggot whose only noble act in life is reminding others of the penalty for stealing from the sultan." The janissary pushed Vlad toward the thief. "This maggot will take several days to die. See how the stake follows the base of the spine?"

Vlad gagged, willed himself not to vomit.

The janissary pointed to a shady spot under a nearby tree. "Sit here until sundown, brave little prince. Mark the stages of dying. Return tomorrow and do the same. Until the maggot dies. Pray the sultan in his mercy does not kill you in this manner."

The thief took four days to die. The first day, he begged for death, cried for Allah, and cursed the sultan. On the second, Vlad wrapped a scarf around his own face, the stench of piss, shit, and putrid flesh made him vomit too often. By the third day the thief's face was coated in a roiling mass of flies.

Vlad heard the thief's every moan, plea, and prayer. Each one was a spike to his heart. But later, his heart detached from his mind. He had no choice. His manliness was being tested.

On the fourth day, Vlad was able to gaze at the lump of flesh without emotion. Neither pity nor revulsion pierced his heart. The janissary's lesson proved effective. He had dulled Vlad's senses, hardened him, and set him on the path to becoming a warrior.

Vlad's next lesson in torture came the following week.

The janissary pushed the wooden pole and grease pot at Vlad. "Your turn."

At first, Vlad's hands trembled as he smeared grease on the pole. But as he aimed the point at the victim all his pent-up rage gushed forth. Mehmed, the Turks, his humiliations, their punishments—these wrongs formed a cold vengeful mass inside of him. With steely resolve, his mind fixed on the injustices endured by his people, Vlad calmly rammed the pole into the man's backside.

The man screamed, scattering the birds on the roof, but to Vlad it was a victory song. For the first time in his life, he felt a rush of power flood through his body, and this deluge submerged his soul.

"Bring the pole through his spine and out his chest," said the janissary. "There are many ways to impale. Many ways to torture. You will learn them all."

He did. Vlad was an apt student. He impaled thieves. Skinned rebels alive. Roasted a bandit over a bonfire.

"Pray the sultan does not kill you this way," said the janissary after each lesson.

Vlad knew otherwise. Live Wallachian princes were better bargaining tools than dead ones.

The last torture lesson, however, changed his mind about his worth.

"Today you learn about *toca.*" The janissary turned to a guard. "Do it."

The soldier gabbed Vlad and held him down.

Vlad's breath came fast, his eyes wide as the soldiers bound his feet and hands. "I don't understand."

"You will, little prince." The janissary crossed his arms.

They lay Vlad on a table, stuffed a rag between his teeth, and poured water over his mouth.

Every muscle taut, Vlad twisted and wrenched. He struggled for air but inhaled only water. The solders held his head still, the water drowning Vlad's scream. His back arched off the plank, his bulging eyes pleaded for mercy, but they were merciless and poured more water on the soaked rag.

Vlad vowed to kill them—to do all that was humanly and inhumanly possible—take up the Order of the Dragon, summon the forces of evil, anything to avenge them.

The smiling janissary plucked the water-drenched rag from Vlad's mouth. "Effective, yes?" He untied the ropes.

Vlad rolled on his side, gagging, coughing, and spitting. The janissary's scare tactic was a whetstone honing Vlad's fury into a sword sharp with vengeance.

RADU THE HANDSOME. It was an endearing nickname inspired by his muscular physique, smoldering eyes, and natural charm. Mehmed celebrated Radu's first chin hair with a visit to the harem. Radu attended private parties, accompanied Mehmed on outings, and was excused from learning the art of torture.

Radu befriended everyone. Vlad, no one. Their rift widened. Especially where it concerned their father, Dracul.

Radu dashed his goblet against the wall. "Father is selfish. He cares only about protecting his title."

"Don't be stupid. Father is protecting our homeland against John Hunyadi," said Vlad. "The man wants the Wallachian, Polish, and Hungarian crowns for himself."

"Father's lust for war goes too far."

Radu's accusation was a punch to Vlad's gut. "You repeat Mehmed's words." Vlad tapped his head. "Mehmed twists your mind against Father."

"What kind of father betrays the sultan knowing his sons might die because of it?"

"You fool, you understand nothing!" Vlad lunged at Radu.

"Guards!" Radu ducked, spun on his heels, and fled the room.

Vlad watched Radu retreat down the marble hallway. "Run away, coward. The guards can't save you from Mehmed," he murmured under his breath.

DRINKING AND SEX. Mehmed indulged in both. He found comfort losing himself in drunken debauchery. It numbed the pain. His father, realizing his son was not ready to be sultan, returned to power. Mehmed became a sultan-in-waiting again.

He still had power over some people though.

"Radu the Handsome." Mehmed climbed into Radu's cot and snuggled close. "Let me in."

Radu pushed him away. "I'm tired. Go away."

"You want it as much as I, my pretty pet." Mehmed wrapped his hand around Radu's cock, felt it stiffen.

"Stop it." Radu bucked against it but felt only the tug of pleasure.

"Mmm." Mehmed kissed the back of his neck. "You'll be as tight as a virgin."

Radu jumped out of bed, his cock rigid. "If I had a sword I would kill you."

Mehmed stood, swayed, and grabbed his scimitar from the floor. "How dare you speak to me like that."

Vlad pounced from the bed. "You're drunk. The sultan will be furious you violate the Koran."

"Shut up, Vlad. This is between Radu and me." Mehmed pushed Radu against the wall with the tip of his blade. "Get on your knees."

Radu dropped to the floor and Mehmed, bracing himself against the wall with his free hand, opened his robe. "The women say my cum tastes like honey."

Radu shoved him. Mehmed staggered back, swiped the

scimitar through the air. Radu scrambled to his feet and raced from the room, the floor speckled with blood.

"Let him be." Vlad circled Mehmed. "Take your drunken cock to the harem."

"Fuck you. You do not understand the love I have for your brother." Mehmed's scimitar slashed the air.

Vlad ducked, felt the scimitar swish over his head, saw a lock of his hair fall to the floor. "You dishonor the sultan and Islam." He advanced, retreated, danced around the staggering Mehmed in hopes of buying time for Radu.

"Get out of my way or I'll kill you." Mehmed swung again.

Vlad sidestepped the blade. "You're drunk. Don't be stupid. The sultan will kill Radu and I at his good pleasure not yours."

Mehmed sprung forward, his blade at Vlad's throat. "Afraid?"

Vlad lifted his chin and glared. "Of you? Never."

Mehmed's laugh became a gag. He retched at Vlad's feet, green-flecked yellow foam spraying the marble. "You're nothing but a lowly prince of an insignificant land. My people have kept yours in check for over a hundred years. We will dominate you for a thousand more." He heaved again, vomit splattering his robe. "One day you will pay me ten thousand ducats while I rape your women and take your boys to serve in my army." He wiped vomit from his mouth and staggered from the room. "Radu! I will find you!"

Radu returned at sunrise.

Vlad, heavy-eyed from waiting up all night, sighed with relief. "Where did you go?"

"I hid in a tree near the seraglio." Radu threw himself on the bed.

Vlad sat beside him. "Are you hurt?"

"A scratch." Radu rolled over on his belly.

"I told you Mehmed wanted—"

"Shut up."

RADU, reeking of wine and hookah, stumbled into the room and collapsed on the bed.

"Again?" Vlad slammed closed *One Thousand and One Nights*. "You've become as wicked as Mehmed."

Radu pulled off his turban. "If the future sultan says drink, you drink. If the future sultan says here is a woman, you fuck. If the future sultan says he wants an orgy, you fuck more."

Vlad stood over the bed, his hands on his hips. "You dishonor Father."

"Father would be proud. I learned Turkish ways and made Turkish friends. I succeed where you do not." Radu sat up, thumped his chest. "I, not you, am Mehmed's beloved friend. I am the friend of the future sultan. We even share the same women."

Heat surged through Vlad's limbs, tightening his fists. "And the same bed."

Radu reddened and looked away. "You don't understand."

"I understand that you're a cock-sucking sycophant who lets Mehmed shove his power up your kowtowing ass."

"Go to hell, brother."

"You'll go first, mark my words." Vlad stomped out of the room.

MEHMED TOLD them the grim news in December. "Vladislav Dăneşti's mercenaries murdered your father and brother in November."

Radu ran into Mehmed's arms and wept.

Vlad looked down at his book, tears blurring the text. He

stood, the chair falling away beneath him, and upended the desk, ink bottle shards splattering black ink over the white marble. He kicked the table, broke the carved leg. "I'll kill him! I'll skin him alive! Set him on fire! Impale him so he suffers for *days*!"

The following morning, a friend from Wallachia paid Vlad a visit.

"Cazan, welcome." Vlad embraced the Wallachian boyar, wondered at the bundle gripped in his hands, and gestured to the chair. "Do you have news?"

"Terrible news, my lord." A travel-weary Cazan dropped into the seat.

"I already know Vladislav Dăneşti killed Father and Mircea. Do you know the details?" Vlad poured Cazan a cup of water.

Cazan gulped it down and wiped his lips. "John Hunyadi and Vladislav Dăneşti conspired together—those pig-breathing scoundrels spread lies about your father, claimed his loyalties were womanish—changeable and faithless— claimed your father made secret deals with the sultan and that Mircea—the most valiant young man I ever knew—fled like a coward into the woods instead of rescuing the Polish king. John Hunyadi twisted your father's words making it seem like Dracul condemned himself. Many boyars turned against him and joined Hunyadi and Dăneşti at Tîrgoviste. Your father suspected treachery and closed the town gate. But it was too late. The two-faced boyars living in the castle rose up against him." Cazan stared down into the empty cup.

Vlad swallowed. "And then? I want details."

Cazan exhaled loudly, blinked back a tear. "They captured Mircea. Bound his feet and hands. Tied a sack over his head and buried him alive."

Tears bubbled up from a deep well of grief and rolled down Vlad's face. "And Father?"

"He fled into the woods toward Bucharest. Hunyadi's

men caught up to him at Balteni and killed him as he crossed the marsh."

Vlad smeared his tears across his cheeks. "Where is Father's body?"

Cazan shook his head. "No one knows. An old woman claims several villagers pulled his body from the muck and carried it back to the village."

Vlad rubbed his hand across his mouth. "What happened to Mother?"

"Princess Cneajna escaped and is in hiding."

Vlad looked away, anger churning his grief into a vengeful promise. "We both know that's not true." He closed his eyes, gathered his strength, then with a stoicism beyond his years pointed to the bundle. "What's that?"

Cazan pushed the parcel forward. "Your destiny."

Vlad untied the hemp and removed the cloth wrapping. "Father's Toledo sword." His hand curled around the gilded hilt. "Emperor Sigismund gave this to him the year of my birth."

Cazan reached into his cloak and withdrew another bundle. "This too."

Vlad did not need to unwrap it. He knew what it was, the weight of its responsibility falling upon his sixteen-year-old shoulders. It bound him to a holy oath. Consecrated his life's purpose. Ordained his future.

Vlad lifted the golden medallion by its thick chain. "*O quam misericors est Deus.*" Vlad ran his thumb over the inscription. "Oh, how merciful is God. *Justus et Pius.* Just and pious." He traced the lines of the Cross of Lorraine from its winged fire-breathing dragon outstretching its claws to the curve of the dragon's tail. "Christ is ever victorious over the forces of darkness." He lifted the chain over his head, positioned the medallion in the middle of his chest. "Mark this day, Cazan. You are my witness. I swear an oath to God I will avenge my family's deaths by killing Vladislav Dăneşti. I vow to uphold the Order of the Dragon oath, and I vow to regain my father's crown for I am Vlad, son of the dragon."

The opportunity to make good on his vow came one month later when Sultan Murad, impressed by Vlad's courage, tenacity, and stoicism made Vlad an officer in the Turkish army and told him to retake his father's throne.

## 18

# Ilona

**Winter 1467**
**Buda Castle, Hungary**

Songs, shouts, and music rise into the air, the breeze carrying their joy all the way to the castle's courtyard. Everyone in Buda celebrates the first of the twelve days of Christmas.

I want to dance a jig in the square. Eat roasted pork from a street vendor. I cannot. Ladies must be content with more sophisticated celebrations.

"Well, aren't you looking smug." Margit pokes at her embroidery. "Did Matthias find another fat old man for you to wed?"

"Perhaps two fat brothers." I wink. "One for both of us."

Margit rolls her eyes and scowls. "Aunt Erzsébet says your reputation is ruined because the marriage was consummated in the carriage."

"It wasn't." I draw the needle through a blouse.

"Do you have proof?"

"Margit." Aunt Orsulya looks up from her stitchery. "Are you calling Ilona a liar?"

"They were alone for hours." Margit yanks hard on the needle and breaks the thread.

The hours after the attack are a blur. A wool merchant traveling with his wife found me dazed, weeping, and surrounded by the dead. After telling them my name—no small feat, they insisted—they brought me to the castle. Matthias ordered the forests searched, promised death to anyone caught with the stolen goods or heard bragging about the slaughter.

The attack was a diplomatic nightmare. The Captain of the Guard demanded I identify the bandits' language. They hoped to blame the massacre on feuding Venetian or Milanese factions. I did not lie to them. Nor did I tell the truth. I said the language was unknown to me. Two days after the attack Matthias sent Vlad back to Solomon's Tower in Visegrád.

"Margit, enough," snaps Aunt Orsulya.

Margit drops her embroidery on her lap and turns to me. "Do you know Vlad Dracula has returned to Buda?"

"No." His letters never mentioned a trip to the castle.

Aunt Orsulya nods. "Matthias summoned him because the pope demands a crusade."

"Not to mention he needs Dracula to figure out how a single mercenary convinced a hundred cutthroats to seize a Slovakian village." Zsazsa threads her needle with bright green floss. "Luckily, Matthias thwarted the attack—he does employ the best spies—and hung every guilty man and woman."

"A king is only as clever as his best—or in Dracula's case, most shrewd—advisor," says Aunt Orsulya.

"Just like another devious person I know." Margit glares at me.

Instead of taking the bait, I attack my embroidery with a vigorous stitch, pricking my finger in the process. I suck the bright crimson droplet from my fingertip before it stains the linen's pristine whiteness.

Aunt Orsulya sets down her embroidery and puts her hands on her hips. "You girls act like Dracula is the only rooster in the hen house. He's not. Besides, it doesn't matter who you marry. Old man. Young man. Prince or count. Men are all the same. Brutal beasts with two desires—fornicating and fighting. Anyway, the decision is Matthias's alone. Not Erzsébet's."

We lower our heads and sew in silence until heavy footfall makes us look up.

"Lady Ilona." The king's squire bows. "His Highness summons you."

I stare at the squire. "Me?"

Aunt Orsulya nudges me. "Don't sit there like a stunned child, Ilona, His Highness expects you at his good pleasure not yours."

My stomach churning with worry, I smooth my dress, and follow the squire out of the room. Either Matthias will scold me about Prince Vlad's letters or announce another betrothal. Both drag my feet.

Matthias sits at a sunny table scattered with gold chess pieces. "Come, sweet and troublesome cousin." His arms open wide for a hug.

I rush over; pay no attention to his chess partner whose face is hidden in the shadows.

Matthias kisses both cheeks and clasps my hands. "You are more beautiful every day, Ilona. I'm glad your harrowing experience did not steal the rose from your cheeks." His head dips forward. "Do not forget to welcome this worthy man."

I twist about and gasp. "My lord, what a pleasure to see you."

Vlad Dracula wears an odd smile, half smirk, half grin. He is unshaven, hair tied behind him, and dressed in a tunic and loose robe, a gold medallion peeking between the lapels.

"Will you set the board for us?" Matthias leans back in the chair.

The kings are toppled, rooks upended, knights knocked down, bishops tipped over, the pawns in disarray. Only a queen stands in the middle of the checkered board. The black queen.

I exhale my anxiety and gather the chessmen, only to inhale the scent of man and ale, smoke and fire, and the musk of competition.

Matthias crosses his arms. "My noble prisoner is adamant about wedding you. His persistence is quite maddening. Treasonous, in truth."

Prince Vlad laughs and reaches for the black queen the same moment I do. "This is mine." His forefinger traces the queen's chiseled curves.

I draw back my hand, my cheeks flaming over his lewd fingering.

King Matthias scratches the blonde stubble on his face. "Vlad insists your temperament is perfect for the royal rigors of his fiefdoms."

I position each chess piece, except for the queen, which Vlad cradles in this hand, and set the white queen in her square before Matthias. "The prince is an excellent judge of character."

"That he is." Matthias takes a swig of ale. "We settled our dispute with the game of kings."

"What?" My betrothal, my life, my heart decided with a chess game!

"Not one game. Several." Vlad curls his fingers around the queen and kisses the exposed marble nub. "For luck." He stands the queen in the square.

Matthias slams his fist on the table and laughs. "I let you win."

Vlad, grins and bangs his fist down as well. "I promised to become a Catholic."

I step back and press my hands to my cheeks. "I am

betrothed to Prince Vlad?" I look from Matthias to Prince Vlad. "You're no longer a prisoner?"

"Yes, sweet cousin," says Matthias as though I am a small child in need of reassurance. "Vlad is a free man; however, this will not be public knowledge until a more politically advantageous time."

Prince Vlad tilts his head, his eyes warm with affection. "Our nuptials will be a small affair after Easter."

I cannot stop smiling. I want to throw my arms around Prince Vlad and sprinkle his face with kisses.

Prince Vlad settles back in the chair and crosses his arms. "One day your Wallachian subjects will hail you Princess of Wallachia."

I clasp my hands together, hold them to my heart. "You bestow me with a great honor."

"The title or the husband?" Vlad's voice is gruff and superior, much different than the smooth tones I am used to hearing.

It is another test.

"Both." I meet his cool green eyes and watch them melt into playfulness.

"You will learn Romanian." His tone is all business, but his eyes promise fun.

"I will begin lessons this very afternoon." I dip my head.

Matthias taps the chessboard. "Good day, Lady Ilona."

"Thank you, Your Highness." I curtsy. "I look forward to seeing you at tonight's masquerade."

"Yes, until then." Matthias rubs his chin. "What shall we play for next?"

I leave the king and prince to decide the fates of people and countries over the marble chessboard.

"Lady Ilona," Matthias calls as I am about to leave. "Your complete discretion is necessary. I will make the announcement."

"As you wish, Your Highness." Discretion?! I want to

shout from the top of the turret. Climb the bronze statue of King Sigismund to proclaim my joy. Dance through the courtyards. Vlad Dracula and I will wed after Easter! I am the luckiest girl in Christendom! I will marry the man who makes my body simmer, my heart sing, and my soul sparkle! I will be a princess! My sons destined to be princes and heirs to the Wallachian throne! I squeeze shut my eyes and shake with pent-up joy. How will I ever keep this a secret?

I return to the sewing circle.

"Why did Matthias summon you?" Aunt Orsulya is all politeness.

"Matthias wanted his chessboard set." I pick up my embroidery, my joy threatening to leak out from my mask of composure.

"His chessboard? You expect us to believe that?" Margit points her needle at me but speaks to the other ladies. "Look at her. She's as stoic as that Greek philosopher...um..."

"Seneca." I need to do something before my self-control crumbles like the walls of Jericho. "What indulgence will you give up for Lent, aunt?"

"The second cup of wine." Aunt Orsulya grits her teeth.

Everyone laughs and for a fleeting instant Margit and I are not rivals but loving sisters untouched by jealousy. Then a twinge, part guilt and part pity, wedges into my belly. When Margit finds out about my betrothal, she will unleash her fury.

## 19

I am Artemis, goddess of the hunt, my body swathed in white linen and laced with silver cords that hug my curves. I sling the basket of quivers over my shoulder and adjust the laurel wreath circling my head. Bernádett did a wonderful job weaving my braids with shimmering ribbons.

My glittering costume matches my sparkling mood. Aunt Orsulya says I glow. Happiness does that!

Keeping such a delicious secret makes me ravenous and so I savor every mouthful of fish soup, fig-stuffed pork, spiced swan, honeyed lamb, and apple crepe.

Even the music is sweeter. The minstrel's songs about love and honor make me by turns blush, giggle, and sigh. My happiness soars to such heights not even the thespians' anemic version of the passions of Christ mars my mood.

Yet nothing compares to dancing with my betrothed. Vlad's eyes are alight with innuendo as I melt into his arms. When his hand closes around mine to spin me around, I imagine his hand other places, shameful places. When his cheek brushes against mine, I wonder what it would be like to kiss him, to feel his lips on mine, to taste—

"Thinking about our wedding night?" Prince Vlad dances me toward a shadowed alcove.

The tips of my ears burn with embarrassment. "I was thinking of a Bible verse."

Prince Vlad quirks an eyebrow. "Which book?"

"One from the *Song of Solomon*," I giggle.

Vlad presses his lips to my ear. "How fair and how pleasant art thou, O love for delights! This thy statue is like a palm tree, and thy breasts to cluster of grapes." His gaze drops to my heaving bosom. "I will go up to the palm tree, I will take hold of the boughs thereof: now also thy breasts shall be as clusters of the vine, and the smell of thy nose like apples; and the roof of thy mouth like the best wine for my beloved, that goeth down sweetly, causing the lips of those that are asleep to speak."

His recitation is thick sweet cream pouring over my body, lusty images dripping down my skin, and soaking my maidenhead.

"Solomon was a lustful king." My voice is husky.

"And most beloved by God." Vlad bends over my hand, the raven-feathered plumes on his costume tickling my skin. "The next forty days will pass with tedious slowness." His lips whisk across my hand with the lightness of a breeze. "My beloved, I hate to leave your side, but our intimate proximity conquers my honor in ways I am loath to defend." He spins about and disappears into the crowd.

Margit, dressed as the pagan Earth Mother, Boldo-gasszony, sashays toward me in a daringly draped fabric bedecked with foliage and flowers.

"Prince Vlad left you alone." Margit adjusts a flower above her breast. "Your charms must no longer charm."

I shrug and feign indifference. If only I could slap that smug grin off her face.

Margit plucks an arrow from my basket and taps the

point. "You are Artemis to Vlad's Apollo, brother and sister. How prophetic." She pokes the arrow into my side.

I flinch but do not step away. "You are very dull this evening."

Margit snaps the arrow in half, drops it to the ground, and stomps away.

I leave the party soon after Aunt Erzsébet—inspired by her always well-timed exits—and return to my room.

A young ladies' maid, twelve-years at most, leaps from the chair. "My lady, Bernádett has not yet returned."

I had given Bernádett the evening off.

"Good. She deserves some fun." I turn my back to let her unlace my dress.

The girl fumbles with the golden cords. "Forgive me, my lady. I am sure Bernádett is not as clumsy."

"You've had a long day. I will prepare myself for bed. The rest of the night is yours."

With a relieved thank you she departs. Lost in a cloud of happy imaginings, I pull off my costume and slip my night-gown over my head.

There is a knock at the door just as I begin unraveling my braids.

"Bernádett?" I crack open the door.

Prince Vlad slips inside and slides the iron bolt across.

"My lord." My back to the door, I wrap my arms around my body. "What are you doing here?"

Vlad's emerald gaze sears right through my nightgown. "My beloved." He steps forward and his lips brush from the nap of my neck to my earlobe. "Do not deny me." His mouth hovers over my mine.

I draw in his breath, inhale his scent of forest, rosemary, and musk, and wait for his kiss. My body softens and molds to his, my lips part, my gaze pleading as his thumb traces the bow of my lips.

Prince Vlad's mouth lowers and I feel the first touch of

his lips. It is buttery soft, his lips whisking across mine. Each pass over my lip burns and chills. Each feather light touch is like a single granule of sugar—a tantalizing hint of the sweetness to come.

I am greedy and push into him. He deepens the kiss, the warmth and tingle a thousand times more intense than our handkerchief kiss. His tongue darts inside and I gasp. My skin is alive, sparkling with heat and a curious longing that melds my body into his. His tongue explores my mouth and I follow his lead, flick my tongue across his.

Prince Vlad sighs and quickens his thrusts. I meet each parry, open my mouth wider. It is a dual, one he excels in, for when he nips at my bottom lip, my skin glitters with a sensation that burrows between my legs.

His fingertips caress my cheeks, trail down my neck, and brush across my breasts.

"Oh." I break the kiss and stare at him, wide-eyed.

He stares back with liquid eyes and boldly touches my breasts again. I am panting, and push against him, needing to feel the weight of his hand, which cups my breasts and thumbs across my rigid nipples. Our mouths lock together, lips and tongues fervent. The womanly place between my legs throb and tug, and a lifetime of practicing modesty dissolves.

"No." I try to push him away. "I must be a virgin on our wedding night."

"You will be." Vlad's hand slides over my belly and nestles between my thighs. "It's important my wife be receptive to my desires." His fingers burrow deep, only the thick linen nightgown between my maidenhead and his flesh.

My fingers squeeze around his arm, my legs stiffening as a velvety throb folds into pleats of pleasure. My head lulls back, the sensation making my spine liquid and my legs rigid. "This is wrong." It is the whispered plea of my religious upbringing.

"Ilona, look at me." Prince Vlad's steady tempo continues. "I am not breaching your maidenhood. I am only caressing the fabric of your nightgown."

I moan, my nethermost smoldering and my buttocks rocking into his rhythm. The tension increases, my center molten, desire gathering and stoking into a blaze my flesh must enter.

"Give yourself over, Ilona," he purrs in my ear. "You are mine."

My flesh erupts, waves of joy pummel my body, soak my shuddering flesh with tingling pleasure. I throw my head back, my hips thrusting into his hand, and moan.

"Kiss me," says Vlad still rubbing me.

I smash my mouth on his, feel his tongue thrust to the rhythm of his fingers. Another wave crests, stronger than the first, and rips through me. I cry out in rapture, my knees buckling, senseless to everything but my overcome flesh.

A wide smile on his face, Vlad scoops me in his arms, crosses the chamber, and sets me on the bed.

I bury my face in my hands. What must he think of me? I act like a harlot.

Prince Vlad pulls my hands away. "Never hide orgasm's glow, especially since it assures the conception of many children. Good night, my lady." He kisses my forehead and departs.

I shiver, ashamed and thrilled in equal measure.

I PULL out the third uneven stitch. It is impossible to embroider neatly when all I can think about is my upcoming wedding. Especially the wedding night.

My skin warms remembering the way Vlad touched me, gave me indescribable pleasure. I once heard the ladies at court tell a bride that the first time is painful, but I do not understand how this is possible.

The door swings wide, and Aunt Erzsébet charges into my chambers like an angry bull. "Is it true? Are you betrothed to Vlad Dracula?"

I gather my courage by smoothing my wedding present to Vlad—an embroidered shirt—over my knee. "The nuptials will be held after Easter."

Aunt Erzsébet's mouth drops open. "So soon? What trickery did you use to change Matthias's mind?"

"None. Vlad Dracula won me in a chess match."

"A game of chess?" Her rage deflated, Aunt Erzsébet drops into the chair next to mine. Both hands on her cheeks, she shakes her head and looks to the ceiling. "Men."

"I was as surprised as you."

Aunt Erzsébet's eyes narrow. "Surprised but happy, I dare say." She puffs out her exasperation. "My son is clever, he knows your temperament is better suited to Prince Vlad than Margit's." Aunt Erzsébet inspects my needlework. "Excellent workmanship. The blackbirds on the sleeves are tiny yet artful." She taps the cuffs. "What will you embroider here?"

"Dragons." I lift one sleeve to show the stitched outline.

Aunt Erzsébet nods much too vigorously. "The merging of both families. Dracula will be impressed."

I give her a tight smile yet wonder at the reason for my aunt's sudden niceness.

She watches my needle go in and out of the linen.

The air thickens between us, congeals my suspicions about her motives.

I forgo manners for directness and stop mid stitch. "What is it?"

Aunt Erzsébet straightens her spine. "Have you heard about the strange circumstances which surrounded the death of Dracula's mistress?"

My belly tightens. "I don't pay attention to gossip."

Aunt Erzsébet pats my shoulder. "That's unwise. There is always some truth in gossip. Even if that particular truth is subjective." Her fingers slide down the veil of my hennin with the comfortable familiarity of a loving mother. "Nobleman, merchant, farmer—each sees events through eyes distorted by power, wealth, poverty, or prejudice. Ask three different people to recount an event and they will give you three different answers. Any shrewd person knows not to trust the eye or heart when life, limb, or wealth are at risk."

I chew my lip, finally decide to swallow whatever sour insight she offers. "I'm listening."

"Good." Aunt Erzsébet spins the vesuvianite ring on her finger. "Before Dracula was captured and imprisoned, he took refuge at one of his most impenetrable castles—a large fortress perched on a mountaintop with no rear entrance. The back wall of the castle abuts the vertical drop into the Argeş River far below. Dracula thought he was safe until messengers told him Radu's army was *en route* with cannons. Dracula's mistress—a Wallachian woman of no consequence— threatened to jump out the window rather than become one of the sultan's concubines. They argued when he told her the only means of escape was through a secret tunnel. Then, so the story goes, she screamed like a she-devil and leapt off the ledge and fell to her death, her body smashed on the rocky riverbank below."

"A fanciful tale about a foolish woman," I said. "I don't believe it."

"You miss the point, my dear. Though we might never know what really happened that day, one thing is certain, Dracula's mistress did not understand the problems that come from being a ruler." Aunt Erzsébet's cool wrinkled hand closes around mine. "Are you the sort of wife willing to go to hell and back for your husband?"

"Without a doubt."

Aunt Erzsébet tilts her head and scrunches her face as

though I am a foolish child not a bride in love with the groom. "Loyalty to your husband is not always that easy."

My other hand sandwiches hers. "You always stood by Uncle John and no one disputes that you are Matthias's greatest champion. Dear Aunt, I aspire to be like you, to possess your courage and loyalty."

"You are a shrewd but naïve young woman." Aunt Erzsébet sets her hand heavily over mine, our hands stacked. "You marry a man with a dark soul and a darker past."

"If you believe this then why did you want Margit to marry him?"

Aunt Erzsébet sighs and releases my hands. "Margit does not possess your shrewd sensibilities. She would be oblivious to those moral dilemmas that will plague you."

"What moral dilemmas?" I resist the desire to rub my cold hands back into warmth.

"A storm rages inside Vlad Dracula, one you must learn to control and subdue. You can only do this if you learn what feeds and soothes the fury in his soul. Study his moods while your breasts are firm and your thighs sweet, and while the marriage bed is daily stained with the vigor of lust. Only by understanding his deepest desires, fears, and longings will you discover the best way to inspire and calm him. By doing so he will come to need you more than he has ever needed anyone in his life."

"What about love?"

"Need trumps love every time." Her cool fingers brush the curve of my cheek. "And yet sometimes they are one in the same."

"I will try my best."

"You must do more than try, Ilona. It must be your mission. If not, Dracula will treat you like all men treat senseless wives. They put their mistresses first, in their beds and in their hearts. Do you want that?"

"That would be horrible." I sink into my thick wool shawl, her presumption like ice in my limbs.

Aunt Erzsébet purses her lips. "Then submit to Dracula's baser needs. Play the whore in his bed but be the princess in the great hall. And give him male children."

I burn with guilt and shame. "How do I do that?"

"Tie a string around his sack—not too tight." Her voice is matter-of-fact, as though she recites a guest list for a party. "He will enjoy this." She clears her throat. "Also, the ancient Greek physician, Galen of Pergamon, believed a wife must enjoy the act in order to conceive."

I look at the mouse hole, wish to disappear into it.

"I'm only telling you these things because your mother asked me to prepare you for the intimacies of marriage. Do her honor by listening to me." Aunt Erzsébet's voice is fringed with annoyance. "Vlad is not a young man. He should come to you only once a week. Do not encourage him to visit more often as this will decrease the chances of siring a male child. You must abstain during Lent, on Sundays, religious days, and the days before and after receiving communion."

"Is it any surprise a man takes a mistress?"

Aunt Erzsébet snorts. "Those wenches are not godly women and—"

The door bangs open and Margit barges in.

"You whore!" She grabs a silver goblet from the table and hurls it.

I duck. Air whooshes past my ear, and the goblet crashes against the wall behind me.

"You thieving jezebel!" Margit's red face contorts with anger. "You stole my bridegroom!" Spittle flies from her mouth.

"Get out." I leap to my feet, my embroidery falling to the floor.

"Calm yourself, Margit." Aunt Erzsébet pats the air. "It is not Ilona's fault."

Margit stomps across the room. "You seduced him. Wiggled your breasts—"

"Enough." Aunt Erzsébet steps between us.

"You probably spread your legs—"

"I. Said. Enough." Aunt Erzsébet rests her hands against Margit's shoulders. "You were never betrothed to Vlad Dracula, and I never promised you would be," she says through clenched teeth.

Margit's eyes throw daggers at Aunt Erzsébet. "You said—"

"Circumstances change. Ilona must marry first." Aunt Erzsébet pats Margit's shoulders as though petting a dog. "Do not fret. Matthias will find you a suitable husband."

Margit aims a frosty look at me. "I will never curtsy to you."

"No one expects you to." Aunt Erzsébet stops her pawing to center Margit's silver and enamel necklace. "Dracula is a prince in name only. Radu is the real prince of Wallachia."

Margit shrugs away from Aunt Erzsébet's fussing. "You marry a nobody without any power." Her blue-eyed glare, as cold as the Danube in winter, holds an icy promise of revenge.

## 20

"**M**ore gifts?" Bernádett closes my chamber door after Aunt Erzsébet's ladies-in-waiting deliver yet another bolt of costly fabric. "Turkish rugs. Your favorite sweets. Does she think your loyalty is so easily got?"

I unfurl the embroidered fabric, the gold threads glittering in the gray light of a cloudy afternoon. "She must suspect I will not always be a princess without a fiefdom." I hold one end of the fabric to my bosom and splay the rest like a dress. "Prince Vlad will like this."

Bernádett holds up a length of complementary violet ribbon. "I will summon the dressmaker."

"If only you could summon Prince Vlad as easily." I crush the fabric in my fist with frustration. I see Vlad only during daily mass, which he attends as a condition of his conversion to Catholicism.

"Your aunts are protecting your virginity, my lady."

I fling my arm toward the door. "Is a guard necessary? Does Prince Vlad really believe a courtier is foolish enough to kidnap me before the wedding?"

It is a prank, a Wallachian custom.

Bernádett shivers. "God save the man who tries to steal Prince Vlad's bride."

My breath catches as I recall della Scala's fate.

M&#x1D67; &#x1D11A;&#x1D11E;&#x1D123;&#x1D123;&#x1D11E;&#x1D121;&#x1D11E; &#x1D123;&#x1D121;&#x1D132;!

My WEDDING DAY!

My trembling hand smooths the pear-colored wedding dress. The embroidery is flawless, from the snow-white lambs on the bodice to the red Easter eggs on the sleeves to the moss-hued dragon and black raven—signifying the merging of our two families—on the cuffs. Beneath the veil my hair is braided with white blooms, green buds, and tiny pearl strands. My lips are stained with beet juice, my breath sweetened with a compote of marjoram and mint.

Aunt Erzsébet enters my room and smiles approvingly. "It's time." She gestures to the open window where the ledge drips rain. "Even the weather heralds good luck."

I cross the crocus and lilac-strewn floor, each step crushing the flowers and releasing their fragrance. I cannot stop smiling, my emotions as taut as the hemp string on a bow, my body waiting to fly arrow-like to my new life with Vlad.

The ceremony rushes by in a dazzling blur of contract signing, hand clasping, and singing. The cardinal tells me to submit to my husband. Vlad slips a ring engraved with our merged family crests onto my finger.

After the feast, we listen to the Romanian *ţigani lăutari* playing flutes, violins, cimbalom, and bagpipe. One melody is so fast the guests cannot keep pace, and I laugh with a spontaneous joy. Another melody has such a haunting beauty, tears well in my eyes.

I look to Vlad to see if he too is moved by the song but instead his brows are pulled straight with frustration. "What's wrong, my lord?"

"I am the happiest of men." The creases at the corner of his eyes say otherwise.

"You don't look happy."

"It has nothing to do with our nuptials." He smiles tightly, his mouth stretched into his public smile, not his private irrepressible grin that always warms my insides.

His aloofness unbalances me. I feel as wobbly as a rope-dancer whose foot slipped.

I lean close. "Now that we are husband and wife you must share your burdens."

"Is that so?" Vlad picks up my hand and grazes his teeth across my fingertips.

The suggestive sensation mixes with my worry, quickening my pulse and confusing me. "Your problems are mine."

"I just learned that Matthias's tax reforms caused Wallachian farmers to riot."

"Do not trouble yourself with the poor's problems," I purr.

In a blink, his eyes harden, and he drops my hand. "It is best you understand a few simple truths, Princess Ilona. Kings like your cousin neither understand nor care that for the poor a single coin of tax one day means no food the next. Have you ever gone without food?"

"No, my lord." Ignorance heats my cheeks. Ashamed, I survey the tables laden with trenchers of meat, vegetables, and fruit.

"Then you do not understand the poor's suffering. Kings levy taxes and dispense justice on a whim, and yet a king's way of life depends on the people he burdens most. Do you know any destitute folk, my lady?"

"Only the servants."

"They are fortunate. Always fed. Their beds beneath a sturdy roof. I speak of the baser workers, Ilona. You know them, just not their names. The farmer whose wheat made this bread, the child hewing wood for your fire, the young man cutting stones for the castle—his grandfather having laid its foundation—the maiden sweeping the cathedral steps. The nobility are the real *strigoi* of the land—they suck their people's lifeblood. The noble class—what an ironic name—are worse than common thieves, worse than the beggar woman with a never-aging babe at her breast, worse than the gypsies telling happy fortunes for coin. You can outrun, outwit, or fight these low types but you cannot evade the lords who rape their lands and—" Vlad frowns and shakes his head. "Forgive me, I've upset you."

I stop gnawing on my lip. "I never thought about it that way. Your righteous anger makes me love you even more."

The emeralds in his eyes melt into verdant pools of affection. "Either you are a crafty flatterer or the most perfect wife."

"I will be whatever is required."

Vlad bursts out laughing. He lifts a quail off the platter, rips it apart, and offers me a choice piece of flesh. "Oh, to be that bird on which your lips nibble," he says when I pull off a morsel.

At the appointed hour and after much foolery, good wishes, and prayers, we leave for Vlad's chambers. Our mansion in Pest—King Matthias's wedding present—is still noisy and dusty with hammering carpenters.

Vlad's chambers are aglow with candles and fragrant with scattered rose petals. Plush furs cover the red velvet bed.

I stand transfixed. This is my first visit to his chambers. Will his belongings whisper his secrets? Vibrant Turkish rugs murmur of his admiration of Turkish artistry. The carved writing desk stacked with books and paper mumble his enjoyment of reading. The decorative chests and tables topped with jeweled coffers and sculptures confide his appreciation of beauty. I feel like I know him a little better.

"Bernádett will prepare me for bed." I nod toward my nightgown, delivered earlier and folded on the table.

"Not tonight. Modesty in not permitted in my bedroom."
Vlad pushes my nightgown off the table then stands in front
of the blazing hearth. "Come, wife."

I set my hand over my fluttering stomach and recall Aunt
Erzsébet's advice to drink lots of wine and lie on my back.

Vlad pulls me close, then circles around me and sprinkles
kisses on the nape of my neck. Shivers shimmy down my
spine. He removes the headscarf signifying my new marital
status and uncoils my braids.

"Do you love me?" He lips brush against my shoulder.

"Heart, mind, and soul." My skin prickles under his
touch.

"But you don't really know me." His hands slide up my
arms.

My body melts into his, my curves cleaved with his. "I
know you saved me from marrying Luigi della Scala."

"Did I?" Vlad nibbles my earlobe.

"It was you under the mask. I saw your eyes," I whisper
as his tongue dances down the length of my neck. "I also
know you are a fearless warrior and Father's good friend. I
know you care about your people. I know—"

"You know very little." Vlad tugs on the laces of my dress.

"What little I know, I love." My breath is light with anticipation, my body already heavy with need.

Vlad pushes down my sleeves. "Love is a girlish senti-
ment. It does not satisfy a husband." He unbuckles my belt,
drops it to the floor.

"What does?" I wish he would tear off my clothes, my
skin aches to feel his touch.

Vlad's hands wander across my heaving bosom. "Obedience. Courage. Respect." He removes my bodice and draws
light circles around my pale pink flesh.

My nipples grow to points, eager to be stroked. "Why do I
need courage?"

Vlad tugs at my gown and it puddles at my feet. He turns my cheek, skims his lips across. "To satisfy me." His mouth covers mine with a deep kiss.

I meet his tongue, thrust for thrust, a hungry plundering that weakens my legs. His hands glide over my stiff nipples, stroke my belly and hips, and slide around to grab my buttocks.

My skin erupts into a single tingling need, wraps around my hips and thighs, and nestles into my core. I tug on his clothes, ravenous to feel all of him on all of me.

Vlad scoops me up, kisses the tip of my nose, then sets me lightly on the bed. "Patience." He undresses quickly.

I reach out to touch his chest, sculpted, hard, and downy, and trace the line of dark hair below his waist.

He drops his britches. "Do you approve?"

"Oh yes." It is thick and rigid, and I look away in shame at my wantonness.

"Good." He spreads apart my thighs and brushes his hands lightly across my womanly whorls.

My buttocks rise off the bed, straining forward, needing to feel more. He smiles with that irrepressible grin I already adore and burrows his fingers deep until finding a place coiled with pleasure.

"Ilona," he whispers sliding and circling around this place. "My beautiful wife."

My pants drift into moans, the sensation like a thousand quills brushing across every inch of my skin. His finger slides into me and I gasp, tighten my bottom.

Vlad's hand slithers around my bottom, caressing it gently, until I shake. Three sensations overpower me. His finger slicking in and out of my maidenhood, a rubbing at the entrance, and my quivering buttocks. I explode into a paroxysm of bliss, throw back my head, and writhe.

Vlad wraps my legs around his waist and plunges deep

while my nethers pulse, his thrusts spiraling me into another frenzied crescendo.

The next morning, I snake my arm out to touch my beloved but he is gone. "Husband?" I roll over.

Vlad stands naked by the window, the scars on his back a reminder of all I do not know about him. "Fresh air promotes good health." He turns, a small bird caught in his fist.

"They're such a nuisance when they fly inside."

"This bird is more than a nuisance, it reminds me of Radu. Weak. Common. Small." Vlad picks up a small knife from the desk and flashes me a wolfish grin. "Ilona, we are legally cleaved in mind and body. The blackbird of Corvinus joining with my grandfather's eagle. This foul fowl of my brother's reign must be destroyed." He spears the bird on the knife. "I promise you, *iubirea mea*, one day you will be the reigning princess of Wallachia."

The bird squeaks, its wings flutter for a moment before wilting. Smiling, Vlad sets the impaled bird on the desk, the death of the Radu Bird adding length and girth to his manhood.

"And now, dear wife, let us give thanks for a new day with my preferred morning rite."

I receive his fleshly sacrament with eagerness. It is not until our passions are spent, my flesh sore, the sun high overhead, that I look again at the spiked sparrow. The dead bird glares at us with contempt.

## 21

# Vlad

**Winter 1450**
**Bogdan's castle, Moldavia**

"To my sister, Crina, and cousin Vlad." Prince Bogdan of Moldavia hoisted a goblet of spiced wine.

The betrothal between Vlad and Crina heralded a new beginning, one strengthening an important ally.

"To family, new and old." Lifting his chalice with one hand, the nineteen-year-old Vlad touched the medallion on his chest with the other, and silently renewed his promise to avenge his family's deaths.

Crina stared at the floor and mumbled her cheers.

Vlad had regained his Wallachian crown.

He succeeded in sending the murdering usurper Vladislav Dăneşti into hiding.

But Vlad's victory against the man who murdered his family was cut short. Vlad's reign lasted only two months. In that time he learned a bitter lesson. The sweet taste of sovereignty was impossible to maintain without local alliances and military support.

The Wallachian boyars insisted Vlad defend his claim to

the throne. The Transylvanian vice-governor, Nicolae of Ocna, demanded Vlad disclose the whereabouts of John Hunyadi.

The son of Dracul should not have to justify his sovereignty to anyone! Yet the boyars would not be appeased until Vlad hunted down and killed Dăneşti.

Vlad did his best, but eight weeks was not enough time to track Dăneşti. It was, however, time enough to earn Vlad the title, Dracula, Son of the Dragon.

While Vlad wasted time forming alliances, Dăneşti regrouped with fresh forces from Hungary and rallied loyal boyars. They decimated Vlad's paltry military by Christmas.

"*Noroc.*" Vlad Bogdan's son, Stephen, a pious seventeen-year-old with a long nose and several unruly chin hairs, hoisted his glass with the others.

Vlad drank heartily, his gaze lingering on the angelic-faced Crina.

"Stay with us," said Stephen. "Continue your education. Our Polish scribes just returned from Venice and Rome. Our monks will teach you our people's history."

"I would be honored. It's time to replace the Islamic *adhan* with Christian church bells."

VLAD LIFTED his hand from Crina's linen-covered breast. "Why are you crying?"

Crina squeezed her eyes shut, her body stiff. "Just put it in and be done with it."

"Am I hurting you? Love making is pleasant not painful." Vlad propped his head on his hand, drew circles over her shoulder and wondered if the Turkish courtesan who had showed him how to turn an icy virgin into a heated lover had neglected an important detail.

"Just do it," Crina whimpered.

Vlad lifted Crina's nightgown to her waist and pushed in. It was tight and dry, and he exploded with release.

Crina burst into tears, drew up the covers, and curled into a tight ball.

Massages, caresses, sweet talk, gifts; nothing melted the frigid Crina. Vlad stopped trying and took his pleasures with the blacksmith's daughter, a fifteen-year-old jezebel with breasts as ripe as pears and a tongue as juicy as a summer plum.

Vlad needed a legitimate male heir so he bedded Crina every morning except for Sundays and holy days when she crossed her legs and laid the Bible on her curly mound. Vlad found their daily conjoining helpful. It took the edge off his urges just enough that he was able to revel for hours in the arms of the lascivious blacksmith's daughter.

After one such lusty night, Vlad returned to find Stephen waiting by the hearth.

"You're up late, cousin." Vlad tossed his snow-dusted mantle to a servant, poured himself wine, and flopped into a chair.

"Yes, but for different reasons than you." Stephen spoke without a hint of disappointment. He knew men like Vlad needed more than just one woman. "I have been thinking about how alike we are."

"Alike?" Vlad banged down the goblet. "I was the sultan's hostage. My family murdered by Dănești. I know the joys of victory and the pain of defeat. Your father and mother live. You wear no battle scars. You have not yet lay with a woman."

Stephen reeled back.

"We are practically twins." Vlad howled with laughter.

Stephen chuckled and shook his finger at him. "Identical twins with the same royal destiny."

"To thrones and crowns." Vlad hoisted his goblet.

"Better yet, we will make a pledge." Stephen thumped

his chest. "We will promise to help one another resist the tyranny of Hungarian and Polish kings bent on stealing our lands."

Vlad studied his cousin's face for signs of a hidden agenda but found only honest naiveté. "We must also vow to fight the Turkish invasion."

Stephen pumped his fist. "Your threat is mine."

Vlad's smile was grim; he wished every king realized that Wallachia was a door, which once breached by the ambitious Sultan Mehmed, would be the beginning of the end for all of Christendom. "Bring us a Bible," Vlad said to a servant. "Wake my wife, the prince, and princess. We need witnesses."

Half a goblet later they plodded in with sleep thick eyes and yawns.

"This is an untimely oath." Crina clutched the wool shawl tight to her neck.

"Nonsense, sister," said Prince Bogdan. "Important vows of alliance do not wait on daylight."

Vlad placed his hand on the Bible. "I, Prince Vlad, son of Vlad Dracul the Great, sovereign and ruler of Ungro-Wallachia and of the duchies of Făgăras and Amlaş, do pledge friendship and loyalty to my cousin Stephen cel Mare, of the House of Musat and heir to Moldavia as we seek to secure our respective thrones, the rightful legacy of our fathers. Not gifts, nor promises, nor affection, nor hate, shall deter us from assisting one another nor will we refuse to come to the aid of the other in times of trouble."

Vlad kissed the book, passed it to Stephen, who swore the same.

THE POLISH KING invaded Moldavia in June.

Prince Bogdan sent Stephen and Vlad to lead the battle.

They returned victorious, the combat sharpening their military skills and solidifying their friendship.

Once again, Vlad's days were busy with history lessons, parties, and lusty hours with the blacksmith's daughter. Those carefree days ended forever one chilly and bloody October day.

"Prince Vlad! Prince Vlad!" A servant pounded on Vlad's chamber door. "They are murdered! Dead!"

Vlad leapt from the bed, leaving the blacksmith's daughter with her legs in the air, and flung open the door. "Who's murdered?"

"Prince Bogdan and Princess Oltea." The servant was wild-eyed, his face pale with fear.

Vlad seized the boy by his shirt. "That's impossible. They are at a friend's wedding. You lie."

The boy shook his head. "I swear, my lord, on my life. Prince Stephen just returned from Suceava. He begs your presence in his chambers."

Vlad released the boy, closed the door, and turned to the blacksmith's daughter. "You must leave. Say nothing about what you heard. Your life depends on it." He donned a robe, strode from the chambers, and headed for Stephen's room.

Vlad found Stephen shoving clothes into a satchel.

"We were ambushed by Petru Aaron and his men." Stephen kicked at a table. "He's my uncle—my father's bastard brother, and he conspired with the groom."

Vlad narrowed his eyes. "Why are you still alive?"

Stephen spun on his heels. "I would be dead too except I was in the guest chambers when it happened. I heard screaming and ran to the great hall thinking something was amiss. But…" He shook his head, blinked back tears. "God in his infinite mercy whispered a warning. Instead of racing in, I hid in a shadowed nook and watched Petru Aaron force Father to his knees and run a spear through his neck."

Vlad's eyes bulged. "Why didn't you stop him?"

"Fight fifty armed men? I'm no fool. A dead heir does not benefit Father. Or Moldavia." Stephen opened a cabinet door, took a small worn Bible from the shelf, kissed it, and placed it on top of his clothes. "I barely escaped. We must leave. They're searching for me."

Vlad rubbed his chin, his mind's eye seeing all the possible routes of escape. "We will take the Bârgău Pass to Braşov. We can stay with boyars loyal to my father."

"Braşov?" Stephen grimaced. "That's John Hunyadi's domain. His mercenaries roam the countryside. We would be offering ourselves like a stuffed sow on a silver tray. Hunyadi wants your head, Vlad."

"Precisely." Vlad folded his arms. "Which is why it's the last place Petru Aaron's men will look for us."

Vlad returned to his chamber, arranged for Crina to be taken to her cousin's home, and packed his cantle and pack saddlebag.

Vlad and Stephen slipped from the castle, saddled their horses, and raced toward Bârgău Pass. When the mountain peaks glowed orange in the twilight they slowed their pace. Moonlight guided them a bit farther, but only until the forest's thick canopy swallowed their path in darkness.

They took turns sleeping while the other stood watch. They were lucky. Neither beast nor mercenary made an appearance. They moved on before dawn, stopping once to purchase the day's provisions.

They traveled through narrow gorges where mountain goats grazed on rocky slopes, eagles soared, and lynxes prowled. They shared their ambitions, debated religion, and plotted revenge. The second night they stayed at a small inn, ate heartily, and mapped a southerly route.

"We will avoid Bistriţa." Vlad crossed his arms. "I have no desire to run into Hunyadi's mercenaries." Vlad looked past Stephen to the rosy-cheeked whore leaning against the wall.

She hooked her finger over the dress's neckline and tugged down to expose her large brown nipple. Vlad's loins ached but bedding a whore was foolish. A few coins turned a peddler of flesh into a supplier of information.

Stephen followed Vlad's gaze. "You have time for a tumble. Our clothes are homespun and the horse's tack without a crest. We are rather forgettable."

Vlad dragged his eyes away from the luscious breast. "Too risky. Nothing gets past a sharp-eyed whore." He rubbed his stubbled chin. "Hunyadi fell out of favor with the Hungarian king. Had his Viceroy of Hungary and Governor of Transylvania titles revoked. The once formidable John Hunyadi now lords only over his wife Erzsébet, two sons, and few provinces."

"Capturing you would be a triumph," said Stephen.

"Exactly, which is why we'll go the long way around."

The next day they crossed into Hunyadi's lands. They skirted the villages, passing only a few weary shepherds tending their flocks.

Night fell early. Thick gray clouds pressed down and forced Vlad and Stephen to abandon the footpath for the protection of the forest. They made camp in a small clearing near a stream and ate their porridge while listening to a nocturnal symphony of hooting owls, howling wolves, and yowling lynxes.

A twig snapped.`

Vlad clenched the hilt of his sword. "Identify yourself."

"I am unarmed." The voice came from the darkness. "A harmless pilgrim." A tall red-haired man stepped into the clearing, his empty hands outstretched.

"What are those?" Vlad aimed the sword at the odd trinkets hanging from his waist.

"Tools of my trade, good sir." He patted his belt.

"What trade is that?" Vlad tossed a leaf into the air and sliced it in half with his sword.

The stranger blinked, unimpressed by the sharpness of Vlad's blade. "Knowledge."

Stephen jumped up and drew his sword. "You're a spy."

The stranger tugged at the white fur around his neck. "Spies carry falsehoods. I carry mysteries of the world."

"Ah, I know who you are." Stephen re-sheathed his sword and sat back down. "Your appearance gives you away. You are a Şolomonar. A practitioner of alchemy."

"I am." He dipped his head. "A hungry Şolomonar."

"Help yourself." Vlad gestured to the pot on the fire.

Stephen tossed the Şolomonar a wineskin. "What brings you from your mountain cave to practice the art of wizardry?"

"A *strigoi* terrorizes a village not far from here." The Şolomonar scooped a bowlful of porridge. "It steals the life force of their women. Several robust maidens grow pale from blood loss."

Vlad rolled his eyes. "You are in the presence of learned men, sir. We do not believe in fairy stories. S*trigoi* are no more real than dragons and *jinn*."

"Learned men, you say?" The Şolomonar scratched his red beard, his brow creased with confusion. "Then perhaps you can explain why scholars of art, mathematics, and philosophy continue to debate the world's great mysteries?"

"There are no mysteries." Vlad wiped out his empty bowl. "Only spheres of understanding. The unschooled know little. The scholar some. The expert more. A mystery, therefore, is something not yet understood. Eventually, man will awaken, and then they will solve all the world's mysteries."

"You are a philosopher." The Şolomonar smiled approvingly. "Do you think one of these woke men will discover why *strigoi* rise from the grave? Will they tell us how a body neither alive nor dead—existing in some hellish realm—is able to steal the livings' life force? Do you believe these woke men will explain why a *moroi* takes demonic possession of an innocent?"

"Yes."

"You have much faith in mankind."

"I have no faith in mankind." Vlad tasted the injustices of his youth at the back of his throat. "I do have faith in man's fondness for evil. And evil pushes men to cross moral boundaries that good men fear to look upon."

"I have no quarrel there." The Şolomonar turned to Stephen. "You are silent."

Stephen shrugged. "My companion is the better philosopher."

"Perhaps, but you have a noble energy that foretells a great destiny." The Şolomonar rubbed his chin, his gaze fixed on Stephen. "The fruits of your labors will not be harvested for several years."

Vlad bit back his laughter.

Stephen jabbed his thumb toward Vlad. "What predictions do you have for my companion?"

The Şolomonar's face darkened as his eyes bore into Vlad's. "Two reside within. One shall perish. The other will live for eternity."

"You get a prophecy, I get a riddle." Vlad nudged Stephen with his boot.

The Şolomonar rose and rinsed his bowl in the stream. "Thank you for your hospitality, my lords." He set the bowl by the fire. "I wish you both prosperity and many children."

"May God speed you on your journey," said Stephen.

"And you." The Şolomonar walked beyond the firelight's glow.

"Şolomonar!" Vlad called. "Is it true your people possess a book containing the secrets of the natural world?"

"The unnatural as well." His words faded into the forest with him.

Vlad turned to Stephen. "I…"

Stephen yawned. "What?"

"I'll keep first watch." It was best he kept his curiosity about the book to himself.

A LOYAL BOYAR near Braşov offered Vlad and Stephen accommodation. It was a short stay.

Days later, a breathless, ashen-faced priest arrived at the home. "Hunyadi d-d-discovered y-y-your w-w-whereabouts." He looked over his shoulder into the forest, his fingers gripping a wooden crucifix. "M-m-mercenaries are headed this w-w-way."

Vlad and Stephan fled without saying goodbye to the boyar. They arrived in the village of Gioagiu—their satchels yet unpacked—when the innkeeper told them an assassin for Hunyadi was tethering his horse in the stable. Vlad and Stephen climbed out the window and raced into the forest. The assassin missed them by the shake of a dog's tail.

A year passed. Vlad and Stephen moved from house to house. They made midnight journeys to attend secret meetings in hopes of finding allies and raising support.

But some trips Vlad made alone, and they had nothing to do with diplomacy.

For two days, Vlad squatted unseen in a dense thicket. No one went in or out of the narrow mountain crevice.

This was the entrance to the Şolomonari lair. It had to be. Every barely visible footstep, every half bent twig led here.

Satisfied the Şolomonari were far away, possibly on some godly mission, Vlad approached the cave. He swept aside a tangle of branches at its entrance. Odd characters were carved into the rock.

Vlad ran his hand over it. A subtle force seeped into his fingertips and slide serpent-like up his arm. The sensation—

part itch, part warmth—blossomed outward into his body, before it gathered and curled at the nape of his neck.

Vlad swallowed, touched his neck as though expecting to feel something, a scratch, a lump…something. There was nothing. As though it, whatever *it* was, already became part of him.

Energy coursing through his limbs, Vlad pushed his way between the narrow rocky crevice. Inside, he held his breath and listened for signs of life.

The cave was silent, expectant, as though it waited for him. The same odd script covered the walls from floor to ceiling. Warnings? Incantations? Wisdom? Vlad circled the cave in awe, then stood in the center, hands on his hips.

Maybe all this writing was the book? Vlad circled the cave again and again, held the lantern at different levels. On the fourth circuit, with the light above his head, he noticed a fissure near the ceiling. Beneath, footholds were carved into the stone. How had he missed them?

His heart pounding, Vlad scaled the wall, and thrust his hand inside the cleft. Something was wedged inside. He coaxed it out, unwound the wool around it.

The *Book of the Şolomonari.*

Vlad's breath caught in his throat. The world hummed in his ear. Vlad jumped down, sat on the ground, and opened the book. More of the same writing. Heady with exhilaration, muscles coiled for action, Vlad emerged from the cave and squinted into the sun.

The forest was preternaturally quiet, as though it held its collective breath. Vlad clutched the book to his chest and inhaled its ancient scent, the fragrance of Solomon; king, necromancer, scholar, and beloved of God. With this book he could not fail to save his country and people. With this book he could fight Sultan Mehmed. With this book he would become someone the world would never forget.

THE JANUARY SNOW FELL FAST, wet, and thick when the messenger arrived with a letter for Vlad.

Vlad turned it over in his hand, rubbed his thumb over Hunyadi's waxed signet, and fought back the dread in his gut. "He must have a spy under every rug and stone."

"Better a letter than an assassin." Stephen paced the room.

Vlad broke the seal and read. Twice. He dropped the letter in his lap, clasped his hands together, and tapped his steepled index fingers on his lips. He stared at nothing, but his mind went everywhere. To every possible motive.

His face blanched with worry, Stephen's eyes darted the room. "Are we surrounded?"

Vlad blinked, his mind made up. "Hunyadi seeks my counsel. He believes Mehmed wants to invade Hungary."

Stephen's shoulders slumped with relief. "You know Mehmed better than anyone. Is that his intent?"

Vlad exhaled a grunt. "Mehmed wants—has always wanted—to conquer the entire world."

"What will you do?" Stephen gestured to the letter.

Vlad closed his eyes and rubbed the bridge of his nose. "The only thing I can do."

## 22

# Ilona

**Spring 1467
Buda Castle, Hungary**

I kneel before Jesus and pray. Or rather I try to pray. Other thoughts occupy my mind. Shameful thoughts.

Beside me, Margit's lips move in silent prayer.

I try again. I must stop thinking about last night that I may honor Vlad's request.

"You are the wife of a deposed sovereign, Ilona," he had said this morning before I left for the chapel. "You must pray for the people of Wallachia and for the lands of Făgăras and Amlaş. You must pray that I, the true prince, will reunite with my people."

"If you like." I had kissed him on the cheek.

"This is not a frivolous request." His fingers had squeezed my hand and his eyes had hardened. "It is your duty to beseech God with fervent prayers. You must pray for the farmers, merchants, and boyars. You are a princess now, and along with the benefits of nobility comes the burden of pleading the case of your people before God."

"I will pray most fervently," I had said, his serious face and tone made me uneasy. "Come with me, my lord. Surely God cannot refuse two devout supplicants. Together we—"

His warm lips had silenced me.

Vlad broke the kiss with a quick nip to my bottom lip. "Your prayers come from a virtuous heart because you never felt treachery's sting nor vengeance's burden. I have tasted hatred, thus my prayers are not as pure as yours."

"But you're a Catholic now. Any prayer you utter is as worthy as mine."

"I wish it were so." Vlad had arranged the veil over my hair. "Your duties as Princess of Wallachia begin today. Plead to God for my restoration."

With his request echoing in my ear, I squeeze shut my eyes and focus my thoughts. I pray for the boyars, the wives, children, farmers, merchants, shepherds, and guildsmen. I pray for Wallachia, Făgăras and Amlaş. I pray with such fervency that God's approval warms my soul and fills me with peace.

Margit hooks her arm around mine as we walk out the chapel door. "Are the marital duties dispensed with already?"

"I..." I look away.

"Tell me everything." Margit leans in. "Please, Ilona. What is it like? The ladies at court either giggle or roll their eyes when I ask." She puts her mouth to my ear. "Did you see it?"

I nod, my face ablaze with embarrassment.

"Tell me." Margit's tone is more demand than request.

Two years ago, when Margit was less viperous, I would have shared every detail. But I no longer trust her. Neither do I want her as an enemy. "Walk with me."

We go to the courtyard and wander through the gardens.

Margit frowns as she studies my face in the bright afternoon light. "You don't look any different."

"I feel different. He…we…I don't know if I can explain it."

"You must." Margit affects a charming pout. "Did it hurt?"

"For a moment only but then…"

Margit's eyes grow wide as saucers. "Then…"

"There is an ache inside of you. Not a painful ache, more like a tension. This grows until you think you will burst from the agony—"

"How awful." Margit wrinkles her nose.

I glance about, mindful of eavesdroppers. "Do you know how good it feels when you scratch an itch?"

"Yes." Margit's eyes taper.

"It's a thousand times better."

Margit's lips twist. "Mmm…Do you want to do it again?"

"Yes." The tips of my ears burn with shame. I don't dare tell Margit that Vlad took me four times since yesterday, three last night and once this morning.

"The ladies claim only a skilled lover can pleasure a woman," says Margit. "Yet to hear them talk you would think not one in twenty have any skill at all."

"Princess Ilona," calls a familiar voice.

Hearing my new title gives me a happy start. "My lord."

"Lady Margit, good afternoon," says Vlad, elegant and robust in a moss colored frock.

Margit giggles and curtsies. "Prince Vlad, have I detained your bride too long?"

"Not at all." My husband kisses my hand. "I trust your daily devotions are complete."

"They are, my lord."

Vlad gives me his most infectious grin and loops his arm through mine. "Shall we take a turn about the courtyard?"

I blush, recalling when he turned me over and took me from behind. "I am honored."

We take our leave from Margit, whose stare feels like icicles at my back, and wander the cobbled pathway, pausing to greet courtiers enjoying the mild weather.

"I have another task for you, my lady," Vlad whispers as we walk the halls to his chambers.

"Do you need a button sewn or hem mended?"

"Nothing as tedious as that." Vlad bolts the door. "Sit on the bed." His luminous emerald eyes soften as he kneels before me. "You prayed for Wallachia and for my people?"

I stroke his cheek, rough with stubble. "Most ardently."

"You prayed for the restoration of my throne?" Vlad lifts my foot and slips off my high platform shoe.

"Yes, I even reminded God why you are the better prince." The subservience of his action makes me uneasy and yet my nethers tighten with expectation.

Vlad chuckles, removes my hose and kisses my toe. "It is time I worship at your altar, my lady."

He inches up the stiff embroidered silk skirt and, with exquisite slowness, grazes my shin with his lips. First one. Next the other. Back and forth and upwards. My nethers pulse, and I sigh as his tongue grazes my knees.

He draws apart my legs and pushes up my skirt in tiny increments, all the while nibbling at the sensitive flesh on my inner thighs.

I crush the silk in my fist, the pulsing ache tightening. His lips linger and tease and move closer to my core. Surely he will stop this sinful path to my most private of places, discard his robe, and consummate our vows as God intended.

I cannot stop him—don't want to stop him—my decadent desire to feel his mouth at my moist junction burning away all sensible thought.

Vlad's lips brush against the hollow between my thighs. I throw back my head, adrift to a throbbing need.

He flicks his tongue over that most sensitive spot. "Look at yourself."

"No." My face burns with shame.

"It is not a request. I demand you look." His fingers spread the cleft apart.

I drop my gaze and see glistening pink petals of flesh.

"Beautiful," he murmurs and lowers his mouth.

I grab his head, my fingers entwining in his hair, and writhe and moan like a whore. He lingers and teases. Slow precise sucks followed by quick flicks of his tongue. When he permits my release I do not recognize the sound of my own joyful cry. Emboldened by desire, I pull him to me, my hands tearing at his clothes, eager for the length of him.

Vlad moves his robe aside. "Tell me what you want."

"You. I want you." It is the faintest of whispers.

"Tell me exactly what you want me to do."

"I want you to…" I bite my lips, feel my face burn.

Vlad whispers the words he wants to hear. "Say it."

I am horrified and excited in equal measure. How can he want his bride to utter such vile words? Yet I must. And I do.

"Again. Louder," he says.

I say the words again and this time every syllable excites me, their vulgarity rousing and freeing.

I am swept away once more.

"Do not be ashamed." Vlad arranges the folds of his garment after our lust is sated. "Any act bringing pleasure to a man and his wife is moral."

I smooth my skirt. "I never imagined the act could be so…"

"Gratifying?" He gathers his hair into a low ponytail at the nape of his neck.

"Debased."

A shadow passes over his face and his eyes harden. "Prudish wives are of little worth to men of great passions."

I wince. "My lord, I did not mean to suggest that…I want nothing more than to be a good wife. You are so proper, admire virtue, and demand decency. I did not know this other side of you."

"You know nothing of the other side of me." Vlad bows stiffly, crosses the chamber, and opens the door where his manservant, Rareș, waits to accompany us to dinner.

My stomach knots. Married less than two days and I have already angered my husband. How foolish of me. Aunt Erzsébet's advised me to become his confidant, not his critic. I am about to apologize but think better of it. Better I do not question his baser desires ever again.

Vlad does not speak to me until we reach the great hall when draws me near. "It's such an amusement knowing my seed sticks to your thighs while we prattle with courtiers." A thin smile slides up one cheek.

I murmur those wicked words. Vlad's eyes twinkle with delight. My shoulders loosen with relief. All is well with us once again.

We part ways moments after, Vlad to discuss Sultan Mehmed's latest conquests with the Venetian emissary, and I to talk with friends.

"How do you find marriage so far?" Aunt Erzsébet crosses her arms.

Our lust is unquenchable. My woman parts are sore. His moods change from sunny to stormy in a heartbeat. "Interesting."

She stares at me in surprise, her lips poised to ask another question when a French envoy and two advisors join us. The conversation is boring. They chatter about the Diet's meeting in March, the new treasury tax, and the problems arising from restructuring royal revenues. With feigned regrets I part company to join sister Jusztina, who came to town for my wedding.

I return to Vlad's side when the meal arrives. He is witty and charming with guests and yet pays no attention to me. I set my hand on his knee, but he removes it without even a glance my way.

The second course is no different. By the third course I no longer taste the food. By the fourth my stomach clenches with worry. What did I do this time to provoke Vlad Dracula's displeasure?

## 23

The meal concludes with King Matthias's announcement that fair weather permits dancing outside under the stars. Vlad and I join the others in a courtyard strung with lanterns and lively with music.

Vlad bows low, takes my hand, and we dance without speaking until a twirl brings us face to face.

Vlad lifts his arm as I dip under. "Do you think your duties as princess of Wallachia involve only spreading your legs?" His voice is chilly.

"No, my lord," I swallow.

"Then why did you leave the conversation with the French envoy and his advisors?" He walks around me, his clap blending with twenty men.

Hands clasped high, we promenade forward, separating at the end of the line.

"I wanted to speak to Jusztina," I explain when we partner again.

"Your personal desires are secondary." He scowls. "In truth, they are unimportant."

My lips tremble, and my heavy feet stumble. "Forgive me, my lord."

"Mind your emotions and smile, Ilona. You are my eyes and ears now. A practical princess never leaves an important discussion."

"Yes, my lord." I battle to keep the smile from slipping off my face.

"An unwarranted twitch, a raised eyebrow, a pause too long; you must report all you hear and see. These festivities are a time to gather information, not flaunt the latest Venetian styles or play the coquette."

Shoulder to shoulder we circle about, our eyes fixed upon one another.

"I beg forgiveness."

Vlad lifts his hand and spins me to the right. "Forgiveness is the invention of gods and the prerogative of fools." His lips curve into a sad smile. "You are a princess now. All selfish desires ended with your oath before God and the sealing of our marital contract."

I blink back a tear. "I will not make the same mistake again."

The music ends, Vlad bows, and heads toward a knot of Matthias's closest friends. I am left to do the only thing I can do—must do. I locate an elderly courtier—a confidant of Aunt Erzsébet—in the crowd and flatter him until he begs a dance.

"Did you hear about the two papal emissaries caught stealing?" He wheezes between spins.

"Disgraceful, isn't it?" I pretend to know the gossip. "Whoever would have suspected it from such devout men?"

"That's what I said." The courtier spills details between coughing fits.

My next three dance partners have no useful information, but the fourth shares a tidbit. By evening's end I feel as satisfied as after prayers this morning. Flattery loosens mouths, as well as a sincere request for advice. Nobles do love giving advice.

Vlad comes to my side. "May I escort you to your chambers?"

My chambers?

"I would be honored." Though my stomach clenches, I do not question him, instead I brandish an impish smile. "I learned many interesting things tonight."

Vlad quirks his eyebrow. "No doubt from the foppish courtier and bald noble."

"You know who I danced with?"

Vlad wraps his arm around my waist. "I recall every one of your dancing partners since the day we were introduced."

My mouth hangs open for a moment. "I don't know whether to be flattered or worried."

"I suppose that depends on your faithfulness." He winks.

"Then I am flattered." My stomach uncoils and I sense I am fully forgiven. "I learned that Matthias wants Marcin Bylica to be his court astrologer."

"I'm not surprised. He is well-respected."

"But he's Polish."

"And one of the best." Vlad turns the iron door handle and frowns. "You must keep this door locked at all times." He strides inside and beckons to Bernádett. "Find another place to sleep tonight."

"If I may get a blanket, my lord." Bernádett scurries to the chest, yanks out a thick woolen, and dashes from the room.

Vlad bolts the door. "How long has the girl served you?"

"Since I was a child."

"Is she Hungarian?"

"She is a distant relation." I do not question his inquiry. "Father brought her here after her mother died."

"Do you trust her?" Vlad unclasps his belt, drops it on the floor, and shrugs off his velvet robe.

I lift my chin. "If I didn't, she would not be my ladies' maid."

"Good enough." Vlad removes his boots and breeches,

and pulls his linen tunic over his head. Naked and stiff with arousal he sits in the middle of my bed, adjusts the pillows, and stares expectantly. "Well?"

"Do you expect me to undress myself?"

"Something wrong with your hands?" Vlad interlocks his fingers behind his head.

"Is there something wrong with yours?"

"They're occupied at the moment." Vlad crosses his ankles. "What do you know about astrology?"

"Only that it has something to do with the stars." I tug at the silk cord securing my bodice.

"Astrology is more than that. The position of the sun, moon, and stars affect many things—a person's temperament, the probable outcome of an event. Wars are lost because the stars are not favorable. Battles are won because they are." Vlad's gaze roams up and down my body. "Take your time," he says as I fumble with my skirt. "The pleasure is in the disrobing, which I insist you prolong."

My face flushes. "Did you have a court astrologer?"

"All great and intelligent leaders do."

The skirt puddles at my feet and I step out of it, only my tunic and platform shoes remain on.

"Slowly," he says as I push my linen tunic from my shoulder.

"Like this?" I slide one shoulder off, a hint of breast exposed.

"The other." It is a command.

With a slowness that causes his chest to heave and eyes to glaze, I do as asked. I catch the tunic before it falls, lowering it bit by bit, until my nipples are exposed.

"Your hair." His voice is husky with desire.

I remove the pins, drop each on the rug. Dark locks tumble over my shoulders and down my back in unruly waves.

Vlad draws a circle in the air with his finger. I turn around.

"Stop." His voice is thick and low.

I stand with my back to him, my skin prickling under his gaze.

"Straight spine, firm thighs, plump buttocks, and a generous curve from waist to hip."

"I am not livestock, your lord." I wiggle my buttocks. "Are you inspecting my breeding or my ability to breed?"

"I'm assessing your natural aptitude for vigorous activities."

I bend down and touch my toes.

Vlad sucks air through his teeth. "Come here, wife. We have an heir to make."

We indulge our lust well into the night before falling asleep in each other's arms.

Vlad is gone when I awake. Chilled without him, I burrow under the fur blanket, recall last night's lovemaking, and giggle.

Bernádett peeks into the room. "Good morning, my lady. Are you in need of a bath?"

"Oh Bernádett, how did you know?"

"One of Aunt Erzsébet's ladies told me brides always ask for more baths." She opens the door and two burly servants drag in a copper bathtub. Many steaming buckets later, I throw off the blankets and swing my legs over the side of the bed.

Bernádett's eyes bulge. "Does Prince Vlad demand you remove your nightgown to complete his husbandly duty?"

I sink into the hot water. "I...um...yes."

"I worry my lady will be bothered by the prince's excessive attentions." She sponges my shoulders. "I know a midwife who claims there are only certain days during a woman's cycle when a man's seed takes hold." She drags the soapy cloth down my arm. "Shall I summon her?"

"I do not mind his attentions." I rest my head against the rim and close my eyes.

"I've heard most men lose interest in their wives once the deflowering is over and the seed planted. They prefer fornicating with their mistresses."

Despite the hot water Bernádett pours down my back, a cold fear clamps around my heart. What if I am not enough? I could not bear the pain of his betrayal if he took a mistress. "Don't tell me about most men. My Vlad is not most men."

The silence prickles my skin. I open one eye.

Bernádett wrings out the washcloth. "I agree, my lady, Prince Vlad is assuredly not like most men."

WEEKS PASS in a cloud of bliss. Vlad teaches me the history of his lands, gently corrects my mispronounced Romanian, and discusses books and philosophies. We hawk and picnic and stroll in the courtyards. Each night we frolic in bed, and often in the afternoons. Like today as I watch gossamer clouds move across an azure sky.

Midway through the royal rabbit hunt, Vlad leads me to a secluded knoll where we indulge in fleshy delights.

"I don't remember ever being happier in my life." I roll onto my side.

Vlad brushes away a tendril of hair from my face. "That's because your needs are few."

"Are you not happy, my lord?"

Vlad sits up and runs his hand through his hair. "I am a ruler without a throne, a warrior without a war, and a prince without a legitimate heir. No, Ilona, I am not happy." He sets a finger on my lips. "I am, however, most satisfied with you."

Satisfied?! Satisfaction is for wine, a meal, or a book. Not a bride.

"I love you, my lord." I sit up, grab his hand, and press it to my breast. "Do you feel my heart? It belongs to you. Each beat."

Vlad's eyes dissolve into moss-green pools. "You confuse fornication with love. Love grows over time and at great cost. You are young and virtuous. Life has been kind to you. You do not yet understand the pain and pleasure of authentic love."

My hackles rise like a cat. "Do not dismiss my feelings simply because I have no experience with romance. Love—be it for God or country, sister or father—share common elements. The warmth in one's belly, a fullness in the heart, the empty ache in the bosom when a loved one departs this world. Is that not love? Since we first met, I have felt this... tension, like a cord pulling us together, a connection of body and soul, almost instinctual."

Vlad's cheek brushes mine. "Like a wolf howls at the moon."

I wiggle his nose. "I hope your love never wanes."

"I'm the moon? Well, that explains why my wolf wife has such a ferocious appetite for lovemaking." Vlad growls and nips at my neck.

He pushes me back to the ground, slips his hand beneath my skirt, and brings me to ecstasy in moments.

Afterwards, I brush twigs and leaves from my clothes and recall Aunt Erzsébet's advice. A storm rages inside Vlad Dracula. One I must learn to control. But how will I do that if Vlad does not accept my declaration of love?

## 24

*Smack!* Icy gusts slam the open shutters against the wall. Despite the howling storm, I fling off the fur blanket and hurry across the room to close them.

"Leave them be," Vlad says from the bed.

"It's so windy it rains sideways." I point to the floor. "You'll be able to fish in this puddle soon."

"I find comfort in storms." His voice is as bright and sunny as it is dark and dreary outside. "The wind heartens me, and the rain sheds tears I cannot."

"Tears?" A blast of frigid air scatters cold mist over my skin. I dart away from the window.

Vlad leaps off the bed like a lynx and drapes a mink cape over my shoulders. "Do you have something to tell me, Ilona?"

I snuggle into the fur. "Mmm, let me think. You already know about the envoy from Florence who keeps a black-skinned mistress, and I told you about Matthias's latest lover, the large-breasted daughter of an elderly courtier."

He nips at my ear. "I'm not talking about Egyptian whores and feeble-minded wenches."

"What then, my lord? I never keep anything from you."

Vlad's arms encircle me, and his fingers splay wide across my belly. "Are your courses timely?"

"My courses?" I chew on my lip. When was the last time I bled?

"Six weeks have passed," he murmurs.

The realization comes in a flash, more startling than the lightning gilding the room. "I'm with child?!" I spin about. Joy pours over me like a waterfall. "How…?" I stare at him amazed. "Did you count the weeks?"

"I counted the days." With a wolfish grin, Vlad carries me squealing to bed. He sets me down and flutters kisses over my belly. "Give me a healthy son, Princess Ilona." He drops his head between my thighs, his fingers and tongue making me squeal again.

I CANNOT SHARE my joyful news. Vlad forbids it. Says we must wait until my belly is round. But Bernádett figures it out the day my breasts burst from my bodice.

That same afternoon, Aunt Erzsébet touches my hard, rounded belly. "Pray each day for your unborn child and cease all marital relations."

Heat blooms in my cheeks. Vlad beds me once a day, sometimes twice. "Why?"

"It will harm the babe." Aunt Erzsébet palpates my stomach. "How far along are you?"

"Almost five months." I arch my back and cup the swell that is not yet noticeable under my skirts.

"Dracula was prudent to keep it quiet. Many babes are lost in the first few months. Have you felt the quickening?"

"I think so."

Aunt Erzsébet's face lights up. "Good. You must be careful, Ilona. No horseback riding. No hawking. Prince Vlad will be furious if his child is lost to your negligence. Do not worry about his manly needs, he will find his pleasures elsewhere during your lying-in. Men always do."

Her advice feels like a punch to my gut. No! Not my Vlad. I am enough for him.

"Is it true?" I ask Vlad after relating Aunt Erzsébet's advice.

"She's an old fool." He strokes my cheek. "But she is right about one thing. No more horseback riding after the seventh month."

Vlad takes great interest in my pregnancy. He interviews midwifes. He commissions the royal carpenter to make a cradle from cedar, the sacred wood of Noah's Ark and the Ark of the Covenant. He orders oranges, pomegranates, and figs be delivered from afar.

Months pass. My belly ripens. Our lovemaking decreases. I am not too worried because Vlad showers me with gifts.

When the court astrologer predicts a son, Vlad buys me costly perfumes. When an old gypsy prophesies of his long lineage he orders an ermine collar made for my cloak. Not all gifts are extravagant. The best ones are humble. A tray of perfect red, yellow, and orange fall leaves collected from the forest. A branch of ice-glazed red berries. A bucket of fresh snow. The first loaf of bread hot from the oven. My favorite gift, however, is when Vlad reads to me.

Vlad pauses his translation of Ovid's tale about Theseus to spread his hand over my distended belly. "He kicks like a warrior."

"I wish this wee warrior wouldn't kick my ribs quite so vigorously." I slurp juice from an orange wedge.

A proud smile darts across Vlad's face. "Our manse in Pest is almost complete. It's time you see your new lying-in chamber." He thrusts his tongue inside for a sweet kiss.

We make the trip the next day. A fleet of servants in livery waits in the courtyard. I lumber through each room, wide-eyed and delighted by the furnishings. Many are new, commissioned by Vlad. Others glow with an aged patina.

Vlad notes every detail as we tour the manse, from the arches' curvature to the marble columns' smoothness to the tile floor's symmetry.

At the base of an impressive curved staircase, Vlad looks at me with lust-clouded eyes. "Both our chambers are upstairs. Each has an exceptional view of the Danube and courtyard. Shall we anoint it with our pleasures?" He loops his arm through mine.

I look up the long flight of stairs and heave a loud sigh. If that's what Vlad wants...

Vlad presses his lips to my ear. "Your time must be near. I have never known you to sigh with weariness when I suggest lovemaking."

"This belly weighs me down like an anchor." I pat my rock hard belly.

Vlad encloses my hands. "An anchor securing the Dracul lineage."

I PLOD through the crowded party with the grace of a bear. My face is bloated and my back hurts. The narrow-waisted maidens flitting around Vlad make me want to snarl. How dare they flirt with my husband! Even Margit takes advantage of my fatigue. She bats her eyes, smiles, whispers in his ear, and affects provocative poses. Jealousy claws at me like a bear scratching a tree.

Aunt Erzsébet takes a seat beside me. "I hear Dracula employs only servants from Wallachia."

"You heard correctly." My eyes stay fixed on Margit. My glowering does not thwart her flirtatious flouncing. In truth, it increases it.

"Dracula sees treachery everywhere. Or at least, the

opportunity for it. Be vigilant. Trust no one. Spies are everywhere."

I drag my eyes away from Margit and Vlad. "I know. Vlad reminds me all the time."

"Heed his warning." Aunt Erzsébet twists her green vesuvianite ring. "You are well-suited for one another, a love match from all appearances." Her eyes soften into a faraway look, as though remembering her marriage to John Hunyadi. "Be steadfast, Ilona. Ambitious men like Dracula are difficult to live with. You will need patience, understanding, and tolerance to cope with all the troubles that come with such a strong-willed and stubborn man." She looks at me. "Can you do that?"

Troubles to come? Whatever does she mean by that?

## 25

# Vlad

**Winter 1451**
**Hunyadi's Castle in Hunedoara, Transylvania**

Twenty-year-old Vlad Dracula stared agape at John Hunyadi's castle. Words left him. This was the majestic castle of his dreams. The one he imagined building, living in, rearing children in, and ruling his people from.

Vlad studied its architecture. A narrow bridge crossed a moat. There was a profusion of windows and balconies amid the fine checked walls, and conical spires sat like pointed hats atop the soaring towers. The castle was situated in a near impregnable location near the Zlaşti River, and its defense towers were wide enough to accommodate traction trebuchets and mangonels. A low approving whistle emitted between Vlad's lips. All it needed was tunnels to be perfect.

Vlad spoke over his shoulder to his men waiting behind him. "Let's find out why the great John Hunyadi needs a deposed prince's help." He started over the drawbridge.

"State your business." A guard shouted from atop the bartizan.

"I am Prince Vlad Dracula. I come at Hunyadi's request. He's expecting me."

The portcullis clanged upwards, and Dracula's entourage entered the courtyard where armed guards and Hunyadi's chancellor met them.

After surrendering their weapons, the chancellor led them inside. Vlad felt the same awe as when he had first walked into the sultan's palace in Edirne, Anatolia. Although his face was smooth with indifference, his eyes feasted on the marble columns, vaulted ceilings, ornate lamps, and ivory-inlayed buffets.

One day, he thought, I too will surround myself with the artistry of power and prosperity.

Vlad's purposeful stride faltered for a moment upon entering the great hall. It was enormous, a chamber for a titan. Intimidating in its vast display of standards, portraits, and seals. Though stripped of his two former titles, it was clear Hunyadi was confident his status would rise again.

Vlad swallowed, breathed deep and stood tall, chest out, shoulders back. His chin in the air, he strode through the crowd of nobles, courtiers, and petitioners.

Hunyadi, lording over the room from a massive fur-draped chair, studied Dracula's arrogant approach. A shrewd judge of character, Hunyadi noted Vlad's haughty stride and knew it was authentic. He found Vlad's eyes bright and sharp with a courage borne of suffering and vengeance. Vlad's ambition equaled his own.

Formal introductions dispensed with, Hunyadi got right to the point. "Is it true you served five times in the Turkish army?"

"If you had competent spies you would know the answer." Vlad pretended annoyance. "Tell me, my lord, do you assess my honesty or your informants' because I did not travel all this way to answer a trivial question."

Hunyadi bit back a smile and leaned forward. "Then I will ask a weighty one. Do you seek your father's throne?"

Vlad puffed out his chest and spoke slowly. "It is mine by birthright."

Hunyadi smirked. "A throne belongs to the man earning it. An experienced warrior can take the throne—as you did a year ago—but only a skillful diplomat keeps it."

Vlad's mouth twitched, the truth piercing his pride. He kept silent, ready to turn on his heels if Hunyadi continued to malign him.

Hunyadi was glad he wiped the smug smile from the young prince's face. "Youthful ambition is best honed with the help of a clever mentor."

Vlad rubbed his chin with pretended skepticism. "Why would a clever mentor care about a young man's ambition?"

"He wouldn't." Hunyadi leaned back in the chair. "Not unless something could be gained, like a young man's intimate knowledge of their mutual enemy."

There it was, the reason for Hunyadi's complete turnaround. He needed Vlad. Needed Vlad's expertise in Turkish ways and tactics. Needed his insight on Mehmed.

Vlad had different needs. He needed allies. He needed power, the kind that amassed armies. The kind Hunyadi could give him. That, however, required Vlad to give up his vendetta against Hunyadi, to overlook Hunyadi's hand in his father's and brother's death.

Vlad's predicament—much like those faced by his father —humbled him. But not enough to lessen the bravado he would need to win Hunyadi's respect.

"*Düşmanımın düşmanı dostumdur.*" Vlad folded his arms. "The enemy of my enemy is my friend."

"An apt adage, and especially appropriate when our mutual enemy prefers war to peace." Hunyadi watched Vlad for signs of indecision or duplicity. A quick flinch, sudden squint, or tensed jaw. All he saw was Vlad's arrogance.

Vlad did not speak—silence was an effective negotiating strategy—and waited for Hunyadi to make an offer. The silence stretched. Courtiers and councilors stopped their side conversations to watch this contest of wills.

Hunyadi ended the standoff with an offer. "A man with personal information about Sultan Mehmed would live in Sibiu without fear for his life."

Vlad remained silent though his heart leapt. Sibiu! His boyhood home.

Seeing Vlad's indifferent expression, Hunyadi sweetened the deal. "He will enjoy a position in my court."

Vlad's lips pressed together, blinked.

Hunyadi tried another tactic. "You will receive a military appointment in my army."

"*Alea iacta est.*" The die is cast. Vlad bowed. Though he was now diplomatically shackled to Hunyadi, at least they were gilded chains. "A gracious offer. Favorable to both parties."

JOHN HUNYADI RATHER LIKED DRACULA. He was impressed by Dracula's gift for foreign languages, his skilled court etiquette, and insights on Turkish military tactics.

The ladies at court fell for Vlad's charms. His seductive tales about life in a harem inspired them to lift their skirts and spread their thighs. His recitation of Turkish poetry made the virgins swoon.

Not all of Dracula's time was spent at court. He often visited his wife in Sibiu and whooped for joy during one trip when Crina announced she was with child. For once in his life, Dracula felt like things were finally going his way. Even his trip to Hungary was a success. Vlad swore allegiance to King Ladislas—a formidable alliance—after which the king appointed him protector of the Transylvanian Diet. For the first time since he could remember, Vlad was happy. Truly happy.

That happiness leached from his heart during the return trip to Hunyadi's castle when a messenger delivered a letter from his home.

A son! Dracula ripped open the letter with eager hands.

*Prince Vlad,*

*I regret to inform you that Lady Crina died in childbirth. Your son, cut from his mother's womb, lived less than a day.*

Vlad crumbled the letter in his fist and took off at a gallop. He couldn't let his men see his tears.

## Fall 1453

"A ROW of impaled bodies rings the city like Satan's halo." The rotund emissary's hands drew a large circle in the air.

The fall of Constantinople. The councilors stared dumbfounded, horrified, their faces pale with alarm. Hunyadi, sweat beading on his forehead, guzzled his wine.

Dracula tapped his foot impatiently. The emissary's news was weeks old. Dracula had heard the same reports first hand when survivors of the Marmora Sea battle had passed through his town. "Lining a road with impaled bodies is a common Turkish tactic meant to frighten the enemy into surrendering."

The emissary lifted his pudgy palms skyward. "Our God had better tactics. Divine strategies."

Hunyadi winced, the emissary's overly dramatic reporting had lost its gloss. "Which were…"

The emissary twisted his wrist, curled his fingers, and shook his fists. "God's wrath made the cathedral of Saint

Sophia glow a brilliant crimson, whereupon Sultan Mehmed fell quaking to his knees in fear and postponed the attack."

Vlad rolled his eyes. He leaned close to Hunyadi. "Mehmed does not ascribe to his own faith in Allah, let alone fear our God."

The emissary spread his arms wide. "And then God covered the land in divine darkness. His third miracle defies explanation. As the priests carried the Blessed Virgin from Saint Sophia it fell—for no apparent reason—toppled from the platform to the ground. Lo! It did not break! Not so much as a crack or nick! Try as they might the priests could not lift the Virgin from the ground until every man, woman, and child united in fervent prayers. And then—"

"We need facts about the battle. Facts. Not miracles or divine interventions." Hunyadi waved his hand dismissively. "Tell us how the Turks breeched the wall."

"My lord," interjected János Vitéz, Hunyadi's trusted confidant. "The fourteen-mile wall is defended by seven thousand men, most frail old holy clerics. It was only a matter of t—"

"A monster!" shouted the emissary and slammed his fist on the table. "A monster weapon breached the wall! An iron Goliath with the power to kill a million of the world's finest warriors."

Vlad's heart sank. The rumors were true. His dream of defeating Mehmed, of keeping Wallachia safe from the Turks, was fast becoming a nightmare. "Describe it." The stony-faced Vlad dipped his quill in the inkpot.

"It's a gigantic cannon." The emissary rose from his chair and flung out his arms as if encompassing the room. "It crumbled Constantinople's walls like they were straw."

"Facts not commentary, if you please." Vlad's quill hovered over the paper.

The emissary tugged on his long gray beard. "By my reckoning, it weighs over six-hundred-pounds and is twenty-seven-feet in length. It fired six-hundred-pound projectiles a quarter of a league and took sixty-four oxen to transport and scores of men to operate."

Vlad rubbed the tight knot in the middle of his brow. "How many of these cannons does Mehmed have?"

The emissary stroked his beard. "Seventy, my lord."

"Seventy?" Vlad felt all six hundred pounds of the cannon's weight crush his chest.

Christendom had no such weapon. Mehmed would roll through Wallachia and blow every wall, tower, and town to pebbles and splinters. Reduce Christendom to rubbles.

Impaling his mind like a flaming arrow, Vlad recalled his first meeting Mehmed. *I am Mehmed Celibi, future sultan and ruler of the world.*

Ruler of the world....

Vlad set down his quill, steepled his hands under his chin, and closed his eyes. There had to be a way to stop Mehmed. Even Goliaths had weaknesses.

"Seventy cannons," Hunyadi roared. "Seventy?"

"God save us." Several councilors made the sign of the cross.

"It was a bloody spectacle, my lords." The emissary mopped sweat from his brow and neck. "Families were smashed against the walls of their homes. Crushed like insects. Piles of debris all that was left of many buildings. Men of God moaned in the streets. The Turks raped virgins, pissed on our holy relics, looted the temples and holy places, smashed our icons, shit upon our dead, and hacked families huddled in their homes. They stripped the dead or nearly dead of their clothes. Beat the oldest priests to death, rammed holy vessels into the younger men's—"

"What's the death toll?" Hunyadi interrupted, all too familiar with a conquering army's behavior. He glanced at Dracula. Unlike the white-faced councilors, Dracula's expression was like a wolf studying its prey. Not a trace of fear. Only a cold hunger to devour.

The emissary answered questions all afternoon about the forty-seven-day siege and three-day riot where eighty-thousand Turks—ten thousand of them janissaries—slaughtered over four thousand and enslaved fifty thousand more.

"Some say Mehmed wept over St. Sophia's damage." The emissary shrugged.

"Highly unlikely," Vlad murmured under his breath.

"Others claim he urged its destruction." The emissary gave Vlad a sidelong glance. "But all swear Sultan Mehmed prayed at the altar to Allah and Mohammed before proclaiming himself Mehmed *el-Fātih*."

Vlad winced at the emissary's horrible pronunciation. "Mehmed the Conqueror," he translated and turned to Hunyadi. "Wallachia will be Mehmed's gateway into Hungary. If he succeeds all of Christendom will be at risk."

## 26

# Ilona

**January 1468**
**Dracula's Manse in Pest, Hungary**

Screams echo off the walls. Through the tapestry-covered stones. Across the hall. Down the stairs. Out into the courtyard. My screams.

"Focus your strength downward. The babe is crowning. Bear down with the next pain." The midwife rubs ointment into my nether regions.

Bernádett presses a cool cloth to my brow. "Another push, my lady. Just one more."

Aunt Orsulya hunches over her rosary, her fingers clenched, her lips moving soundlessly for hours.

Margit gnaws her fingernails.

Aunt Erzsébet paces the room. "Everyone, we must all beseech Saint Margaret's blessed help."

I am dying. Only the patron saint of childbirth can help me now. I writhe. My bones ache. My skin hurts. After a day and a half of labor my body is as weak as a newborn kitten.

The midwife crouches at my feet. "My lady, the last pains are always the worst. Your babe waits for the final push. Let your child enter the world." She sticks a knotted cloth between my teeth.

PUSH! A strength surges from somewhere deep within, and my body and soul bears down into an agony so tremendous it blocks all reason.

The searing pressure slips away as the infant emerges.

"A son. A son." The midwife holds the red-faced babe aloft. "A healthy son."

The child lets loose a loud wail. The ladies burst into happy tears. They hug, kiss their crosses, and give thanks to Saint Margaret. The midwife places my son in my arms. I stare down at his tiny pink face, hot tears running down my cheeks, and my heart blooms with instant love. He is perfect and beautiful and mine. Joyful sobs wrack my weary body.

"Lady Ilona is overcome," says Aunt Erzsébet to a servant. "Bring her watered wine. Hurry." She dabs at my tears with a handkerchief then counts the babe's fingers and toes, inspects the shape of his face, and runs a hand over his limbs. "Well done. I will give the good news to Prince Vlad." With a swish of her skirt she departs.

The midwife tugs on the cord and a hot rush of afterbirth slushes out. She checks it, nods her approval, and sets it in a bowl.

"You must rest, Ilona." Zsazsa lifts my son from my heavy arms and the midwife helps me from the birthing stool to the bed.

I collapse in its softness, feel the midwife cover me with clean linen. I doze in and out, hear snatches of conversation.

"So vigorous. A strong little man."

"Bring fresh linens."

"Cleanse the air with fresh herbs."

"Warm the milk bath."

"Bring swaddling."

My eyes flutter open when the midwife palpates my stomach.

She scrutinizes the blood clots. "All is well, my lady. How do you feel?" The midwife sets my milk-bathed babe in my arms.

"Tired but wonderful." I stare down at the babe's corn-flower-blue eyes, which already blink as though determined to take in the world around him. I kiss his wee head, sweet smelling and downy with pale fine hair, and place him at my breast where he latches on my nipple with gusto. Tears flow down my cheeks. My happiness is complete.

Aunt Orsulya, Zsazsa, and Margit arrange their chairs at my bedside.

"May I?" Margit lifts the blanket and strokes the under-side of his wrinkled foot. "He's beautiful, Ilona." Her lower lips quivers. Today, Margit shows her sisterly side; concerned, caring, and without guile.

Zsazsa puts her hand to her ear. "Do you hear that? Prince Vlad is celebrating."

I hear it. The *țigani lăutari's* merry melody drifts up from the great chamber. I smile, close my eyes, and whisper a prayer of gratitude for God's blessings. A devoted husband. A healthy son. Contentment overflows my soul.

A smiling Aunt Erzsébet returns to the room. "Prince Vlad pronounced you the finest wife in all the world."

I point to the bowl holding the umbilical cord. "Will you do the honors?"

"Thank you." Aunt Erzsébet takes the bowl to the fire-place and tosses in the cord where the flames consume it with a fiery dance. "Light more lamps." She speaks to a maidser-vant. "Bring more fragrant herbs." She opens the shutters and a wintery blast swooshes fresh air into a room thick with sweat and fear and birth. "Rejoice in your accomplishment, Ilona. Your great duty is done." She puts on her fur-lined cloak. "I have been away too long."

I reach out to clasp her cool dry hand. "Thank you, Aunt Erzsébet. I pray for King Matthias every day." After she departs, I stare at my sleeping son. Today is the first day of a lifetime of worry for him. How do mothers bear it? I turn to Aunt Orsulya. "Is Matthias's condition much improved?"

"Healing takes time." Aunt Orsulya shakes her head, her lips pressed into a long-suffering frown. "His wounds are deep. Thanks be to God the Moldavian arrows did not strike a vital organ." She tucks the blanket around me. "No more questions. Worry spoils breast milk."

The ladies depart late in the evening. Only Bernádett remains, her cot placed outside the door in case I need help. From downstairs, the duduk music floats upward, the haunting melody honoring the miracle of life. I close my eyes and let the tune carry me to sleep.

"Ilona." Vlad, wrapped in a thick robe and smelling of wine, sits on the bed. "Remove the swaddling. I want to marvel at him."

Though my eyes are thick with fatigue, my heart warms with pleasure that Vlad visits so soon. "He sleeps."

"Remove the swaddling." It is a command.

Alarmed by his tone, I sit up and obediently unwind the cloth. The babe flails his thin pale arms and cries in protest. Vlad runs a slow hand over his son's head, strokes each limb, and wriggles his finger into the infant's fist. He cups the tiny feet in his hands, leans over and kisses the sole of each foot. The baby howls, loud robust bawls that upset my composure.

"He's strong." Vlad grins wide, his eyes sparkling with pride. "With lungs like that he will be able to command great armies." He kisses his head. "You may swaddle him now. I will name him Vlad."

"I can think of no better name." I re-wrap the babe and put him to my breast.

"You will nurse him. I will not have a malnourished wet nurse suckle my infant son."

My eyes widen. "I...yes... of course, my lord."

Vlad strokes my cheek with his thumb. "You made me very happy today."

Pleased by this, I press my face into his warm palm. And then I remember Matthias. "Tell me about Matthias. Will he recover? My aunts refused to give me any details during my lying-in. They said worrying brings on early labor."

"Those silly women and their superstitions." Vlad scowls, then nestles beside me. "Matthias caught three arrows in the back and collapsed in the middle of battle. Fortunately, his physicians treated him immediately." Vlad pats my arm. "He is expected to make a full recovery."

"Was Hungary victorious?" I hope Matthias's wounds had not been for naught.

Vlad's face contorts, crumpled with pained disappointment. "Hungary suffered an embarrassing defeat."

"Defeat? How can that be?"

"Because Matthias made stupid mistakes." Vlad's nostrils flare. "They were defeated despite having five hundred cannons, and plenty of siege engines, catapults, and battering rams. Matthias lost ten thousand of forty thousand soldiers— many from Wallachia. A forty-day battle, and they were crushed like bugs." Vlad balls his fist.

"What happened?"

"Matthias is no match for a shrewd strategist like Prince Stephen. A few blocked roads and a couple evacuated villages was all it took to weaken Matthias's army." Vlad grunted and shook his head. "The only good that came out of their humiliating defeat was that several nobles distinguished themselves in combat. I hear Stefan Báthory fought well."

"Will Matthias retaliate?"

"He already did. On Christmas day he sent mercenaries to torture the rebels celebrating their victory at a village inn." Vlad turns his fist as though he holds a sword. "I wish I had been there. It would have given me great satisfaction to run a sword through Stephen's black heart."

"Did the man wrong you?"

"That man is my cousin—his Aunt Crina, my first wife." Vlad's body tenses, muscles coiled with anger. "For a brief time after my first reign we were inseparable, the best of friends. We swore an oath to support each other and fight the Turks. I honored our oath. He did not. I have no tolerance for duplicitous men, cousin or not."

"I understand." I set a light hand on his arm.

"Do you?" Vlad leans away, his face pinched with annoyance. "You're familiar with betrayal, are you?" Sarcasm drips from his lips.

I drop my gaze. "Not really."

"Betrayal murders families and destroys dynasties," he snarls. "Betrayal is insidious. Inescapable. It lurks in council chambers, the great halls, private chambers... even beneath the sheets." His eyes flash with a past hurt. "Did you know Matthias offered sanctuary to Petru Aaron? Did you know this same man beheaded Stephen's mother and father—his own half-brother— during a wedding feast? You know nothing of betrayal." He grunts, rubs the tightness between his eyes. "You grew up surrounded by great wealth and loving relatives."

"As will our son," I say lightly to soothe his quick temper.

"Circumstances can change, Ilona." The hard line of Vlad's mouth softens when he looks at our son. "Extraordinary isn't it, how the birth of a son makes a man ponder the burdens and privileges of fulfilling his family's destiny."

I have no experience with betrayal but continuing the family line I understand. "This child will be a great man. How can he not? The blood of two great families runs through his veins."

"Greatness is nothing without honor."

I recall Vlad's hatred of his dishonorable brother Radu. "We will teach our son honor."

"Not all sons learn their father's lessons." Vlad strokes our babe's head. "Sons are a worthy burden bringing both pleasure and pain. The pain is watching him struggle with the hard lessons of life. The pleasure is...well, everything else. His worthiness will come from his immortalizing the Drăculești name, continuing the family lineage that it may live forever."

Lulled by his tender insight, I add my own. "Jesus had no children and he lives forever."

Vlad stiffens and pulls away. "I bare my soul and you reply with a myth?"

"Jesus is no myth." I clutch the babe to my breast, shielding him from Vlad's blasphemy. "You converted to Catholicism." My voice quivers. "Was that a lie?"

Vlad holds my chin. "I have killed for you, wife. I officially renounced the Orthodoxy of my people to marry you. Listen well. Allah. God. Yahweh. There are many names for god. A multitude of sacred books, canons, and scriptures. There are even more ways to honor one's god—chanting over fire, the *Salah,* ritual ablution, sacrificing animals, eating consecrated bread. Why is one deemed better than another? Who is your god, Ilona? Describe him."

My arms and legs are as heavy as my eyes. My mind is foggy and weary from the pendulum of emotions that swung from worry to fear to elation since my first labor pain. I am too tired for this conversation. Too tired to think clearly. But I must. Vlad wants to talk. Needs to talk. "The artists illuminating the manuscripts in Matthias's library depict God as an old man with a white beard wearing a red robe and holding an orb. *The Book of Hours* depicts him this way as well."

"God as earthly king." Vlad lets loose a throaty guffaw. "*The Book of Hours* is nothing more than a collection of prayers with colorful miniatures for entertaining the dull-minded." Vlad makes a show of swinging his head as though looking for eavesdroppers. "Are you aware that your royal cousin stoops to devious methods to procuring his books? Don't look so shocked, Ilona. Do you really believe a Carthusian monk willingly parted with his manuscript touting the virtues of a king?"

First religion and now accusations about Matthias? I am determined to lighten the mood. "I don't know. Are you willing to part with that book in your room? The one that is always open? You must read it every day."

A shadow passes over Vlad's face. "I will never part with that book."

"What is it? Theology? Philosophy? Warfare." I nudge his side. "Poems?"

"All of them." Vlad strokes my cheek. "You look tired, *iubirea mea*. I'll stay here until you fall asleep."

"*Iubirea mea*. You've called me this before. What does it mean?"

"My love." He whisks a light kiss across my forehead.

I rest my head on his chest, sighing with happiness when he slips his arm around me. Enfolded in his love, I close my eyes and sleep.

The following day, Aunt Erzsébet, Aunt Orsulya, and Margit take little Vlad—Vlăduţ as Aunt Erzsébet calls him—to be baptized.

While I rest in bed awaiting their return the midwife brings thistle tea. "When is the wet nurse due to arrive?"

"I will not need one." I close my eyes and think creamy thoughts...

I am jolted awake to the sound of my wailing, anointed babe carried into the room.

Aunt Erzsébet sets Vlăduţ in my arms where he latches on, his tiny mouth sucking mightily. A thousand needles prickle within my breasts. Vlăduţ begins gulping, rivulets of milk run from his mouth, over pink lips, and down his chin.

"You make motherhood look easy." Margit's voice is honey, but her eyes glare sour with envy.

Bernádett blinks back tears. "God blesses your marriage."

"Where's the wet nurse?" Aunt Erzsébet lips pinch tight with displeasure. "Why isn't she here?"

"Vlad doesn't want me to have one."

Aunt Erzsébet cringes. "No wet nurse? The man over-steps. Babies are a woman's domain." She touches her forehead and shakes her head. "Ilona, you can set limits. You don't have to agree to everything he wants."

But somehow, I fear what will happen if I do not.

## 27

"Tighter." A thousand butterflies flutter in my stomach. This is my first formal appearance since Vlăduţ's birth. "How do I look?"

"Motherhood becomes you, my lady." Bernádett adjusts the veil flowing from my gold-threaded hennin.

I look down at my milk-full breasts, eager to flaunt my impressive cleavage. "Motherhood added a few new curves." I suck in my stomach. "But this waist. Ugh, Aunt Erzsébet says it will never return to its former size."

"A daughter steals her mother's beauty," says my new lady-in-waiting, Gizella, the heart-faced daughter of a Wallachian boyar. She clasps an emerald pendant, a gift from Vlad, around my neck. "A son increases it."

If that were the case, Aunt Erzsébet would be a great beauty.

"Summon me immediately if he cries." I kiss Vlăduţ's chubby cheek as he sleeps in the pillow-soft arms of the placid, rotund *Dădacă*, the skilled white-haired Romanian nursemaid Vlad hired.

"Don't worry, my lady." Bernádett smooths the veil over my back.

"Vlăduţ is in the best of hands." Gizella holds open the door.

I kiss Vlăduţ yet again. I don't want to leave my precious son but I must. I need to charm Vlad back into my bed. I miss the taste of his passionate kisses, the feel of his hands on my body, and the tenor of his wanton whisperings.

I walk toward the great room feeling like a visitor in my own home. Vlad added many furnishings during my lying-in. Tapestries. Banners. Statues. Benches. I recognize the two golden Turkish vases and the turquoise inlayed coffer he had brought to my bedside but nothing else.

"New house, new baby, new nursemaid, new lady-in-waiting." Gizella sighs loudly. "I don't know how you manage to be so calm."

I like Gizella. She is always cheerful and eager to please. "It's easy when my husband finds such good people."

Gizella blushes and lowers her head. "Thank you, my lady."

We are about to pass Vlad's chambers when I stop. I am desperate to discover why Vlad makes such infrequent visits to my lying-in chambers. Do I dare enter his room? I rest my hand on the door handle. It's unlocked.

"Wait there." I point to the bench across the hall.

With wide eyes, Gizella backs across the hall.

My heart throbbing in my throat, I open the door. "I'll only be a minute." I slip inside.

Vlad's chamber is rosy-colored and cool, sunset's pink glow streaming through the open window. His bed is draped with fur blankets, strewn with pillows, and canopied in red velvet. Rare sculptures and fine objects decorate the tables. A tall spray of fresh rosemary—the herb promoting mental clarity—bursts from an urn on the casement ledge. But it is his desk, topped with a candelabrum, a large drawing, and a sheaf of stacked missives that I go to for answers.

I stare down at a diagram of our manse. Thick straight

lines delineate the basements, first, second, and third floors. Five chambers are marked with arrows and X's, and three dotted lines extend from the cellar to the edge of the paper. Tunnels perhaps? Vlad loves tunnels.

An old book is buried beneath a pile of correspondence. It's the same one I mistook for the Bible. The cover is worn, its wood casing peeking through a cracked leather binding. I run my fingers over its scratches and stains. How odd that it has no title, etching, or engraving. Three soft discolored leather straps fasten the book closed. With trembling fingers, I untie them and open the book.

The room darkens—the sun sliding beneath the horizon—and a chill seems to rise from the thick dry pigskin pages.

I study the faded brown and red ink. The script is foreign and dissimilar, as though many hands drew the curves, dashes, and simplistic drawings of birds, snakes, and other lowly creatures. Icy shivers race down my neck and prickle my skin. I close the book, set it down and replace the letters and reorder the stacks. Legs slogging heavily as though through a muddy bog, I cross the room, dread coiling into a tight ball in my belly. Something about that book is...wrong.

I close the door behind me with more questions than answers. Without saying a word, Gizella follows as I descend the stairway.

The great hall is noisy; councilors, boyars, emissaries, pages, squires, Vlad's steward, and chamberlain all gossiping, debating and laughing. Presiding over the gathering, Vlad sits in a carved chair on the dragon-and-raven crested dais. He acknowledges my arrival with a slight tilt of his head.

The nobles are more gracious. They ask about Vlăduţ and inquire about my health. The bachelors flirt with Gizella. The older men compliment me. I hide my disappointment over Vlad's aloofness behind bright smiles and witty repartee. He is busy with affairs of state, I tell myself.

During the meal we sit side by side and yet he pays no

attention to me. I barely eat and dull my hurt with too many cups of wine. I pretend interest in the conversation about the Hungarian taxes levied on Wallachia, Radu's misrule, Sultan Mehmed's latest conquests, the death of Skënderbej, and the odd miracles occurring in several villages.

"That village is the talk of Romania," says a boyar with jowls like a chipmunk.

"Are you referring to the one where the fresco of Madonna and child emerged from a heavenly mist during the Feast of Saint Mark?" The red-bearded boyar crosses himself.

"It's brilliant. And a hell...er, a heavenly way of increasing a town's revenues," says a handsome young Wallachian boyar.

"I know several traders who make a good living selling holy relics," says another.

During the final course, Vlad surprises everyone with an announcement. Mihnea, his eleven-year-old bastard son, became a page in Matthias's court. The boy—who I have not yet met—was taken to a remote monastery months before Vlad's capture. After we married, Vlad sent for him.

I leave the great hall later that evening, my throat choked with misery over Vlad's indifference. I burst into tears before reaching my chambers. I am a failure. Only nine months wed and my husband already lost interest.

I rush into the room, order Bernádett and Dădacă rip open my bodice, and thrust a huge leaking breast into Vlăduț greedy mouth. How can I follow Aunt Erzsébet's advice to become my husband's confidant when he ignores me? I lie in bed with Vlăduț in the crook of my arm and weep.

I awake determined to rekindle our attraction, but the next evening is the same.

Days. Weeks. One month. I dress for the evening meal and play the gracious hostess. Occasionally, Vlad speaks to me. I hang on to these brief exchanges, clutch them tight in hopes it foretells a change of heart. Each night I pray Vlad comes to my room. I wait in vain. My tears dry up. Vlad has a mistress. There can be no other reason for his absence from my bed.

I do not complain to Gizella or Bernádett, but when I am alone I hurl vases against the wall in frustration. Bernádett never comments as she cleans up the shattered pieces of my heart.

COLD WIND and needle sharp rain batter the manse. The nursery, however, is warm and calm. Vlăduṭ, wrapped in a wool blanket, suckles at my breast.

Bernádett embroiders tiny lapis birds on a pale blue blanket. Gizella writes a letter. *Dădacă* tidies the room. All is well until Vlad bangs open the door and stalks in. Vlăduṭ turns his head, his mouth still attached to my nipple.

Vlad holds out his hands. "Give me my son." His tone is more suited for the battlefield than a nursery.

I smile sweetly. "Vlăduṭ is nursing, my lord."

Vlad's nostrils flair. "Lady Ilona…"

Frightened by Vlad's tone, I shift Vlăduṭ, warm from milk and love, to Vlad's arms. He lays him on the bed and unwraps his swaddling.

I leap from the chair. "Vlăduṭ will catch a chill."

Vlad frowns and quirks an eyebrow, picks up the naked babe, and cradles him in his arms. "Today Vlăduṭ receives his first lesson."

"What lesson? He is not yet three-months." My breath comes heavy and my body stiffens.

"He will learn to endure the climes of a land he will one day rule." Vlad walks through the doorway.

Bernádett, Gizella, and I look wide-eyed at one another.

I grab the discarded swaddling and race after Vlad. "You're taking Vlăduṭ outside?"

Vlad does not reply and begins speaking Turkish to Vlăduț as he descends the stairs.

"My lord, consider the harsh weather." I clasp my hands in prayer. "Do not subject our babe to its contagions. Teach this lesson when the weather is more suitable to his delicate condition."

"There is nothing delicate about my son." He shrugs his fur cape to the floor and strolls into the courtyard as though it is a balmy spring day.

The hail falls fast and hard, bounces this way and that, blankets the ground with an icy layer, yet Vlad strides to the middle of the courtyard. He lifts Vlăduț aloft and intones a strange incantation.

Vlăduț shrieks. His pudgy limbs flail and jerk.

"What are you doing?" I clutch Vlad's arm. "Stop this! He'll get sick!" Tears and rain pour down my face. "I beg of you, please stop."

"Vlăduț, first born legitimate son of Prince Vlad Dracula, has no use for tears." Vlad lowers the babe until they are eye to eye.

Vlăduț is drenched and red-faced from crying. His bright green eyes—the same as his father's—glare with indignation. I touch his wee cold foot.

"My son will have a life filled with betrayal and battles, battles he must fight in the rain and snow. Battles won and lost because of his courage and bravery. Because of his ability to lead men. He must be a wellspring for their courage. A source of inspiration. Victorious or not."

I kneel, the icy mud soaking through my heavy skirt and chilling my skin. Vlad's coldness sends spasms of shivers through my body. "Please…"

Vlad peers down with disdain. "You know nothing about the agony and thrills of battle. Nothing of leadership. Look at my son. Imagine his future. Will his bastard brother Mihnea betray him one day? Will his undoing be a front facing wound or a coward's wound in the back? Will he learn the lessons I teach? Or mock them?" Vlad's voice is thick and sharp, his eyes frosty with memory.

My husband is a frightening mystery. I am not strong enough to understand his dark secrets and true motivations. Age and experience make us strangers. And yet, I still feel pulled toward him, a strange bond that is more air than earth. I blink away tears. "Your son will be b-b-brave, strong, fearless like his father. A w-w-warrior. A p-p-prince." I speak through chattering teeth.

Vlad bestows that roguish grin which always twists my heart and extends his hand. "Rise, wife." He kisses Vlăduț on both cheeks and returns his howling heir to my arms.

Our eyes lock, a mutual understanding between us. I break the look I have yearned for all these lonely nights to tend to my baby. I rush inside where Bernádett, Gizella, and Dădacă wait with blankets. Dădacă wraps Vlăduț in fur and soothes his cries with croons and a slow rocking motion.

Vlad, his face slick with rain, watches our fussing with amusement. "My son is strong and robust, a true descendant of the Drăculeşti family." Vlad grips my forearm as I turn to leave and tugs me close. "Never question the lessons I must instill in my son."

"Yes, my lord." I shiver, my lower lip quivering from dismay and cold.

"I look forward to seeing you at supper this evening." Vlad turns my chin and presses his mouth to mine, his tongue pushing inside.

It is like our first kiss, insistent and needy. My knees buckle and my body warms—oh, I want him again.

Vlad pulls away, bows with a gallant flourish, and walks away. Flustered and desirous, I return to my chambers where Gizella rings a tiny bell above a laughing Vlăduț.

"He's a sturdy babe, my lady," says Gizella. "It is our way and will make him strong."

"*Da*," says Dădacă. "He will soon like it."

Bernádett peels off my mud-soaked dress and drapes a woolen shawl over my shoulders. "I think exposing a babe to a storm is cruel."

Her comment makes me bristle and though I do not like this premature initiation of endurance, I defend my husband. "Vlăduț is no common babe. He is the rightful heir of Wallachia, the future prince who must be braver and stronger than his people. Eager and able to lead in battle."

That evening, Vlad is attentive at dinner and my loins ache for the weight of his body and the touch of his hands. But he does not come to my chambers and once again my tears soak the pillow.

The following day Vlad and I visit Buda castle where he meets with Matthias to discuss affairs of state while I keep a sharp ear out for the latest scandals.

I leave Vlăduț with Bernádett and Dădacă in the Buda nursery and go to the ladies' chamber, the best place for hearing gossip. As usual, Aunt Orsulya plays cards with Zsazsa, and Aunt Erzsébet's ladies-in-waiting chatter about courtiers and emissaries. Margit is there as well, bragging about the young noble currently negotiating her betrothal.

"His name is Mátyus Maróti. Look, sister." Margit unsnaps a filigree locket hanging from a golden chain around her neck.

I peer at the miniature of a fair-haired and round-faced young man with bug eyes and a bulbous nose. "Very handsome."

"He has strategic land holdings and a large castle in Gyönk." She strokes the miniature. "I wonder if his hair is as blonde as mine? Miniatures never give a precise likeness, do they?"

"When do you wed?" I ask.

Margit kisses his portrait before snapping shut the locket. "Who knows? Aunt Erzsébet says there are still many matters to discuss." She wraps cool fingers around my wrist, tugs me close, and whispers in my ear. "I'm worried about the negotiations."

"Why?"

"A certain complication might be discovered." Margit purses her lips and lifts her brows, but she looks more happy than worried. "I'm not a..." Margit's gaze drops to her lap, the unspoken word hanging in the air.

I suck air through my teeth and turn the chair about to prevent one particular lady-in-waiting from reading our lips. "A one-time indiscretion?"

Margit shakes her head, her expression gleeful.

"You took a lover?" I whisper.

Margit's eyes shift sideways, her lips puckered.

"If Matthias finds out..." I do not need to tell her how angry he will be. "You must end it."

Margit lifts her chin, blue eyes blazing. "I don't want to."

I take Margit's hand. "Is he married?"

"Yes."

I take a deep breath. "Do you love him?"

"I love what we do together." Her smile is devilish.

"Why would you jeopardize everything for lust?"

"Revenge." Margit's face is as smooth as a blade and sharp with meaning.

I snatch my hand away. My insides shrivel. I cannot breathe. The room blurs, the world spins...

Not Vlad. He would never...would he?

Aunt Erzsébet's arrival ends my frozen trance. I rise in a daze, curtsy, and the room comes back into focus. I refuse to be bested by Margit.

"I am certain your paramour's wife," my words drip honey, "tolerates her husband's dalliances secure in her position." I leave the room with a haughty chin and sick stomach.

I flee to the nursery where Vlăduţ gulps my milk while tears well in my eyes. How is it possible that my breasts produce the milk of life when the swill of disgust brews in my heart?

Aunt Orsulya enters the nursery and draws a chair to my side. "What did Margit say to you?"

I wipe tears across my cheek. "Is Vlad unfaithful?"

Aunt Orsulya snorts. "All husbands are unfaithful."

My insides tangle into a knot. "But with my own sister?"

"What? Preposterous." Aunt Orsulya shakes her head. "Is this what she told you?"

I put the milk-drunk Vlăduţ over my shoulder and pat his back. "I thought...Margit implied ..."

"Bah." Aunt Orsulya flaps her hand. "She is jealous of you and upset that Mátyus Maróti is not titled. Land and wealth are not enough for her. Margit wants a crown. I do not know if Prince Vlad has a mistress—there is no gossip to support that. However, I do know that some men are not content with one woman, even one giving them a son." She strokes Vlăduţ's face. "Men's desires for new conquests and new victories extend past the battlefield. Be realistic, Ilona. Expect infidelities. Whether it's one mistress or a harem, another woman does not threaten your position."

Aunt Orsulya's words add fresh gnashes to my injured heart. How can I tell her that her advice is opposite of Aunt Erzsébet's? How can I explain that I love Vlad so much it hurts? That his loving and needing someone else is like a living death for me?

Aunt Orsulya takes Vlăduţ into her arms. "Go back to the ladies' chambers. I'll be there in a bit."

I kiss Aunt Orsulya's cheek. "Thank you for putting things into perspective," I lie, and hurry from the nursery to a place where I can weep in private. Where only the saints and Jesus see my suffering.

The chapel door closes behind me with a hollow thud.

"I am a failure. I cannot satisfy my husband. I allow my

sister to taunt me." My whispered confessions sound trite in the sanctified space.

The crucified Jesus, stone saints, and Blessed Mother are oblivious to my sufferings. Prayers offer no comfort. Hot tears of self-pity roll down my cheeks until the door creaks open. I wipe them away, squeeze my eyes shut, and bow my head pretending fervent prayer.

The pew squeaks as the intruder sits on the bench.

"Praying for our son?"

My head swings around and my heart pulses in my throat. "I pray for future sons."

Vlad slides next to me and wipes a tear from my cheek. "Why are you crying?"

"Those are tears of devotion." My false smile quivers.

"Devotion to what? God? Our child? Me?" Vlad presses his mouth to mine, pushes his tongue past my closed lips.

I want him; feel that primal desire welling inside me. "Not here."

Vlad runs his finger beneath the edge of my bodice. "You want it, don't you?"

I do. My nipples harden, stretch towards him in anticipation of his fingers and tongue. "Not in front of them." I point to the saints and stand to leave.

Vlad blocks my way, wraps me in his arms, and sprinkles kisses across my neck. "I want you, wife. Here and now." His hands wonder over my bodice.

"This is God's house." I struggle in his grip. "It's wrong."

"The act between husband and wife is a sacrament." Vlad spins me about, lifts my skirt up, and caresses my buttocks. "Show your devotion to me, Ilona."

His touch shoots arrows of pleasure to my nethers, the twinging ache of need overcoming my objections. I bend over the pew and offer my bare buttocks like a gift. Vlad grasps my hips and plunges in. I whimper with pleasure as his length thrusts deep.

"Is this what you were praying for, *iubirea mea*?" He breathes into my ear, his hand sliding around my thigh to stroke my pleasure knot.

I moan and sigh as he teases my slippery core until all piety is gone. Blinded by lust, I stare insensible at the crucified Jesus certain my mounting bliss assures me a place in hell. Together we consecrate our marriage with unholy paroxysms of pleasure.

He wipes our stickiness across my buttocks. "I have stayed too long from your bed."

Two sensations war within me. My skin tingles with the thrill of our naughtiness, yet my soul blisters with guilt.

As we leave the chapel my silent prayer is twofold, forgiveness and gratitude.

## 28

Vlăduţ topples over and bursts into a frustrated cry.

"He is an exceptionally determined young prince. Just like his father." Dădacă props him up again because he wails with frustration if left on his back.

"Vlăduţ is extraordinary, everyone says so." One hand rests on my plump belly, my wanton depravity at Buda chapel igniting Vlad's desire for me again.

This pregnancy is easy. I am neither sick nor tired. Vlad believes it is another boy. But whether conceived between the pews or during the many times afterward, it proves our resurrected bond.

Our lovemaking has taken an unusual turn. Vlad avoids the bed in favor of daring locations. He feasted on my pleasure knot while I leaned against the stable wall. He took me in the courtyard under the stars. I rode him like a horse atop the table in the great chamber. He suckles my breast milk like a babe. We cannot get enough of one another—wet kisses and lusty gropes throughout the day. I've stopped worrying when he is gone for days and sometimes weeks. If he says he meets with boyars, I believe him.

Rareş, Vlad's manservant, rouses my happy thoughts and

enters the nursery. "My lady, my master requires your presence."

My pulse quickens with delight. It is not often I have the privilege of entering his inner sanctum.

The room is a treasure of colorful tapestries, marble busts, bronze statues, weaponry schematics, and Transylvanian maps. A manly musk mingles with the tang of wine and whiff of ale.

Vlad sits in a plush velvet chair, a wine goblet and map in front of him. "I have a surprise."

I kiss his bristly cheek. "A map?"

"Not just any map." Vlad hooks his arm around my waist and pats his knee.

I sit on his thigh, and he burrows his face in my bodice and growls. I giggle and feel the familiar heated tightening below. I tug at my skirt but he stays my hand.

"Does this map look familiar?"

I peer at it, giggling as Vlad's hand wanders over my bodice. "It is Pest." Every street, residence, shop, stable, inn, church, and smithy are drawn to scale. Even our manse.

Vlad taps a well-known inn notorious for brawls and debaucheries. "We're going here tonight."

"Whatever for?"

"A bit of scouting." Vlad winks.

"You mean spying." I nip at his nose.

Vlad chuckles, the deep timbre as smooth as a cat's purr. Hypnotic and honeyed, his voice is food for my soul, burrowing deep into the very fiber of my being and feeding my love for him.

"Is this your disguise?" I brush my hand across his chin, scraggly and thick from three-days growth. "This explains why the barber has time to chase my servant girl."

Vlad scratches his cheek. "I thought it rather made me look like a carpet dealer from Serbia."

"Not in these clothes." I tug on his velvet robe. "And am I to be your Serbian wife?"

"You will be my Hungarian wife."

"How is that a disguise?"

"You won't be wearing this blouse." Vlad tugs on the lace cuff dangling from my sleeve. "Or this skirt." He pushes up my skirt and plunges his finger into my wetness.

THE NIGHT IS COOL, and dusk's waning light casts long shadows across the road. Over the clatter of hooves and wheels, dogs bark. Pulled by an old mare, we travel through Pest in our most modest carriage, all Drăculeşti insignia removed. Rareş drives us, his colorful livery exchanged for well-worn undyed clothing. Likewise, Vlad and I dress in sturdy travel attire and plain boots.

I pat the artless bun at the nap of my neck.

"Keep your hands hidden. They are too smooth and groomed for a merchant's wife." Vlad kisses my fingertips, but his attention is fixed out the window.

"Looking for someone?"

Vlad squeezes my hand. "Misfortunes occur when one is not attentive to their surroundings."

Unsavory elements lurk in the gloom, but neither beast nor thief can best Vlad. "I fear no living creature when I'm with you."

Vlad quirks his brow. "What about dead ones? Like the *strigoi*?"

"Unsaved souls who rise from the grave to feed off the living?" I snort with laughter. "We are not in Romania."

"Do you think the *strigoi* limit their mischief to the Carpathian Mountains?"

"I think you want to frighten me enough that I leap into your arms."

"Perhaps." He adjusts the *oglavja* atop his head.

I pat his knee. "I hope you don't intend frightening our children with tales about this bloodthirsty creature."

"Not frighten. Enlighten. Myths speak to our darkest fears and explain the supernatural in ways philosophy and religion fail to do."

Our conversation is cut short, the carriage arriving at the Cow & Sow, an inn popular for its zesty stew and spicy women of ill repute.

"Ready?" Vlad clasps my hand.

My pulse quickens with anticipation. It reminds me of our excursion into Buda castle's labyrinth. This outing will be much more fun, no gruesome dungeon here.

Our arrival is noted with only a few curious glances, which is a fine thing. Our disguises fool them.

I inhale the aromas of sweat and pork, earth and ale, and men and women. Good, honest smells.

"Traveling late, are you?" A chubby red-nosed old man with glassy eyes slaps the empty bench next to him.

Vlad sits down. "A shrewd carpet merchant makes deals at the buyer's leisure not the sellers."

"Carpet, you say?" the man asks over his mug of ale. "Where do you call home?"

"Kosovo, Serbia." Vlad slips into a convincing foreign accent.

"Bastards, all of them." The man's belly bounces with laughter.

"Shut up, Egyid, you drunken ass." Another man, two long hairs sprouting from an enormous mole on his cheek, plops down beside Egyid. "Your father's a Serb."

"And I'm a bastard, aren't I?" Egyid thumps his fist on the table. "Papa stuck Mama good, then disappeared down the Danube." He leans toward me. "Pardon my language, mistress, but you should tell your husband to take you to a better inn. This one is full of drunks and whores."

The proprietress, a stout woman whose ponderous breasts sway in tempo with her stride, cuffs the red-nosed man on the back of his head. "Watch it, you lout, or I'll cut you off—the ale as well."

"Aw, Ildi, don't be cruel. You know how I feel about you." Egyid smacks her substantial bottom.

Vlad flicks an amused glance my way. "I heard your *gulyás* is the best around."

"None better, except for the cooks working in the castle scullery. Two bowls for you?" The proprietress' grin flaunts one brown front tooth. "You'll be wanting ale, yes?"

I bite my lips to keep from laughing. For more than twenty years, I have been confined to castles and ensconced in carriages, forbidden to mingle with common folk. Tonight's adventure is a wish made reality. I don't want to miss a thing.

I run my palms over the crude-hewn table. Its lustrous patina is worn smooth from ale, food, and thousands of hands. I study the patrons; whores in bosom-baring dresses, smudged-faced smiths, and tired-eyed shopkeepers. These are the tax-paying subjects of King Matthias, the ones most affected by the smallest increase in tariffs. The good folk, Vlad says, abused by greedy nobles levying excessive taxes. They wear their poverty on their weary faces, hunched backs, and hitched gaits.

I live in a frivolous world shielded from hunger and oppression. My bed is always warm, my plate heaped with meat, my clothes lavish and fine. My only work is with the needle. I never prepare food, kindle a fire, or even dispose of my own chamber pot.

I look at Vlad, my heart swelling with newfound admiration. Unlike all the other nobles I know, Vlad wants to help his subjects improve their lives. I put my mouth to his ear. "When you rule Wallachia, we will make frequent scouting trips."

Vlad arches an eyebrow. "Have a taste for vulgarity, do you?"

"Ah, look at them. They whisper like lovers." Ildi sets down two mugs of ale. "Are you newly married?"

"Almost two years," I say.

"Well, bless you both." Ildi's gaze drops to my rounded belly, which is concealed under the voluminous gray mantel. "I'll be back with your *gulyás*." She shuffles away.

The men are discussing whether it rains more this year than last when Egyid interrupts the debate with local gossip. A village boy ran into the vicar with a stolen loaf of bread in his hand. The virgin bride gave birth to a full-term baby four months after the nuptials, the cuckolded husband doing business with the very man his wife dallies with. My stomach hurts from laughing.

A customer with a wide curled mustache heaves himself on the bench across from us. "Do you folks travel through Pest often?"

"It's been two years since I traveled this way," says Vlad as Ildi sets down two steaming trenchers of stew. "Not much has changed."

"Ah, but it has." Curly Mustache twists the hairy tips. "The devil himself now lives in our town."

"A devil? Maybe I should make a deal with him."

"He's no devil," says a man with eyebrows like wooly caterpillars. "He's just a banished prince trying to reclaim what is his by rights."

"Bah, we have no rights. Why should they?" Curly Mustache bangs his fist on the table. "If my father leaves me an unprofitable business, is it my right to steal to increase my income? Princes, lords, kings—the whole lot of them can rot in hell. They sit in their stone strongholds bored because they have nothing to do. Their soft life makes them soft—right here." He grabs his crotch. "That's why they start wars. It's the only thing that makes their cocks hard."

"You're an idiot," says Ildi. "Kings don't make war because their cocks don't work. They make war because God told them to fight the infidels."

"What does it matter who sits his hairy ass on the Buda throne? Our lives don't change. I still have to rise before sunset and work like a dog to put food in my young ones' bellies."

"Your bitch doesn't work, just lies on her back in the doorway with her legs spread," says Egyid.

"Don't be talking about his wife that way," says Wooly Eyebrow and everyone laughs.

"Now there's a she-devil." Ildi wipes her hands on her apron.

"Seems to be a lot of devils in this little town." Though his tone is playful, his eyes harden with displeasure.

"The real one lives yonder." Egyid jerks a thick thumb in our manse's direction. "Prince Vlad Dracula. Vlad Țepeș, The Impaler they call him. He's a vile wretch. Skewers babes still bloody from the womb onto poles and eats them raw."

"Only the sons of his enemies," says Wooly Eyebrow. "I don't much like a man who refuses to hire the local folk to muck out his stables or pour his wine."

"Your brains are all addled," says Ilda. "Princes need to hire people they know and trust, ones who won't slit their throat while they're sitting on the privy."

"Lucky son of a bitch," says Egyid. "I only have a pot to shit in."

I look down at my stew, my appetite gone.

"Do you think someone wipes his ass for him?" Curly Mustache pantomimes a back and forth motion that sends the others into fits of laughter.

"Oh, sure. It's a genuine castle position," Egyid wipes gleeful tears from his eyes. "Royal Ass Wiper."

Snorting with hilarity, the men pound the table and clutch

their sides. Vlad joins in but I am not fooled and see the flash of exasperation in his eyes.

"Aren't you hungry, dearie?" Ilda nudges me with her elbow. "You're a pretty thing. Why your skin just glows and your hands…they look smooth as butter."

I curl my fingers into a fist as though to hide them. "Thank you. The *gulyás* is delicious." I dip my bread in. "Who is this Vlad Ţepeş?" I glance at my husband.

Vlad rewards my question with a conspiratorial smile. "The Prince of Wallachia."

"Not anymore," says Egyid. "He was prince for a few years. Maybe not even that long."

"My morning piss was longer than his reign," says Curled Mustache.

"Sounds like you need to see a healer," says Egyid before turning to me. "He's the devil, I tell you. Drinks his enemies' blood from a golden cup."

"So would you," says Curled Mustache, "if you had any gold or balls big enough to kill your enemies."

"My balls are plenty big."

"My cock is bigger."

"Doesn't matter if don't work."

Vlad clears his throat. "I heard King Matthias falsely imprisoned him."

"Don't know anything about that," says Egyid. "Only heard he has a vicious temper and a lust for sadism."

"I heard he married the king's beautiful cousin," says Ildi. "And she already gave him a son."

A whore wiggles herself between two men at our crowded table. "Dracula visits brothels, you know. Likes it rough. Gets his jollies from tying girls up."

"Pardon, missus, if I cause offense," the whore says to me, "but I'm just repeating what I heard."

The *gulyás* congeals in my belly, but I am too well schooled in genteel behavior to let my horror show.

Vlad sops up the rest of his *gulyás* with bread. "He skewers babies, drinks his enemies' blood, and fancies wicked pleasures. You think he's a monster then?"

Wooly Brow flaps his hand. "He's no better or worse than any other prince trying to get his throne back."

"Yes, except The Impaler prefers battles to peace," adds Egyid.

"But you've got to battle for peace," says Ilda.

"That's stupid."

"No, you ass, that's what Greeks call destructive reasoning."

"Greeks fuck everybody in the ass—guess that's a fair amount of destruction."

"Deductive reasoning, clod heads!" Egyid pounds the table.

Ildi stands and smooths her stain-smeared skirt. "You louts don't know anything about princes. They are learned men who make war for reasons we will never understand."

"You saying we're stupid?" says Curly Mustache.

"I'm saying we have no proper learning. Princes read books before they can walk. Their tutors stick a quill in their wee hands before they're weaned."

"How do you know?" asked Egyid.

"My niece—the one that died giving birth to the palace guard's spawn—worked in the scullery. She told me how it is with those lords. The servants all talk, you see, and what happens in the nursery eventually makes it to the scullery." Ildi picks up our trenchers and shuffles away.

"Well," said Egyid, "if learning makes you want to give blades to thousands of young lads and send 'em to their deaths so you can sit your fat ass on a throne then I'm glad I'm stupid. Wouldn't want that sin on my soul."

"That's not sin," said Wooly Eyebrow. "That's power."

"Power? Fucking up thousands of lives?"

The argument digresses into hurling expletives and name-calling.

Vlad and I leave soon after, not speaking to each other until clopping hooves and creaking wheels prevent Rareş from eavesdropping.

"Do you visit brothels and fornicate with whores?" My voice is as brittle as a reed-thin icicle. First Margit's insinuation. And now a common whore's remark. Who is this man I love?

Vlad grunts and stares out the window.

"My lord, please tell me. Did the whore speak the truth?" My body stiffens.

Vlad shifts about, the full moon casting an eerie blue glow on half his face. "It was whores' gossip."

"You told me all gossip has a morsel of truth," I whisper.

Vlad's face contorts as though smelling something foul. "I find it curious that gossip about my sexual appetites is more troubling to you than that of my eating babies and drinking blood."

I recall the awful leaflet proclaiming Vlad a bloodthirsty berserker who skewered babes and ate them raw. And the political reason behind Matthias's concocting and distributing the lies. "Well of course you don't eat your enemies' babies."

"Then you have your answer."

But when I search for the truth in his eyes about his alleged sexual proclivities he turns away.

# 29

## ℭlad

**Summer 1455**
**Hunyadi's castle in Hunedoara, Transylvania**

Vlad Dracula relished strategy meetings. They were more delicious than the finest wine. Especially when it involved talking with cunning strategists like John Hunyadi, János Vitéz, Mihály Szilágy, Hunyadi's eldest son, and Vlad's cousin Stephen.

Hunyadi waved the first letter from the stack in front of him. "This one is a plea for help from the mayor of Sibiu."

"I received the same request," says Mihály Szilágy, a handsome man with a cleft in his chin, an aquiline nose, kind eyes, and thick bushy hair.

"The mayor is an alarmist." János Vitéz crossed his arms. "Mehmed will attack Belgrade before taking Sibiu."

Dracula winced at János Vitéz nonchalance and swallowed the sharp rebuke on the tip of his tongue in favor of a more diplomatic approach. "You're right, however, the mayor's fear is valid. Turkish spies pretending to be merchants have already infiltrated many Wallachian towns."

"They gather intelligence in preparation for an attack," said Stephen, sporting a thin blonde mustache since Vlad last saw him.

"These letters are much the same." Hunyadi fanned out the missives. "And thanks to Vlad's spies we know Dăneşti threw his lot with our enemy and cowers under Sultan Mehmed's robes." Hunyadi pushed two letters toward Vlad. "Letters from the mayors of Făgăras and Amlaş. Dăneşti seized control."

Beneath Dracula's calm veneer, his muscles rippled with rage. "Those fiefdoms are mine by birthright." His voice dripped vengeance. "We must stop Mehmed and Dăneşti."

"We will take care of Mehmed." Hunyadi pointed his finger at Dracula. "You get to do as you like to Dăneşti."

"It will be an honor." Dracula's wolfish grin was so chilling cousin Stephen shuddered.

While Dracula explained the disadvantages of Mehmed's siege engines, Matthias, Hunyadi's chubby twelve-year-old son, slunk into the chamber. He stretched out on a wooden bench, by turns yawning or fidgeting.

By the time the sun disappeared behind the horizon all was decided. Hunyadi's eldest would lead the fight in Croatia. Mihály Szilágy would enlist the Serbs in Belgrade. Stephen would accompany Hunyadi.

And Prince Vlad was given free rein to stop Dăneşti any way he saw fit.

## July 22, 1456
## Forest near Tîrgovişte

"THE COMET that blazed across the sky last month heralds a great victory for you," said the astrologer to Dracula and his assembled advisors.

Dracula balled his fists. He had waited six long years to confront his father's murderer. He was ready, had more skill, shrewdness, military might, and allies than ever before. His mouth watered thinking about the sweet taste of revenge. His cock stiffened as he imagined thrusting a sword through Dănești's traitorous heart.

A ruddy-cheeked young scout, huffing and puffing, ran into the tent.

"Well?" Dracula looked up from the map of Tîrgoviște.

"Your trick was a success, my lord."

"Good." Dracula nodded, his chest expanding with pride.

"It was a brilliant plan, my lord," said a boyar with a face like a bull and the brawn of a bear.

It was. Who else but Dracula could devise a plan to get Dănești and his men to leave the safety of Tîrgoviște's fortified walls? Vlad had sent his captain, his look-a-like in face and form, north with a small group of mercenaries to seize Bran castle. There they had raided the custom offices and confiscated all the monies and goods. Enraged by 'Dracula's' insurrection, Dănești was forced to quell the sedition. Which meant traveling through a narrow pass. The only route between Tîrgoviște and Bran castle.

Dracula turned to the astrologer. "Victory is certain?"

"Without a doubt, my lord. The direction of the double-tailed comet portends your success."

"My lord," said a young boyar known for breaking many a maiden's heart, "our forces are much smaller than Dănești's."

"Small forces have the advantage of speed and stealth," said Dracula. "Do you recall the story of David and Goliath? We will make quick work of Dănești's slow-moving troops." Dracula positioned a small silver marker atop the map. "We will ambush them here." He sniffed the air. "Do you smell it?"

"Smell what?" asked Bull Face.

"The sweet fragrance of blood and victory."

Before dawn the next day, Dracula gathered his soldiers.

"Tomorrow they sing songs for us." Dracula spoke from atop his white warhorse. "Tomorrow your wife and children mourn your fallen body. Tomorrow your friends toast your victory. Tomorrow your favorite whore worships your stiff valor. But today we fight! Today we slay the sultan's bootlicker. Today we purge the Infidels! Today we fight for Christ! Today we battle for all of Christendom!"

DRACULA'S MILITIA hid in trees, without armor, silent and still.

Dăneşti's vanguard marched passed in threes through the narrow winding trail. Dracula's men stayed hidden. They watched soundlessly as the main guard tramped by next. Lagging behind, the rear guard, plodded carelessly forward.

Dracula gave the signal. His men jumped from trees with spears. Sprang from thickets with swords. They smashed surprised faces with cudgels. Hacked armor-slow bodies with axes. The rear guard fled shrieking into the woods. Vlad's archers picked them off from the top of the knoll.

Dracula gouged and stabbed and gutted his way through the mêlée in search of Dăneşti. The slaughter and screams quickened his blood, each gouged stomach and severed limb stirring an almost sensual excitement.

"Where are you, Dăneşti?" Dracula shouted. "Show yourself!"

A rustle of movement in the thicketed hillside caught his eye. "Coward!" Dracula charged after him.

The white-haired Dăneşti waited at the top of the summit. "Dracul's pup finally comes to piddle upon me. What took you so long, little pup?" He flung off his cloak and brandished his sword.

Dracula's rage crystalized into an icy resolve. "If I am my father's pup that makes you Mehmed's ball-licking lapdog."

Dăneşti pointed his sword at Dracula. "That honor belongs to your brother Radu."

Vlad rushed at him.

Dăneşti deflected the slash. "Skill beats youth any day."

Dăneşti misjudged Dracula's cold fury. Underestimated the years Dracula spent as the sultan's ward. Undervalued the training he received by a master swordsman.

"I have skill enough." Dracula circled around him, unhurried and confident.

Dăneşti sidestepped a rock, scooped up his cloak and blocked Dracula's thrust.

Vlad circled a second time, each swipe marking Dăneşti's tempo. Vlad adjusted his stance and swiped his blade.

"I tire of this dance, boy. Shall we—" Dăneşti pivoted and kicked Vlad in the gut.

Vlad lost his balance and stumbled back. He pressed his hand to his stomach and staggered forward.

Dăneşti fell for the trick and rushed forward. Vlad dropped to his knee and sliced his blade across Dăneşti's hamstring. He hit the ground, tried to rise, grimaced in pain, and collapsed. It was a crippling blow.

Ice ran through Vlad's veins as he plunged his blade into Dăneşti's traitorous gut. Vlad grabbed Dăneşti by his hair, jerked him to his knees, and dug the blade into his throat.

"This is for my father," Vlad hissed, "for my brother Mircea, my mother, and for all the heirs coming after me for a thousand years."

"Do it, boy," Dăneşti rasped as blood soaked the ground.

"I am no boy. I am Vlad Dracula, son of Dracul, Prince of Wallachia, ruler of the duchies of Făgăras and Amlaş." Vlad drew the blade across Dăneşti's neck. "Any last words?"

Dăneşti gurgled a bloody profanity.

A shiver of pleasure—as though he held a naked woman

—coursed through Vlad, and he stiffened with expectancy. He lifted his blade high and brought it down.

Prince Vlad Dracula emerged from the woods holding Dănești's severed head. "Victory is ours!"

## 30

# Ilona

## December 1468
## Dracula's Mansion in Pest, Hungary

The baby will not come. Two days now. The ladies cry and pray. It is God's punishment for defiling the chapel with our lust. Two babes born within a year is not a gift but God's punishment.

I have no tears left. Death's icy hands claw at my body. Two midwives—when did the other arrive?—huddle with Aunt Erzsébet in my insensible haze. I will die like Mother. In agony and blood.

Another pain severs reality. My body floats off the bed, my neck arcs back. My mouth opens wide to let a serpent emerge. An inhumane wail shatters the quiet.

Death's hands grab my thighs and ankles. Satan smacks my face. A mountain falls on top of me. I split in two. The mountain becomes a raging river.

"My babe," I whimper into the gray droning fog shrouding the room.

The midwife shows me an unmoving bundle. "A girl."

The babe is lifeless, her face purple with torment. Coiled

around her neck, my daughter's cord of life delivered only death.

I hold out my arms. "Give her to me."

"My lady…"

"Give her to me." I say between clenched teeth, my mind's fog clearing.

The ladies weep, Margit vomits, Bernádett buries her face in her hands. Aunt Orsulya sobs in Zsazsa's arms. Aunt Erzsébet squares her shoulders and departs the room to give Vlad the bad news.

I cradle my perfect daughter, unwind the death cord, kiss her cool head, and baptize her with my hot tears.

I weep and weep and weep and the fog descends again.

"You must eat," the midwife says as Bernádett tries spooning *mămăligă* into my mouth. I turn away and wish death had claimed me. I thrash out when the ladies sponge me clean, stiffen my arms when they put a fresh nightgown over me, and cry when they brush my hair.

"Ilona?" Vlad creeps into the room, his voice low.

"Why are you here?" I turn away. A dead daughter deserves no visit.

Vlad stands at the foot of the bed, his hands clasped behind his back, his face unshaven, his eyes red-rimmed. "I have named our daughter Oana. God is gracious."

"Gracious!?" I snarl like a wounded dog. "Better a dead daughter than a dead son?"

Vlad reels back as though struck with a blade. Stunned, he stares and shakes his head. "God graciously spared your life." Vlad regains his composure, his face turning icy, and speaks to Bernádett sitting by the bed. "I want a daily report of Lady Ilona's recovery." He turns on his heels and stalks to the door. "I expect your swift return to Matthias's court," he says without looking back.

I open my mouth to call him back—to apologize for assuming the worst—but shame squeezes my throat closed.

Bernádett smooths the blanket. "Men are heartless."

"Prince Vlad is not heartless." I was the cruel one to assume he cared more about having another heir than my life.

"He left without—"

Gizella enters the room with Dădacă carrying Vlăduț.

"We passed Prince Vlad in the hall. My lady, I've never seen a man so distraught over a stillborn girl." Gizella sets down a tray of bread and cheese.

Bernádett wrinkles her nose. "You're the daughter of a loyal boyar. You side with him."

"I side with my lady," bristles Gizella before turning to me. "I know many noble ladies whose husbands only visit the lying-in chamber if a son is born."

"A reminder of your blessings." Dădacă places Vlăduț in my outstretched arms.

I burrow my nose into my chubby-cheeked one-year-old with gratitude, but he squirms away to crawl under the blanket. We play peek-a-boo until Dădacă notes my heavy eyes.

"Let Lady Mother rest now, Vlăduț." Dădacă captures him and after he scatters a host of laughing kisses on my face, carries him back to the nursery.

Exhaustion overcomes me. The next morning I wake weeping.

The tears don't stop. Day after day.

Bernádett encourages my tears. Purge your sadness, she says. Stay in bed.

Gizella urges me to resume my normal activities.

Aunt Erzsébet bursts into my lying-in chamber like a general ready to chastise his troops. "I must speak to Lady Ilona in private."

Aunt Erzsébet tosses her thick fur cape over a chair as Gizella and Bernádett flee the room.

"Do you know what day it is?" Each word is blade-sharp.

"The eve of Christmas." My voice is small, like a mouse before a tiger.

"Christmas. And yet there you recline as if you have nothing to do." She flings out her arms. "The babe is buried, Ilona. The time for mourning is past. Get up. Attend the celebration tonight." It is a command.

"I cannot."

Eyes bulging with anger, Aunt Erzsébet stalks toward my bed. "All women have buried a babe or two. Do you think only two sons came from this body?" She touches her velvet-clad stomach. "A man as vigorous and valiant as John Hunyadi did not tolerate a frail wife. I never indulged my sorrows. I was always strong. For him. Why? Because women always buzzed around John like bees eager for the honey of his bed. Ladies of the court were as conniving then as they are today. They wheedle their way into a man's heart with ripe bosoms and splayed legs and are keen to displace the weary wife." Aunt Erzsébet throws back my fur blankets. "John, like Vlad, was a fierce warrior against the Turks, celebrated for his victories and triumphs. And, like Vlad, his ambition was not for riches and airy honors but for power— the power to effect change and right wrongs. It consumed his days and nights. For men like ours, their excess of yellow bile is expressed in conquest. All types of conquest." She lay her cool ring-laden hand over mine. "The torch inside of you— whether love or ambition—ought to blaze with your husband not burn away his admiration. Be his kindling not his ash." She squeezes my fingers. "I've prepared a chamber at Buda for you both." Aunt Erzsébet gives my fingers a final too-hard squeeze before letting go. "I will see you both tonight."

Aunt Erzsébet dons her cape and departs, leaving behind more than just the scent of lilac but the stink of obligation and the stench of responsibility. My stomach knots imagining the many women eager to take care of Vlad's carnal needs. I imagine Margit fluttering her eyelashes at Vlad as she dances with him.

I swing my legs over the bed, stomp across the chamber, throw open the shutters, and suck in the cold as though it will freeze my grief into stone.

Gizella and Bernádett return to find my best dresses strewn across the bed.

"Are you certain you feel well enough?" Bernádett closes the shutters. "You bled so much and I fear—"

"My body is healed enough," I say. "It's time to heal my heart." And save my marriage.

Bernádett wrings her hands. "You should not over exert yourself, especially since…"

"Don't." Gizella's eyes grow wide as she shakes her head at Bernádett.

"My lady ought to know," says Bernádett. "I have never kept anything from her and will not begin today."

A chill—and not from the drafty window—infuses my bones. "Tell me."

Bernádett takes a deep breath as though to draw courage. "During your lying-in as I walked in the courtyard with Vlăduț, I saw three men with axes and shovels napping against the wall. Since there is no construction inside, I can only assume that Prince Vlad digs beneath the manse."

My shoulders slump with relief. "He's probably building a tunnel."

"There's another matter." Bernádett chews on her lip and glances at Gizella.

"It's cruel to repeat such gossip. I won't listen to it." Gizella puts her hands over her ears.

All relief vanishes, and a gut deep intuition claws its way up my throat. "Out with it."

"Lady Margit claims she and Prince Vlad are lovers." Afraid to see my reaction, Bernádett squeezes shut her eyes.

I drop down on the chair and stare at the floor. A hundred

conflicting thoughts collide. Marriage. Duty. Honor. Love. Revenge. I must say the right thing. Must act the right way. Aunt Erzsébet's words come back to me. *Be Vlad's kindling not his ash.* I must inspire him, not accuse.

The answer emerges from the crescent marks left from digging my nails into my palms. Pain helps me think.

"Your honesty is appreciated, Bernádett, but it's old gossip. Nothing more than Margit's pitiable attempts to humiliate me." My voice is thick with concealed anger. "She's jealous that I'm a princess, something she will never be. I am confident of Vlad's love." The lie almost sticks in my throat. "Margit is foolish. If Mátyus Maróti learns of Margit's indiscretions, true or not, she will compromise the marriage contract. Do not believe her lies. I don't."

"Yes, my lady." Bernádett reddens with embarrassment and lowers her head.

I want to hug her and confess that my confidence is false, that it is a pathetic attempt to act like a confident princess and not a jealous wife. "Help me choose a dress."

By midafternoon my physical transformation from grieving mother to gracious princess is complete. But beneath my cherry-red velvet dress with the ermine collar, my milkless breasts and empty womb still ache for my dead daughter.

"You look like a queen," says Vlad as I descend the grand stairway. "Merry Christmas."

A servant holding a palm-sized wooden box steps forward and waits while Vlad lifts the lid.

"Oh." My hand flies to my mouth. "It's beautiful."

Vlad takes the jeweled pendant from its silken nest. "The ruby signifies our love." He fastens the necklace around my neck, his touch on my skin sending frissons of yearning down my spine. I inhale his familiar scent—a forest after the rain, fresh rosemary, and leather—like an elixir. How foolish I was to keep to my room.

"The diamonds represent your purity and faithfulness."
His lips brush across the nape of my neck.

I am glad I decided to end my mourning early. Not for the
ruby and diamond necklace but to feel his love again. I am
more determined than ever to follow Aunt Erzsébet's advice.
I will be his inspiration—or die trying. "It matches my dress
perfectly, my lord."

Vlad's mouth hovers over my ear. "I did not have dress-
wearing in mind when I commissioned it."

My cheeks flame at the thought and my heart rejoices. He
still wants me! I signal Gizella, who presents my gift with
outstretched arms.

Vlad unsnaps the golden broach and admires the miniature of me and Vlăduţ. "Perfectly captured. I will cherish
this."

My heart beating as fast as when we first met, I pin the
broach to his cloak and steal shy glances at him. His eyes are
soft and liquid with love. Surely, Margit's claim must be
false. How could he look at me like that and bed another?

Christmas eve we feast and drink and dance and play
cards. Vlad rewards my coquettish charm and merry wit with
lingering kisses and stolen caresses. By the time we return to
the guest chambers I want only to collapse in bed. I do not.

I slowly peel each piece of clothing off my body as a
glassy-eyed Vlad watches. Wearing only the ruby necklace, I
kneel before him. "My lord, allow me to express my gratitude
for your generous gift." With feather lightness I stroke him
until he sighs my name and twists his fingers in my hair. My
lips take the place of my fingertips as I continue teasing.
Soon Vlad's breath is ragged and his legs tense with building
pleasure.

"Ilona," Vlad moans.

I fondle his tight sac and run my tongue up and down his
length, his grunts making me wet for his girth. I suck on his
smooth roundness and he jerks and groans and fills my mouth

with the brine of manliness. I slurp and lick while he holds my head between his hands, his legs aquiver.

"You can thank me like that anytime," he says with heavy eyes and the sleepy leer of satisfaction.

At first light he wakes me to repeat the act.

After mass we present our Christmas gift to King Matthias. He turns the bone saddle about and runs his finger along its gilded seams. "It's beautiful but is it functional?"

"The finest saddler in Christendom constructed the frame from Wallachia's strongest wood, layered it with birch bark, and covered it all with raw hide." Vlad's voice rumbles with pride.

Matthias traces the intricate ivory carving of Saint George battling the dragon. "Then it shall bear my royal rump during our next victory procession."

Christmas week soars by faster than any hawk. Each day is packed with delightful diversions and delicious delicacies, yet I am eager to go home.

"Your sister captured all the courtiers' hearts," Vlad says while we watch Margit play the innocent virgin in a bawdy play.

I cross my arms. "A bit of a stretch, considering she claims to have taken up with a married man of great reputation." I watch Vlad's reaction, wanting, needing to put this hateful rumor to rest once and for all.

Vlad turns his head, his green eyes as hard and cold as steel. "I did not think I married a fool." He strides away, his icy reply like a frost-covered blanket dropped on my shoulders.

## 31

I shiver under the furs as the sleigh glides homeward in the winter twilight, not from the cold but from Vlad's icy mood. It is my fault. I implied he and Margit were lovers. He stares at the distant forest, his lips occasionally twitching in contemplation. Like all those of royal birth he is skilled at concealing emotions.

Since our first meeting, I have made a study of Vlad's face. I learned that when he broods his eyes narrow and his lower lip shifts upward to form a crease across his chin. I never disturb him then. But when his eyes are soft I know a witty comment will lighten his mood. Like tonight.

I brush my hand over his head, scattering the snowflakes on his curled hair, his style for formal occasions.

"Mmph." Vlad grunts and tilts his head away.

"Who do you think is Margit's lover?" My tone is playful, as though never in a thousand years do I accuse him.

His demeanor changes in an instant and he laughs. "Matthias's court is full of men willing to bed her."

"What will Mátyus Maróti do if he discovers she's not a virgin?"

"Nothing. He can't afford to jeopardize the match. Right

now, his land is of strategic importance to Hungary. This might be his only chance to marry into the Hunyadi royal family. Don't fret about Margit." His shoulder rubs against mine. "The only gossip I'm interested in about Margit is if she spreads her legs for a man able to fund a war."

I nod, my limbs flooding with relief that my gaffe is forgiven. Then I shush Vlăduţ, who fusses despite my rocking.

"Let me." Vlad transfers Vlăduţ to his arms, whispers to him in Romanian, and the boy quiets.

"What are you telling him?" I ask when Vlăduţ giggles.

"I'm telling him a story."

"Not about battles, I hope."

"Life is a battle, Ilona. But this particular story is about my escape across the Bârgău Pass with cousin Stephen."

Vlăduţ's chubby hand escapes from the fleece to tug on Vlad's hair. "*Tati, Tati.*"

"Mmm…Where was I?" Vlad switches to Hungarian. "Ah, yes, the wolves. Wolves as big as this sleigh and gray as a storm circled around our fire. They howled—ahhwoooooo —" Vlad throws his head back and wails into the night sky.

"Oooooo," Vlăduţ imitates.

I smile, proud of my alpha and pup.

"Our steel teeth were longer than any wolf's," says Vlad, "so we were not afraid of man or beast. We made ourselves comfortable, the leaves our cushions and the tree trunks our chairs. Stephen and I had just finished our porridge when a stranger with flame-colored hair steps out of the darkness. He was dressed head to toe in white garments with odd trinkets hanging from his belt. Seeing the stranger had no weapons we asked if he would like some porridge. It was while he ate that Stephen guessed his true identity. You see, this was no common man. He was a wizard with the power to control the winds, summon storms, and foretell futures. But on that night, the wizard was eager to be on his way and complete his fearsome task —stopping a bloodthirsty *strigoi* from attacking maidens in a nearby village."

"A fairy story," I giggle, recalling this mythical creature.

Vlad quirks an eyebrow at me, then shifts his attention back to Vlăduţ. "Despite our plain attire the wizard knows we are princes and tells our futures. He says cousin Stephen will be a great leader—pfft—that's a story for another day. He tells me I will live forever." Vlad taps Vlăduţ's nose. "And here you are, my progeny and destiny, one in a long line assuring the family Drăculeşti is forever upon the earth."

Vlăduţ yawns and burrows into Vlad's cape.

"Before the wizard departed, I asked him a question." Vlad strokes Vlăduţ's forehead. "Is it true that his people possess a book containing ancient secrets of the natural world?"

"What did the wizard say?" I smile at this fiction.

"The stranger said they did, a book of secret incantations and rituals both natural and unnatural." Vlad turns to me, his eyes alight with a frightening intensity.

I force a smile even though his words make my skin crawl with dark foreboding. "Vlăduţ is too young to understand such stories."

"He is not too young to sense its spirit. His mind is a *tabula rasa*, a blank slate influenced by perception and experience. And by stories and expectations."

"Did you tell this story to Mihnea?" I tug Vlăduţ's cap, frosty with snowflakes, over his ears.

"Yes, he's my son."

"I look forward to meeting him."

The muscles undulate beneath Vlad's face, a sign he wrestles with a dilemma. "It's not that simple."

"But it is. Summon him to our manse for dinner."

Vlad's scowl is more suited for a disobedient child than a wife. "That's enough, Ilona. I will not be badgered."

I went too far again. Will I never learn? "Forgive me, my lord, I am still out of sorts since…" I look away.

Vlad sets our sleeping son back in my arms. "There will be other children, *iubirea mea*."

PURPLE-HUED CROCUSES PUSH through sunlit meadows. New leaves sprout from birch trees. Chicks crack open their shells. Lambs bleat in the pastures. It is the season of renewal. Time to renew my request to meet Vlad's bastard son.

"No." Vlad, looks up from letter writing and shakes his head.

I kneel down beside him and kiss his hand. "Why not?"

Vlad strokes his finger across my cheek. "Mihnea's position is precarious. Each royal son you bear reduces his chances to rise in the world. He is second in line to the throne and yet he is my first-born."

"Half siblings don't have to be enemies." I give him my most imploring eyes.

"My father was a bastard who killed all his bastard brothers to become ruler. My father's own bastard, my sworn enemy."

"But if they know each other…"

Vlad runs his fingers through my unbound hair. "One day Mihnea will regard Vlăduț as a rival. Nothing will prevent this. There is a reason why Cain and Abel is one of the first stories of betrayal in the *Book of Genesis*."

I want to ask him if his relationship with Radu makes him certain of this, but instead I rest my hand on Vlad's knee. "You love him."

"Without condition. My blood runs through his veins."

My hand creeps upward. "Will you listen to my reason why I should meet Mihnea?"

"Give me three." Vlad drops his gaze to where my hand

strokes his inner thigh. "Before your caresses cloud my judgment."

"First, Mihnea will feel more loved if you include him in our family. Second, Mihnea must be groomed for a high position at court, working with his half-brother not against. Third—"

"Times up." Vlad sets my hand between his legs.

"My lord, that's not fair," I pout.

"Precisely. Life is not fair." Vlad stiffens under my touch. "Here's my rebuttal. One: no foreign king will align himself with a bastard. Two: his mother was not cousin to the King of Hungary. Three: Mihnea is unimportant, one of many bastards at court."

"But—"

Vlad's finger seals my lips. "When I regain my throne then, and only then, will Mihnea's opportunities increase."

I wrap my lips around his finger, my teeth scraping the tip, and watch his pupils dilate with pleasure. "You ought to humor me in my delicate condition."

Vlad's eyes widen and he lifts me to my feet to give me a deep hungry kiss. I match his ferocity and in moments I am seated on the table. My thighs spread, skirt hoisted up, the letter swept to the floor, Vlad slams into my moist clutch.

One week later, Mihnea arrives at our manse. The meeting is far too formal for my liking but I suspect Vlad seeks to stress the importance of the visit. Cloaked in ermine and glittering with jewels, I sit next to the regally dressed Vlad under the dais in the great chamber. Standing nearby, Dădacă holds a squirmy Vlăduţ.

"Lord father." Mihnea comes forward with the reverence due a king and bows low.

"Rise Mihnea and greet your new mother, Princess Ilona."

The eleven-year-old boy genuflects before me. "Lady Mother, I am pleased to make your acquaintance."

I am struck by the resemblance, both in bearing and

looks. Except Mihnea's eyes lack Vlad's green luminosity and his hair is flecked with gold strands. Their strides, however, are identical, elegant and purposeful. "The pleasure is mine, Mihnea."

Vlad summons Dădacă forward. "This is your brother, Vlad Dracula."

Mihnea, unsure of protocol concerning a toddler, bows stiffly to his half-brother, the legitimate claimant to the Wallachian throne.

"How are your lessons?" Vlad's face brightens as he leans over, an elbow on his knee and his chin resting on his fist.

Mihnea squares his shoulders. "My dancing instructor says I am ready for a heavier blade."

"I'll see to it you have one." Vlad's eyes narrow, his focus hawk-like. "You're not neglecting your scholarly studies, are you?"

Mihnea stands taller. "No, Lord Father. This week we discussed Plato's allegory of the cave."

"Ah, a worthy bit of philosophy. What did you make of it?"

Mihnea screws up his face. "Aahh...I suppose, Lord Father, that I am still seeing shadows on the subject of philosophy."

Vlad chuckles, rises from his chair, and embraces his bastard. "You will stay for the evening meal."

It is an intimate gathering. Just the three of us. I take an immediate liking to Mihnea, a serious boy so in awe of his father he pays rapt attention to every word.

"He is a boy of rare intelligence and courtesy," I say after we bid Mihnea good night.

Vlad holds my hand. "Indeed he is. Unfortunately, he will need to claw and kick his way to success."

My third child is born on a cold winter day. He is tiny and his cries so weak Aunt Erzsébet baptizes him the day of his birth. Vlad names him Nicolae, which means victor of the people. Milk spouts like a fountain from my breasts and by the time my lying-in is over Nicolae is plump.

Vlad visits twice a week but the thread of desire between us no longer quivers. He turns me down when I bare my breasts or spread my thighs. His manly needs are gotten elsewhere. I do not cry this time. Instead, I take Zsazsa's advice and hire a courtesan to teach me tricks. These new tricks please Vlad but their novelty soon wears off, and once again I feel his passionate love slipping away. I am not enough. Or...

I suspect it is Vlad who withholds his deepest needs from me. I feel it in every fiber of my being.

I refuse to allow our marriage to wither into a dull monotony. It is only when are intimacies are vigorous that Vlad and I are closest, when the string between us thickens and quivers. But it is difficult, impossible, to resume our pre-lying-in intimacy when he is gone for days and weeks without warning and refuses to tell me where or why he goes.

It is during such an absence that I attend Margit's going-away party at Buda.

"He's so handsome," says a round-faced maiden. "Don't you miss him?"

Margit has been wed for two months but refuses to leave Buda castle. A frustrated Mátyus Maróti finally appealed to King Matthias, who demanded she join her husband in Gyönk immediately. Or else!

Margit giggles. "I miss more than that." She plops down on one of the trunks. "You all must swear on your honor that you will visit."

The ladies agree to a promise they cannot keep. Ladies do not travel without permission from husbands or fathers.

"I will miss my sister most of all." Margit's arms wrap around my waist. "It's not fair, Ilona. You only have to travel across the Danube. How fortunate you are that Prince Vlad is powerless to retake his throne."

All conversation stops. Everyone, even the servants, wait with bated breath.

"How fortunate you are to be so blissfully ignorant of political secrets." My voice is as soft as a breeze, my smile as wide as the Danube. Not one strained syllable do I utter. Not a drop of annoyance. Outwardly.

Inside, my blood boils with liquid fire.

The ladies' eyes dart about with raised eyebrows and pursed lips. Have you heard the gossip? What does Ilona know that we don't? A few noblewomen frown at Margit and her attempted insult.

The ladies resume their conversations, and I glide from group to group like a skilled diplomat. I listen for an empha- sized word or a sudden gasp, watch for blushing or paling, or a head that shakes no while agreeing. Vlad says whereas the mouth easily deceives the body cannot. Today, however, the noblewomen's gossip has no diplomatic value.

"We need to talk." Margit pulls me aside as the women

leave the chambers for the evening meal. She shuts the door after they go. "Do you forgive me?"

I flap my hand. Her insult made her look bad, not me. "All is forgiven."

"Really?" Margit's lips pinch sideways. "You know about us and you're not angry?"

I recall Vlad's advice: say nothing, you get more information. I blink, tilt my head, my face a smooth mask.

Margit aims a steely gaze at me. "My husband is an awkward boy without any skill. I will miss my lover."

"Perhaps you can teach your husband a few tricks." I clasp my hands together to keep from balling them into fists.

If she implies that Vlad is her lover one more time...

My fists tighten. It's not true. It cannot be true. Margit is jealous, crazed with envy. Like Cain was resentful of Abel. But I have no intention of being a victim to her viciousness.

Margit splays her fingers across her flat belly. "His royal seed takes root in my womb."

My hand uncurls, flattens and rises. I smack Margit's face. Her head bangs against the door.

"Vlad would never have you. Never." I grip her face between my thumb and fingers. "If you carry a child, it is not his. Stop spreading your lies or..." I squeeze her face.

"You're hurting me." Her arrogance distorts into panic.

"This pain is nothing compared to the years you tormented me with your lies." I push against her, wrap a golden tendril of her hair around my finger, and pull. Hard.

"Owww." Margit's eyes well with tears.

"Don't play with fire if you don't want to get scorched." I kiss her hard on the cheek. "I will pray for your soul." I depart the room.

My soul sings. My skin tingles. My heart pounds with an almost sensual excitement. Margit's fear felt wonderful, like a cool bath on a hot day. Invigorating. Washing away years of her cruel comments and insinuations.

Her fear. My power. Every second crystalizes into perfect clarity. Power is a heady feeling. I like it. I like it very much.

I LEAN into Vlad as we climb the steps to Buda castle. "Is it true Matthias brought a new mistress back from Vienna?"

"Unfortunately, that was his only accomplishment." Vlad, looking dashing in emerald green velvet, adjusts his cuffs.

My mouth drops open. "Emperor Frederick denied all Matthias's requests?"

"Only those that mattered most." Vlad holds up two fingers. "Financial support in his fight against George of Poděbrady and his claim as King of the Romans."

"Oh dear," I cringe, "he really wanted that title. I'll make sure to avoid that topic."

"Ask him about the Florentine scrolls he acquired."

"Wonderful, more books for Bibliotheca Corvinus."

"Better still," Vlad's eyes sparkle with a mischievous look I love so well. "Make friends with his new mistress. Royal favorites always have the king's ear."

"An ear?" I nudge Vlad's side. "There's another appendage that is much more...vulnerable."

Vlad bursts out laughing and brings my palm to his lips. "Figured me out have you?"

I rake his stubbled cheek with my fingernails. "Some parts. Others are still a mystery." Like why he disappears for days or refuses to share his deepest secrets.

Inside the great hall we find a laughing King Matthias surrounded by courtiers. At his side, a young woman with rosy cheeks and heart-shaped lips gazes at him with adoring eyes. Her dress is a stitch short of indecency, the neckline plunging so low Matthias's eyes rarely stray from her creamy abundant cleavage.

"Prince Vlad, my cousin Princess Ilona, I present Barbara

Edelpöck." Matthias beams at Barbara like a man in love. Or at least a man satisfied in the bedroom.

We exchange pleasantries for several moments before Matthias draws Vlad away, leaving Barbara and I to ourselves.

"Our men have more interest in politics than dancing." Barbara casts a loving glance as Matthias heads to the small council chambers. "His Highness speaks of you with great affection. I looked forward to our meeting."

"I too looked forward to meeting the women who stole Matthias's heart."

Barbara blushes. "His heart belongs to Hungry, I am just an amusement." Barbara steps forward, her voice quiet. "I confess, what with all the outrageous gossip concerning Prince Vlad, I expected a brutish Hercules. Instead I find him to be quite charming."

"His charm continues to enthrall me." My voice is ripe with innuendo.

Barbara giggles. "We will be great friends, and I do need a friend at court." Barbara sidles close. "His Highness says I can trust you, therefore I must ask, which courtier or lady should I never turn my back on?"

I like Barbara. Neither coquettish nor aloof, she understands her tenuous position as Matthias's mistress, even confiding that her 'position was apt to change according to His Highness' desires.' By evening's end we declare our friendship.

I return to Pest alone the next day. Vlad, at Matthias's request, stays on to discuss the war with Bohemia.

It is not war I think about while sewing in my chambers later that afternoon. It is the three prophesies I was told years ago. The first, that I will be a princess, came true. The second, about receiving pleasure from pain, came true as well. Two painful births produced male heirs. The third, something about a book, is as mysterious as ever. Why would anyone fear a book?

"Forgive my intrusion, my lady. May we speak in confidence?" Gizella wrings her hands.

She puts me in a bad spot, asking for secrecy before I know the subject. "It depends."

Gizella glances over her shoulder at the closed door. "It concerns Bernádett. I know your fondness for her and her long service but..." She chews on her bottom lip.

I pluck at an errant thread. "I'm listening."

"I was told—"

"I do not tolerate malicious gossip."

"This is fact, not gossip, my lady. A trustworthy source told me that Bernádett's mother was a close friend...a very special friend of your father."

Much as I want to believe Father never found fleshly pleasures with another after mother died, Gizella's pained expression forces me to confront the truth. "His mistress?"

"Yes, my lady."

I drop my needle. My God! "Bernádett is my half-sister?"

"No, my lady," Gizella wags her head, her face wincing at my conjecture. "Bernádett was born well before that time. But...well...Bernádett's uncle—her mother's brother—is a Şolomonar." She whispers the last word as though it conjures demons.

"A Şolomonar?" The word is not familiar.

"A wizard who can cure diseases, summon hailstorms, and command the wind." Gizella's voice takes on a prayerful reverence.

"He lived in the castle?"

"Oh no, my lady, they live in an unearthly realm betwixt heaven, hell, and earth, the secret entrance hidden deep in the Carpathian Mountains."

I bite my lip to keep from smiling. More Romanian fairy stories. "So, this reputable source, told you that Bernádett's uncle is a wizard? Gizella, this is worse than gossip, it's superstitious nonsense."

Gizella's head swivels emphatically. "No, my lady. Şolomonari exist. If you meet one you must offer alms and food, because if you scorn them, they punish your wickedness."

"I see." I give her a tight smile and wonder if Dădacă fills my sons' heads with the same foolishness.

"The Şolomonar came to his sister—your father's mistress—and said a nobleman staying at the castle stole their sacred book of secret incantations and ancient wisdom." Gizella grits her teeth.

"My father stole their book?"

"No, Prince Vlad." Her head sinks into her shoulders.

I frown. "Preposterous. Prince Vlad is well-educated." I stab the needle through the fabric. "He does not believe in wizards and witches. Who is your source and how does this concern Bernádett?"

Gizella's lower lip quivers and she blinks back a tear. "My mother."

Gizella is such a mild young woman always eager to please that I regret my harsh tone. I temper my voice and smile an apology. "I met your mother at His Highness' last party. A delightful woman. What prompted your mother to tell you this?"

"I write about Vlăduţ and Nicolae all the time, and Mother begged me to see them. I took her to the nursery, and that's where she saw Bernádett playing with Vlăduţ. Mother told me there was no mistaking the daughter of Mihály Szilágyi's mistress—her red hair, wide set eyes, and narrow chin make her the very image of her mother."

Gizella's story shed light on the so-called 'obscure relative.' It warms my heart knowing Father cared so much for his mistress he did not want her child to die in poverty.

But claiming Bernádett's uncle is a wizard is ridiculous. That Vlad stole their book of secrets even more absurd.

"I'm surprised Bernádett does not speak Romanian." Gizella's brow knits in puzzlement.

"Unused languages are quickly forgotten." I rise from the chair, a cold slimy anxiety swimming in my gut as I recall Bernádett claiming only a vague memory of her mother. "Have you spoken about this to anyone else?"

"No, my lady." Gizella's hands fly to her heart. "What is said in this room stays in this room."

"Thank you." I give her shoulder a squeeze as I walk past to look out the window. Worry, like tentacles, encircles my limbs. I consider the story Vlad told Vlăduţ about crossing the Bârgău Pass with cousin Stephen. They met a wizard in the forest who told their future. Was he a Şolomonar? *The* Şolomonar?

I shiver. Close my eyes. Contemplate the mysterious old book in Vlad's chambers. Is that the Şolomonari book of secrets?

## 33

# Ⱳlad

**August 1456**
**Tîrgovişte Palace, Wallachia**

His lips curled into a satisfied grin as Prince Vlad ran his hands over the carved throne in the great chamber. *His* great chamber. His throne.

Vlad sat down, the weight of his vengeance slipping from his shoulders with a long silent exhalation. He looked over the gathered councilors and emissaries like a proud father. Victory was sweet.

The battles led by John Hunyadi, Mihály Szilágy, and Cousin Stephen—all victorious. Mehmed's military had failed on all fronts. Humiliated, Mehmed ordered his incompetent generals hacked to pieces.

Their battles came with a price. Plague swept like a storm over the villages. Killed more people than Mehmed's army ever could. Including John Hunyadi.

Sovereign and ruler of Ungro-Wallachia and the duchies of

Amlaş and Făgăruş: Prince Vlad, son of Vlad the Great was ordained and anointed at Biserica Domnească. He was twenty-five-years-old.

Dracula would not make the same mistakes of his first brief reign. He wasted no time returning favors, keeping promises, and governing his realms.

With a proud flourish he signed the order to send six thousand Wallachian soldiers to help cousin Stephen recapture the Moldavian throne. The tribute fee of two thousand ducats to Turkish emissaries, however, made his blood boil. It did have one benefit though. It legitimized Dracula's sovereignty to all of Christendom. It validated Dracula's reign.

Empowered by this validation, Dracula sent letters to Wallachian mayors and the Hungarian king extolling his fearless plans for the future.

None of these things guaranteed his sovereignty. His position was still as vulnerable as a baby bird in a nest. Real power and genuine allies took years to obtain. Which left Dracula only a few options.

First, he fortified his monasteries and fortresses. Made them attack-ready. The remote castle nested atop a rocky precipice in the Carpathian Mountains was his pet project. It was the castle of his boyhood dreams.

Second, he sidelined the disloyal flabby-bodied noble class and created a new one. The *Viteji*, The Brave, he dubbed them, were commoners who had demonstrated exceptional valor during battle. Unlike the traitorous boyars who had grown fat and soft from meat, wine, and deceit, the *Viteji's* ambitions were made tough by poverty, hardship, and toil. The two groups hated one another. The old boyars were repulsed by the *Viteji's* cruelty and immorality. The *Viteji* despised the boyars' arrogance and cowardice.

Third, Dracula formed an *armaş*. He granted the men lands and court duties in exchange for punishing lawbreakers, upholding laws, and forcing reluctant boyars into obedience.

Dracula gave the *armaş* their first task. Kill the boyars responsible for burying his brother Mircea alive.

## Easter Sunday 1457

DISLOYAL BOYARS. Ugly wives. Ill-mannered children. Dracula swallowed his disgust for the guests devouring his Easter dinner. He concealed his rage behind a polite smile as their disloyal hands raised goblets and their dishonest lips pledged loyalty with false flattery. And yet Dracula inhaled the stench of their treachery as though it was a field of flowers.

"Such gluttony, you would think they never ate before." Doina, Dracula's broad-hipped mistress with a taste for vulgar pleasures, wrinkled her nose.

"Their greed is their undoing." Dracula's long-awaited revenge made him stiffen with lust.

After the boyars stuffed the last bite of meat into their mouths, Dracula rose from the chair. "As proof of my love and generosity I have gifts for you in the courtyard."

The boyars cheered and banged their fists on the table with excitement.

Dracula swung his arm toward the door. "Go claim your prizes."

They rushed out, leaving behind spilled drinks and fallen chairs.

When the last boyar left, Dracula quaffed his wine, wiped his mouth, and headed for the door.

Doina poured more wine into her goblet. "Where are you going?"

"To celebrate my revenge."

Vlad swaggered into the courtyard, his lips pulled back into a wolfish grin.

"What is the meaning of this?" A boyar lifted his shackled arms.

Their cries and screams were music to Dracula's ears, an anguished symphony of two hundred traitorous boyars and their families.

The *armaş* grabbed the boyars the moment they walked into the courtyard. Before the nobles knew what was happening Dracula's men separated the men from their families.

Hands clasped behind his back, Dracula strode like a general inspecting his troops.

"Rot in hell, Dracula!" shouted a pig-faced boyar bound in chains.

Dracula wended his way past the manacled boyars and trussed up families to a wall stacked with impaling poles. He hefted one, assessed its length and girth.

"Excellent." His face beamed with pride. His new *armaş* had executed his instructions with speed and precision.

"*Voivode.*" A black-toothed mercenary dangled a squalling toddler by one leg. "This one too?"

Dracula nodded. "He's a little worm that will grow into the same poisonous serpent as his father." He cast a critical eye on the pole extending from the mouth of the first victim, a young wife. "Impale the women and children with mercy. Give them a quick death like this one. Their only fault lies in marrying treacherous men. Give no mercy to the old boyars. Impale them that they have plenty of time to reflect on their treason."

"What have we done, *Voivode*? We are obedient to you," wailed a pock-marked boyar.

"I had no hand in killing Mircea," cried another.

"Why are you murdering my innocent wife and children?"

"Allow me to die with honor beside my father."

Dracula crossed the courtyard, satisfaction, anger, and

pity wrestling one other beneath his stoic expression. Victory was bittersweet. Yes, these men were untrustworthy, pathetic, and a liability. Yes, they had to pay for their treason. How unfortunate their wives and children had to pay for their crimes.

Dracula stood tall. "This is a great day for Wallachia. No longer will you suck the lifeblood of my people dry with your greed." Dracula lifted his chin and his lips curled into a twisted grin. "And yet I am compelled to thank you. Your strong arms and backs will restore Wallachia to its former glory. Fear not, you will not die. Not today." Dracula summoned his captain. "The march to Argeş begins at nightfall."

"Yes, *Voivode*." A whistle brought a dozen men to his side.

Vlad went back into the castle, found Doina in her chambers, and bedded her with a vigor not satisfied by a single release.

Afterwards, Doina rubbed her flat belly. "I feel your seed, a son, taking root in my womb."

"Is that so?" Dracula doubted her prediction. But a son, even a bastard, was better than no heir at all. "Satisfy me once more, my pet, and I will show you a marvelous sight."

Later, Vlad and Doina rode out beyond the city walls. Beneath a purple sky, the underbelly of clouds glowed red with the blood of the impaled. Like gory sentinels, rows of impaled bodies jutted from the ground. It was the price of betrayal. Most were impaled from buttocks to mouth. Others from stomach to back, entrails dangling from their bodies. Smaller children were spiked one atop the other, *armaş* practicality at work.

Dracula stopped his horse in front of a moaning white-haired boyar. "Pray God hastens your death, although my wish is that you linger for days."

The boyar's head flopped back as he gurgled unintelligible syllables.

"Eh? Was did you say? Are you thanking me for the fine sight? Look about! From your perch you have a grand view of all the merchants and farmers you raped with your greed." Dracula scowled, annoyed the old boyar lost consciousness. He turned to speak to Doina.

Her back was hunched, her head hanging over the side of the horse as she retched onto the blood-soaked field.

"Doina?"

She righted herself and wiped her mouth. "My lord, the smell does not mix well with the Easter feast."

Dracula inhaled the odors of loosened bowels, piss, blood, and rotting flesh as though savoring fresh cut flowers. "It is the fragrance of victory. The perfume of sovereignty."

Overhead, a loud *caw-caw* pierced twilight's morbid hush. A crow swooped down, alighted atop an impaled young woman and pecked at her eye.

The fortuitous omen warmed Dracula.

"Look. The crow of the Hungarian Corvinus clan approves of my offering." Dracula kicked the horse's flanks and raced toward the town gates where he waited for the green-faced Doina to catch up. "Tomorrow I visit my fortress in Argeș to supervise its renovation."

Doina grimaced and swallowed the bile rising in her throat. "The boyars will have to pass...them." She pointed to the rows of staked victims.

"It's a two-day march to Argeș. I'm certain they will want to say a final farewell to their loved ones." Dracula cleared his throat of a familiar lump. Cruel as it was to make the boyars walk past their murdered families, he wished he had been given the same opportunity to say goodbye to the bodies of his father, mother, and Mircea.

The following morning, a messenger ran into the courtyard

as Dracula mounted his horse. "*Voivode,* I was fishing in the *elesteile* when two farmers recognized my livery and asked if I serve…" The messenger took a deep breath. "Vlad Ţepeş."

"Vlad the Impaler?" Dracula burst into a hearty chortle. His chest puffed out, pleased by the fear-inspiring nickname. "I like it."

"Vlad Ţepeş! Vlad Ţepeş!" The townsfolk hailed as Dracula rode atop his steed.

He stretched his arm to the sky. His people's respect was almost as sweet as victory.

The moment he passed the town gate he relaxed. He needed a break from sniveling courtiers, giggling ladies, and fawning servants. Parties and meetings were tolerable but only if balanced with solitude. Dracula filled his lungs with the fragrance of fields, fresh air, and forest until the cloying castle odors were expunged, then he gave his horse a light kick and raced toward his favorite monastery.

He followed the familiar narrow path through the woodlands, each mile putting distance between him and a prince's every day annoyances and problems. By the time he reached the monastery nestled in the clearing by the river he felt cleansed of castle life.

The monks showed Vlad to his preferred room, a small one-window cell furnished with a clean cot, oak crucifix, and a single lantern atop a rough-hewn table.

Dracula spent three days strategizing how to make his hopes and dreams a reality. He meditated, dined on trout, drank friar-made wine, and planned his next diplomatic venture.

In the evenings by the lantern's glow, he translated more of the Şolomonari's book. What had begun as an amusing curiosity had become a serious obsession. He was enthralled, the book's philosophies made sense of his senseless world, offered answers and a purpose far beyond that of priests, rabbis, or imams. More than that, the book offered divine solutions to his most frustrating problems.

IN THEIR FOUL-SMELLING, filthy Easter clothes the boyars moved scalding bricks hand to hand from the village kiln to the mountain summit. The human chain worked from sun up to sun down, their pace unbroken until one collapsed from exhaustion.

After Dracula approved an increase in the boyars' rations —in hopes they lived longer and worked harder—he rode up the tunnel-like switchback toward the castle. The slender path wended through a forest so dense with trees its leafy canopy blocked the sun.

When he reached the narrow trestle bridge spanning the deep ravine, Dracula stopped to admire the bird's eye view. He inhaled deeply. Let the rarified air purify his spirit. Far below him the Argeş River slithered through the gorge like a snake. He felt like Zeus looking down from Mount Olympus. If only he could throw lightning bolts at the Turks all his problems would be solved. Laughing at the thought, Dracula continued across the trestle.

At the sight of the fortress with its spires rising in the sky like a crown atop the summit, Dracula's heart pounded with excited pride. He jumped from his horse and went in search of the master builder. He found the man hunched by an outside wall measuring its thickness.

Dracula crouched beside him. "Twice as thick. The walls must withstand Turkish cannons."

"Yes, my lord." The master builder held the architectural plans against the wall with one hand and pointed with the other. "Five circulated towers—each large enough for fifty soldiers—will allow crossfire. This tower will be the most difficult to breach." His finger tapped the paper. "Its window is inaccessible, the wall impossible to scale. The topmost chamber has a superior view." Another tap. "I think you can see all the way to Hungary."

Vlad chuckled. "If only."

"It's high enough that if you toss a coin from the window it would shatter into a thousand pieces."

Vlad's smile melted. "I'm not a frivolous upstart. No prince worth his crown throws good money away."

"I only meant—"

Vlad clapped him on the back. "I hope your skill with lime, compass, and level is better than your wit." He pointed to the drawing. "Are these the tunnels?"

"Per your specifications." The master builder's finger skimmed past the battlements. "A passage cut into the side of the well will reach all the way to the exit cave."

Vlad rubbed his palms together. "How much longer until it's complete?"

"Two years."

Vlad sighed. Two years was a long time. "Keep me apprised of any problems or delays."

Vlad strode inside and bound up the circular staircase of the highest turret, his spirit as warm and bright as a summer day.

At the topmost chamber, he peered out its narrow window. He remembered another such view, that of his cell in Egrigöz, Western Anatolia when he was a child. This view was far superior. Tree-covered hills stretched into the vast distance of His land. His people. His destiny.

That night Vlad stayed at a small inn where he ate *impletato*, drank local wine, and bedded a doe-eyed wench eager to submit to rough intimacies.

## 34

# ℑlona

### Spring 1471
### Dracula's Manse in Pest, Hungary

Rain thrashes against the shutters, wind howls like a beast, and thunder rumbles overhead. The weather matches my mood. I am eating alone. Again.

I rise from the table and summon a servant. "Take this food and follow me." When Vlad is busy with a project he forgets to eat. He forgets me. Neither is acceptable.

I find Rareş, Vlad's obedient guard, blocking the door to Vlad's chambers. "My husband needs food."

"My Lord does not wish to be disturbed."

I put my hands on my hips and imitate Aunt Erzsébet's sternest face. "I'm not leaving until you tell him I am here."

The ever stoic Rareş slips around the door. Moments later, I am permitted inside.

Vlad sits at his desk, the lamp's glow throwing dancing shadows on the wall behind him.

"Nourishment feeds the mind." I dismiss the servant once he sets down the tray.

"Starvation inspires it." Vlad puts the quill in the pot and rubs his eyes.

I pull a chair close and pluck a bit of pork from the trencher. "Open."

Vlad opens wide, gratitude shining in his eyes, which drop to my bosom while he chews.

"Diplomacy makes my prince hungry." I hold another morsel before him.

"For power." Quick as a hungry wolf he snatches the pork from my fingers.

I scoop sauce with two curled fingers and drag it across his lips. "I only offer sustenance."

Vlad's eyes glaze as he sucks on my saucy fingers until I sigh with pleasure. "Sustenance comes in many forms." His thumb runs across the top of my chemise.

"Mmm, let me guess..." I stand, discard my thick woolen robe, lift my chemise over my head. Next, I push away the stack of letters, sit on the table before him naked, my feet resting on the carved wood arm of his chair. I balance a chunk of bread on my knee.

Vlad wolves it down and waits like an obedient dog for the next morsel. I place a radish on my shoulder.

After a few more strategic bites, Vlad orders me to lie back and spreads the meal over my body. By the time he eats dessert between my thighs I am gasping with ecstasy. The final course has him thrusting into my wantonness.

"Where is your favorite book?" I ask snuggling next to him in bed afterwards.

Vlad nuzzles my neck. "Book? What book?"

"The old one that is always on your desk."

Vlad pulls away, his wary eyes searching mine. "Why do you ask?"

I shrug, pretend indifference. "No reason. Just curious."

Vlad's hand slides up my thigh. "Curiosity can be dangerous."

"That only makes me more curious." I walk my fingers up his hard curly-haired chest. "Is the book about battle strategies? Religion? Philosophy? Humanism?"

Vlad grabs my busy fingers and kisses the tips. "Yes."

"No wonder it has so many pages." I run my fingers through his wavy hair. "You read many books, my lord, what makes this one special enough it never leaves your chambers?"

"The book is my salvation." Vlad spreads my thighs, settles between them, and slides into me with a satisfied groan.

"You are my salvation." I drape my legs over his shoulder, groaning as his length plunges deep.

This time, I get his salty dessert. I fall asleep in his arms, the taste of his brine in my mouth.

I awake the next morning alone. Vlad is an early riser and often schedules meetings before breakfast. I roll over, my sleepy gaze following the swath of sunlight crossing the chamber and illuminating the cabinet. It's as though God himself lights up the location of this mysterious book. This may be my only chance.

I pad across the chamber. The cabinet door is locked. I smack my palm against it. Where would Vlad hide the key? It is not atop the cabinet. Or inside a vase. Or in the desk drawer.

I slip on Vlad's robe, my finger tapping against my lips as I study his chambers with a critical eye. I check under the bed, lift the Turkish carpet, and feel under the desk and tables. Nothing! The key has to be somewhere. I get on my knees, my cheek to the floor, and look under the cabinet. There's a thin layer of dust. Except for one square.

I pry the tile up with my fingernails and find the key beneath.

Someone knocks on the door.

"My lady, are you awake?" Rareş's voice comes from the hallway.

I am silent. Let him think I still sleep.

"Princess Ilona?" More knocks, louder and more impatient than the first.

Clanging keys send me diving into the bed. I burrow under the furs, the key clutched in my fist.

"My lady?" The door squeaks open a crack. "I am sorry to disturb you, but Prince Vlad demands I retrieve a certain letter."

"Is it morning?" I feign a yawn. "Come in. You don't want to keep him waiting."

Rareş averts his eyes, pretending not to see the tangle of clothes on the floor as he goes to the desk and shuffles through the stack. Before he leaves, I tell him to send for Bernádett, then after locking the door I dash to the cabinet and turn the key.

The book is on the topmost shelf. I carry it to the desk, open to the first page, and copy several lines of the strange text onto a small parchment. Hopefully, it will be enough for someone to decipher and confirm that it is not the Şolomonari's sacred book.

BERNÁDETT BRUSHES dust from my velvet shoes. Gizella arranges my perfumes. Both are distracted. Perfect.

I stuff the scrap of parchment down my bodice. Finally, I have an opportunity to show the strange writing to someone. Barbara Edelpöck's invitation to her Summer Sumptuary Bazaar provides the perfect excuse to visit the palace. It will be easy to slip out of the room while the ladies are engrossed in the latest textiles from Florence and Venice.

I stop by Vlad's chambers before departing for the afternoon.

"A gathering of silk snakes in a brocade nest." Vlad looks up from his book. "I do not envy your having to compete for fabric with Barbara. By rights you, a princess, should outshine Matthias's mistress." He wraps his arms around my waist and burrows his face in my bodice.

"I am certain there will be plenty of fabric that break the ridiculous sumptuary laws." I rake my fingers through his hair and with hammering heart hope his attentions do not dislodge the paper.

I arrive at Barbara Edelpöck's chambers relieved by the size of the gathering. There must be fifty ladies chatting and laughing among the bolts of fabric, trimmings, lace, and food-laden tables.

"Wonderful, isn't it?" Barbara Edelpöck stands on a small platform with a length of silk brocade wrapped around her like cabbage in *töltött káposzta*.

After an hour mingling and gushing over the selections, I sidle close to Barbara. "Do you mind if I slip out for a moment? I want to go to the chapel and ask God for another child."

Barbara heaves a heavy sigh. "Say a prayer for me as well. His Highness wants an heir and so far…" A quick shadow darkens her face. A male child will secure her position and increase her worth.

"I will." I kiss her cheek.

I stop at the chapel where the Blessed Virgin looks down at me with disdain from her niche. I pray, too quickly, too distractedly, the parchment with the copied words like hot embers on my skin. After making the Sign of the Cross, I hurry from the chapel.

My pulse quickens whenever I visit Matthias's library, Bibliotheca Corviniana. Today is no different. Matthias's love of reading led him to amass many manuscripts. Every shelf is overstuffed, and the chests burst. My feet drag, the books calling to me as I cross the expanse to the artist workshop in the back.

"Hello?" I stand at the workshop entrance. "Galeotto Marzio?" The librarian is the only one with the skill to decipher the curious script.

"He's not here this week, my lady." The illuminator lifts his head, his tiny paintbrush poised over the etched sheet of vellum gilded with swirls and dashes.

I chew on my lip, decide to take a chance. "Perhaps you can help." I hold out the paper. "Do you understand this language?"

The illuminator turns it one way, then another. "It's not Latin or Greek or Arabic. Not even Oriental. Is this from the library?"

I did not plan for questions. "One of my ladies copied this script etched into the bottom of an old coffer."

The illuminator scratches his chin. "It may be a language from a faraway land." He returns the paper. "My apologies, my lady, for my inadequacy. I have disappointed you."

I force a bright smile, though my stomach coils with dread. "No apology is needed. I am sure this would puzzle even Galeotto Marzio." I fold the paper. "Thank you for your time. I will tell my ladies this script will remain a mystery."

The illuminator itches his head. "It might be code. Did you ask King Matthias? He is an excellent decoder. All codes have a key—a translator. This may be as simple as a substitution cipher or as complicated as Caesar's shift or a *tabula recta*. Your own noble husband, Prince Vlad, excels at code breaking."

"He is? I will ask him." I say goodbye, slip the paper into my pocket, and with a heavy heart walk back through the library. Someone besides Vlad or Matthias—who will demand the book be added to his library—must be able to translate the text.

And then I know whom to ask. And it is not the person lurking in the hall.

"Enjoying Bibliotheca Corviniana?" Aunt Erzsébet cocks a thin grey eyebrow. "One day my son's library will be as renown as the one in Alexandria."

"Let us pray it does not come to the same unfortunate end."

Aunt Erzsébet looks at me as though I am daft. "The Turks will never get into Buda, dear child. Never." Aunt Erzsébet folds her arms. "It's very kind of you to attend Barbara's little party."

"I would not dream of missing it."

Aunt Erzsébet's brows pinch together. "I'm glad you are friends but remember she will never be queen. When Matthias marries again, and he will, you will need to befriend his wife."

"I will not forgo one friendship for the other."

Aunt Erzsébet snorts. "Don't be a fool. You'll do whatever is politically advantageous." She pats my arm as we walk. "Speaking of which, Margit will visit soon. I insist you forgive any wrong she has done you and focus on rebuilding a relationship."

"For political reasons?" Dread heavy as a cannon ball weighs down my shoulders.

"Your husband needs friendly relatives in every corner of the world, especially remote locations. It's time you mend fences and build bridges with Margit."

"And dig a deep moat," I quip, determined to appear confident.

"Very wise of you." A low snicker rumbles from the back of her throat.

We part with a hug at the junction of two halls, but as she strides away I wonder at Aunt Erzsébet's true motive. She does nothing without an ulterior purpose.

The moment she turns the corner, I double back to my original destination. There is only one person I know with friends in high and low places.

"Aunt Orsulya?" I rap on the door. "It's Ilona. I need your help."

Aunt Orsulya's red-cheeked face peers around the cracked open door. "Come back later."

"Are you ill? Your face is flushed. Should I summon a doctor?" I push the door open. "Oh!" I slam the door behind me and stare open-mouthed at the naked woman in Aunt Orsulya's bed.

"Have you come to join us?" Zsazsa flips back her mussed hair.

"Zsazsa." Aunt Orsulya frowns and bolts the door. "What's wrong, Ilona?" She ties her robe closed.

"I...I'm glad my pious aunt finds pleasures in more than just prayer." I suck in my lips to keep from laughing.

"We pray fervently together." Zsazsa throws her shapely legs over the bed. "Orsulya's prayers always end with 'oh God, oh God.'"

Aunt Orsulya rolls her eyes. "You will be discreet about this."

"I will say nothing." Her secret sin makes her more endearing. "Actually, I came here to ask you where I could find Zsazsa." I settle in the chair and smooth my skirt.

"Does Vlad need a threesome?" Zsazsa crosses the room and makes herself comfortable in a chair, naked and glorious as a queen swathed in taffeta, jewels, and furs. She ages well. Her forty-year-old body curvy and smooth. Her breasts, never having suckled a child, are still taut and high. "Man or woman?"

"No." I recoil. "He would never..." I squeeze my eyes shut blocking out the thought. "Would he?" My eyes flash open.

Zsazsa pats my knee. "I'm teasing you, child. How can I help?"

"Oh, yes. I...I knew that." I shift in my seat, regain my composure. "You know everyone—nobles, merchants, scholars—do you know someone who can translate this." I pull the paper from my pocket.

"Let me see." Zsazsa extends her hand and wiggles her fingers.

Paper in hand, Aunt Orsulya and Zsazsa huddle together, their heads touching, this conspiratorial pose more endearing now I know its meaning.

"The script is most peculiar." Zsazsa taps her chin. "Where did you get it?"

"I copied it from a manuscript."

Zsazsa arches an eyebrow.

"I...it's..." I swallow and look away, feel my cheeks warm.

Zsazsa laughs. "Lady Ilona is embroiled in an intrigue. How delightful." She narrows one eye. "Why didn't you ask Vlad? His reputation as a linguist is much admired."

My twisting lips give me away.

"That's what you get for snooping, Ilona." Zsazsa wags her finger.

Aunt Orsulya swats Zsazsa's shoulder. "You should talk, oh keeper of everyone's secrets."

Zsazsa giggles then studies the script again. "Did you ask the pompous little librarian Galeotto Marzio? I swear his arrogance is a substitute for the size of his prick." She bites the tip of her pinky.

"He wasn't there," I say. "And the illuminator provided no illumination." I recount the conversation.

"A code? This is a mystery. I will make discreet inquiries."

"Thank you." I rise from the chair, kiss both their cheeks, and depart the room, my imagination churning with visions of my aunt and Zsazsa together. Of Vlad with two women. Of me with another woman.

I hurry to Barbara's chambers. I have been gone too long to return to the chapel to ask forgiveness for the moistness between my legs.

# 35

Rareş blocks the door to Vlad's chambers.

"I demand you let me in." I stomp my foot. "I have not seen my husband for two weeks."

I am used to Vlad spending long hours and endless days forging alliances and meeting with emissaries and councilors. But he has never remained holed up in his room for this length of time without coming out.

"I know he's in there." I shake my finger at Rareş. Vlad always departs the manse accompanied by a small retinue of servants and advisors. "I know someone came to see him last night."

The clatter of a carriage had roused me from my sleep. Curious about the late-night visitor, I rushed to the chamber window. A cloaked figure entered the manse. All my worst fears took hold. An assassin. A harlot. A mistress. I ran to my door. It was locked! Bolted from the outside. I slumped to the floor in tears. Cried myself to sleep. The next morning it was unlocked.

"I demand to see Prince Vlad."

"You are not permitted inside." Rareş's hand drops to the hilt of his sword.

My nails dig into my palm, the pain keeping me focused, allowing me to think of a way to get past Rareş.

"Do I look like a threat?" I spread my hands. "Am I dressed for battle?" After finding the door unlocked, I had dressed quickly, not waiting for Bernádett. My hair is braided and coiled into a bun.

Rareş balks, his face crumbled with discomfiture. "No, my lady."

I glance at his defensive stance, then step forward and gaze up into his blue eyes. "Let me in."

"I will not disobey Prince Vlad. Ever. Do not ask me to, my lady. If not for My Lord I would be a poor serf or worse." Rareş squares his already very broad shoulders. "Nothing will ever compel me to disobey him. Not you. Not all the gold in Christendom."

"Prince Vlad is fortunate to have such a faithful manservant." I sigh with pretend concession. "I'll leave you to your post."

Rareş's body relaxes, his shoulders drop, and his mouth curves up. "I will tell My Lord you—*oof*!" His knees buckle and he drops to the ground.

The knee to a groin is a formidable weapon, one Vlad said I should use if I was ever attacked.

"I'm sorry, Rareş. You left me no choice." With only a smidgen of regret, I fling open the door.

The room is dark. The shutters closed against the sun. The odors of unwashed bodies, foul breath, and stale air saturate the room like a fetid fog. Cold fear drenches every inch of my body.

"Vlad?" I race across the room.

"He is ill," says a voice from the shadows.

Vlad is as white as the linen he lays on, his breath shallow and labored.

A wrinkled old man emerges from the dusky corner. "We

thought it was a case of the grippe, my lady, a few days rest all that was needed."

I recognize the man. He is a respected physician from Buda, well acquainted with plagues and afflictions.

I lay my hand on my husband's forehead. "Prince Vlad could not be any colder if he was dead. This is no common grippe."

The physician pinches the bridge of his nose. "His illness is most vexing."

"My lord, can you speak?" I stroke Vlad's icy cheek, thick from two-weeks' beard growth.

Vlad's eyelids flutter.

I turn to the physician. "What are you doing for him?"

"We have tried everything, but the usual tonics and leeching do not improve his health. I spoke with other physicians and even consulted ancient texts in Matthias's library. Prince Vlad's ailment is a mystery."

"Why wasn't I told?"

"Prince Vlad forbad us."

"He's dying, you idiot!" I pick up the pitcher of water from the nightstand and heave it at the physician.

The physician ducks. "My lady—"

"Get out! Get out! Damn you. Damn you to hell! Bring another physician, a young one whose brain is not addled from old age!" I stomp to the door and swing it wide.

I grind my finger into Rareş's chest. "If Prince Vlad dies, I will behead you myself."

A wheeze makes me spin around. Vlad! I rush back to the bed, take his cold hand in mine. "I will get a better physician."

"Vh..." Vlad's voice is rough, more groan than word.

"Do not speak." I rest my hand on his chest, feel its faint rise and fall.

"Vörös," he whispers.

"Is this the physician you want?"

"Ap...oth..." Vlad struggles with each syllable.

"Vörös is an apothecary? In Buda?"

Vlad grunts.

"In Pest?"

His head lolls to the left, all consciousness gone.

RAREŞ BOUNDS UP THE STAIRS, dust clinging to his leather boots. "Vörös refuses to come." He wipes sweat from his brow. "He says only the wife of Vlad Dracula may purchase the cure."

"Insufferable beast." I ball my fists, wish I could hit something. "I'll buy his damned cure and then behead him." I return to Vlad's bedside, kiss his icy cheek. "Stoke the fire, Rareş, and cover his feet when he throws off the blankets. I'm going to pay a visit to this insolent apothecary."

Gizella and Bernádett, waiting across the hall, follow me as I hoist up my skirt and run down the steps.

"There is terrible gossip about Vörös," says Bernádett, "They say he's not a real apothecary. His patients are not Christian."

"Vörös is from Wallachia," says Gizella. "His patients are simple folk who cling to the old ways."

"Pagan ways. Witchcraft," mutters Bernádett.

"You're too eager to believe rumors." Gizella frowns, her voice hitched with irritation.

"You're too eager to send my mistress into harm's way." Bernádett bristles.

"Stop it," I bark. "I don't care if I have to make a deal with the devil himself, I will do as my husband asks."

My heart gallops in time with the horses thundering through the streets. I urge my steed past the armed guards accompanying me on my race across town. I try to pray, but my spirit burns with so much fearful fury my 'let him live' plea is without divine direction. Lost in anguish.

"This is the place." I pull back on the reins, slide from the saddle, and tramp toward the apothecary's shop.

It is a modest dwelling of whitewashed stone beneath a steep thatched roof, its gable painted the same circular flower motif as the doorframe.

I pound on the door. "It is Princess Ilona. I come at Prince Vlad's request."

A shrunken old man with hair as white as snow opens the door. "Alone," he says, his grizzled chin jutting to the guards behind me.

With a flick of my eyes, the guards take a defensive position near the door.

"Are you Vörös?"

"*Da.*" He shuffles inside, his gait lopsided and hitched.

I follow him, my gaze taking in the sagging shelves, each crowded with pottery, coffers, leather bags, and jugs. The fireplace mantel, painted vivid blues, greens, and reds, is crammed with casks and stoneware. Behind the counter, a thick drapery cordons off the living quarters.

"You must help me." I make prayerful hands. "Prince Vlad is dying."

"*Da. Da.*" Vörös hobbles to the fireplace.

"Do you want to know his symptoms?"

"*Nu,*" he mumbles.

"No? Why not? How will you be able to prescribe the proper tonic?"

"I know what he suffers from." Vörös runs his fingers over the vessels and flasks.

"How?"

"I know where he comes from." Vörös stops at a clay pot, feels its shape.

I wring my hands, my fingernails scratching my skin. "He is cold. Cold as ice. Blankets fail to warm him."

"*Da*." Vörös picks up the pot, rubs his finger along a crack.

"He won't eat and drinks only when water is dribbled into his mouth."

"*Da*." Vörös sniffs the jar's contents.

"He barely speaks."

"*Da. Da*. I know this. I know his illness. Are you deaf?"

"No." But I almost certain Vörös is partially blind.

He squints at me. "Tell me, my lady, are you worried for Vlad Țepeș or worried about your own future?"

Vlad Țepeș. Vlad the Impaler. The moniker feels like thorns in my heart. "I am Princess Ilona, wife of Prince Vlad and cousin of King Matthias of Hungary." I lift my chin, determined not to let the old apothecary have the upper hand. "Your question is impertinent. If you cannot help, I will leave."

Vörös nods and grins, as though he approves of my pride. "The cure." He holds up a clay jar.

I step forward, hand outstretched.

The apothecary clutches the jar to his chest. "There is a formidable fee. Vlad Țepeș did that which is beyond his knowing." He jiggled the jar. "This will heal his body but not his spirit."

The apothecary talks in riddles. Either too full of self-importance or addled by old age.

"Yes, yes. His body is sick. I will pay the price, whatever it is." No price is too high to save my beloved's life. I reach into my pocket, my fingers curling around the small leather sack filled with gold.

A tall redheaded woman appears from behind the thick drapery. "The cost is not paid in coin."

"You!" I reel back when I realize where I know her from. "You told me my husband would live forever." I am ready to turn on my heels and leave this shop of charlatans.

"*Da.*" Her bright blue eyes shine with superiority. "The day of King Matthias's coronation."

I look her up and down, puzzled by her elegant clothing, at odds with this humble shop. "Who are you?"

She walks around the counter to stand in front of me. "I am Vörös's granddaughter."

"Do you know Prince Vlad?"

She takes the jar from the old man. "We are acquainted." Her words ooze from lips with a tone that makes me thinks she knows my husband in ways she should not.

"I demand to know the meaning of your prophecy."

"I am a seer not an interpreter." She uncorks the jar. "Do you want the cure or not?"

"Yes, my husband is dying."

She tilts her head, her blue-eyed stare reaching into my soul. "The cure comes at great cost to the one procuring it."

I stare right back. I will not be intimidated. "I will pay any price to save my husband."

The woman points at me. "All that is hidden within will appear."

More riddles.

"Fine." I reach for the clay pot.

The moment my fingers touch the lid, the woman snatches my hand, presses it against the rim, and chants in a strange language. I am spellbound, unable to move, stilled by the hypnotic melody.

"It is done." She inserts the stopper and pushes the jar into my hands. "Dracula must drink the contents as soon as possible."

I sit by his bedside through the night. Fear for Vlad's life kills my appetite and murders my sleep. I wave away offers of food and advice to nap.

For the thousandth time, I set my hand on Vlad's cold skin in hopes of detecting a bit of warmth.

His skin warms by sunrise.

I order the servants to stoke the fire, bring fresh water, and cut fresh sprigs of rosemary. I lay down beside him, my hand on his arm, and fall asleep.

"Ilona."

My eyes fly open. Vlad looks at me with cloudy eyes, and his mouth twitches into the smallest smile.

I squeeze his arm. "You will live, my love."

By evening, all his color and warmth returns. On the second day, Vlad sits up and drinks a restoring broth. By the third day, he demands a full explanation of his recovery. And a bath.

"Ilona, I am well again." Vlad flicks water at me from the tub. "Why do you look so grim?"

I force a smile. "I will be completely happy when you are fully recovered." It is a lie. Too many questions plague my mind.

How did you get this mystical illness? Why do you consort with pagans? How do you know the redheaded woman? I ask none of these questions. I fear the answers.

## 36

# Vlad

## Winter 1457
## Tîrgovişte castle, Wallachia

"Drink up." Vlad Dracula lifted his wine goblet.

Mihály Szilágy drank. "Excellent. Local?"

"From the *podgorie* region of Wallachia." Dracula settled back in his chair with a proud grin.

Impressing Mihály was no small feat. The man was an accomplished military strategist, fierce warrior, shrewd diplomat, and an epicure of life's finer pleasures.

Despite the thirty-year age difference Mihály and Vlad became good friends. Shared political interests forged their relationship. But their sacred duty to repel the Turks and unite against the scheming Saxon merchants was the whetstone sharpening their almost father-son bond.

"Because of your help, Vlad, my men crushed the merchants' rebellion at Bistriţa." Mihály smacked his fist into his palm. "But your bastard half-brother…" He smacked twice more. "He works against you by looking under every rock for boyars disloyal to you and promising them the world."

"He's weak. His promises, empty. Those boyars are nothing but leeches feasting on the lifeblood of the poor. I have the love of farmers and guildsmen." Vlad thumped his chest. "They are Wallachia's true muscle. It is their strong backs that chop down trees for farming and till the fertile soil. I doubt my bastard half-brother will gain their support. Not when I exempt their villages from taxes, built their churches, and made the land safe again."

Mihály downed his wine and poured more. "There's a rumor of a golden cup that sits on a sweet water well and is never stolen."

Vlad laughed. "The thieves are too afraid of my punishments."

Mihály stroked his beard. "Do you ever wonder if they are too harsh?"

The muscles rippled under Vlad's cheek as he considered Mihály's question. He beckoned to the servant nearby. "Do you think my punishments are just?"

The ruddy-faced lad's face drained of color. "Perfectly just, my lord."

Vlad swirled his goblet, pretending indifference. "Which is your favorite?"

"My lord?" The serving boy's eyes bugged out.

"Which punishment do you enjoy watching?"

"They are all excellent, my lord," the serving boy squeaked before clearing his throat. "The criminals staked around the castle inspire honesty. The two rapists pretending to be traveling monks that you boiled alive last week deserved nothing less. My sisters were relieved when your guards caught them."

Vlad flicked a satisfied look at Mihály, then turned back to the lad. "How would you like to die?"

"My lord?" The boy swayed, blinking rapidly with distress.

287

"If you did something criminal, how would you like to die?" Vlad's tone was chillingly casual.

The lad was clever. Prince Vlad chose only the brightest to work in his castles.

"Your question confounds my unschooled mind." The lad knew he was being tested. "Preferring a swift head chopping-off shows cowardice, which you do not tolerate. Choosing impalement reveals my arrogance in believing I'm strong enough to linger for days. Forgive me, my lord, but I prefer to leave a fitting punishment to your good judgment."

Vlad banged his fist on the table and roared with laughter. "You see, Mihály, even my servants have learned the art of diplomacy."

His body flooding with relief, the servant retreated to the corner and prayed his answer earned him a better position. Others had earned favor the same way.

Two topics kept Vlad and Mihály talking well into the night: The complications of Saxon merchant's buying allegiance from local nobility; and King Habsburg murdering László, John Hunyadi's eldest, which made the fifteen-year-old Matthias the best contender for the Hungarian throne.

"How are you planning on getting Matthias out of Buda prison?" Vlad sincerely hoped the chubby distracted youth had matured.

"Erzsébet and I are planning a rebellion. My sister," Mihály wiggled his little finger, "has more political sense in this finger than most diplomats. Thanks to her, we have the backing of the entire Hungarian Diet."

As the crescent moon traveled over Vlad's castle, their conversation turned to personal matters. Vlad shared concern about his mistress's impending birth. Mihály shared his sorrow over his own mistress's death from plague.

"I want to do right by her daughter," said Mihály.

"Is she yours?" asked Vlad.

"No, heaven forbid, I have enough daughters. Jusztina is

fourteen this year. Ilona is eleven and far too clever for her age. Margit is eight-years-old and already a beauty. I have no sons—not even a bastard." Mihály Szilágy lifted his goblet. "Except for you, Vlad, who I love like a son."

Vlad pressed his hand to his heart. "I can think of no greater honor."

VLAD'S HEART warmed and swelled. He held back tears as he gazed down at the bundle in his arms. "His name will be Mihnea, after my beloved brother."

Doina beamed. She gave Vlad what no other woman had. An heir.

Vlad put his nose to Mihnea's head, inhaled the fragrance of baby, more intoxicating than any wine. "Matthias is King of Hungary now. Remember my telling you how vital it is to my reign that—"

"I'm weary, my lord. Childbirth is exhausting work." Doina closed her eyes.

Vlad grunted a frown. He wanted to discuss the consequences of Matthias's rule. "Another time." He set a soft kiss on Mihnea's smooth cheek, then passed him to the midwife.

Vlad returned to his chambers, joy over his newborn son replaced by aggravation over political problems. There must be a way to bring strategic trade towns into obedience. The last diplomatic visit failed. Even worse, spies reported these towns sheltered his bastard half-bother. Whole towns were turning treasonous!

Vlad sunk into his chair and read yet another letter from a town protesting the trade tariffs. He pinched the space between his eyes. He did not blame the merchants and villagers. They were unschooled. Easily manipulated by profit-seeking merchants. Commoners did not understand how a land without taxes and tariffs undermined livelihoods, crushed aspirations, and weakened the principality.

Vlad crushed the letter in his palm and lobbed it into the fireplace. He had to teach them all a lesson in sovereignty. From the tax-evading merchants to the disloyal boyars to his bastard half-brother.

He knew just how to do it.

DRACULA and his *armaş* raced across the countryside. They galloped over grassy mountain passes, forded rivers raging with melted snow, and trekked through leafy forests in search of Vlad's bastard half-brother and his accomplices. Dracula's *armaş* burned the villages who harbored the bastard. Slaughtered the boyars and tax-evading merchants and confiscated their property.

In Bod, they hacked up the villagers, Vlad himself dismembering a man who spit on him. They impaled the traitors. The highest-ranking nobles they skewered on the tallest poles.

"Go to hell, Dracula." The boyar's mouth bubbled blood.

"Foul words to match your foul morals." Vlad reined his horse. "Tell me, how far do you see from your great height?"

"Fuck you."

Dracula swept his arm over the row of impaled and dying boyars. "You conspired with my bastard half-brother, plotted against the rightful sovereign knowing treason ends in death. May God have mercy on your souls."

Dracula never found his bastard half-brother. The Saxon merchants, however, found another way to revolt.

## 37

## Tîrgovişte

The messenger's legs shook under his breeches. "Two hundred Saxon merchants refuse to unpack their merchandise for inspection before going to Brăila."

Five letters in his hand, Dracula looked up from a desk piled with parchments, books, and maps. He regarded the tall youth with interest. Boy-men like him, with broad shoulders, large hands, and round honest faces were the lifeblood of Wallachia. "What is your name?"

The boy squared his shoulders and marshaled his courage. "Rareş Dobre, my lord."

Dracula stacked the letters by importance. "Tell me, Rareş Dobre, if you were prince how would you punish treason?"

Rareş remembered his father's advice: Stupidity often resulted in impalement, whereas cleverness brought favor. "God save Wallachia if the likes of me were ever prince." Encouraged by Vlad's chuckle, Rareş knees stopped knocking. "But if the impossible did happen, I would follow the example of a righteous sovereign—you, Prince Vlad—and seize their goods—my princely right—and impale them."

Rareş scratched his nose. "Or I would use the great pot you devised—the one with holes in the side—and boil the very wicked to death."

Vlad quirked an eyebrow. "How do you determine the 'very wicked'?"

"Why those not agreeing with the impaling, my lord."

Dracula bit back a smile. "Both suitable punishments. Deliver those instructions to the commander in Brăila, witness the Saxon seditionists' deaths, then report back here." Vlad plucked the most important letter from off the stack. "There will be a job working for me when you return."

Rareş's eyes widened, and he bowed low. "It will be an honor, my lord."

Dracula dismissed the boy, opened the first letter, and pumped his fist in the air. Yes! King Matthias's diplomats had decided to pay an official visit. This bode well for his continued alliance with Hungary.

Dracula rubbed his hands together after reading the letter from his spy in Mantua. Cardinal Eneo Silvio Bartolomeo Piccolomini, the newly elected pope, was planning a new crusade against the Turks. Dracula had waited years for the chance to defend the Order of the Dragon's godly edicts.

Dracula read the third letter. Poured more wine in his goblet. Dăneşti's brother, Dan, gathered forces in Braşov in hopes of overthrowing him.

Dracula muttered under his breath half way through the fourth letter. Mihály Szilágy wrote that his nephew, Matthias, the new boy-king, rejected advice from his councilors. His uncle included.

Dracula gulped down his wine while reading the fifth letter from his chancellor. His new mistress in Argeş was demanding special foods because she was with child. Dracula put his head in his hands and groaned. He liked the girl well enough. She enjoyed being spanked and shackled to the bed while he fucked her. But this...No, this was traitorous.

Two days later Dracula arrived at his mountaintop retreat in Argeş and entered his mistress's chambers without knocking. "You're with child?"

"I am, my lord." The slim-hipped young woman laid her palm on her flat belly.

Dracula pushed her hand away and replaced it with his own. "Flat and hard as stone tile. How many months?"

She giggled. "I don't know. Many, I suspect."

Dracula's hand moved upwards and squeezed her tiny pert breasts. "Your breasts have not changed."

She giggled again, louder this time. "Every woman is different. My mother showed no outward signs until her sixth month."

Vlad cupped her breasts. "Why are you demanding costly lemons, oranges, and pomegranates?"

"The midwife said those fruits assure a healthy child." She tugged on his mustache. "I've missed our naughty games." She lifted her skirt to her knees. "Tie my ankles to the bed."

Prince Vlad pressed his need into her. "After my physician confirms your condition."

The mistress spun about and ground her rump into his groin. "Take me now, my lord. Fuck me."

Dracula nuzzled her neck. "I'm going to bend you over and make you squeal. Later." He stepped back and walked from the room.

Dracula returned with the physician and two guards shortly after.

"She is not with child," said the physician after conducting an examination.

"I am. I swear it." The mistress, naked from the exam, yanked the blanket to her chin. "What does a man know about a woman's body? Let me summon the midwife. She will confirm my condition." Tears rolled down her pale cheeks.

He didn't want to do this. But he had no choice.

Vlad withdrew his dagger. "Who is this midwife?"

"The midwife is her cousin," said the physician. "She's young and inexperienced and has only attended three births."

Dracula touched the dagger's tip to his mistress's belly. Hopefully, it would frighten her into confessing her lie. "I have been gone five months. If there is a babe in your womb it is a weak and sickly thing."

"You would kill your son? He hides in my womb. I felt the quickening." Her voice cracking into a thin squeak, she drew her legs to her chest.

Dracula took deep breaths, his fingers squeezing the dagger's hilt. "How dare you live in my home, eat my food, drink my wine, and lie to me." He glared at her. "Did you think you could fool me?" He thumped his chest. "I know where and when I have been."

The mistress pressed her hands together in prayer. "I swear upon God, I am with child."

Dracula blew out his rage like a bull. "Perhaps you are with child, but it is not with mine." Dracula signaled his guards. "Hold her down." He ripped the blanket away.

The mistress whimpered as the guards held her ankles and wrists.

Vlad stared into her lying eyes. "Did you fuck a guard during my absence? Do I need to remind you that claiming to be pregnant with a prince's child when it's someone else's is high treason?"

"What? High treason?" The mistress's eyes bulged with terror.

Dracula lowered his blade.

"No! Not that! NOT THAT!" she sobbed and thrashed about.

Her screams curdled Dracula's blood. Still it did not stop him. He slit open her belly with painstaking slowness, cutting upward until reaching her sternum. She was unconscious by the time he splayed wide the bloody flaps of her womb. "What is that?"

The physician poked at the tiny bloody sac. "A fetus of no more than three months."

"An ambitious mistress who deceives her master is worse than a traitorous boyar." Dracula wiped the blade with the sheet, then crossed the room to stare out the narrow window. He did not see the forested mountains under a clear blue sky but saw only the blood of treachery. "She deserves a proper Orthodox burial." He left the room.

## 38

# Ilona

## Winter 1473
## Dracula's Mansion in Pest, Hungary

Vlad looks up from his writing desk, his face creased into a deep scowl. "I'm busy, Ilona. Is this important?"

Our marriage, I want to shout. Instead, I bend over his desk in hopes my low-cut dress improves his mood. "It's been two weeks since we've spent time together. I miss you."

Vlad runs his fingers through his hair. "It's not a good time. I'm in a vile mood." He crumbles a paper in his fist and throws it into the fireplace.

"A grim husband is better company than no husband at all."

Vlad grunts. "Did you come from a party? Your dress is rather…daring."

"I wore it for you. Do you remember when I wore it last?"

"I'm not in the mood for riddles, Ilona."

I walk my fingers across the desk and onto his hand. "I wore it to Matthias's birthday gala, remember? All the courtiers begged me for a dance, and you teased me about being a shameless seductress."

"You grow more beautiful every year." Vlad captures my hand and lifts it to his lips. "I hope you are never fool enough to take them up on their offers."

"You would kill them."

Vlad squeezes my fingers. "Which is why they will try to bed you. The more danger, the greater the pleasure."

"Speaking of pleasure…" I ease the sleeve off my shoulder.

Vlad drops my hand and points to the stack of correspondence. "Not tonight."

I tug up the sleeve. His rejection—one of many—feels like a blow to my gut. My eyes grow hot with tears I must not let him see. "Some other time." My lips quiver into a forced smile.

Vlad looks away.

"Have I displeased you, my lord?" I am a sob away from unleashing a torrent of tears that if released will puddle at Vlad's feet.

"I would tell you if you did." Vlad takes a letter from the pile and begins to read.

I have been dismissed.

"Good night, my lord." I sniff, walk away, tears brimming.

The passion is gone, and I have no idea why. Our love-making is dull and sporadic. It is my fault. I have not done what Aunt Erzsébet said I must: satisfy his secret desires and be his confidante.

"Is your maidservant still dallying with my barber?" Vlad asks as I head for the door.

I wipe my eyes and turn around. "Your barber? I thought Flora was with a groomsman."

"She's a whore. Dismiss her."

"She told me he wants to wed her."

Vlad snorts. "Don't be stupid. Men always speak of

marriage when they want to bed an unmarried maid. Dismiss her."

"I will not." I put my hands on my hips. "Flora is a good maidservant and a harmless girl whose only fault is her lack of judgment with men."

"Harmless? You're a fool. A maidservant spreading her legs for any man she fancies is immoral."

"How dare you pass such cruel judgment." My cheeks burn with rage. "Flora is moral. She attends services in Pest and confesses her sins weekly. She's just trying to find a husband."

"By fucking any man she fancies?" Vlad walks around his desk. "Tell me, wife, will it be acceptable if the fire dies while she's fucking a potential husband in the stables? Will it be acceptable if she leaves your chambers untidy or frocks soiled to suck on her would-be husband's cock? What will you tell a visiting dignitary when he finds Flora rutting like an animal with his guard?"

"Stop. Enough." I clap my hands over my ears and rush to the door.

Vlad races past and bars my exit. He yanks my hands from my ears and grabs my wrists. "Act like the Princess of Wallachia, not a spoiled child."

"Let me go." I yank my arms, but his grip tightens.

Vlad's gaze drops to my bosom, which heaves beneath the snug bodice.

"You're hurting me." I twist away.

Vlad pushes his arousal into me, his breath ragged, his eyes glazed.

My pain makes him lusty?!

"You beast!"

Like a dog caught with stolen meat from the scullery, Vlad freezes, shame etched on his face. He flings open the door and strong-arms me from the room. "Lady Ilona is no longer permitted in my chambers," he says to Rareș and slams the door.

I stare at the door unable to move, to think. A loud crash —like a vase thrown against the door—sends me stumbling backwards. A thousand horrid thoughts spin out of control. More crashes and bangs. Vlad tears apart the room. I flee down the hall, his Turkish rants echoing in my ears.

AUNT ERZSÉBET HOLDS her embroidery inches from her eyes. "Odd, isn't it? I can see a hawk in the sky but not a thread at the end of my nose." She thrusts the needlework at me. "Idle hands make for an apathetic princess."

I heavy sigh escapes my lips as I thread her needle.

"What's wrong? Are you worried Barbara will eat until she's plump as a sow during her lying-in?" Though her tone is light, Aunt Erzsébet's brow crumples with concern.

"Barbara does seem to be enjoying herself." I smile, pretend my whole world has not fallen to pieces. "I was always clumsy and weary the last few months of pregnancy."

Aunt Erzsébet glances at my flat belly. "Is Dracula content with only two sons?'

"Three. You forget Mihnea."

"Pfft, a bastard." Aunt Erzsébet flaps her hand. "Another pawn to move around the chess board."

I shrug, give her back the threaded needle, and pick up my own.

"I bait you and you don't reply?" Aunt Erzsébet *tsk-tsks*. "What's troubling you? Is it Vlăduț? Nicolae? A marital problem? Did you find out Vlad has a mistress?"

"What?" I drop my sewing. "He does?"

Aunt Erzsébet gives my shoulder a comforting squeeze. "All men have mistresses."

"Who is she?" My heart beats against my chest like a wild bird in a cage.

"You misunderstand, my dear. I make an assumption. Nothing more. Is that what's got you out of sorts? Does Vlad no longer visit your chambers?"

I blink back hot tears. "Weeks go by where we exchange only two or three words."

Aunt Erzsébet's eyes soften and she nods knowingly. "I wife always assumes the worst, doesn't she? Take heart, he is probably busy wooing nobles with a financial stake in his return to power."

I resume my needlework. "What do you know?"

"There are whispers of Radu's dreadful misrule. If Dracula seeks to claim his throne he must make sure his chessboard is poised for victory."

Men and their politics.

"Anyway," says Aunt Erzsébet, "even if he does have a mistress you should use it to advantage."

My jaw drops.

"Close your mouth, dear, it's very unbecoming."

"How—"

"If the woman is lowborn with a taste for vulgar pleasure, use it against him when he accuses you of having less than impeccable scruples."

I square my shoulders and scowl. Attacking Vlad's faults will never work.

"It's the silly ladies at court you must be wary of. If the woman knows more court gossip than you then she becomes a valuable asset to him. Worse still is the maiden or young widow with an ambitious father bent on replacing you. Get a food taster if that happens."

"No one will replace me." I yank the needle through the fabric and tear the thread.

"A delicate hand is required in all things. Especially when dealing with the vices of men."

I spend the rest of my Buda castle visit eavesdropping and watching the women who flirt with Vlad.

I hate myself for it. I hate the jealousy and suspicions that strangle my dignity. The redheaded woman was right. All that was hidden did surface. My jealous nature emerged from the depths of my soul and swallows my confidence whole.

That evening I look, really look, at the other dinner guests and my heart sinks with the awful realization. The older couples no longer dote upon one another, their sweetest laughter and brightest smiles only for dashing emissaries and blushing maidens.

Vlad takes my hand to dance, yet his smile does not reach his eyes. When was the last time I saw those green eyes sparkle with lust? When was the last time he whispered sexy promises in my ear? Or stole a caress?

How stupid to think his passion would forever flame hot. I resign myself to the cruel truths of matrimony.

## 39

The sun warms my face as I descend wearily from the carriage. As usual Vlad will be busy writing letters and meeting advisors, but I must interrupt him anyway. He will want to know.

Yawning, I trudge through the manse, exhausted by last night's vigil. I must not complain though. Vlad works from morning until evening. On rare occasions he visits my room, but our lovemaking is dull. Sometimes he does not reach completion. I am left equally unsatisfied. It's my fault. My breasts no longer bounce, and my waist is soft from childbirth.

A week ago, I wept in Bernádett's arms and mourned the sorry state of my marriage. Bernádett stroked my back and agreed when I told her Vlad no longer desired me.

Gizella disagreed. "Mama says a wife must find ways to ignite her husband's lust. Replace the sparkle of virginity with the dazzle of novelty. Mama says the more powerful the man, the more his need to conquer new lands—even if that's the valley between a mistress's legs or the hummocks of his wife's ass."

Novelty. How am I supposed to initiate that, I think while treading the steps to Vlad's chambers.

Vlad, dressed in linen tunic and velvet robe, looks up from The Book, the one I suspect he stole from the Şolomonari. "Boy or girl?"

"Barbara gave birth to a healthy son."

Vlad beckons me forward, his eyes sparkling with good humor. "I'll send a gift to Matthias in honor of his first bastard." Vlad curls his fingers around my hand. "His name?"

"John Corvinus."

"Matthias ought to find a suitable wife and produce a legitimate heir or this bastard might lay claim to the Hungarian crown one day." Vlad kisses my fingertips and grins like a wolf. "I want to show you something."

My fatigue evaporates like morning dew on a hot summer day.

"Come."

Together we walk downstairs and through the wide hallway. Vlad stops at the armory. He pulls a key from his pocket and unlocks the iron lattice door.

I hide my disappointment with a loving smile. I have no interest in weaponry.

Vlad lights each lantern, row after row of weapons emerging from the darkness to join the burnished glow of steel and iron. Then Vlad slides closed the bolt, takes my hand, and strolls around the room. He names each weapon—arming sword, broad sword, long sword, poignard, rondle, scimitar, flanged mace, flail, halberd, war hammer, morning star, pike, lance, spear, crossbow, longbow.

I comment on each. How sharp. So heavy. My god. Impressive.

Vlad hefts an arming sword in his hand and taps the tip. "I received a letter from cousin Stephen today about Radu." Vlad aims the point at me. "Touch it."

It's cold and sharp, like my husband's mind.

"Radu's health and influence are wilting. He relies on Mehmed's army and wealth to keep him in power." Vlad exchanges the arming sword for an ivory-hilted stiletto. "My brother is nothing but Mehmed's lap dog now. Stephen is itching to overthrow him and install Basarab Laiotă as ruler."

This is terrible news. More of Stephen's betrayal.

"Basarab Laiotă? One of your Dănesti rivals?" I keep my voice light, though his cheery demeanor is puzzling.

"*Da.*" Vlad turns the dagger over in his hand and runs a finger along the flat side of the blade. "Stephen is planning to attack Bucharest soon."

"This is good news?" Surely, I am missing the forest for the trees.

Vlad touches the sharp tip to my neck. "Basarab Laiotă is weak. He'll be licking Mehmed's boots in no time." Vlad flicks the blade. My gold beads and precious jewels scatter across the floor.

I recoil, and my hand flies to my throat.

Vlad snatches my wrist and wrenches me close. "Are you afraid of me?" One side of his mouth curls into a frightening grin.

I stare into his wild eyes and my legs shake. "I fear the Prince of Wallachia. I do not fear my husband."

"We are one in the same," he growls. "Look around, Ilona. I have weapons but no soldiers. An armory but no battle. I have only one fixed and constant purpose. To regain my throne." Vlad lays the blade's broad side atop my shoulder. He pushes the blade down, forces me to my knees.

Who is this man? His eyes are icy green. His wolf grin, vicious. He looks absolutely feral. Fear flows through me, pools between my legs, and spins like an eddy.

"What will you do to help my cause, *iubirea mea*?" Vlad taps the blade on my bodice.

"Anything you want." I am aroused and frightened, the two feelings uniting into a single throbbing need.

A low growl rises from his depths, but this only inflames my lust.

"Why point the dagger at me when our aspirations are the same?" I ask. "Our destinies are enfolded. Two sons engraft our union. My ambitions for them may even exceed your own. It is you who should kneel before me because it is my womb that joined two mighty families and birthed your progeny."

"Kneel to you?" Vlad's mouth twists in astonished amusement. "I think not."

"Then neither shall I." I sit down, spread out my silk skirt, and throw my head back to look up at him. "Our children are the foundation of your legacy." I thump the cold stone with my fist.

The low rumble in his throat rushes forth into joyful laughter. "You are my true wife, Ilona. My greatest love. No other woman would have courage enough to defy me with a sword to her heart." He straddles my legs. "Do you have the courage to satisfy my darkest desires?"

"Yes," I say without giving it a moment's thought. Had I not waited our entire marriage for the opportunity to become his greatest confidant? "A thousand times yes."

With eyes hungry and feverish with desire, Vlad slices my pearl-encrusted bodice in half. "Tell me, *iubirea mea*, have you figured out that I have the Şolomonari's book?" He aims the blade's tip at my embellished belt.

I gasp, shame's heat torches my cheeks. "You know?"

Like a pendulum, Vlad pivots the blade up and down the length of my torso. He grins, and with a flick of his wrist, slashes my blouse from top to bottom. My blouse falls open and exposes my breasts.

"Zsazsa and I have an understanding. She tells me everything." Vlad presses the blade's flat side to my nipple, stiffening them to an eager point. "Do you want to know the book's secrets?" Another flick and my belt falls to the ground.

"Yes." I am panting now, my lips burning for a kiss, my loins aching for him, my soul yearning to fold itself into his.

Vlad splits the sleeves of my dress. "Its knowledge comes with a price." He slices each layer of my skirt.

"I will pay it." I am naked now, my clothing in tatters around me, my need ravenous. I will say anything, do anything.

Vlad bends over me, takes my wrists and sets a soft kiss on the underside. "The first payment is due now." He locks me in manacles, lifts my arms over my head, and latches them to some contraption above me. "The Şolomonari's book is only for the strong minded. For those of unwavering ambitions." He kneels between my thighs.

"I'm as strong-willed and ambitious as you." I arch my back, thrusting out my breasts that he may feast on them.

A slow devious grin creeps up his face. "I hope so, *iubirea mea*." He draws the dagger up my thigh and leaves a heated pink trail.

My skin tingles with the sensation, the sting melting into my moist junction and leaving me heaving for more. Vlad lowers his head to my breast, bites my nipple, tugging it out with his teeth. It hurts but I want more and twist my body to offer the other nipple. Vlad gives it a quick noncommittal flick then returns to the first, renewing his biting pull.

I say the words he loves to hear. A whore's words.

I am unprepared for what follows. My raw desire sweeps my husband away, replaces him with a rough warlord. He slaps my buttocks. I yelp, and yet my core explodes with desire. My moan prompts another slap, this one followed by soft caresses. He smears his fingers between my legs and slaps a third time, the two sensations spiraling me into an insatiable frenzy. He does this again and again and again. By the time Vlad plunges into me I am shouting the whore's words like a mantra.

Vlad strips me of all modesty and dignity, which lies as shredded as my torn clothing. I am born anew, christened by a painful pleasure that releases all inhibitions and sends my body and soul to glorious new heights. That which is darkest has surfaced.

After our lust is spent, my body sore, and our wickedness satisfied, Vlad removes the manacles. I grab the stiletto laying next to me and press it to his heart. "Tell me about the Șolomonari's book."

# 40

Vlad does not tell me about the *Book of the Şolomonari*. Instead, he covers my nakedness with his robe and asks me about the strength of my faith.

I nestle close and rub my nose against his cheek. "I never miss mass, receive the sacraments, and always confess my sins."

"Those are rituals." Vlad caresses my cheek. "I'm referring to a spiritual belief with the strength to transform."

This is not about feeling good after praying the rosary. He speaks about a more complex faith.

"I confess, my mouth recites," I say. "My knees bend, and my hands make the Sign of the Cross but my mind is often elsewhere."

Vlad kisses my hand. "That's the problem with rituals, they are performed by rote and without mindfulness. Exposure to another faith, like Islam, might have made you more mindful, more aware of the power behind ritual."

"Or gotten me excommunicated." I give his earlobe a playful pinch. "What does faith have to do with the *Book of the Şolomonari*?"

"My salvation, deliverance from my many sins, requires

faith in ritual." He says this as lightly as if commenting on the weather, and yet my skin prickles with foreboding.

"You are already saved, my lord."

"Am I?" He snorts, doubtful. "I sacrificed too many people in the name of justice."

I press my finger against his lips. "Don't talk like this. Don't second guess the decisions you were forced to make for the good of Wallachia."

Vlad nibbles on my finger. "Not just Wallachia. All of Christendom. Don't you see? Mehmed grows bolder every year. His ambition exceeds Julius Caesar and Alexander the Great." Vlad scratches the air, his fingers curled into claws. "I itch for a crusade, Ilona. It's time to strike back at Mehmed. Before he conscripts all our strongest boys, kidnaps our women, and taxes Wallachian towns to death."

"You must not let that happen."

Vlad holds out his hands. "They might as well be manacled."

"It's time Matthias pardons you." Love for my cousin king wilts like a plucked flower. As long as Matthias keeps up the pretense of Vlad's imprisonment, my husband is powerless. I gather Vlad's hands in mine and press them to my bosom. "How infuriating. All these diplomatic contrivances, family rivalries, ancient feuds, and lines on a map prevent you from protecting us from a Turkish invasion. How many sons must be seized, wives raped, and villages burned until they wake up to the inevitable?"

"Even one more is too many." Vlad shakes his head, stands, and helps me to my feet. "Ah, if only I could live forever I would awaken the sleeping world." He wraps his robe tight around me, scoops me up, and cradles me in his arms.

"My lord," I say as he carries me upstairs. "You didn't tell me anything about the *Book of the Şolomonari*."

Vlad nuzzles my neck. "I did. You just weren't ready to hear."

That evening I sit on the velvet bench in our private chapel and ponder the gilded stars on the indigo ceiling. What was I not ready to hear? The stars have no answer. I look to the painted angels, cherubs, and seraphim on the oak paneling. They are silent as well.

I kneel down and gaze at the altar where a pale, emaciated Jesus hangs limp from a carved cross. I do not like that crucifix, even if it was made by a famous Venetian artist. It is too gruesome with its bright red blood gushing from His wounds and heart. When I complained, Vlad said blood and faith are forever joined. One begets the other. He told the artist to add more.

I stare at bloody Christ and pray. "Father in Heaven, today I submitted to my husband's shameful desires and it was...wonderful. Is our wickedness abhorrent to You? Immoral? Why do I find pleasure in it?" I squeeze my eyes shut. This is no prayer. I try again. "Almighty Father, grant me the strength to be a good mother, a virtuous princess, and a loving and obedient wife. Thank you for blessing me with two healthy sons and an exceptional husband. Give me the strength to ease the pain buried deep within him and give me the boldness to meet his desires in all things." I stare at bloody Jesus. "I adore my husband. I will do anything for him."

Even if it requires worshipping before his savage appetites.

VLĂDUŢ AND MIRCEA hover like Goliaths over the miniature battle of clay soldiers, horses, and lead cannons set up on the patterned Turkish carpet.

"No, Nicolae!" Vlăduţ slams his little fist down, already

showing his father's exacting nature. "The archer doesn't belong there. The *armaș* must be in wedge formation."

Nicolae covers the tiny archer with a chubby hand. "No, mine!"

"*Mami*," whines Vlăduț. "Tell Nicolae to do what I say. I'm the general."

"Vlăduț, he's too little to understand tactical formations, and wasn't it only last week you learned about them yourself?"

"*Mami*," pouts Vlăduț. "Tell him to—" His head snaps around when the nursery door opens. "*Tati*." Vlăduț drops the clay soldier and runs headlong into his father's legs. He throws his arms around them.

Nicolae, two years younger and half as fast, thumps his brother on the back. "My *Tati*. My *Tati*!" He lifts his arms and shakes his hands until Vlad scoops him up and kisses his plump cheek.

"Pick me up too, *Tati*." Vlăduț, his chin resting on Vlad's hip, gazes up with devotion.

Vlad ruffles his hair. "A man does not address his father like a child."

"Yes, Lord Father." Vlăduț's seriousness is made comical by his two missing front teeth.

Vlad lifts him up, a child on each hip. "What did you learn today?"

"I learned that writing legibly is impossible," says Vlăduț. "I practiced making D's and V's all morning but the tutor said they were dreadfully...mmmm...dreadfully killed."

"Killed or executed?"

Vlăduț squeezes on eye closed, his face scrunched in thought. "Executed. But, Lord Father, I don't understand how I kill letters."

"Some words have several meanings. Your tutor meant your letters are not well written." Vlad sets both his sons back on the floor. "You may both dine with your mother and

I tonight but only if you can properly execute all your letters."

"Me. Me." Nicolae jumps up and down.

"Yes, Nicolae, you must also practice writing." Vlad bows with an exaggerated flourish. "Lady Ilona, will you accompany me for a walk in the garden?"

After kisses and hugs Vlad and I leave our energetic sons in the indulgent care of Dădacă, Bernádett, and Gizella.

"This isn't the way to the garden," I say.

Vlad scrapes his teeth against my fingertips, sending a pleasurable tingle up my arm.

"I lied." Vlad gives me an impish grin, the one he wooed me with, the one I fell in-love with, and the one that is resurrected by our ferocious passions. "The political winds have begun blowing in my favor, *iubirea mea*. When it comes time for me to battle Radu the manse will be vulnerable to assaults by mercenaries wanting to take our sons hostage. This. Must. Not. Happen." Memories of misery and humiliation flare in his eyes. "My sons must not suffer the torments I had to endure." He kneads the bridge of his nose and blows out a grunt. "My sons must not be bargaining chips."

Fear constricts my throat. It's up to me to protect our sons.

Vlad nuzzles my neck. "The first thing mercenaries will do if they breach the manse is search our private chambers. They'll look for trap doors and a secret tunnel. If they don't find one they'll loot the treasury and armory, and then hit the scullery for food."

"Where will the boys and I be if all this happens?"

"Long gone through the tunnel." Vlad flings open the well-used door down the hall and around the corner from the great chambers.

My mouth falls open. "Surely the entrance to the tunnel is not here."

## 41

# Vlad

### Winter 1460
### Carpathian Valley of Braşov, Transylvania

The blood-splatted captain clutched his gory sword. "My lord?"

Prince Vlad fixed his gaze on the snow-covered Carpathian Mountains and inhaled the coldness of an imperfect triumph. "Burn every building, every tree, every blade of grass." His fist clenched, he renewed his silent promise to rid his land from princely pretenders and traitorous boyars. Only then could his people enjoy a prosperous future. He peered down at his blood-slick sword and scowled. Dan, a member of the rival Dăneşti clan and brother to the man responsible for murdering his father, had eluded him. Again! "Kill the treasonous boyars, their wives, and children. Burn everything. Only fire will purify my land of its traitors."

Braşov burned.

Dracula's eyes reddened. The women's screams scorched his heart, and the cries of the damned blistered his soul, but there was no other way. Better blood and battle than Turkish subjugation.

"My lord." A messenger emerged from the haze of ash and smoke. "A copy of the papal bull." He doubled over with a fit of coughing.

Dracula, his nose and mouth covered with a cloth, grunted his thanks, pulled off his gauntlets and read. "Good news." He smacked the letter as he entered his tent. "Pope Pius calls for a three-year crusade against Sultan Mehmed."

Rareş set Dracula's sword and rondel on the table. "This new pope is truly God's vassal."

"And a savvy vassal at that." He waved the paper before tossing it aside. "Says here he will forgive the sins of all crusaders. King, prince, archer, longbow-men, lancer, bombardier, cook, servant, or slave."

Rareş removed Dracula's surcoat. "Surely every king in Christendom will join the crusade."

"Not likely." Dracula shifted from foot to foot with impatience while Rareş unstrapped the shin greaves. "The French king struggles for succession in Naples. Emperor Frederick is more interested in stealing Matthias's Hungarian golden crown than battling for Christ's thorny one."

Rareş unfastened Dracula's metal arm plates, unbuckled the first of the two-part cuirass, untied the skirt of mail, unfastened the mail doublet—constructed by notable armorer Antonio Missaglias of Milan—and freed his boot spurs. "What about the other kings?"

"The French battle Portugal's bastard king," spat Dracula in disgust. "The Polish king believes the Turks will never reach his land. He's an idiot."

"What about the others?" Rareş offered Vlad a pitcher of water.

"England is a divided island. The Houses of Plantagenet, York, and Lancaster have neither money nor men to spare in their vicious war against one another." Dracula guzzled the water.

"What about the Grand Duke of Moscow?"

"Bah, he's a fool. He refuses to spend money until the Turks batter at his castle gate."

"It's too late by then."

"Exactly." Dracula dipped his fingers into the steaming tub. "You are much smarter than these so-called educated kings, Rareş."

"Thank you, my lord." Rareş backed out of the tent to give Dracula the privacy he required.

The moment the tent flap fell closed Dracula lifted his father's medallion from his chest. "I will answer Pope Pius' call, Father." He rubbed his thumb over the dragon-draped cross engraving, burnishing his ambitions to a shine. "I will fulfill your oath to the Order of the Dragon."

Vlad pressed the medallion into his skin until it left a circular imprint. This was his ritual. It brought comfort and a renewed sense of purpose. He leaned back, closed his eyes, and wondered, not for the first time, how his name would be recorded in history. Would he be hailed a hero or denounced a tyrant? Or would those earthly terms have no meaning once he discovered the Şolomonari's secrets? After all, King Solomon commanded demons to do his bidding.

The sun descended against the flame-colored horizon while Dracula ate supper with his captains. The table was situated near the impaled traitors. Too close for Dracula. Too far away for his gloating captains. Dracula said nothing. If this gruesome meal inspired his officers to continue their hunt for Dan so be it.

The captains lifted their goblets. "To Prince Vlad! To Wallachia!"

Dracula's mouth pressed into a thin smile. He found no victory in the massacre. Found no triumph in Dan's narrow escape.

"We swear on our lives we will find Dan and bring him to you," shouted a blonde-bearded captain drunk on killing and wine.

The others banged their fists on the table.

"Your rule shall surpass Alexander the Great," hollered a captain with blood-matted hair.

"Like Genghis Kahn who united the Mongol clans, you will unite the kingdoms of Wallachia, Transylvania, and Moldavia, and conquer your enemies," proclaimed another.

Their fists pounded the table. *Thump. Thump. Thump.*

"Your military command rivals Julius Caesar!"

*Thump. Thump. Thump.*

"The spirit of Augustus takes residence in your person!"

*Thump. Thump. Thump.*

Dracula raised his goblet. "Let us drink to the blood of the conquered."

The blonde-bearded captain jumped from the table, traipsed through the grove of the impaled, and stopped before a pole dripping with blood. He tilted his goblet into the rivulet, then swaggered back to the table and kneeled before Vlad Dracula.

"Hail to you, my prince. You will conquer the world. Your name will live forever." He offered the cup to Dracula.

*Thump. Thump. Thump.* Faster and faster. The captains shouted praises and noble epithets.

Dracula held the goblet aloft. "To my enemies; to Dan; to those I have killed; to those waiting for my blade; to my noble allies; to my fierce captains and their resolute soldiers; to our dream."

The captains hoisted their cups. "*Noroc.*"

Dracula lifted the blood-infused cup to his lips and drank, the shouts of his men a divine choir to his ears.

## Summer 1460: Outskirts of Rucăr, Transylvania

DRACULA'S and Dan's armies faced off in a verdant valley

nestled between rolling hills. The summer sun heated weapons and tempers.

For Dracula it was more than a battle between prince and usurper, between the families of Dănești and Drăculești. It was a war determining Wallachia's independence *from* or servitude *to* the sultan. For Dracula, it was nothing less than a fight between Good and Evil.

Dracula gave the order to charge.

He galloped across the battlefield, skirted the onslaught, and rushed into the thick of the rear guard where Dan always hid behind his men. Dracula headed for his target, Dan's plumed-topped turban rising above the guards.

Their horses reared, threw off their surprised riders.

Dracula thrust his long sword under Dan's arm, snagged Dan's strap like a fish on a hook. He yanked hard, pulled Dan from his horse, and galloped from the camp.

A quarter mile away, Dracula trussed Dan's legs like a deer. He tied the rope to his saddle, mounted his horse again and dragged Dan's body into the battlefield.

Dracula rode tall, his sword in the air, his heart pumping with the thrill of triumphant revenge.

"Look!" Dan's soldiers pointed at their unconscious leader hauled like game across the field.

They fled. Into the meadows. Into the forest. Scattered like roaches.

Dracula arrived in his camp. "Wake him up. Make him kneel."

Two soldiers lifted Dan to his knees. A third splashed a bucket of water on his face.

A wolf smile spanning his face, Dracula loomed over his dazed and bleeding enemy. "Any last words before you die?"

Dan spat out blood. "You are a scourge upon Wallachia, Dracula. A wicked tyrant. Your own people hate you. You are not fit to live, let alone rule."

Dracula rolled his eyes. "The problem with idiots like you

is their inability to fathom genius. You and your boyars are thieves. Worse than thieves. You are leeches. Your greed sucks the lifeblood of farmers and tradesman. Your arrogance keeps them down, prevents and undermines their potential. A good ruler is a sculptor, molding his people like clay into a great masterpiece. You, Dan, are a slinger of mud."

"It's your vile mud." Dan spewed more blood on the ground. "I slung it far and wide across the land. I told everyone you drank the blood of the innocent at Mount Tîmpa—like a *strigoi*—as you basked in your glory."

"The only glory I feel will be watching you die." Dracula tossed a shovel at his feet. "Dig."

Dan dug. Shovelful after shovelful. When his grave was deep enough, he wiped the black soil from his mouth. "What have you done with my men? Impaled them?"

"Ask them yourself when you see them in hell," said Dracula.

Dan dropped the shovel. "I swear on my grave, I did not bury your brother alive."

Dracula studied Dan's terrified face for truth yet saw only an equivocator's lies. "Maybe you did not shovel the dirt over his head, but you murdered him just the same."

Dan peered into his grave. "By the grace of God and by all you hold honorable, I beg of you, kill me first."

Dracula nodded, gripped the sword with both hands and swung. Dan's head dropped to the ground, his blue eyes fixed on the gathering clouds above. With a nudge of Dracula's boot, Dan's head tumbled into the grave.

### Fall 1460

DRACULA STARED AT THE TREATY. Disappointment twisted like a knife in his gut. His people deserved better. But this was the best he could wrangle from the money-grubbing Saxon merchants.

His heart heavy, Dracula dashed his signature across the treaty. His merchant tax—gone. His private wealth used to pay restitution for damaged property. It boiled his blood. At least the Saxon merchants agreed to maintain a militia in case of Turkish attack.

The celebratory meal eaten, Dracula spent the night at his family home in Sighişoara. The narrow hallways stirred long forgotten memories. The horror and excitement of watching criminal executions. The awe and pride of listening to his father strategize with boyars. The thrill of sledding down snow-packed hills. The satisfaction of felling birds with a slingshot. Simple pleasures for carefree times.

Dracula sunk into the chair and looked out the narrow window. A sparrow clung to the ledge. Long ago there was another sparrow...

He was four-years-old, angry and ashamed because Father had struck his hand with a switch. A broken toy? Rude behavior? Some childish infraction Vlad no longer remembered.

On the verge of tears, Vlad had escaped to the courtyard where he found a wounded sparrow flopping on the ground. He had cradled the bird in his stinging hand, its fear melting into his own smarting palm. Poor little sparrow. Doomed to die by cat or bird of prey. Doomed to linger in pain if he took the sparrow inside. Vlad had pulled a small pointed stick from his pocket, his pretend sword, and jabbed it into the bird. Again and again. Until the sparrow stopped moving. The sting on Vlad's hand disappeared, the mercy killing a balm to his own hurt and pain.

"My lord?" Rareş voice broke the spell of the past.

Dracula blinked away the memory. "Enter."

"A messenger from Mihály Szilágy's militia just arrived."

Dracula brightened. "Send him in."

The messenger, a reed-thin young lad, bowed low.

Dracula stretched out his arm, eager for the letter.

"I have no letter, my lord, only terrible news." His face taut with anxiety, the lad shifted from foot to foot. "General Szilágy was taken prisoner by the bey, Ali Mihaloğlu when—"

"Mihaloğlu?" A frigid wind gusted through Vlad's body. Mihaloğlu was one of Mehmed's foremost commanders.

"*Da*, my lord. The Turks attacked near Pojejena. I hid— on General Szilágy's order, I swear, my lord—that I could give a true account of the battle." The boy thumped his chest. "I am no coward. I wanted to fight."

Despite the cold grip of foreboding, Vlad nodded approvingly. "Go on."

"It was a massacre." The lad grabbed both sides of his head. "Mihaloğlu's army was enormous! Too many to count. They impaled every soldier but one. General Szilágy."

Dracula's mouth went dry. Mihály...

"Mihaloğlu took him away in chains." The messenger pressed his thumb into his chest. "I was supposed to report back here but instead I trailed the Turks to Constantinople."

"They didn't see you following them?"

"No, my lord. I'm too skinny." The lad turned to the side. "I hid behind trees."

Vlad cocked his head. "How did you pass through the gates?"

"I had no coins for the entrance fee so I waited in hopes a kindly merchant would let me join their group."

"Merchants are not kindly."

"Never threw me even a crumb, my lord. The next day, I kneeled down and prayed. God heard my prayers, and a troupe of drunken minstrels let me join their group. I ran straight to the sultan's palace and waited—two days, my lord —until a Hungarian emissary came out. He said he was on his way to tell King Matthias that General Lord Szilágy was dead—sawed in half—for refusing to confess secrets." The boy blinked back tears.

"You are a brave and intelligent boy." Dracula gave him a handful of coin before opening the door. "Rareş, first get this boy something to eat. Then find him a job." Legs heavy with sorrow, Dracula trudged up the narrow steps to his chambers. He bolted shut the door, sank into the chair, and wept.

Mihály Szilágy was dead. Tortured by Mehmed. Vlad doubled over, his heart twisting and shredding, the agony all too familiar. Father, Mother, Mircea: all slaughtered.

A thick loneliness wrapped around Vlad. Mihály...like a father to him.

Vlad Dracula and Mihály Szilágy were smelted from the same metal. Forged with the same philosophies. Hammered by the same diplomatic struggles. Sharpened by the same ambitions.

Dracula buried his head in his hands and mourned the loss of his greatest friend. He did not leave his chambers, refused food, and called only for more wine.

The following morning Dracula left his childhood home —where two years prior Mihály Szilágy had made his battle headquarters—and rode to Cârta monastery. He needed a place to mourn in private.

This time the monastery on the Olt River, with its tall stone tower, chapel, and wooden lodgings did not mend his spirits. Neither did meditating or reading. Not even translating the *Book of the Şolomonari* brought Dracula comfort.

There was only one way to soothe his heartache and honor his dearest friend. Avenge Mihály Szilágy's murder. End, once and for all, Mehmed's quest for world domination.

## 42

## Ilona

**Summer 1473**
**Dracula's Mansion in Pest, Hungary**

"No one will suspect a tunnel's entrance here." Vlad flashes his wolfish grin.

My gaze sweeps across the small, cold, foul-smelling privy. A wood bench with a single hole adjoins the far wall. A decorative wood plank buts up against it.

I cover my nose. "Where is it?"

Vlad pulls me inside, bolts the door, and points to the hole in the bench.

"No." My hands fly to my mouth. "You expect us to climb down there? Where we urinate and defecate?"

Vlad chuckles. "It was my original idea but the size of the hole would have to be too big. No, *iubirea mea*, this is the entrance." He runs his fingers along the decorative plank fixed against the wall. "Here is one latch. Can you find the other?"

My fingers slide along the plank. I snort with unladylike delight, it evoking a memory of our first tunnel excursion into Buda's labyrinth. "Found it."

The metal latch is tiny, hidden between the ridges and gray stone. I lift the latch. "Now what?"

"Push down."

The decorative plank descends behind the seat by way of a chiseled groove.

"Very clever. A tunnel next to the pit." I cover my nose and peer into the blackness.

"This way, my lady." Eyes alight with glee, Vlad gathers his robes tight around him, lies across the bench, and rolls into the blackness. "Roll twice." His deep voice sounds like it's coming from the bottom of a well.

How did Vlad build this tunnel without my knowing? And while I was doing my business over this very hole!

I gather my skirt, a difficult task because it is more voluminous than Vlad's robe, lie upon the bench and roll.

Once. Twice. I land in Vlad's arms.

He plants a robust kiss on my lips. "You must close the entrance immediately." He sets me on my feet.

"How? I can't see anything."

Vlad takes my hand and guides it to a ledge cut into the stone. "Tinderbox and lantern." With a deftness perfected from primitive conditions on the battlefield, he strikes flint against steel. The spark jumps onto a charcloth, and a few gentle puffs ignites the slim timber splint.

"Pull the lever down." Vlad holds aloft the lantern. "Practice this until you do it quickly." He loops his arm through mine as though we are about to enter a grand gala. "Shall we?"

We walk in a halo of light, the ground sloping first gently, then steeply as we continue.

"Do not talk," whispers Vlad. "Let the tunnel speak to you. Hear its space. Listen to its breath."

I hear nothing but my skirt *whisk-whisk-whisk* across the ground.

Then I hear it. Feel it. The soundless din of an emptiness

that is full of expectancy. The tunnel is alive, warmed by our bodies, inhales our breath, and yet needs nothing from us.

This tunnel is unlike Buda's cavernous labyrinth of ancient drawings and sculptures. This escape route is roughly hewn and smells of damp earth and rock. It does, however, have several grottos, which Vlad hurries past.

"Surely we have walked the length of our manse and courtyards by now." My voice echoes as though disembodied.

"Yes." His whisper sounds like a hiss.

The tunnel ends at a wall of hard-packed dirt.

"The tunnel is not finished?" I gesture to the small trowel on the ground.

A wry smile flits across Vlad's face. He strokes his beard and says nothing.

There is no door, no obvious door, so I look for a latch. Vlad drums his fingers against the wall pretending impatience.

"Ah, found it." I drop to my knees, brush away the thin veneer of soil over a wooden hatch. "Too easy." I pull on the handle and the hatch flies open. "Dirt?" I sink my fingers into the cool black earth. "It's a trick? Where is the exit?"

"Where indeed." Vlad rocks back on his heels, his grin twisted with amusement.

Refusing to be bested, I stare into the darkness. "How many grottos are there?"

"Five."

"Does each have a false door?"

"All but one."

I stand, brush off the dirt, and tug on his arm. "Show me."

I lift my skirt to keep up as Vlad races back down the tunnel. He turns into the first grotto and holds up the lantern. On the ground beside a carved door lay one of Vlăduţ's toy soldiers.

I rap on the door. "Is it a fake?"

"Hopefully looking for a latch that doesn't exist will stall them for a few minutes."

We move on to the next grotto where a bloody handprint stains an old timber door.

I open the door and peer into darkness. "Another trick."

"The tunnel goes about twenty feet."

"More time wasters."

The third grotto has a hole cut into the ceiling, a rope ladder unfurled to the ground.

"False passages will give you and the boys more time to escape." Vlad gives the rope ladder a tug.

The next cavern is stacked to the ceiling with crates. Vlad opens a few, and I look inside. Blankets, dried beans, hard cheeses, casks of wine, and water—the normal provisions. The last crate is empty.

Vlad lowers the lantern inside. "Do you see it?"

"See what?"

Vlad pushes a wooden slat. The bottom swings open and a black chasm yawns wide below.

"A tunnel beneath a tunnel. You're a genius." I hoist my skirts to my thighs.

"That's why I love you." Vlad waits as I climb into the crate. He follows close, the lantern lighting the steep stairs.

The tunnel is narrow, a shade wider than Vlad's shoulders.

"It's designed that you don't need any light." Vlad spreads his fingertips. "Darkness is only frightening when you lose your bearings. You have only to touch both walls and run."

"Headfirst into the exit?" My fingertips graze the smooth rock.

"Ten feet from the exit, the stones are rough. Try it. Run." He extinguishes the lantern and gives me a nudge. "Courage, *iubirea mea.*"

I start at a brisk walk, then a jog, finally running as fast as my skirt allows. My soul exhilarates in the thrill. My skin tingles with pleasure. I am free! Desire pulses between my legs.

Rough stones. I stop, panting, sweat beading at my temple. "We're here," I gasp though I see only a black abyss.

Vlad's arms snake around me, his breath hot on my neck. "Vlăduţ and Mircea must have their sword with them."

My neck relaxes into his shoulder, this dark jaunt fueling my lust. "Who can escape with us?"

"You and the children are all that matter." He turns my cheek and thrusts his tongue into my eager mouth. Without sight, his taste and touch sharpen, the only sensations in this void. He brushes a strand of hair from my cheek. "Kindness be damned. Do not try to save Bernádett or Gizella. It might be our sons' undoing."

"I understand." I recalled Father's words after he showed me Buda's labyrinth. *Save yourself. No one else matters.*

Vlad presses my hand to a wood door. "Feel it."

I giggle as his other hand wanders over my breasts. "How can I ever concentrate if you keep doing that?"

"I want you, Ilona." Vlad murmurs in my ear, his need pressed into my back.

I am wet with wanting. Ready to receive him. Then I feel the latch. The door creaks open with a tug, and a sliver of half-light reveals a narrow ladder spiraling into the ceiling.

"It opens into a barn floor of a trusted friend. Do not go to Buda palace. The mercenaries will expect it and have men stationed nearby to abduct you." Vlad nibbles my ear.

I wiggle my buttocks into him. "Where do you want us to go?"

"To Oradea monastery." Vlad slips his fingers under my bodice, finds a nipple and rubs. "It's a day and half's ride. Send word to Matthias from there and go to Buda only with an armed company of soldiers."

I arch my back and sigh. "Have you discussed this with him?"

Vlad rubs the other nipple, already taut with pleasure. "Our sons' lives have great political value to him."

"We are all pawns in this royal chess match."

"The secret, *iubirea mea*, is to make certain you are the player, not the one being played." His hand slides out of my bodice.

We return, walking this time, and Vlad tells me about the difficulties encountered with the tunnel's construction.

"Who designed it?" I ask.

"Me. What good is a secret passage if someone else knows its secrets?"

"What about the diggers and laborers?"

"Sadly, all died of tunnel fever shortly after completion."

"I have never heard of—oh…yes, a terrible illness. I hope they did not suffer long." My voice falters, and I am glad Vlad cannot see me wincing.

It is an unfortunate and unavoidable truth. Workers give their life for their masters. Food tasters, lime burners, leech collectors, fullers, and tanners; all dangerous trades. So it must be with diggers of secret tunnels.

"They died without pain. I had their wages delivered to their families." Vlad stops at a grotto nearest the stairs, lights the lantern, and walks inside.

My mouth drops open. A thick featherbed lays on the floor. Atop its fur blanket is a long velvet rope, a small metal hoop, leather straps, several feathers, a cat o' nine whip of silk, and a linen sack. Vlad unties the sack and scatters a handful of rose petals.

"No one can hear us down here, *iubirea mea*."

I drop to my knees and hoist my skirt to my waist. "Do it." I command, my body already tingling with anticipation.

Vlad lets out a lecherous groan then smacks my bare buttocks with the cat o-nine tails.

"Harder." I shake my ass. "Or I won't use the ring on your cock."

"Like this?" Vlad strikes hard, the sting sending vibrations of desire into my core.

Much later, only the scents of crushed roses and our decadent pleasures linger in the air, the echoes of our rapture having seeped into the cold earth.

## 43

The sun beats down on the inner courtyard while Gizella, Bernádett, and I toss balls to Vlăduț and Nicolae.

"Lady Mother, he's cheating." Vlăduț balls his fists when Nicolae swats the ball away.

"Vlăduț, he—" I hear shouts and put my finger to my lips.

We stop and listen. The shouts come from the front courtyard. Gizella takes Nicolae's hand and slides me a worried look.

No thief dare enters our home. Vlad's reputation is renown, and yet a sliver of fear pricks my composure.

More shouts. The sliver widens, chills my blood.

I clasp Vlăduț's hand. "Everyone, come with me."

Together we follow the shouts toward the main entrance hall.

Bernádett, her face fear-blanched, leans close. "I'm afraid."

"There are guards at the gate." I pull a sword, a gift from a loyal boyar, from its wall mount and wrap my fingers around its jewel-encrusted hilt. I'm surprised, it is much heavier than the one I practice with.

Vlăduț's eyes are as round as platters. "Do you know how to use it?"

I jab the air, and Vlăduț squeals with delight.

"May I have one, too? Lord Father only lets me practice with a wood sword."

"Your father will give you a real sword when you are ready and not a day earlier." I tussle his hair.

"What's going on?" I move past the servants hovering around the door.

Hands on his hips, Vlad stands in the middle of the courtyard. Clad in linen tunic and breeches, his hair falls loose over his shoulders. My breath catches at his dominant stance.

Opposite him, three of our guards and one Buda palace guard loom over a man on his knees.

"Lord Father." Vlăduț pushes by me.

Vlad turns his head and beckons us forward. He scoops up Vlăduț and kisses the top of his head. "Tell me, son, which man is the criminal?"

Vlăduț puffs out his lips, looks back and forth from the guards to the kneeling man. "The ugly man in old clothes."

"Neither clothing or appearance make a criminal." Vlad shifts his gaze at me, sees my sword, his face warm with proud surprise.

Vlăduț scrunches his face. "Then who?"

"The guard invading my home." Vlad takes my blade and points it at the Buda palace guard. "Instead of asking permission to enter and explaining the reason for the intrusion, the guard took it upon himself to enter a prince's home. This shows a lack of respect to me, my family, and for those in my employ." He sets Vlăduț back on his feet.

"Prince Vlad, forgive my transgression." The Buda guard's voice quivers with fear. "I was wrong, but I was intent on catching the thief and didn't think to ask your permission."

Vlad's face looks as if he sucks on a sour lemon. "You

didn't think. A problematic trait for someone guarding Buda castle. I will be doing His Majesty a favor by relieving him of such an idiot." Vlad hefts the hilt by both hands and swings.

The Buda guard's head drops to the ground.

Vlăduț screeches with delight, jumps up and down. "Do it again. Do it again."

Vlad turns to our guards. "Release the thief."

The thief's breeches are wet with fear. "Thank you, Prince Vlad." He drops to his knees and kisses Vlad's boots. "God bless you. God bless your family."

Vlad scowls. "You ran all the way from Buda, forded a river, and scaled my wall. Such athleticism should be put to more lawful use." Vlad taps the thief's leg with the sword's broad side. "If I ever find you in my courtyard again, I will kill you. And your death will not be as swift as his." He nudges the Buda guard's head.

Tears soak the thief's cheeks. "Yes, my lord. Thank you, my lord. Bless you, my lord."

Vlad takes Vlăduț's hand as we walk inside. "*Quis custodiet ipsos?*"

Vlăduț wrinkles his nose and scratches his head. "Who will guard the guards?"

"You are already a Latin scholar." Vlad beams with pride.

"I don't want to be a scholar, I want to be a warrior."

"Princes must be both." Vlad bends down on one knee and runs his thumb over Vlăduț's palms. "Too soft. I will tell the teacher to give you a real blade."

"Thank you, Lord Father. I will make you proud. I will kill Turks and all the bad men."

A shadow darkens Vlad's face, and I wonder if he is thinking about his own unfulfilled vows, promises to the Order of the Dragon, promises to avenge my father's death.

"We will kill them together." Vlad meets my eye and presses his lips together with a hopeful smile. With a nudge Vlăduț scurries back to the house. "This afternoon's exercise in swordsmanship sharpens my desires for another sport."

"What sport is that, my lord?" I run my tongue over my lips, eager for the taste of him. Swords and blood set fire to my basest desires. Vlad's show of strength and power makes me hungry for him.

One side of his mouth curves upward. "Your favorite kind." He throws me over his shoulder, strides inside, and bounds up the stairs two at a time.

I am wet with desire as he pushes me over the desk, lifts my skirt, and pokes the blade's tip into my buttocks. With his other hand he shines my pleasure knot, the two points of sensation driving me skyward to paradise. My body tenses and throbs until I explode in rapture.

Vlad's hand flicks across my buttocks, then shows me the drop of blood on his finger.

"Is that mine?" I still tingle and glisten.

"It is, *iubirea mea*." He thrusts hard into me and takes me to paradise several more times.

Much later and after we take our meal together in bed, Vlad gets the *Book of the Şolomonari* from his desk.

"Why did you steal it?" Complete honesty is a great benefit of our relationship. When two people indulge their darkest desires, there is no room for falseness and pretense.

Vlad opens the book, his hand drifting across the pages with a loving touch. "Wisdom like this should not be hidden away. It should be available to those who are worthy."

"You."

"Yes, me. I can end a battle by summoning a storm. I can rid villages of *strigoi*. Cure disease." He taps the book. "These secrets can bring prosperity to my people."

"Those are God's dominions not yours."

"God does these things through the Şolomonari. Why not me? There is nothing unnatural here." Vlad's eyes reflect the light of infinite possibilities. "If you believe God is a divine

entity without limit, creator of heaven and earth, then everything—everything—he made is ours for the taking."

I never win a religious debate with Vlad, but I try anyway.
"But from what you've read to me, these wisdoms bear no
resemblance to Catholic doctrines."

Vlad links his fingers through mine. "This transcends any
one religion, Ilona." He lifts his arms, our fingers entwined,
his green eyes holding me captive. "The secret to life is all
around us. I want to know the unknowable. Don't you?"

Do I? It will require abandoning a lifetime of Catholic
indoctrination. "Only if you are by my side."

"I FORBID IT." Vlad blocks the doorway, his arms crossed, his
face hard.

My lips twitch. "Then you force me to defy you."

Vlad swears in Turkish yet his green eyes sparkle. "I'll
lock you in your chambers."

"The one in the tunnel?" I whisper in this ear. "Sounds
like fun."

"You're incorrigible." He shakes his head in mock exasperation.

Our taste for rough intimacies brings new life to our
marriage. Vlad seeks my company during mealtimes, for a
game of cards, and conversation. He indulges my whims and
showers me with gifts. He teaches me sword fighting, a skill,
he insists, that may save my life. His affection and trust
embolden me, and he pays the price. My boldness either
arouses or annoys him.

Vlad tugs me close. "Why must you do this, Ilona?"

"I do it for you," I whisper. "To repair your damaged
reputation. Dismiss my ladies and I'll tell you why I must do
this."

With a word, Bernádett and Gizella scurry from the room.

Vlad sits down and gives me an expectant look. "Explain."

"You murdered the Buda guard without just cause. The lesson is lost if the student is dead, my lord."

His mouth twists, his muscles undulating under his skin. "I—"

I set my fingers on his lips. "You murdered the Buda guard whose only fault was his single-minded purpose. A trait you admire. Allow me to make restitution to his family. He had a wife and three children. It will be an act of Christian charity on your behalf."

"I will send a messenger."

"Too cold-hearted. I must visit the widow myself. I'll hold her hand, offer my handkerchief, and weep with her."

Vlad's eyes taper. "You will undermine my penalty for trespassing."

"Not at all. We will cry about fate and the burdens of being a wife. We will cry because we do not understand our beneficent God, who, in His mercy, brought her husband to His bosom early." I sit on his lap and rake my nails over his day-old beard. "I will press enough coin into the wife's hand that her children will never go hungry again."

Vlad searches my eyes. "What's the real reason for this noble charity?"

"You know me too well." I smooth my skirt and take a deep breath. "The day after you killed the guard I went to the chapel. In the middle of my prayer for you—"

"For me?" He quirks an eyebrow.

"I pray for you every day." I pat his cheek. "Yesterday, in the middle of my prayer all the candles went out. I thought nothing of it, a draft from under the door." I run my fingers through his hair. "I was asking God to absolve you of sins committed in His name during battle..."

"Go on." Vlad's voice is gruff even though he leans into my caresses.

"I had just made the Sign of the Cross when the blood on the crucified Jesus glowed red. Everything, every pew and relic, disappeared in the blackness but Christ's blood."

Vlad rolls his eyes. "It's not Christ's blood, it is paint."

"Not that day. It was blood. A sign from God."

Vlad kisses my palm. "What is your interpretation, oh Great Diviner?"

"Bloody Jesus wants me to visit the Buda guard's widow."

Vlad shifts in the chair, his expression swinging from amusement to admiration. "If the chapel walls ever ooze blood tell me immediately." Vlad plants a kiss on my forehead. "Go visit her."

I OFFER my heartfelt condolences to the young widow. Together we weep over life's cruelties and God's will.

"Prince Vlad's knows this will never replace your husband." I press a small purse full of coins into her hands.

She unties the string, her eyes widening with surprise. "This is more than—" Fresh tears stream down her cheeks as she clutches the purse to her breast.

Feeling like a fraud, I depart with heavy legs and heart. My intent was genuine—restitution had to be made—but my soul sinks into a quagmire over my dubious motives.

"That was very kind of you, my lady," says Gizella as the carriage rattles homeward.

"Even if it's motivated by pity and guilt?"

Gizella presses her lips together, concern knitted across her brow. "Smiths burn their hands while forging royal swords. Stonemasons break their arms when building castles. Workers die falling off a buttress. Soldiers die for king and country. Do you pity them? Feel guilt for their accidents?

Nobility is bound by higher rules than common folk. Kings and princes must sacrifice a few to save many."

I nod, her point well-reasoned. "You think like a princess."

Gizella pulls up her sleeve and points to the blue veins on her pale wrist. "No royal blood here. I must settle for a handsome boyar with a castle and property."

I blink, suddenly seeing Gizella not as my lady's maid but as an unmarried woman longing for a husband. "I will tell Prince Vlad it is time he found you a suitable husband."

Gizella's brows shoot up and her hands cover her heart. "Thank you, my lady."

I have done two good deeds today, yet I receive no satisfaction from either. Making restitution to a widow, finding Gizella a husband, these are trivial gestures. They make scant difference in a world plagued by war, hunger, and sickness. No wonder Vlad seeks the wisdom in the Şolomonari's book. How can he, or any sovereign, come to terms with all the pain and death they order in the name of leadership and righteousness?

There is not enough coin in all the world to atone for the deaths of thousands and thousands.

## 44

The tub sits in a wide ribbon of morning sun that divides my chambers into light and shadow. I sink into the steamy bath, the sunlight and water enveloping me in a cocoon of serenity.

Except Bernádett's sulky frown spoils my enjoyment.

"What's bothering you?" I rest my head on a pillow.

Bernádett tucks a red lock of hair behind her ear. "The guard's beheading brought back a long-buried memory of when I was a child."

Any hope for a calming bath vanishes like a sizzling drop of water on a cold floor. "What of?"

"I recall Mother telling me about a noble who sliced off women's nipples and shoved burning pokers into their nether parts for the sin of adultery." Bernádett pours hot rose-scented water over my shoulders.

"Stories like that are meant to frighten daughters into staying chaste."

"It wasn't a story, my lady." Bernádett's soapy ministrations stop. "Mother told me his name…Prince Vlad."

"You are mistaken." My voice is as cold as the water is

hot. "Your mother needed a name, someone everyone knew, to make the story believable."

"But—"

"Prince Vlad would never do that. It's a story, Bernádett, like all those other lies about him. Surely, living in the manse all these years you see he is not the tyrant others made him out to be."

"Yes, my lady." Her voice is stiff. Her eyes, downcast.

"Your mother did what many mothers do to protect their daughters. My nanny frightened me with stories about a child-eating Bába living in the labyrinth." I chew on my lip. What else does she remember about her mother? Does she know her mother was Father's mistress? Or that her uncle was a Şolomonar? How much does Bernádett remember about her childhood?

Gizella brings towels into the room and the moment for divulging secrets scurries away like a mouse in a hole.

Gizella wraps a towel around me. Bernádett fetches my clothes. Two women who serve my every need and whim: I know very little about either of them.

"You are safe here," I whisper reassuringly to Bernádett as she helps me into my dress.

As Gizella fixes my hair I recall the outrageous stories told at the Cow & Sow, the inn we visited in disguise. They claimed Vlad drank blood and ate babies. Vlad had scoffed at those stories. Yet, he has told me before that there is always a scrap of truth in every outrageous lie. The whore's story proved true. Vlad likes to tie me up. But if one story is true does that mean all the stories are true?

I swallow hard, dry-mouthed, a sour fear wedged in my throat. There is much I do not know about Vlad—details about his first two reigns, the horrors of his childhood imprisonment.

But I know one thing about my husband. Vlad would

never slice off a woman's nipples. Or burn her womb. I intend to get to the bottom of these stories. This morning. At breakfast.

Sunlight winks through the gathering clouds, our table lit with brief bright flares.

I spread a dollop of apricot jam on a thick slab of bread. "Why do people make-up fanciful stories about their rulers?" My voice is as warm and breezy as a summer morning.

Vlad cocks his head, his eyes narrow, searching for the intent behind my question. "I should imagine there are three reasons. They either want to glorify, vilify, or make their king more like them."

"You tell me all the time that these stories have a bit of truth to them. Even the most horrific." I dab the napkin to my sticky sweet lips.

Vlad leans back in the chair and rubs his chin. "I will tell you two different stories and you will tell me which is true and which false. If you are correct, I will not ask the name of the person spreading outrageous tales about me."

I drop my napkin, my cheeks burning at being found out. This hasn't gone to plan at all. "If I'm wrong?"

"The disrespectful person will be dealt with." Vlad rubs his hands together with a cat-drank-the-cream grin.

Breakfast curdles in my stomach, and I shift uneasily in the chair. I don't want Bernádett to be 'dealt with.'

"Fine." My voice is light, pretending indifference.

If Vlad sees right through me, he gives no sign.

"Here is the first story. One day, two Genoan diplomats wearing fine robes and elegant hats visited my court. Their hats had two layers, an elegant outer covering and a close-fitting cap beneath. The diplomats removed only their outer hat, bowed low, and heaped flowery praises on me. I asked why they ignored protocol by keeping on their caps. They claimed their own custom forbad them from removing the cap for anyone, be he a pope or a sultan. To show the Genoan diplomats my respect for their lack of respect, I had their caps nailed into their skulls."

My heart races, my mind jumping from one plausible explanation to the next.

"Story two." Vlad gives me no time to respond. "While heading to my castle I met three barefoot Benedictine monks. Brothers Hans, Michael, and Jacob. When I inquired about their abbey they proudly admitted to being banished, exiled for reading Saint Bernard's writings and converting to Catholicism. Curious as to why they would forsake their Romanian faith, I invited them to my castle to discuss religious philosophy. They accepted and followed me home. After supper we discussed salvation. I asked how God views my killing all the terrible sinners and evildoers. Would I be deemed a saint for ridding the land of the ungodly?" Vlad leans back, fingers locked behind his head. "Brother Michael said all who are repentant receive salvation and cites the biblical villain Barabbas as proof. This, the story goes, made me happy. Brother Hans, on the other hand, proclaimed me a ruthless tyrant, a despot, the spawn of Satan. He claimed I ruled without remorse or compassion, a murderer of women, children, and babes. He damned me to Hell's eternal flames."

I cringe at this, yet Vlad's smile thickens.

"Brother Hans demanded I justify my cruelty. I explained that felling a tree does not prevent its roots from growing, and that Wallachia was like a field, fertile and rich, which must be cleared before new seeds could be sown. Treacherous boyars and wicked thieves were the trees invading the field and preventing new growth. I was merely a diligent farmer, keeping my fields free of choking roots that stunted my people's opportunity for economic success. Brother Hans was so enraged his face turned as red as a beet, and he shouted that my crimes were so great, so intolerable, and so evil that the entire populace of heaven—every seraphim and cherub, every saint and every celestial inhabitant—would rage against my entrance to heaven. Unmoved by his despicable insults, I tell Brother Hans he was a traitor to our Orthodox religion and must be punished. Then I beat him to death with my bare fists, skewered his body on a pole, and stuck it in front of the monastery." Vlad unfolds his arms to smack both palms on the table. "Which story is true?"

"Mmmm…." My fingers drum the table, tap across the taut layers of truth, lies, and exaggerations. I must answer correctly for Bernádett's sake.

"No stalling."

"I'm composing my answer." I drum louder. Then it comes to me, as clear as a mountain stream. "The story of the Genoan diplomats refusing to remove their skull caps is true. Their refusal, especially after you gave them a second chance, showed their contempt for your court and was an intolerable breach of protocol. Diplomats know better than to insult a sovereign. The story of the monks is also true. As I see it, Brother Hans was not a godly man because he preferred insults and damning to kindness and forgiving. Brother Hans forgot the Old Testament. He forgot that God loved Solomon, a vengeful ruler with seven hundred wives. Since Brother Hans knew the penalty for insulting his prince, he left you no choice." I sit up straight. "The stories are also false."

Vlad's mouth twitches into a half smile.

"Their falseness is in the details not told, the facts left out. Perhaps Brother Hans attacked you. Perhaps the Genoan diplomats were actually mercenaries. Two things, however, are quite obvious. Although the stories are meant to slander you, they reveal your masterful leadership." I grin, my teeth clamped in nervous anticipation.

Vlad claps slowly, his half smile unleashed into an expansive grin. "Your answer is masterful as well. And because of it, I will leave you to reprimand the person spreading old stories about me." Vlad stands up and takes my hand. "Your diplomatic answer also merits the next lesson in the *Book of the Şolomonari*...a trip to see their ritual."

## 45

# Vlad

**Winter 1462**
**Dracula's Castle in Tîrgovişte, Wallachia**

"These demands are absurd." Dracula thrusts the letter with such force it flew off the edge. "Mehmed has no intention of reaching an agreement." Dracula would not make the same mistake as his father. He would never trust a sultan. Any sultan.

R. Farma, Dracula's trusted advisor, snatched the letter as it fluttered off the table. He was a thin man with an angular face, hawkish nose, and the eyes of a hungry lynx. What he lacked in brawn he made up for in shrewd intellect.

Dracula gulped his wine, which did not take the edge off the hot sharp anger rising from deep within. "Does Mehmed really think I'll agree to meet Hamza Pasha, his chief falconer, no less, at Sin Giorgiu to sign a treaty? A small army could hide inside its parapets, even more in its four towers."

R. Farma tapped the map of the island fortress, its only access a single bridge over the Danube. "Any ideas?"

Dracula banged the goblet on the table and spun the map about. "There has to be a way..."

R. Farma cleared his throat after several silent moments. "What do we do about Thomas Catavolinos?"

"That duplicitous Greek can't suspect a thing. We can't kill him either. Mehmed will know we're on to his trick if he doesn't receive his daily updates." Dracula rubbed his palms together. "I will play Mehmed's game, but by my rules, not his."

R. Farma, twirling the ends of his waxed mustache, grinned with anticipation with what he knew would be a cunningly brilliant plan. "Will these rules require siege equipment?"

Vlad stood, laced his fingers at the back of his neck. "No."

R. Farma brows jumped to his receding hairline. "How do you expect to breach the walls?"

His earlier anger cooling to cold calculation, Vlad bent forward over the map and walked his fingers over the road to Sin Giorgiu. "We won't need to breach the walls. The Turks will let us walk through the gate."

DRESSED in extravagant finery and thick furs, Dracula's diplomatic party rode toward Sin Giorgiu. Neither fallen trees nor muddy bogs delayed their steady progress.

A few leagues from Sin Giorgiu in a grove of trees, a red-faced and shivering Thomas Catavolinos slowed his horse. He tugged off his gloves. "My hands are as frozen as the twixt between my wife's thighs. Take pity on this old man and let's pause to build a fire where I can warm my fingers."

Dracula's loud exhalation steamed cold in the frigid air. "Warm them at the fortress."

Thomas Catavolinos drew alongside Dracula. "Warm hands are better for enticing a wench to grease my cock."

Though Dracula's neck hair bristled with catlike instincts, he kept his voice easy. "I will not keep Hamza Pasha waiting because his fair-weather envoy's cold hands will not entice a hot woman."

Thomas Catavolinos's laugh rang hollow, practiced, and much too loudly.

Muscles tensed for the inevitable, Dracula glanced at his three closest men, who boxed in Thomas Catavolinos with practiced skill.

Several birds flew out of the snow-coated brambles.

"Good men of my court," shouted Dracula, his pulse quickening with excitement. "Tonight we feast with the Bey of Nicopolis."

It was the signal.

Dracula's entourage gripped their swords, alert to every flittering ice-glazed branch, each crunch of snow, any odd sound.

Mehmed's mercenaries sprung from the trees, scimitars flashing.

Thomas Catavolinos's hand, miraculously thawed, went for his sword. Dracula swung his flanged mace, knocked Thomas Catavolinos from his horse.

Dracula's entourage threw off their foppish disguises. The elite members of the *armaş* grabbed their morning stars and gripped their swords.

Mehmed's mercenaries sucked in their collective breath and exhaled expletives. They had expected an easy slaughter of dandified diplomats. Not Dracula's *armaş*.

Cries and shouts and clanging swords rose above the hoary trees as Turkish blood seeped into the snow.

Hamza Pasha stood outside the fray and watched his ambush fail with a chill that had nothing to do with the weather. He spun about, three steps away from disappearing behind a snow-covered thicket when he heard his name shouted over the clamor. He turned and watched Dracula, a main-gauche in one hand and a rapier in the other, hack his way through the fray. His people taught him well. Too well.

With elegant artistry, Dracula crossed his blades, warded off a blow before swinging around to plunge his rapier into an unsuspecting Turk. Hamza Pasha knew Vlad Dracula was happiest during battle, knew he was a warrior prince with a philosopher's soul. But Pasha Hamza was not ready to die. He ran.

"Pasha Hamza!" Dracula raced toward the fleeing pasha. "Face me, coward!"

Hamza Pasha stopped, spun about, and lifted his scimitar with resigned determination. Though he was no match for the young prince, Hamza Pasha lunged. Dracula parried it as effortlessly as a hawk's swoop. Hamza Pasha swiped with a diagonal cut but Dracula's full pass tore the blade from the pasha's fist.

Hamza Pasha dropped to his knees, his contempt spit out in Turkish. "We intercepted your letters promising fealty to King Matthias." He gazed down at the sword Dracula held to his throat. "The son repeats the father's treachery."

Dracula winced, the memory of the punishments he endured by the sultan as raw as though it happened yesterday. Fortunately, there was a difference. The Turks did not have his son. "Are you ready to die?" He pressed the blade to the pasha's throat.

Hamza Pasha lifted his haughty chin, his eyes scornful pinpoints. "Be smart, Prince Vlad. Give into Mehmed-*i sānī*, the greatest ruler the world will ever know. Surrender now and we will negotiate a fair truce."

Dracula guffawed, impressed by the old man's courage. "It takes a fearless man to negotiate with his knees in the mud and a sword kissing his throat."

"It is Mehmed-*i sānī* you should kiss," said Hamza Pasha.

"My brother Radu has done enough of that for the both of us," Dracula growled.

"My lord." The blood-splattered *armaş* captain ran forward. "Every Turk is dead." He jabbed his thumb over his shoulders behind him. "It was too easy, my lord. We cut them down like saplings. Not enough skill in them for us to work up a sweat."

"Good, you can work up a sweat between a wench's thighs at Sin Giurgiu." Dracula's attention returned to the pasha. "Lock him and Catavolinos, if he's still alive, in manacles and take them back to Tîrgovişte." He knocked the pasha unconscious with his main-gauche.

The captain nudged the pasha's leg. "The dungeon, my lord?"

"Too good for them. Give them a lofty view from a very tall stick." Dracula regarded the pasha's body, surprised he did not feel the rush of triumph. "Tell the men to proceed with part two of the plan."

Dracula's cavalry arrived a few hours later. They found a pile of snow-dusted naked dead bodies on the road, and the *armaş* dressed as Turkish mercenaries.

Dracula, wearing the pasha's turban, satin robe, and sable cloak, pointed to the feeble glow of light behind the thick gray clouds. "Wait for the signal." He turned to the Turkish-dressed captain. "It's time."

They left the cavalry hidden in the grove and galloped out onto the wide plain toward Sin Giurgiu.

"*Kapıyı aç!*" Open the gate! Dracula shouted in flawless Turkish. "This land is cursed with cold winds and frigid women."

"Identify yourself." From the top of the guardhouse, a soldier aimed his bow and arrow at Dracula.

"I am Omar Pahsazada, son of Hamza, the Bey of Nicopolis." Dracul's voice oozed a haughty authority. "I have a letter from Mehmed-*i sānī*."

"My apologies, Pahsazada bey." The guard lowered his bow. "We are expecting someone else."

The gate lifted.

Dracula and his disguised *armaş* went inside and dispersed through the fortress. Within moments they set fire to the hay and lit anything that ignited. The occupants, panicked by the sudden fires, ran about shouting for buckets.

"We're under attack," shouted the guard commander. His realization came too late.

Hiding in the grove, Dracula's cavalry saw the gray smoke plumes in the sky and charged toward the fortress. They arrived to the victory music of screams and shouts as Dracula hoisted his flag above the tower wall.

### Spring 1462: Dracula's Castle in Tîrgovişte, Wallachia

"I DO IT FOR CHRISTIANITY." Dracula slammed his fist on the throne.

The Hungarian envoy reeled back, silently cursing his bad luck at having been tasked with delivering this message. "King Matthias is awed—amazed, in truth—with your triumphs against the Turks. He praised your victories to emissaries from Vienna, Ferrara, Milan, Bologna, Prague, and Rome. His Majesty was amused by the sack of noses and ears you sent as proof of your victories."

"I did not send them for Matthias's entertainment." Dracula spoke through clenched teeth. He focused on his thumbnail scratching at the gilded arm of the chair until he reined in his anger. He looked up, his face a steely mask of control. "I need soldiers, weapons, and money."

The envoy winced, pretended embarrassment. "King Matthias's treasury is depleted and—"

"Depleted." Dracula rolled his eyes. "I hope King

Matthias beheaded his treasurer for such a gross misappropriation of funds." He stuffed down the urge to pummel the lying envoy. "Every day King Matthias waits is another day the Turks advance toward Hungary. Wallachia is the door. Do you want the sultan's army to go through it? Last month, Vizier Mahmud's military—eighteen thousand troops—burned our villages, raped our women, and enslaved our boys. My men fought back. Decimated their forces. Next time we might not be as lucky. Because as sure as the sun sets in the west, the sultan will continue his forward march into Hungary. My people do not have the luxury of waiting. And neither will King Matthias when the sultan burns his villages."

Beads of sweat glistened on the envoy's forehead. "King Matthias is well aware—"

"If Wallachia falls every king and prince north of here is at risk. My victories keep your people safe." Dracula spread his hands wide. "Does King Matthias question my allegiance?"

The beads turned into rivulets that ran down the side of the envoy's face. A calm Prince Vlad was more frightening than an angry one. "I told you all I know. I await a message you may have for His Majesty."

Dracula beckoned the sweaty envoy forward. "Tell King Matthias I am willing to wed one of his family members."

The envoy cleared his fear-clogged throat. "The king has no daughters."

"No, but his deceased uncle, Mihály Szilágy, has three."

## Summer 1462: Dracula's Castle in Tîrgovişte, Wallachia

SULTAN MEHMED'S humiliating defeat at Giorgiu did not go unpunished. He sent his finest commanders, Mihaloğlu Ali,

Turahanoğlu Omer, Delioğlu Umur, the grand Vizier Mahmud, to attack Wallachia. Sultan Mehmed also sent Radu.

Thousands of janissaries, hundreds of bodyguards, thousands of slave solders, archers, and spear-bearing *azabs* amassed in Philippoupolis, Bulgaria. The sixty-thousand-strong army had one task: Decimate the legions of *Kazîglu Bey*, Lord Impaler.

"Our *armaş* is too small." R. Farma, his lynx eyes predatory, paced back and forth in the crowded council chambers.

"Which is why the Turks will not expect our farmers, women, and children to attack." Dracula forced a confident smile despite the nagging doubt that gnawed like a rat at his moral code. Wallachia had no choice. Everyone had to fight if they hoped to beat back the Turks.

"Farmers have no weapons," said Galeş, a young boyar with small eyes that sunk beneath a protruding brow.

"They have scythes and axes and hammers. If they can kill a deer with a bow and arrow, they can kill a Turk." Dracula's gaze raked over his advisors. "We will prevail because we are David to Mehmed's Goliath."

The bewildered boyars exchanged glances thick with unspoken doubts.

Dracula stood and circled the table. "Does anyone know why the young shepherd David was able to slay the giant warrior Goliath?"

"Lucky shot?" laughed an old boyar with more white hair sprouting from his ears than his head.

"Power of God," suggested Galeş.

"Neither." Dracula pressed his palms to the table, bent forward, and met every skeptical face. "Allow me to refresh your memory about a lesson in strategy. Goliath wore heavy armor over his slow-moving girth. In his hands he held weapons for hand-to-hand combat. David was young, light, and agile. As a shepherd he killed rabbits, birds, and other small prey with a single stone. He whipped his sling over his head and raced down the mountain—his mountain—nimble as a goat. Goliath never expected David to attack him from far away."

The boyars' eyes flickered with understanding. A few bobbed their heads.

"The sultan's army is Goliath, slow and ponderous. Their one hundred and twenty cannons will sink in Romanian mud. Our dense forests, narrow passes, and sodden marshes will slow them down." Dracula made a fist and slammed it into his palm. "We are David. Small and swift. We know every craggy path, sweet stream, and hidden mountain trail. Just as Goliath did not expect David to use a sling against him, the Turks will not expect our swift attacks." Dracula banged his fist down on the table, sent wine goblets jumping. "Our archers will rain down arrows from between the trees." He banged again. "We attack at night." A third bang. "We attack in the rain." Bang. "Our forests, our mountains, our villages, our people; these are our greatest assets. What use are the sultan's cannons if their oxen die from poisoned water? What advantage are his siege engines if the road is impassable? What benefit are thousands of armed men if they have no food? What use is an army of slave soldiers when our criminals will be pardoned for killing every Turk crossing their path? We!" *Thump*. "Will!" *Thump*. "Destroy!" *Thump*. "Them!"

## 46

# Ilona

**Late Winter 1474**
**Forest in Hungary**

"I'm not cold, your body keeps me warm." I snuggle against Vlad as we ride on one horse over the snow-dusted, moonlit path.

"Good, we still have farther to go." One hand holds the reins, the other cups the small swell of my belly.

"I think there's snow in my boot." I wiggle my foot, which feels colder than the other.

"You did tell me you wanted to feel the snow on your ass. Did I get carried away?" Vlad's hand settles between my thighs.

"Not at all." My loins warm with the memory of our quick romp in the snow. The horse's gait had aroused me to such an extent I suggested we dismount and mount each other. Vlad had pushed me to my knees in the snow and lifted my skirt. The cold's biting sting felt so good I asked Vlad to scatter snow on my bare buttocks. Instead, he piled it high, patted my nethers with snow, and slammed his heat into me with wild abandon.

"How many times have you seen this ritual?" I pluck an ice-glossed twig from my wool cape.

"Shhh." Vlad stops the horse and points ahead. "Look."

I squint into a dark woodland of elm, ash, and oak. A shadow shifts, takes shape, and three stags, their enormous antlers not yet shed, step into the clearing ahead, the huge silver moon silhouetting their majesty.

It is a fortunate sign.

The second horse tethered behind us snorts and blows impatiently. The three stags turn their heads in perfect unison and bound away.

"As to your question," Vlad clicks his tongue and the horse resumes walking. "I've watched the ritual every year."

The Şolomonari's perform the ritual in Gemenc forest, home to giant stags, ferocious boars, elegant storks, rare butterflies, and palm-sized beetles.

"Are we close?" My eager curiosity ebbs away, a spine-prickling unease in its place.

"Soon." Dracula gives my shoulder a reassuring pat. "You'll know when you see the willows and poplars."

I rest my head against him and am about to close my eyes when the baby moves inside me. "Your third son is strong."

Vlad rests his hand on my belly. "Do not pamper him. My mother coddled Radu and it made him weak-willed in all things."

"Don't blame your mother for the love between Sultan Mehmed and Radu. Aunt Orsulya had a sheltered and peaceful childhood and she prefers women. Or at least she prefers Zsazsa." I wiggle friskily; proving him wrong always requires a playful touch.

Vlad grumbles a concession under his breath.

"Is there any mention of that kind of love in the *Book of the Şolomonari*?"

"No." His muscles tense, and he speeds the horses. "It's not a book of erotica, Ilona."

"Well it should be. Love is a physical and spiritual mystery after all." I rub his thigh, which seems tauter, readier, than a moment ago.

"One of many," he murmurs.

We fall silent for a while and enjoy the forest symphony of rustling branches, hooting owls, and hammering woodpeckers.

Elm, ash, and oak soon give way to drooping ice-glazed willows and snow-dusted towering poplars. My unease sharpens, stretches tight, my soul detecting something my other senses do not.

Vlad stops the horse. "Do you smell it?" His voice lifts with childlike excitement.

I sniff the air. "I smell the forest...oh, there it is. Smoke."

"We walk the rest of the way." Vlad dismounts, lifts me down, tethers the horses, and leads me through the trees. "Wait here. I'll be right back." With a quick cheek kiss he disappears into the arboreal gloom.

My nervousness swells into dread. The night suffocates, the air dank with expectancy. Branches stretch claw-like toward me, their human prey. I hug my body, protect myself from *it*. The air stills, the forest holds its frigid breath.

I stare into the icy darkness, one lungful from a scream.

"Ilona."

I stumble back. Vlad emerges from behind a frosted bramble like a specter, puts his finger to his lips, and beckons me forward. We walk into the shadows, my heart pounding, my skin pricked with alertness. I want to see the Şolomonari ritual. Need to understand Vlad's obsession. But the bone deep chill within me senses danger.

Vlad and I ease between the concealing boughs of a willow, its ice-heavy branches drooping to the ground.

Seven Şolomonari in white robes stand on the riverbank and chant a haunting plainsong not too unlike a priestly choir.

Except they croon such macabre notes every hair on my body bristles.

Vlad is serene, his face soft with wonderment. One prolonged eerie note later, the seven Şolomonari lift their torches skyward.

"They burn bundles of dried salvia next," Vlad whispers. "Then they'll drink mint tea and chew on fresh salvia leaves."

In the distance a wolf howls. A Şolomonar tilts back his head and answers. I clutch Vlad's cloak, not from fear but because I remember Vlad's wolf howl while telling a story to Vlăduţ.

Vlad gives me a hard look, as though he knows my thoughts. "Şolomonari are descendants of the ancient Dacians, a clan whose essence springs from the wolf."

"What's happening?" I point to the river where a thick mist swirls above the water.

"The summoning." His voice is reverent, almost dreamy.

The mist shimmers as it blooms ever outward and closes in on the Şolomonari. They throw their torches into the blaze and lift their wineskins to their mouths. The mist responds by thickening, condensing its luminous spectrum of greens and blues.

"What is it?" I whisper despite an ancient knowing from deep in my soul of souls.

"The door to the other realm."

The Şolomonar closest to the riverbank melts into the otherworldly mist.

Sensing my fear, Vlad holds my hand, and I watch enthralled and appalled while the mist swallows every Şolomonar. I squeeze his fingers tight as the mist stretches across the clearing and into the forest.

"Does it know?" I ask as vaporous fingers reach forward, thinning as it dissolves through the trees.

Vlad wrinkles his nose. "Does the mist know what?"

I shrug, afraid to say I believe the mist is sentient. Aware.

Yet that is impossible. "I don't know. I…" I look back at the clearing. "They're gone."

The clearing is empty. No trace but for a pile of ash. I follow Vlad out from under the willow branches and toward the vacant circle.

"The mist took them." I wrap my arms around myself, a sinister cold melting into my bones.

"The mist is the door." Vlad stirred the ash pile with his boot. "The year I had finally decided to run into the mist you were pregnant with Vlăduţ. I couldn't go. Didn't know if I could return." Vlad squats down, picks up a stone, and rubs his thumb across the smooth gray surface. "Şolomonari are flesh and blood, as tangible as this stone, and yet they vanish like the *moroi*, phantoms of the dead." He stares up at me, his green eyes bright. "Do you understand my obsession? Why I must discover their secrets?"

"For Wallachia or for yourself?"

"They are one in the same." Vlad stands, tosses the gray stone back in the ash. "Ancient wisdom is more than just controlling demons, summoning storms, or curing people of supernatural ills. It's about communicating with the divine. There once was a time when men spoke to God and angels walked the earth. The Şolomonari's book is the connection to that divine."

"Have you tried any of the rituals?" Was it a Şolomonari's ritual that infected Vlad with the mystical illness that almost killed him?

"One. A simple restorative to chase away my inner demons." He taps his temple.

Vlad's inner demons are many, the result of too many years held captive by Sultan Murad and King Matthias. Too many betrayals. Too much sorrow. The murders of his father, mother, and eldest brother.

"It worked?"

"I've come to accept aspects of my life with less...rage." The moonlight bathes his sad smile in blue shadows.

I slide my hands down his grizzled cheek. Wiggle his chin. "Please do not attempt any extreme rituals."

"I will promise no such thing. It's why I've kept the book, Ilona."

Vlad and Sultan Mehmed are more alike than they know. Each bent on conquering. Of achieving more than others. I don't tell him this. No one wants to be told they are like their enemy.

As the horses plod through the narrow path an unnerving sensation claws down my spine, scratching raw a primal fear. I glance over my shoulder and my heart stops.

The mist follows us, reaches toward us, one serpent-shaped finger slithering around trees and gliding over the trail in pursuit.

"The mist!" My heart in my throat, I dig my gloved fingers into Vlad's arm.

Vlad looks back and clicks his tongue. The horse breaks into a gallop.

"It's gaining on us!" I pound his arm. "Go faster. Faster!"

Vlad urges the horse faster, my heart galloping in time. The steed outruns the mist, and by the time we reach the road it is gone.

"What would have happened if it had caught us?" The question stammers out between trembling lips.

"The mist is a door to the other realm," says Vlad after a few moments of silence. "Maybe it wants me to enter." He grunts a sigh. "But without knowing what's on the other side, I can't. Not with you and the boys to care for. Not with Wallachia in trouble."

"Maybe one day we will enter together. When we know what to expect," I say to appease him.

"You would come with me?" Vlad's voice is pitched with astonishment.

"I would go anywhere with you."

The journey home is quiet and gives me time to reflect on Vlad's desire to understand and control the earth's most mysterious forces. He is a knowledge seeker, a ravenous reader, a commander, and an imaginative thinker. Learning is his air: curiosity, his lungs.

Weary from our nocturnal travels after returning home, I curl under the blankets for a nap.

Seven Şolomonari dance in my dreams. They howl at the sky as the mist spins around them like a gyre. All they leave behind is a crimson fire, which I walk towards. Yet it is not flames I come upon. The earth spews blood that sizzles and burns like fire. I wake in a sweat, terror slashing at me like a wild beast.

## 47

**Late Spring 1474**

A chubby fist curls around my finger as I kiss lavender-scented cheeks. My Luminita. Vlad names her, says she is a tiny spark kindled from my bright torch.

"She's beautiful." Vlad sits beside me on the bed, an oblong gift in his hand.

"Unwrap it for me. I don't want to wake our sleeping angel." I have no need of gifts. I have everything. A loving husband. Two healthy sons. A daughter.

Vlad unties the ribbon, lifts the lid, and tilts the box.

I wrinkle my nose. "A dagger?"

"Yes, your very own. Hold it. Feel its weight in your hand." Vlad takes Luminita from my arms and nuzzles her warm head.

I trade a warm soft babe for a cool sharp weapon and lift the jewel-encrusted hilt from its silken nest. "Exquisite." My fingers brush across the carved golden hilt before sliding off the sheath of the four-inch blade. "Who is the voluptuous woman holding the severed head?"

"Judith."

"Who?"

"The Jewess who beheaded Holoferes, a general of Nebuchadnezzar. He was bent on starving to death the inhabitants of Bethulia. Judith seduced the general, then while he slept she cut off his head and saved her people."

"I don't recall that story in the Bible." One finger follows the curves of the intricate carving.

"The Council of Nicea rejected that particular text from the canon." Vlad snorts with derision. "A horde of ignorant, self-seeking clerics if you ask me."

I slide the sheath back on. "Thank you. I will treasure this gift."

"It is not for treasuring, *iubirea mea*. It is for using."

"What?" I blink, unsure if I heard correctly. "Why?"

Vlad's brow lowers, weighty with purpose. "Luminita was conceived in the armory, the result of our fierce passions. You will wear it. Keep it concealed in your skirts. Sew pockets if you must."

I swallow hard. "Are the children and I in danger?"

"I smell change in the air." Vlad closes his eyes and inhales, his lips thinning into a smile. "It's the scent of blood and battle, a perfume that heralds my return to the throne." He kisses Luminita's cheek. "After your lying-in, I will teach you how to use the blade."

I force a wan smile. "Not for chopping heads, I hope."

"For wounding and killing. I'll show you how to kill like an assassin, even when a man wears full armor." Vlad passes Luminita back to me. "I hope Luminita will be as beautiful and brave as her mother, although I doubt it is possible." Vlad stands. "I await your return to my bed."

ON THE LAST day of my lying-in, Rareş raps on my chamber

door. "Prince Vlad demands you appear at supper." His characteristic smile, part smirk, part guileless grin leaves me clueless. "Your ladies are also invited."

I choose my most fetching frock. It is as pink as a virgin's cheeks and presents my milk-full breasts like a creamy gift.

Gizella secures my pearl and emerald necklace. "This is new."

"Another gift from Vlad." I blush, recalling the lewd act I engaged in to pleasure Vlad. When he had suggested it, I had been mortified, but after wine, his tongue, and a smear of my own slippery nectar I let him send me into a paroxysm of vulgar bliss. I cleared my throat, the memory causing my buttocks to clench.

Bernádett and Gizella don their best livery, and together we join eight of his most trusted friends for dinner. Each is a man of valor and intelligence. Each refuse to kowtow to Sultan Mehmed. Each denies Radu's sovereignty.

At a table laden with trenchers of meat, fowl, fish, venison, platters of vegetables, bowls of stews, and trays of stuffed pastries, I indulge in tasty food and delicious conversation.

"A toast." Wearing a cat-ate-the-mouse grin, Vlad hoists a golden chalice. "To my faithful boyars, my devoted wife, my allies far and near, to the King of Hungary, my cousin Stephen, and..." He smacks his fist on the table, "to my brother Radu for deserting his castle in Bucharest."

Everyone speaks at once.

Vlad stays their questions with an outward palm. "I received a letter from Prince Stephen today. His campaign against Radu was victorious. Radu fled Bucharest. He left everything behind; his wife and daughter, his standards and banners, his robes and armor, and his jewels and prizes."

"Who wears the Wallachian crown now?" asks Andrei, an unmarried chisel-jawed young boyar who has been flirting with Gizella since we sat down.

"My old rival Basarab Laiotă." Vlad flashes his wolf grin.

R. Farma nods, unsurprised. "I suppose Radu went running to Sultan Mehmed, and is this very moment scheming his comeback."

"Radu's days are numbered." The dashing Andrei steals a glance at Gizella. "Disease weakens his body and mind."

"True," says R. Farma with a catlike purr, "but we all know Basarab Laiotă will kowtow to Sultan Mehmed with almost the same passion as Radu."

A sprightly gray-bearded boyar snorts. "Bah, Basarab and Dăneşti are cockfighting for the Wallachian henhouse."

R. Farma stands and raises his goblet. "King Matthias knows there is only one warrior with enough experience and skill to keep out the Turks. Prince Vlad."

The chamber erupts into a clamor of approval and table banging.

Vlad's sparkling eyes sweep over the guests, resting briefly on me. "It is time for the return of the true prince."

Later that evening after returning to my chambers, Bernádett stands by the hearth and gnaws on her lips. "My lady on the throne, how wonderful. I will have many more duties, I suppose."

I pat her arm. "Yes, and a new position, more money, and your own staff."

"My own staff?" Bernádett's face brightens for a moment before darkening with worry. "That would be wonderful, my lady."

Gizella joins us by the hearth. "Since we are discussing the future, I must tell you that should Andrei ask, I am willing. Most willing." Her teeth rake over her lips with a naughty smile.

"It would be a good match. I'll ask Prince Vlad." I turn to Bernádett. "Should I ask about finding a husband for you, as well?"

Bernádett's brows jump to her hairline. "I…I…" She stares dumbstruck at me.

"Is that a yes?" She deserves a husband and a family after years of faithful service.

Bernádett drops her gaze. "Do not trouble Prince Vlad with such foolish matters."

## 48

**Winter 1474**

A bloodcurdling shriek comes from the mezzanine. I drop the platter of food.

Bernádett, screaming and wild-eyed, flies down the steps and falls at my feet. "Nooooooo!"

Panic punches my belly, has me stammering. "W-w-what happened?" I grip the bannister to steady myself, dread slithering around my body and crushing my bones.

"Luminita...your beautiful Luminita." Bernádett's voice fractures with each weeping gasp.

My mind stops. My body acts. I kick off my platform shoes, hitch up my skirt, and race to the second floor.

Too many steps. The hall is too long! The nursery too far!

I hurl myself around the corner, see the teary-eyed servants backed against the walls. "No. No. No."

Dădacă, crouched on the floor, buries her face in her hands and rocks back and forth. "My lady...my lady..." Sobs choke her voice.

"Luminita!" I run into the bright ray of sunlight gilding her bassinet.

My joy, my sweet, my little light is as still as a statue. I touch her face, serene but for a hint of a smile—that milk drunk smile before falling asleep. Her chubby hands grasp the blanket. I lift my cherub, hold her limp body to my breast and put my finger under her nose. There is no breath. No rise and fall of her chest.

"My baby, my baby. Sweet Luminita, wake up, wake up, your *mami* is here." I kiss her forehead, cheeks, and lips. "*Mami* is here. Please no…God…please no…" The howl of the damned spews from my throat. My knees give out. I sink to the floor and rock my daughter. Back and forth…back and forth…Luminita…My daughter…The world melts away…

Two arms lift me from the floor. Two hands pull Luminita away.

"Nooooo…" I claw the air.

Vlad passes Luminita's body to the priest and gathers me in his arms. "She's in heaven now, *iubirea mea*. Heaven is the best place for angels." He strokes my hair while I sob into his chest.

The nursery is dark when he carries me to his chambers and sets me on the bed.

"Drink." He holds a chalice to my lips. "More."

My head grows heavy and my limbs won't move, yet I feel the steady rise and fall of Vlad's chest…

I wake groggy and drained of energy. Outside, angry gray clouds smother the sunlight.

"Vlad." Hot tears pouring down my cheeks, I open my arms.

Vlad is slumped over, his red-rimmed eyes shadowed purple. He pushes the plate of bread and cheese across the table. "Eat."

"I'm not hungry." My lips tremble and phlegm runs from my nose. "My belly is too full of grief."

Vlad glares at me, his jaw tight with anger. "Luminita will be buried today. You will attend."

"No." My head shakes, twitching with each ragged breath. "I will not see her in a coffin." My chest heaves and tightens, my grief like a vice, squeezing-squeezing.

Vlad's eyes taper into slits. "You will attend. You are a princess. You must bear all tragedies with dignity and grace."

"To see her little body interred in a crypt? No. I refuse to listen to the priest's speech of heaven and God's will. I will tear his heart out if I have to listen to one damned word of it."

Vlad's sorrow slips from his face, transforms into a cold cruelty I have never seen before. He knocks the chair to the floor, crosses the chamber, and wrenches me from the bed, his fingers a vise around my wrist. "You will get up and attend our daughter's funeral rites."

"NO!" I try to yank my arm away.

Vlad jerks me close, his eyes ice, his grip unyielding, his face sinister. "Behave like a princess, wife." He twists my arm. "Grieve later. Today you will honor our daughter with your presence." His fingernails dig into my skin as he lifts my chin. "The world is harsh. God is cruel." His lips smash into mine. A loveless kiss.

"I hate you." My hand flies at his face but Vlad catches it.

Nostrils flaring, Vlad releases me. "Do not confuse your emotional weakness with my request for moral strength."

I stalk to the table, grab a vase and hurl it at the wall. "NO!"

Vlad quirks an eyebrow.

I snatch a small ivory-inlaid coffer and fling it against the wall. "NO!"

Vlad selects a small marble vase from his desk and sets it in my hands. "Do it like you mean it."

The vase is heavy, though not near as heavy as the weight of my sorrow. I look for a target and then launch the marble vase at a stone frieze of Christ and his apostles. It shatters. Stone fragments scatter everywhere.

"Feel better?" Vlad crosses his arms, a strange glint in his eye.

"Yes. No. I hate God, and I hate you." I put on his robe and tie the sash. "I will attend Luminta's funeral but do not expect to see me again for a month." I walk to the door.

"On the contrary, *iubirea mea*, we must attend Matthias's Christmas festivities in a few days."

SNOWFLAKES fall like icy tears as we glide across the frozen Danube. I huddle beneath my furs and shiver. It's no use, after Luminita's death I cannot get warm. Neither wool or fur or wine melts the ice lodged in my soul. Vlad, impervious to cold, adjusts a fur blanket over the napping Vlăduț and Nicolae.

I long to share my heart with Vlad. Need his comforting words. Since my tirade he avoids private conversation. At first, I was furious because he was angry at me. But today his soft eyes suggest a different reason. He gives me time to collect myself, to fortify my emotional wall, to lock away my treasured sorrow and find a safe place for its key.

"Vlad..." It is a sigh.

Vlad closes his eyes for a long moment and breathes deeply. His hand finds mine under the fur blanket. "I know, *iubirea mea*. I know." He turns to me, his eyes red, and pulls me close while my shoulders shake with soundless sobs.

Vlad squeezes my hand. "Be strong, my princess. Bury your pain deep. No one expects you to be happy, but we must make an appearance." He blots my tears as the sleigh nears the palace. "A princess must hold her head high no matter the condition of her heart."

Ivy, holly, and yew garlands drape Buda castle's great hall. Magicians, jugglers, and minstrels entertain bejeweled guests. Pork, beef, fish, and fowl steam hot on the tables.

There are pies, custards, meat-filled dumplings, and fruit-sweet tarts enough to feed the whole of Hungary. It is a lavish celebration I no longer admire. Too many poor go hungry these winter months.

Margit, her face flushed from wine, wends her way around the tables toward me. Her bug-eyed husband, Mátyus Maróti, holds her elbow to steady her staggering walk.

"Oh, how I miss all this." Margit flings her arms into the air. "The people, the entertainers, the extravagance. It's glorious. Matthias spares no expense." She throws an icy scowl at her husband.

"The benefits of being a king, my sweet." Mátyus Maróti's tone is one of resigned tolerance.

A moment later Mátyus Maróti and Vlad seek out King Matthias, leaving Margit and I staring at each other.

"I'm sorry for your loss." Margit puffs out her lower lip in a pathetic show of false sorrow. "But you should count your blessings. You have two sons. I don't have any children." Margit frowns into her goblet. "I live on Hungary's most fertile soil and yet my husband's seed doesn't sprout a single crop."

"You were pregnant when you left Buda." I tap my chin. "With your secret lover's child, wasn't it?" Vlad's child she had insinuated.

Margit's cheeks flush even redder. She quaffs her goblet and smacks her lips. "Oh, that. I was mistaken."

"About the lover or the pregnancy?" I want to watch her squirm, hear shame in her voice.

Margit swipes another goblet from a passing servant, shoves the empty one at him. "I was a foolish girl then. I have a woman's problems now. Mátyus demands a child. But...he...it's up, it's down, it's off before he plows my field. I've consulted midwives, even a whore." Margit wrinkles her nose. "I'm desperate enough to lay with a stable boy."

I try to pity her, but I cannot. It serves her right. "Have you?"

"No." Margit bristles. "Disgusting." Her eyes fix on my emerald necklace. "Look at you. Glittering with jewels. Princess of Wallachia. Where's your throne?" She smirks and leans close. "You stole him from me, probably sucked his cock in a closet. He was mine." Her eyes narrow into slits. "I used to be jealous, you know. Then I heard the rumors." Her face scrunches. "Deplorable."

Rumors? I roll my eyes and turn to leave.

Margit snags hold of my forearm. "I heard he teaches you to kill like an assassin. That you debase yourself by playing the whore to his disgusting pleasures. That he takes you in unnatural ways." Her eyes glitter with malice.

I take a page out of Vlad's own battle strategy book. I fight fire with fire. To end this once and for all. To make her so fearful of me that she will cower forever. "It's true. Vlad taught me how to kill. I can gut you in an instant. I have the knife right here." I pat my skirt. "He is my husband and master, and I do his bidding. And my reward is that he does mine." I flick my eyes furtively from left to right. "Though he does not yet sit on the Wallachian throne, he wields a covert influence and power enough to…." My mouth moves to her ear. "To harm his enemies and my enemies." My cheek brushes hers. "As you know, Vlad is a master of vengeance."

Margit swallows and backs away, my whisper louder than cathedral bells.

The horror in her eyes tingles my skin with wicked satisfaction. I bite back a grin, appalled to be happy about her misery. May God have mercy on my soul.

We depart Buda two days later, our tedious obligation done. I long for solitude and the comfort of my own bed. And Luminita's crypt needs fresh greenery.

"I had an interesting conversation with Matthias." Vlad settles back in the carriage. "He confessed to being displeased with Basarab Laiotă. Seems the foot-licking usurper of my kingdom has become a sniveling sycophant who sucks on Sultan Mehmed's toes."

"You predicted this months ago." I rest my hand on his leg.

"*Da*. But I did not predict Pope Sixtus asking Matthias to start a crusade against the sultan. And I never imagined Matthias agreeing."

"What changed Matthias's mind?"

"He finally understands that Sultan Mehmed will invade all of Christendom—Hungary, Moldavia, Venice, Transylvania, Wallachia, Poland, and Bohemia." Vlad takes my hand and rubs it across his rough unshaven face. "Only one man is capable of stopping Mehmed."

I gasp. Suddenly understand. "The man sitting beside me?"

"My sitting is never idle." Vlad taps the side of his head. "A thousand battle schemes gather like storm clouds inside me. My fury will rain down upon Mehmed with such force his army will drown in the quagmire of my tactical superiority."

I suck air through my teeth. Squeeze my fingers around his. "You'll go to battle." And leave me.

"The second Matthias gives me an official pardon."

"My mind is divided, my lord. The selfish half doesn't want you to leave. The selfless half is excited it is finally happening for you…for us."

Vlad strokes my cheek. "My mind is wholly focused on killing Mehmed. Last time we met on the battlefield he scurried away like a cur with his tail between his legs. This time, he will swallow my blade." He sets a soft kiss on my lips. "And I will reclaim my throne."

I BREATHE IN LILAC, warm milk, and baby. Cheeks wet with tears, I press my daughter's blanket to my breast. Luminita rests eternally in a stone crypt and yet her sweet scent lives on.

Gizella hovers nearby, her lips quivering. "My lady, please let me put away Luminita's clothes."

"I need to do this." I set a pink embroidered dress in the trunk.

Her clothes and swaddling folded, I take a last look before lowering the lid as though it is made of glass. I wipe my eyes and draw a ragged breath. "It is done."

"My lady…" Gizella blows her nose.

"Let's discuss something pleasant. Have you decided on a wedding date?"

"Lord Andrei says we must delay the wedding until after Prince Vlad's crusade against the Turks." Gizella sighs. "Saving Christendom, evidently, is more important than a wedding."

"Not to a bride." I give her hand an affectionate squeeze. "Waiting is never easy." I am still waiting for Matthias to formally pardon Vlad.

"I do hope Prince Vlad's victory is quick. I miss my homeland. How good it will be to hear my native language." Gizella claps her hands. "And live in Prince Vlad's castles. And serve Princess Ilona." She squeals. "It's like a dream come true."

I smile, Gizella's enthusiasm is catching.

Gizella points to the chest. "My lady, I think we ought to put some fragrant herbs in the trunk before we store it. I'll get some from the scullery."

Gizella passes Bernádett in the doorway.

"Why did God take your beautiful Luminita?" Bernádett kneels beside the trunk. "I don't understand. She was healthy. Was it the cost of sin?"

"Sin? Whose sin?" I leap up, press my fingers to my chest. "My sin?"

"Oh, my lady, that's not what I meant. It's only…well, God's love *is* mysterious."

"More like capricious. The only mystery is God's so-called divine judgment." I fold my arms. "God is—"

"Radu is dead." Vlad bursts into the nursery.

I spin around. "Does that mean…" My hand flies to my mouth.

"Yes, my lady. Only one person prevents me from retaking my throne."

"Matthias." It's more hiss than whisper.

Vlad nods. "I'm a royal pardon away from making you a real princess."

"Will he do it?"

## 49

# Vlad

## June 17, 1462
## Carpathian Mountains South of Tîrgovişte, Wallachia

An inky darkness pooled as the sun sunk beneath the horizon. Thick storm clouds smothered the starlight. But that did not prevent Dracula from inspiring the nineteen thousand men-in-arms gathered to hear his speech.

"Tonight we invade the sultan's camp," Dracula shouted. "Tonight we punish the Turks! Tonight your children and your children's children will sing your praises forever! Tonight you will praise God with songs of clashing steel! You will worship God with prayers in the shape of pointed arrows! You will honor God with blood sacraments!"

The men roared their support.

"If you die while your blade scrapes the infidel's bone—if you die while blood spills from a Turk's body—know this! You die with honor! You die with glory! You die for Christendom!"

Like a heavenly choir, the cheers of valiant men on a godly mission rose like thunder over the treetops.

It was a two-pronged night attack. From one side, Dracula's men would lead the raid into the Turkish camp. His trusted boyar Galeş, would attack from the other side. The Turks would be corralled. And slaughtered.

Dracula's men, dressed in clothing taken from captured Turkish soldiers, entered the camp and scattered like seeds in the wind, fast and silent. They set fire to the tents, the signal for Galeş to attack from the rear.

The Turks woke to smoke, fire, and screams. They stumbled, groggy-eyed from their blazing tents. Dracula's men cut them down with swords, morning stars, hammers, and axes. They slashed every Turk in their path. Cleaved limbs from half-dressed janissaries. Chopped heads off of captains putting on armor. Hacked down foot soldiers running to escape. Slave, soldier, cook, janissary, whore. It didn't matter. Dracula's men killed them all, even their stallions, camels, and cannon-pulling bison.

The Turks raised the alarms too late. Much too late.

Dracula did not have time to gloat over the fallen bodies, mangled corpses, blood-drenched wounded, and trampled slaves. He ran through the camp in search of Sultan Mehmed's red tent.

Kill Mehmed first. Then Radu.

A blood-splattered soldier ran up to Dracula. "Prince Vlad."

Dracula squinted, the face before him was too dirty and bloody to recognize, but he knew the voice. "Rareş?"

Rareş smeared the gore away with this arm. "No one has seen Galeş's men. The Turks are escaping out the rear."

Dracula clenched his fists, fury contorting his face. "Galeş will die for his cowardice."

Surprised panic was not enough to win the day. If the Turks managed to marshal, Dracula's men would be outnumbered two to one.

"Retreat," ordered Dracula through his teeth. Better a half victory than a total defeat.

Within minutes, Dracula's nineteen thousand warriors melted like specters into the dark Vlasia forest.

While the sun struggled to break though the heavy morning clouds, Dracula and his personal guard examined each soldier's wound. Those with frontal wounds received money. Those with wounds on the back—evidence of cowardice—were impaled. The first to die—Galeş and his gutless officers.

Their cowardice cost Dracula what might have been his greatest victory. The night raid would have annihilated Mehmed's forces.

R. Farma strode toward Dracula. "The sultan fled his camp. They left all their dead." His hawkish nose creased with disgust.

Dracula blinked. Knew in an instant Mehmed's plan. "He's planning on attacking Tîrgovişte."

"Do we have enough soldiers to defend it?" asked a captain.

"No." Dracula stomped into this tent, his advisors and captains following him inside.

Dracula studied the map on the table. He did not have enough soldiers or cannons.

"My lord," R. Farma slunk through the crowd of men like a cat. "What should we do with all the dead Turks?"

Dracula straightened and laughed, a rumbling chuckle that made R. Farma shiver. "I have an idea."

## June 18, 1462: Outskirts of Tîrgovişte, Wallachia

"If it is *Kazîglu Bey*, Lord Impaler, they want, then it is *Kazîglu Bey* they will get." From atop is horse, Dracula looked out over the field of death stretching half a league wide.

Thousands upon thousands of impaled Turks stood erected like hell's scarecrows. Row after row. The skewered dead, dying, and decomposed would remind Mehmed of Dracula's dominance.

Victims stared sightless into the countryside, the crows having pecked out their eyes. The tattered flesh of skeletal corpses flapped like fabric in the breeze. Flies swarmed around oozing wounds. Limbs torn off by hungry wolves. Not all were dead. Some still lived. They whimpered, moaned, and begged for death, a gruesome chorus that joined the stench like a foul beacon of hell.

Death had a name that day: Dracula. Fear had another: Vlad Ţepeş.

Dracula trotted past the row of carcasses and felt no pity for the cowards, thieves, deserters, and infidels. Each long stake was a mast, each victim thrust through a flag.

"Does my show of strength offend your womanish sensitivities?" Dracula asked when a young boyar put a handkerchief to his nose.

"No, my lord." He jammed the handkerchief back into his shirt.

Dracula breathed deeply. "Ah, the fragrance of victory. A warrior's perfume. Twenty thousand bodies. An impressive welcoming party, don't you agree?"

"Terrifying." The boyar averted his eyes.

"Have you ever witnessed such a glorious sight?" Dracula asked the commanders and boyars accompanying him.

"Better than a thousand cannons." R. Farma nodded and curled his fingers into a fist. "This will crush the Turks' spirits."

"The defense of the damned." A gypsy captain stopped his horse to slice a D into a naked Turk's chest.

"A wall of the wicked," said another.

Dracula gripped his reins. Would his plan work? Would

this forest of the impaled frighten thousands of superstitious Turks into fleeing?

MEHMED'S ADVANCE guard arrived the next morning, took one look at the horrific spectacle, and fled in terror. Sultan Mehmed, skeptical of their report, rode out to verify it for himself.

From atop a knoll, Mehmed wrinkled his nose at the stench carried on the breeze. "Incredible." His respect for Dracula tripled. The audacity! The surly youth he knew long ago had become a master of vengeance and a lord of terror.

Grand Vizier Mahmud shook his head. "What sort of man does this?"

"One capable of conquering the world." Sultan Mehmed clenched the reins. "This land is cursed. The ground oozes blood. The trees weep bile. I imagine even the battlements are mortared with bones. I will let *Kazîglu Bey* have his land." He turned to Radu. "For now."

Radu rubbed his hands together. "Battle is not the only way to conquer a land and its people."

DRACULA'S TRIUMPHANT mood lasted less than a week.

"I swear upon my life, Prince Vlad, I'm telling the truth." The messenger kneeled before him. "Prince Stephen of Moldavia made an agreement with Sultan Mehmed. Both armies march on the fortress at Chilia this very moment."

The boyars' mouths dropped open. Dracula's generals grimaced. Prince Stephen of Moldavia betrayed Dracula?! How was it possible? They had all heard the story of Vlad's and Stephen's narrow escape across Bârgău Pass. They knew of their sacred vow against Sultan Mehmed. What political madness made Prince Stephen break his oath?

Dracula blinked, the room's sudden silence forcing him to bury the deafening rage welling inside him. Unable to look at his advisors, Dracula fixed his attention on the map of the Danube and channeled his anger into strategy. "It appears my cousin places no value on friendship, kinship, and even less on oaths. He will suffer for this betrayal."

# 50

## Ilona

**Summer 1475**
**Dracula's Mansion in Pest, Hungary**

I am naked from the waist up, my hips and legs draped in pin-tucked velvet when Vlad stalks into my chambers. The dressmaker, aghast, throws a length of lace over my breasts.

"I have arrived at a fortunate time." Vlad's lips twitch with amusement. "Out. Out." He flaps his hand.

The dressmaker, her apprentice, Gizella, and Bernádett drop the fabric and hurry from the room.

Vlad holds up a letter, flicks the corner that I may notice Matthias's seal. "My wait is over." Vlad holds the letter just out of reach. "Ah-ah. You need both hands."

I drop the lace, snatch the letter, and skim the document. "Matthias exonerates you of all crimes." I squeal with delight and throw my arms around his neck.

Vlad twirls me about the room. "I'm free! My time...our time was finally come." His gaze drops to my breasts. "God's bones, Ilona, remove these pins or I will rip this frippery in two."

Vlad paces the room like a caged wolf while I pull out the pins holding the skirt together. At long last! Our dream is realized. I fumble with the pins, my hands shaking with excitement.

"First I will fight alongside Matthias's men against the Turks. Then I will fight for my throne."

Pins slip from my fingers and scatter on the floor. I lift the puddle of velvet at my feet and clutch it to my breast. I gulp for air but the room has none. The world spins…

"Ilona?" Vlad leads me to a chair.

I collapse, my limbs liquid. "When do you leave?"

"A few months." Vlad kneels before me, palms my cheek. "What's wrong?"

I shiver and burrow into the velvet. "I'm overjoyed. You and I have waited many years. Too many years. Now the time has come, our dreams made real, and I…"

"Are you afraid?"

"No. I fear nothing." I drop my head in shame. "And I fear everything." I open my palms, lifting and lowering as though mimicking a scale. "Both feelings are equally strong, like two warring spirits within me. One side fears I will go mad worrying about your safety." I make a fist. "The other is fearless and impatient to sit on the Wallachian throne. I have prayed for this day. Prayed for ambitious things I should not."

"What things?" Vlad tilts his head, his eyes searching mine.

"That our sons will rise to great heights. With a prince for a father and a king for a cousin anything is in their reach." I grab Vlad's hand. "Margit has no children. Jusztina is married to a noble of little consequence. Matthias has no legitimate heirs—may never have a legitimate heir—making our sons contenders for the throne of Hungary."

Vlad kisses my fingertips. "The thought has crossed my mind."

"And yet my vaulting ambition stirs another fear." I cover

my heart. "Our sons are in danger. All around them are men who will try to deceive and manipulate and seduce them. Vlăduț and Nicolae are chess pieces in a game they do not understand."

"Then we will make sure they are never pawns." Vlad smooths back my hair and kisses my forehead. "There is plenty of time to plan our sons' rise to power. But right now, I want to celebrate my freedom with you."

"How?"

Vlad pulls the velvet from my body and pounces on my nipples.

THE MANSE BUSTLES WITH DIPLOMATS, boyars, and envoys. Meetings last late into the night.

Fearful of Sultan Mehmed's new attacks, rulers from Venice, Milan, and Rome send their emissaries to hear Vlad's advice. Christendom is under assault, and only one man is capable of thwarting the sultan's plan for world domination. Vlad Dracula.

My husband's past military strategies—once vilified by Saxons and the Hungarian Diet—are now proclaimed righteous, admirable, and inventive.

Vlad spends countless hours with Matthias, advisors, and nobles discussing tactics and logistics, weapons and militias, and alliances. Each day Vlad is one step closer to retaking his throne.

I occupy my days with a sneakier kind of meeting. I gather gossip in the ladies' chambers at Buda.

Bernádett rises from her chair. "I will check on the boys."

"Again?" I pull the thread taut.

Bernádett lowers her voice. "Vlăduț and Nicolae are used to being the center of attention. I want to make sure they are properly entertained."

With my nod she hurries off.

A middle-aged noblewoman with a face as round as her body turns to me. "You're fortunate to have a servant who cares for your children with such devotion."

I agree, but suspicion gnaws at me. It's the second time today Bernádett asked to check on the boys. Vlăduţ and Nicolae are intelligent, curious, and independent. They do not need to be entertained, only corralled.

I set aside my embroidery and hurry from the room in time to see Bernádett's skirt swooshing around the corner. Away from the nursery.

I follow her all the way up the hallway. At the end, Bernádett disappears down the narrow stairwell. I know just where she's going.

After waiting a few moments, I descend, and tiptoe over the well-worn stone floors that lead to the bottlery.

How had she managed to keep her affliction hidden? Bernádett drinks in secret!

I peep around one of the tall racks stacked with wine barrels but do not see her. I inch my way to the next row. Still no sign of her. Did I mistake where she went?

Then I hear her giggle.

My hands pressed against the oak, I peer between two casks.

Bernádett sits on a barrel, her skirt to her waist, her legs locked around the hips of the chief bottler's apprentice.

My heart sinks. Bernádett is ruined. No decent man will want her now...unless the apprentice promises marriage. I gawk, dumbfounded. Pious Bernádett ruts like a whore. How long has she had a lover?

"You're certain she doesn't know?" The apprentice thrusts into her.

"My lady doesn't suspect a thing," Bernádett arches her back. "Oooh, yes, like that."

I do now. Well, at least she found love. Or least the joys of sex.

I slink from the bottlery and return to the ladies' chamber where I find Aunt Erzsébet patting Barbara Edelpöck's shoulder in the corner of the room. A teary-eyed Barbara waves me over.

I sit beside her, sick with worry that something happened to her baby. "What's wrong?"

Barbara blinks back tears. "Lady Erzsébet just told me Matthias announced his engagement to Beatrice of Naples."

"Oh dear." I clasp her hand, her fingers laden with all the rings Matthias commissioned for her.

"He warned me that one day this would happen but somehow I thought...I hoped..." Barbara covers her mouth and shakes her head, which sets all her curls bouncing.

"My son must do his royal duty." Aunt Erzsébet speaks with uncharacteristic gentleness. Ever the skilled diplomat, she knows the importance of being a friend to both her son's bedmates. "It doesn't mean he loves you any less."

Barbara's hand slides to her flat belly. "I will redouble my efforts to give His Highness another son."

"A splendid idea." Aunt Erzsébet nods encouragingly.

A fine idea, if Beatrice of Naples is barren. If not, John and any future sons will be bastards, royal outsiders.

"Excuse me, I need to get something from my chambers." Barbara's lips quiver.

"Poor girl," says Aunt Erzsébet when she departs. "Her future is now quite precarious."

Aunt Erzsébet shifts in her seat, clears her throat, and speaks loudly. "Have you chosen the jewels for your crown, Princess of Wallachia?"

Every lady turns my way, their needles motionless, as they wait for my reply.

Aunt Erzsébet catches me off guard. I am mute, surprised by the question and confused by her motive.

Aunt Erzsébet touches my headdress. "How lovely you will look in a crown. And Vlăduţ and Mircea will make such fine young princes. You must look to your sons' futures. I do hope Dracula's bastard doesn't become a problem. I hear he's an efficient squire and possesses his father's temperament."

She's playing me, and I don't like it one bit. Two can play at this game.

"Oh, Aunt Erzsébet, Mihnea is an extraordinary fifteen-year-old." I press my palm to my heart and sigh with happiness. "He's dutiful, honorable, intelligent, and kind to his half-brothers."

And he will never supplant my legitimate sons.

"How wonderful." Aunt Erzsébet's voice is as sweet and thick as honey. "Are you planning to accompany Prince Vlad on his crusade?"

I aim a steely-eyed glance at Aunt Erzsébet. Her brows jump to her hairline as though my angry look stings.

"Prince Vlad wants me to remain in Pest," I say. These gossip-loving noblewomen will be buzzing for days no matter how I answer.

"That's probably for the best," says Aunt Erzsébet. "Although, I confess, there are benefits to accompanying one's husband to battle."

"What kind of benefits?" asks a very young lady with a heart-shaped face and honest eyes.

"A wife may share in her husband's victories." Aunt Erzsébet settles back in her chair like a queen lording over her court. "And provide wifely comfort during those bleak times when men usually find solace with one of the lice-infested whores following the army."

A newly wed wife of a lieutenant general blanches. "Surely, these whores do not follow them very far?"

"They follow the army everywhere." Aunt Erzsébet sighs and shakes her head. "They camp nearby and walk about with their womanly wares on display. The soldiers get very lonely.

Why, whores earn more during a military campaign than working in a whore house or on the streets." Aunt Erzsébet twists the green vesuvianite ring on her finger. "Whores do their best business with the officers."

Aunt Erzsébet does love to poke the hornet's nest.

"My husband would never have a whore." The lieutenant general's bride jabs her needle into the fabric.

Two silver-haired wives exchange a knowing cackle.

"He loves me," says the bride, her face flushed.

"It's not about love," says the silver-haired wife. "It's about need."

"I'm sure your husband is different." A middle-aged matron tosses a scolding glare to the other women.

They cluck their agreement and reassure the bride's fears.

I clear my throat. "What are the disadvantages?"

"The blood." Aunt Erzsébet closes her eyes. "It flows like a river, the crimson fluid mixing with vomit, excrement, and death." She swallows, her voice brittle and faraway. "The smell." Her whole face contorts, eyes, nose, and mouth pinched tight. "Rotting entrails, putrid wounds, festering gnashes." Her eyes open, yet it seems she looks at a faraway battlefield. "Severed limbs, headless corpses, mangled bodies." She covers her ears with her hands. "I can still hear them moaning, crying, screaming...begging for death."

A dimpled young woman gags, pushes a handkerchief to her mouth. The others are silent, wide-eyed, and horrified.

This is war. Our husbands are warriors. Why are they surprised by brutish behavior?

Aunt Erzsébet shakes her head as though casting off the memory. "Don't worry yourselves, gentle souls. My honest account of battle was for the wife of Vlad the Impaler. You see, Lady Ilona deserves our admiration. She tamed the beast. Her love made Dracula a good Catholic, a loving husband, and a devoted father."

I did not tame the beast. Far from it. My husband released the beast within me.

It is with horror that I realize Aunt Erzsébet's battlefield description fills me with eagerness to join Vlad on his crusade.

## 51

"Please take me with you." I pace the room as the barber scrapes the blade down Vlad's jawline.

The sharp edge at his throat, Vlad's only reaction is an arched brow. Until he dismisses the barber.

"No," he says. "Ask me a hundred times and the answer is still the same."

"Why?"

Vlad looks in the mirror at his short beard, angled to intimidate. "For our sons' safety."

"They will be safe in Buda castle. I know you built the tunnels here but—"

"They need to be in their own home where they are respected and loved." Vlad's voice is razor-sharp. "Where their safety is the only priority."

I dare not argue. Vlad spent too many years imprisoned as a child. The hurt, anxiety, and humiliation will always be with him. The physical, spiritual, and emotional torments he suffered will haunt him forever. His mind will not be changed.

"What about me? How can I make it through the day wondering if you're fucking some whore?"

Vlad dons his robe. "I don't have time for this." He buckles his belt, cinches it around his hard stomach.

"Aunt Erzsébet said—"

"Not now, wife." He snatches a sheaf of documents from the desk, strides across the chambers, and holds open the door.

"When?" I follow him.

Vlad's nostrils flare, his green eyes crystalline cold, and turns to Rareş. "See Lady Ilona safely to her chambers." He strides away, his swaggering walk making me even more determined.

I glance at Rareş, who clears his throat, tugs on his collar, and looks away.

I am determined to accompany Vlad on campaign. I need a plan, a convincing argument. Vlad is a complex man of many faces. But to whom do I make my appeal, the charming prince, stern warlord, loving husband, or doting father?

"Rareş," I say pretending Vlad did not just dismiss me so rudely, "I would prefer you escort me to the boys' study."

Vlăduţ jams a quill into the inkpot when I enter the room. "Lady Mother. Look at this." He pats the paper in front of him.

"What is it?" I look over his shoulder.

"Geometry. Lord Father says it's very important."

Nicolae slides off his chair. "*Mami,* I can't bear to solve one more equation. My head hurts." He puts his hands over his ears and swings his head to and fro.

"Show Lady Mother your sketch." Vlăduţ pushes a paper to the edge of the desk.

Nicolae holds up a charcoal rendering of a cannon.

"Nicolae, this is exceptional." I stare, astonished by the detail. "How were you able to draw it with such accuracy?"

"The envoy who saw the invasion of Constantinople told me all about it. This is the cannon that collapsed the walls.

*Tati* says he will make an even bigger cannon when he sits on his throne again."

"Your father will commission the finest cannon ever made." Of that, I am absolutely certain.

Vlăduţ stands and stretches his arms over his head. "Lord Father said he and the sultan shared the same tutors —*hocalar*, he calls them. He said together they learned about everything in the world. And more."

"This is true." I marvel at his expressions and gestures, which are much like Vlad's.

"Then why is the sultan his greatest enemy? Why did the sultan befriend only Radu?"

"Some friendships demand a price so excessive it's not worth the cost."

Vlăduţ rubs his chin like his father. "Like honor?"

"Yes, honor. Do you understand honor? It's a simple word for a complicated idea, one only time and experience can teach."

"Mmph," Vlăduţ grunts. "Did you know Mihnea is joining the crusade? He visited two days ago and showed us the new horse and armor Lord Father gave him. When will be I be able to ride alongside Lord Father into battle like Mihnea?"

"Not for several more years." I cross the room and look out the window and over the courtyard to the rooftops of Pest.

My sons will leave me for foreign lands and distant battles one day, their only protection alliances, armor, and acumen. Like Father. Like Uncle John Hunyadi. Like King Matthias. Like my husband and every noble boy of a certain age. They will leave behind mothers, lovers, and wives who wring their hands while waiting for word of their wellbeing.

"My lady." The tutor pushes a chair under the desk. "Prince Vlad wants Lord Vlad and Lord Nicolae to join him in the great room when they are finished their lessons."

"Make your father proud," I smile at my sons. "Listen and learn."

They bound after their tutor from the room, leaving me alone.

I pace the boys' study, determined to find a way to convince Vlad of letting me go with him on the crusade. I run my fingers over the books lining the bookshelf. Mathematics, religion, theology, rhetoric, Julius Caesar's battle strategies. Not one book whispers a suggestion.

A moment later, a warm breeze wafts in the window, and with it a daring idea.

GIZELLA RUSHES INTO MY CHAMBERS. "The generals adjourn for the evening."

Finally! I felt guilty about making Gizella keep vigil in the hallway while Vlad and his generals worked past midnight every night this week. I thank her, bid her good night, and lock my chamber door.

I remove the jeweled dagger from its hiding spot in the cabinet, slip it inside my skirt's secret pocket, and head to Vlad's chambers.

"I want to see Prince Vlad," I say to a guard posted at Vlad's door.

The guard raps three times and Rareş pokes out his head. "Prince Vlad is busy, my lady."

I smile sweetly. "I need only a moment of his time."

"Permit Princess Ilona to enter." Vlad's voice comes from within.

I enter, find Vlad hunching over a large map. He lifts his head, his eyes sparkling with vigor despite the dark shadows beneath. Even weariness does not dampen his enthusiasm. Nothing as mundane as fatigue slows down my husband.

"You must rest, my lord." I stand in the middle of the

room, unsure of his mood. "You should not begin the campaign exhausted."

"Sleep is over rated. It interferes with ambition and suspends life." His lips lift into a lopsided grin, our earlier quarrel forgotten. "To what do I owe the pleasure of this unexpected visit?"

I glance over my shoulder. The door is closed. Good. There must be no witnesses to my bold scheme. I straighten my shoulders and inhale courage. "I demand you allow me to accompany you to battle."

Vlad snorts. "You demand, do you? Well, I command you stop your persistent nagging."

Nagging? I bristle at the word, yet I am determined and slip my hand into the secret pocket. My fingers wrap around the hilt, withdraw the dagger, and point the blade at my husband. "And I command that you do. I will be a help not a hindrance. I will mend and wash your clothes, rub your shoulders when they are knotted from troubles. I will comfort the wounded and pray for the dying."

Vlad straightens up, pushes the map away. "There are servants, surgeons, and priests for that." He steps forward, his face devoid of emotion.

"I will comfort you in our special way." I push out my breasts.

"Comfort such as that can be had easily enough." The corner of his mouth twitches as he takes another step towards me.

I turn the blade sideways. "I didn't think I wed a fool."

Vlad presses his lips together in an unsuccessful effort to appear unmoved.

"Come no closer, husband. I can defend myself. You taught me well."

Vlad's eyes flick from the knife to my face, any pretense of indifference lost to an irrepressible grin. "Is that so?"

"I know where to plunge the blade and how to deliver a fatal wound."

"Where might that be?"

My mouth opens in reply. Vlad springs forward. He twists my wrist, wrenches the dagger from my hands, and whirls me about. In half a heartbeat, his one muscled arm tightens around me, one hand holding the blade at my throat.

"This is why you will not accompany me," he growls in my ear.

"God's bones." I burst out laughing before he squeezes the breath almost out of me.

"Your life is no laughing matter, Ilona." He eases his hold, although the cold blade is still at my skin. "The briefest lapse and you are dead. Gutted. Throat slit." Vlad trails the steel tip across the lace trim of my neckline. "In a blink of an eye, a mercenary will slice off your breast—a violence I was falsely accused of." He flattens the blade and drags it over the taffeta bodice to my belly. "In a split second, a mercenary will tear open your womb—a violent act which I do admit to." Vlad rubs his cheek against mine, the bristly hairs sending a shiver down my legs. "You will not accompany me." His breath tickles my ear. "Your presence will make me weak. How will I leave our bed when the warmth of your skin encourages lust instead of leadership? How will I rally my men into ruthlessness after hearing the sweetness of your voice? How can I expect my men to endure misery when your bosom waits to comfort me? No, *iubirea mea*, you must not go, much as I will miss you." Vlad drops the dagger and turns me about until we are face to face.

My breath is ragged, his show of skill frightening. I am no match for a mercenary. "You will be careful, won't you?" My fingernail traces the thin swath of beard angled along his jaw.

"No. Caution does not win battles. Caution will not restore my throne. I will, however, be vigilant in all matters."

I brush my lips across his. "I love you."

"Ilona, words and deeds cannot express my love for you. You are my heart, my soul, my joy." His kisses me deeply, his tongue urgent, his lips needy.

My body responds in an instant. I cling tight to him, suck in his breath, my mouth craving the taste of his lips, the scrape of his teeth.

Vlad pulls away and flicks his lust-glazed eyes at his desk. "Before we indulge, there is a matter we must discuss. Margit's husband, Mátyus Maróti, joined the crusade. You once told me that Margit is unhappy—"

"She's miserable. He cannot perform his husbandly duties. His sword lacks your...penetration." I nip at his chin.

"Shall I appoint him to the advance guard? Make her a young widow?"

"Oh." I blink. Is it that easy to change my sister's life?

A rear-guard position keeps Mátyus Maróti out of harm's way. Margit remains unhappily married and unable to conceive. Sending the inexperienced Mátyus Maróti to the front lines is a death sentence giving Margit a second chance to marry and conceive children. Who may one day compete with mine for titles and power.

"I don't know," I say.

"Decide. Now."

"Keep him far from battle." Revenge tastes sweeter than honey.

Vlad's lips twist into a proud smirk. "You've become as ambitious and heartless as Erzsébet Hunyadi."

I flutter my eyes. "Whatever do you mean?" I drop to my knees and part his robe. "My only ambition tonight is making you beg for mercy."

Vlad's fingers entwine in my hair as he pulls my head forward.

## 52

**Fall 1475**

"Lady Ilona." Someone knocks on my door.

I roll over, my lids heavy with sleep.

"Lady Ilona." Now that someone bangs.

I force open my eyes, see only indigo and lavender shadows in the full moon's ghostly light. It is well past midnight, the time when *strigoi*, if they do exist, walk the earth.

Bernádett's black silhouette shuffles to the door and asks thickly, "Who is it?"

"Rareş."

Bernádett opens the door, the scrape and groan of wood planks against metal and stone too loud in the dead of night.

"Prince Vlad requires my lady's presence at once." Rareş holds a single candle.

"My lady sleeps soundly." Bernádett yawns. "As every sane person does at this hour."

"I'm awake." I roll over.

"Prince Vlad requests you bring the gift honoring your

daughter's birth," says Rareş before Bernádett shuts the door on him.

I rub my eyes. Gift? Then I remember.

"Men," Bernádett grunts as she helps me with my robe. "When their need arises it's never at the woman's convenience."

"A good woman does not whine about a man's needs and is eager to dispense her passion to the man filling her goblet." I give her an impish grin.

"My lady?" She pretends not to understand my pun about her lover's occupation.

"Never mind. Go back to bed." I wait until Bernádett returns to the small room adjoining my chambers before taking the locked chest from the cupboard. After removing the jeweled dagger, I slide it with trembling fingers under my sash and conceal it between the folds of my robe.

Rareş and I move like specters through the dark hallway, the candle's trembling flame struggling to light our path. A draft blows it out the moment Rareş pulls open Vlad's door.

The room is dim, a candelabrum and the hearth's glow the only light. Vlad is dressed in a loose robe, his hair unbound over his shoulders, his hands clasped behind his back as he faces the fire. His dark silhouette is gilded in gold, as though he absorbs its radiance.

The door thuds shut.

"Place it on the table." Vlad does not turn around.

I set down the dagger and go to him. Vlad draws me close, his arms encircling me as we watch the flames dance and sizzle.

"Matthias appointed me commander of his crusade. I will leave earlier than planned."

I lean my head against his chest. "Why?"

"I must set up my headquarters, recruit boyars, and prepare for the return to my throne." He unties my sash and glides the robe off my shoulders. "I need a promise from you."

"Anything, my lord."

"This is no small promise, *iubirea mea*." Vlad strokes my bare breasts and nibbles my neck. "This is an oath, one more important than our wedding vows."

I sigh, my body already aquiver with lustful anticipation. "Whatever you ask I will do."

Vlad's hand moves downward, descending to that needy place between my thighs. "The promise comes with a task."

I rock against his fingers. "Anything, my love."

Vlad turns my chin, our lips meet, and his tongue pushes into my mouth as his fingers below push into my moistness. Locked in this embrace, my passion gathers like a storm.

Vlad breaks the kiss. "I need your courage, *iubirea mea*. And I need your blood."

## 53

# Vlad

**Summer 1462**
**Dracula's Castle in Tîrgovişte, Wallachia**

The Curse of Dracula. That's what the Turk's called it. The Curse of Dracula infested the Turk's homeward bound ships with a deadly plague. The Curse of Dracula sent Sultan Mehmed fleeing back to Adrianople like a wounded dog. The Curse of Dracula caused putrid pus to ooze from Prince Stephen's wounded leg. The Curse of Dracula infected enemy soldiers with a mysterious and fatal disease. The Curse of Dracula punished all invaders of Prince Vlad's domain.

And yet despite Dracula's triumph he was not victorious.

"Radu tunnels like a worm across the countryside. He slithers into the homes of fickle boyars and makes secret alliances and deals in the sultan's name." R. Farma pushed a paper across the table. "The defectors."

Dracula scanned the list. "These are the same boyars who hid in their forest castles while we battled for their freedom." His fist slammed the table. "Imbeciles! These self-serving cretins have zero understanding of the long-term consequences of dancing with the devil."

R. Farma unfolded another paper. "Radu is promising peace through diplomacy. He promises that their children will never be conscripted into the army, that their lands will never be destroyed or used for war, that their castles and villages will never be used to house an army. He promises the merchants more profit and the end of taxes supporting the military."

"No wonder they're easily swayed." Dracula leaned back in the chair and brought his prayerful hands to his lips in thought. "What else?"

"Reduced punishment for crimes."

Dracula closed his eyes and recalled Radu as a child. The sniveling, cowardly, weak-minded, decadent boy had not changed. He should have pretended to be asleep the night Mehmed climbed into Radu's bed. Maybe Radu would have learned to hate Mehmed. Instead, Mehmed seduced him with wine and opiates and orgies until…Dracula shook his head and opened his eyes. "I should have killed him then," he mumbled.

"My lord?" asked R. Farma.

Dracula cleared his throat. "The boyars choose a corrupt peace over moral righteousness. They choose diluted Turkish evil over concentrated Christian good. They choose submissive vassalage to dynamic independence."

A week later Radu proclaimed himself the de facto Prince of Wallachia.

### September 1462: Castle in Arghiş, Wallachia

A CANNON BLAST shook the tower.

Vlad flung the empty wine goblet across the room

where it clattered and skittered across the floor. "I conquered the sultan. Freed my people from Turkish enslavement. And how do they thank me? By following Radu."

"Farmers are eager to return to plow and field." R. Farma glanced at the goblet, familiar with Dracula's angry outbursts. "Merchants are impatient to sell, and the boyars want to get back to their sports and venery. They don't understand your vision."

"Refuse to understand, you mean." Dracula stared out the narrow window into the Arghiş River far below. "Was it a mistake to come here?"

"You had no choice after the assassination attempt," said another advisor.

His hands pressed on either side of the window, Dracula marveled at the vertical tower that dropped thousands of feet into the emerald ocean of trees. "Radu will think I am a coward for hiding behind these thick walls."

"This is the best place," said R. Farma. "And the squads you sent have already delayed the approaching Turkish militia."

Hands braced against the wall, Dracula leaned far out to inhale the green and lofty air. "Any word yet from King Matthias?"

"His army moves slowly and is still quite far away," said a second advisor as another cannon blast rumbled through the castle.

Dracula's gaze swept over the forest to nearby Poenari Hill where Turkish janissaries had set up their bombards and cherry wood cannons. "Let's hope they get here before Radu's janissaries figure out how to breach the fortress."

"What?" Doina, Dracula's mistress, leapt up from the chair. "You told me this castle was impenetrable."

"It is, but every fortress has a weakness." Dracula cast an exasperated glance at his grim-faced advisors.

Doina gulped down her fourth goblet of wine. "I'm afraid, my lord."

"Fear makes poor decisions." Dracula leaned against the wall. "Anger is more practical."

Both walls and floor vibrated with another cannon hit.

Doina ran weeping into Dracula's arms. "When will they stop?"

"They won't." Dracula stroked her back.

Doina looked up through a veil of tears, her chin on Dracula's chest. "What if they breach the castle? Don't let them take me. They'll put me in a harem. Force me to do unspeakable acts. Demand I worship their god."

"No, they'll rape and kill you," said Dracula.

"Noooo." Doina crumbled to the floor as an arrow whizzed over her head.

Dracula snatched it up. "There's a note attached." He unwound the leather string and unrolled the paper.

"Threat or truce?" asked R. Farma.

"Neither. It says, 'I am a distant relative who long ago was taken by the sultan and conscripted into their army. I am a janissary now, but my family and heart will forever belong to my homeland. I urge you to escape. God bless you, Prince Vlad.'" Dracula snapped the bow in half and touched the letter to the wall torch where it burned to ashes. "We need to go. We'll use the tunnel."

Doina heaved herself from the floor, her face wet with tears and pale with a new fear. "*Nu. Nu-nu-nu.*" She walked backwards, her head swinging back and forth. "Please, not that."

"It's the only way." Dracula stuffed a folded map into his satchel. "Do you want to stay here and die?"

"*Nu.*" Wild-eyed, Doina reeled backwards.

Dracula's advisors waited at the door with downcast eyes. R. Farma wondered why Dracula had not sent his mistress away with Mihnea.

Dracula beckoned her foreword. "You put everyone here in danger each moment you delay. Put aside your childish fears."

"*Nu...nu.*" Doina lifted her skirt and climbed onto the window ledge, one hand braced against the stone casement.

Dracula's heart thudded in his chest. "What are you doing?"

"I'm not going. I can't." Her voice choked with heaving sobs. "I... can't breathe in the tunnels. I can't.... breathe." Doina clawed at her throat.

"Please, Doina, get down and come with me." Dracula moved slowly across the room. A few more steps... "I'll carry you through the tunnels, my sweet."

Doina squeezed shut her eyes. "I would rather my dead body be eaten by fish than go in the tunnel."

Vlad stretched out his arm. "Get down. I will help you conquer your fear."

A cannon blast shook the tower. Doina's knee buckled, her foot slipped on the smooth stone. Her hands scratched the air.

Vlad lunged. "Doina!"

Doina disappeared over the ledge.

"Doina," he shouted into the chasm. "NO!" Dracula beat the stones with his fist. "Why?!" He stared at her splayed body on the river's rocky embankment far below...

The mother of his child, his lover...dead.

"May God have mercy on her soul." R. Farma crossed himself. He shifted from foot to foot, uneasy after waiting too long for Dracula to turn around. Every minute lost decreased their odds of escape.

Dracula steadied his heaving breath and racing heart. "Good bye, my sweet," he whispered before turning to face his horror-stricken advisors. "Let's go." He took a torch from the wall and strode through the doorway.

They followed as Dracula raced down the narrow circular

staircase, through the unlit deserted corridors, and into a small courtyard.

"Follow me exactly." Dracula threw his leg over the well's stone wall, found the first foothold and began his descent.

"Brilliant." An advisor climbed in after him.

Dracula sucked in his gut and squeezed through the narrow fissure. His back scraped across the rough rock until he emerged into the tunnel. He stared into the darkness, his heart heaving with pent up grief. Doina would never had made it even this far. Damn the woman for not overcoming her fears! Thank God, Mihnea showed no signs of inheriting his mother's cowardice. Mihnea...no one knew he hid on the island monastery in Arghiş.

R. Farma cleared his throat. "We're all here, my lord."

Dracula swallowed the sorrow wedged in his throat. "Grab a torch and follow me."

Torches lit, they moved briskly through the maze of tunnels. Dracula led the way, each step forward giving him more time to bury his grief next to all the others. Father, Mother, Mircea, Mihály, and now Doina. All dead because of the Turks.

Seven bearded men in wolf skin coats waited at the exit. With the surefootedness of a mountain goat and bear-like strength, the robust and loyal Dobrin brothers guided Dracula and his advisors over the Făgăras Mountains. They trekked across rocky ridges, steep slopes, snow-covered thickets, ice-glazed rocks, and frigid rivers. Their journey ended at the remote Piatra Craiului fortress only a few miles south of Braşov.

"Rally the militia." Dracula flung his coat over a chair. "And find out what the hell happened to Matthias's army."

### Braşov Town Hall

EVERY SEAT WAS TAKEN. Each bench filled. Nobles, advisors, boyars, and envoys stood with crossed arms and grim looks around the table in Braşov's town hall where the air was hot with frustration and cold with false politeness.

Five weeks of talks had come and gone. The nineteen-year-old King Matthias possessed the shrewdness of a diplomat and the patience of a saint. He knew Dracula had nothing to offer but promises, his fearsome reputation, and his ridiculous warning that a Radu-ruled Wallachia would open the door to a Turkish invasion.

King Matthias settled back in the chair. "Are we in agreement then?"

Dracula stiffened. He could not let this boy dictate all the terms. "I don't trust Jan Jiškra. I want another commander to lead your soldiers."

"There's no one else. Return to Piatra Craiului. Gather your men and meet my army in Dîmboviţa where our combined forces will form the vanguard of our crusade against Radu."

"Agreed. So be it." Dracula searched Matthias's deep set and shifty eyes and wondered if he had just made the worst deal of his life.

KÖNIGSTEIN FORTRESS ENJOYED an unusual defensible location. Built on the edge of a high plateau atop a sheer thousand-foot drop into the Valley of the Saxons, it was a short step down for a titan but a challenge for an army to descend.

It took hours for the pulleys to lower all Dracula's soldiers and armaments to the valley floor.

"Ready?" asked Dracula.

He and his last three soldiers peered over the cliff as they waited for the pulley to come to the top.

The wind shifted. The hair on Dracula's neck bristled. He twisted around to the clanging swish of swords unsheathed.

Where moments ago only a few of Jan Jiškra's men stood, now fifty soldiers pointed their blades at him.

"What's the meaning of this?" Dracula's fingers curled around the hilt of his sword.

"Prince Vlad," said the bulbous-nosed Jan Jiškra with an ugly smirk, "by the order of King Matthias, I hereby arrest you."

Dracula's soldiers drew their weapons, but Dracula stayed them. Four against fifty was too many. Even for his fiercest *armaş* captains. Dracula tossed his sword and dagger to the ground. "What are my crimes?"

Jan Jiškra pawed his scraggly beard. "Your crimes?" He flung out his arm. "Your crimes are more vast in scope and measure than the view, my lord." His blade tip scraped a thin bloody line down Dracula's throat. "Had it been my choice, I would bring your head to King Matthias." He dragged the blade to Vlad's stomach. "Regrettably, he bids me to escort you to Buda's dungeons."

"I'm flattered King Matthias insists I travel with such an impressive cadre of soldiers." Dracula squared his shoulders and lifted his chin. "But know this, no dungeon, no chains, no manacles will ever hold me."

# 54

## Ilona

**Fall 1475**
**Dracula's Mansion in Pest, Hungary**

Blood. Vlad needs my blood.

"Blood?" I am not thinking clearly with Vlad's fingers inside me and my body aching for release.

"We will swear a blood oath." Vlad stops his penetrating attentions.

"Yes…later. First, I beg you to finish this task."

Vlad lifts his hand, inhales. "Mmm…we have the rest of the night to finish the task many times over." His fingers curl around mine. "I need a blood oath."

A blood covenant is sacred and binding, a promise of biblical proportions. I will do anything for Vlad, but this fills me with a bone-deep dread.

"What sort of oath requires my blood?"

Vlad leads me to the small table, where tridents of red and green light glint off my dagger's jeweled hilt. And where two documents and two quills are arranged with military precision. The ink bottle is missing.

Vlad sits, and slides one paper forward. "Read. Both documents are identical."

I read the first three sentences, look up, mouth agape and hands trembling.

The candlelight flares in his eyes, his deepest desire blazing his truth. My eyes squeeze shut but it does not stop my grisly imaginings. I can't do this. It's wrong. Immoral. Ungodly.

"Reading is best accomplished with open eyes." Vlad's light tone belies the darkness of his request.

My shoulder sink into my sigh. "I need more than open eyes. I need an open mind." I read the document twice. The true cost of loving Vlad Dracula is never more clear than tonight. "Are you certain you want me to do this?"

"It's the only way." Vlad runs his fingers through his hair, the stray strands of gray shimmering in the pallid light.

"What if I fail? What if something goes wrong? What if— "

Vlad silences my fear with a warm finger to my lips. "I trust you, Ilona. You're the only one who can do this. You must do this for me." His gaze is pleading and hypnotic, warm and comforting, pulling me in.

Like it always does.

I inhale, each breath like jagged shards. I cannot deny him. He is my air. The fire in my soul. The reason my heart beats.

"I'll do it. I swear to you." I lift the quill, the plume's lightness a perverse contrast to the spiritual weight of the oath.

Vlad smiles grimly and takes hold of my jeweled dagger. "I need your arm."

I straighten my elbow, surrendering more than just my bare arm but yielding to dark forces and unholy regencies. Relinquishing all I have ever been taught and been trained to believe.

Vlad kisses my wrist and gazes at me with tender affection. "Ready?"

"Do it." I focus not on my skin but on the blade, the steel as lustrous and skillfully wrought as our marriage.

His needle-thin cut across my arm seeps bright red blood. It is a crimson testament to my unwavering devotion. Vlad sucks my scarlet fluid through the quill.

"Sign both documents." A trickle of blood runs from his mouth as he places the quill into my shaking hand. I sign in my own blood, my name a covenant that must never be broken.

Vlad flips the dagger and offers me the hilt. "Your turn."

The only blood I've ever drawn from him is from raking my nails across his back while in the throes of heavenly ecstasy. This bloodletting is a hellish misery.

"I can't." I wince. "You do it."

"*Da*, you must, *iubirea mea*," Vlad's lips twitch with exasperation. "It's vital to the vow."

Inhaling my courage, I snatch the hilt, our fates forever sealed, our souls forever joined.

Vlad straightens his arm and nods encouragingly.

A morbid but giddy excitement surges through me that I cannot explain. I take another deep breath and draw the blade swiftly across his forearm. A two-inch long sliver of crimson rises from his skin.

"Well done." Vlad grins from ear to ear.

With the second quill, I suck his lifeblood into the plume until I taste its metallic tang.

*Wladislaus Dragwlya*. The sight of my husband's bloody signature is more condemning than my own.

"Are we done?" I shift in my chair. What more can a husband want from his wife? What more can a prince demand of his princess?

"No." Vlad retrieves the *Book of the Şolomonari* from the cupboard and lays it reverently on the table.

The book. The compendium of divine wisdom, ancient incantations, and unholy alchemy will set him free. Give him the solace he has searched a lifetime for. Purify his soul. So why does it terrify me? Its origins are from King Solomon. And he was beloved by God.

Vlad places my hand on the book, covers it with his own. "Repeat after me. We are husband and wife in a covenant before the Divine. Should one deceive the other so the Divine shall deceive the deceiver."

I echo his words, feel a strange energy flutter within.

Vlad's breath is ragged, his eyes lust-glazed. I feel it too. I want him. Need to share his breath, his heartbeat, his skin, his pain.

I go to the hearth and stretch my arms over my head. "Release your pain, my love."

He does.

Hours later as I lie sweaty, sated, and weak from his ministrations, I curl under his arm. Vlad is my salvation as well. He gave me love, children, a title, a destiny, a purpose, a blissful way to release my deepest cravings. Genteel Ilona, false Ilona is put aside that the true Ilona may soar in uninhibited fleshly rapture.

"Fold your copy of the oath as many times as possible." Vlad draws circles on my arm. "Keep it in an amulet around your neck. Sew mine into the shirt I wear under my armor." He pushes a kiss onto my forehead. "You're the bravest woman I know. I have complete confidence that should I die in battle you will complete the Şolomonari ritual."

The molten warmth of afterglow seeps out my pores and turns to ice. "You won't die. We have a country to rule."

## 55

**Winter 1476**

Aparade of advisors, boyars, legates, generals, and messengers come and go all day long. Vlad rarely has time for me, but I do not complain. Ambitious goals require sacrifice. Vlad does, however, send for Vlăduț and Nicolae to join him with the captains in the armory and the advisors in the small council chamber. Learning starts early for heir apparents.

"Lord Father never loses. Never." Vlăduț runs into my chambers one afternoon. "The sultan cowers when he hears Father's name. His janissaries' piss their breeches. They're all afraid of *Kazîglu Bey*, Lord Impaler!" Vlăduț pulls out his sword, a real one, and stabs the air.

I laugh, marveling at how my spirited eight-year-old is already much like his father.

Vlăduț dashes across the room, slashing the sword. "I will be as great as Lord Father. I will slaughter any Turk daring to step even a toe on my land."

"Even if you kill innocent people?" Bernádett looks up from her sewing.

"Lord Father says it is better to be feared than loved." With an arrogant expression identical to Vlad's, Vlăduț twists his sword. "Are you questioning the wisdom of Lord Father?"

"No, my lord, I would never do that." Bernádett offers a meek smile.

"Grrrrr." Vlăduț bares his white teeth, then swivels his blade toward Gizella. "Lord Father says traitors are everywhere. I must be vigilant."

Gizella giggles. "No traitors here, my lord."

I put my needlework down. "Come here."

"*Mami*?" Vlăduț's squeaks, the warrior replaced by the child.

"There is no man greater than your father. No man more fearless or determined to protect Christendom. Mind his words and you will become equally great." I kiss his cheek.

A knock sends Gizella to the door.

"Prince Vlad requests your presence," says Rareş with his usual stoicism.

My heart sinks. It is time. And I'm not ready.

With a brave smile, I follow Rareş through the crowded great chamber, but I enter the small council chambers alone.

Vlad is alone, seated at the end of the long mahogany table. "I leave tomorrow."

My knees buckle, and I grab the edge of the table. "So soon?"

"The army amasses in Arghiş." Vlad interlocks his hands behind his head and narrows his eyes. "Something wrong?"

"No." I will my legs to stiffen and straighten my spine. "It's happening."

"At long last." Vlad brandishes a grin, happiness shining in his eyes. "Remember, no matter what Matthias says, you will not take our sons to Buda. They must remain here with my guards."

I nod. Vlad's caution is not excessive, but a result of his own traumatic childhood.

"Show me your dagger." He glances at my skirt.

I grimace. "I'm not wearing it."

"Ilona…"

"Don't mistake my love of fashion for disobedience."

Vlad springs from the chair and stalks toward me. "Any fashion is destroyed when the wearer bleeds." He takes my hands, kisses each one. "Practice escaping through the tunnel. In the dark. Without lanterns. Without a single candlestick. An attack will come without warning, day or night. Watch for suspicious behavior. Servants, even ours, can be bought with enough money. Most of all, be patient. When my throne is secure I will send for you and the boys. And if…" His eyes narrow into a droop.

I swallow. Force myself to say what he needs to hear. "If that horror comes to pass, be confident that only the devil himself and his demon army will prevent me from completing the Şolomonari ritual."

Vlad rubs my filigree cross between his fingers. "Have you reconciled both beliefs?"

"I suppose." The Bible demands faith, obedience, and prayer. Simple enough. The *Book of the Şolomonari* demands a sophisticated understanding of time, space, and the interconnection of all things—things quite beyond me. Each book espouses a truth. Their truth. But where the Bible reads like a child's primer, the *Book of the Şolomonari* is a master's compendium. "I will combine both Christian dogma and Şolomonari philosophies. Like mixing water in wine."

"Which is the wine?" Vlad quirks an eyebrow.

THE CRESCENT MOON is halfway across the sky when Vlad knocks on my door. I open the door myself—all my ladies and servants dismissed for the night—wearing a linen nightdress of such fine weave it covers my skin like a translucent mist.

Vlad drinks in my body like a man parched for its fleshly sweetness. "This bit of gauze leaves little to the imagination." He skims the neckline with eager fingers.

Hungry for his touch and scent, I fling my arms around his neck.

"*Iubirea mea*, my soul, my heart." Vlad scrapes his teeth over my earlobe.

Molten desire courses through every inch of my body. I want him, my need more urgent than ever before.

Vlad trails his tongue down my neck, blows his hot breath through the linen until he hovers over a rigid nipple, ripe and eager for plucking.

I press his head to my breast. He takes my nipple in his mouth and sucks. Hard. Vlad shifts to the other nipple, latches on like a famished babe, tugging until I grunt with the painful pleasure.

Vlad backs away, smiling at the two round wet spots. I untie his robe, wrap my fingers around his length and tug with deliberate slowness.

Vlad groans, pushes away my hand. "Patience is a virtue." He quotes a line from a hundred-year-old poem.

"I am no longer a virtuous woman, your own lustful ambitions transformed me into an impatient disciple of all your desires." I drop to my knees and pull him into my mouth.

I control him, dominate him, tease and torment him until his legs tremble and his fingers tug my hair. His breath comes faster and faster—

Vlad shoves me back. "*Nu*." He breath is ragged, his eyes glazed with lust. "Not like this."

I cross my wrists and hold them up as an offering.

"Not that either." Vlad scoops me into his arms, strides to the bed, and rips open my nightgown with one yank.

I lie back, amazed by the pure adoration shining in his eyes.

"Vlad…" I hold out my arms.

"Not yet," he rasps.

My toes are first. He brushes his fingertips against them, moves along my arch, and encircles my ankles. My calves and thighs are next. Followed by my hands and arms. His touch is feather light and makes me squirm for more.

"I'm committing to memory that which I love best." Vlad draws circles on my belly. "After each battle I will close my eyes and relive this night, recall every curve and dimple." His fingers slide downward. "I'll remember the whorl of hairs here…here…and here."

Panting, my hips roll upward, and my fingers dig into his hard shoulders.

"*Iubirea mea*," says Vlad. "I will also remember your taste."

He lowers his head and begins anew his journey of memorizing. No inch of my skin is omitted. No crevice or curve not tasted and licked. I lose count of the blissful peaks, each rapture coming like slow waves on a riverbank. By the time he pours himself inside me, I am content to move at his unhurried pace until our spirits join in ecstasy.

I wake at dawn. Alone.

I fling off the blankets and go to the window. The courtyard is already crowded with servants, officers, stable hands, and horses. Day by day, step-by-step, Vlad moves toward his rightful destiny. My destiny. Our sons' destiny.

"Kill them all," I whisper. "Kill every murdering Turk and traitorous boyar. Destroy their unholy ambitions to take away our freedoms. Obliterate their desire to enslave and destroy our faith, country, and family. Teach them a lesson they will never forget."

THE DAY IS cloudless and warm by mid-morning. The entire household staff—guardsmen, emissaries, advisors, elderly boyars, wives, and handmaids—gather in the courtyard to bid Vlad and his entourage farewell.

My forty-four-year-old husband never looked more handsome. The gray strands sparkling in the sunshine are a testament to his wisdom. The tiny creases around his twinkling eyes accentuate his experience. His stride is purposeful, energetic with youthful vigor. My heart aches with pride and love.

Vlad makes a short speech about the crusade. He praises Stephen Báthory, Mihnea, his captains, men-in-arms, and the standard bearers all eager to depart with him.

As the men mount their warhorses, Vlad, hands clasped behind his back, stands before Vlăduț and Nicolae. "What will you do if the enemy tries to kidnap you?"

Vlăduț draws his sword and lunges. "I will stab him through the heart and call him an infidel."

"I will skin him alive," shouts Nicolae.

"Good." Vlad beams. "Listen to your mother. Pay attention to your tutors. I gave them permission to beat you for insolence and laziness."

"Yes, Lord Father," they reply. "May God bless you with many victories."

Vlad turns to me. At his request, my eyes are dry, and I wear my costliest gown, silk brocade threaded with gold and encircled with an ermine collar. Jewels adorn my neck, wrists, and fingers. Even my hair glitters with pinned gems. Also at his request, I did not bathe, my thighs glazed with his seed.

Vlad squeezes my hands, his emerald eyes intent with unspoken words of love and promise. Perhaps those watching thought it strange we did not speak. We had no need. Our eyes hold countless memories of shared pain, pleasures, and promises. We are bound body and soul. United in purpose. Nothing will sever our love.

Vlad bows low, mounts his steed and, with a click of his tongue, gallops out of the courtyard.

"*Mami*." Nicolae tugs at my sleeve. "When will Lord Father return?"

## 56

**November 1476**

*My dearest Ilona,*

*I write with great joy today with news of a happy event, one more heartwarming than all my many victorious battles against the Turks thus far.*

*My erstwhile friend and cousin Stephen, Prince of Moldavia, begged forgiveness for his previous treachery. After I trounced the Turks in Tîrgovişte, my repentant cousin swore allegiance to me once again and together we renewed our pledge to defeat the Turks. Despite all my previous doubts I am confident in our restored friendship.*

My head bobs in approval of Vlad's crafty words. Because letters are often intercepted, he relies on my reading between the lines. Vlad will never trust cousin Stephen again. The betrayal went too deep, and Vlad does not forgive such a gross violation without real evidence of loyalty. I read the next sentence.

*There is more excellent news to report. Stephen Báthory, a man I now call friend, ally, and commander, assisted me in securing Bucharest. Together our strength and skill led to defeating the usurper Basarab Laiotă.*

My mouth twitches. Skill, indeed! Báthory has limited experience in battle and none leading an army, and yet Vlad praises him as though they had equal talent for leadership.

*By the time you read this letter I will be Prince of Wallachia once again.*

I check the date of the letter. November seventeenth.

*It is with immense joy and love that I summon you and our sons to my manse in Sibiu, Transylvania. You will stay there until I am confident all the boyars join me in what will surely be a glorious and prosperous new beginning for Wallachia.*

*Make haste in securing the manse in Pest and attend to those necessities I spoke of before leaving. Soon, my dear wife, we will be together again.*

*V*

I LEAP FROM THE CHAIR, hollering and cheering so loud I must wake the dead.

THE TRIP from Pest to Sibiu is eighty-seven leagues. We begin at dawn each day, not stopping until the sun is low in the sky. Usually we stay at a faithful boyar's home. Other times a monastery. Sometimes, if we are far from a town or friends, we huddle under furs while soldiers guard our conveyance. No one complains. Quite the opposite. Every day brings us closer to Vlad.

"Read the letters again, Lady Mother." Nicolae wiggles next to me.

"You've already heard them three times." Vlăduț elbows his brother in the ribs. "You should have them memorized by now."

Gizella opens the small coffer at our feet. "I wouldn't mind hearing the highlights again."

I lift out the thick sheaf of letters and tap the top. "This one describes your father saving the people of Sabaç from Turkish tyranny. This one," I wag the paper, "explains how he drove the Turks from Srebrenica."

"Read that one." Vlăduț—who's forbidden to unsheathe his sword in this small wagon—jabs and slices at the air with a clenched fist as though dueling. "Take that! Yah!" He swishes his imaginary sword about. "Read the good part."

My finger skims down the page. "'Dressed as Turks, my soldiers mingled with the merchants and Turkish soldiers during market day. They created quite a confusion with their antics, disrupting the stalls, shouting and dancing, and making a nuisance of themselves. The Turks suspected nothing, and we slaughtered them with ease, some while using the chamber pot.'"

"Lord Father is the cleverest man in the world," says Nicolae.

"What about the traitors?" asks Vlăduț. "Did he kill them too?"

"He impales them on a long pole," Bernádett snorts. "That's why he is called Vlad Țepeș, Vlad the Impaler."

"Die-die-die." Nicolae bounces up and down.

I choose another letter. "This one is about cousin Stephen—"

Vlăduţ spits. "The craven traitor."

"They've reconciled," I say.

Vlăduţ scrunches his nose. "Why?"

"Cousin Stephen begged forgiveness for his great wrong and joined your father's campaign."

"Crush the usurper." Vlăduţ balls his fists.

"This letter," I pull another from the stack, "describes the mayor of Braşov begging for a treaty. And this one describes the battle in Prahova Valley where your father and Stephen Báthory met Basarab Laiotă's forces and won."

"When can I fight, Lady Mother?" Vlăduţ touches his sheathed blade. "Why did Lord Father choose Mihnea over me?"

"You're only nine-years-old, his eldest legitimate son. Mihnea is sixteen, a man, and a bastard with little claim to the throne."

Nicolae tugs at my sleeve. "Tell the part where Father sits on his throne."

"The moment your father frees Tîrgovişte, the wretched Basarab Laiotă flees like a whipped bitch, which makes your father Prince of Wallachia once again."

Nicolae and Gizella clap. Vlăduţ hoots and cheers.

I laugh as well and touch my flat belly. If only…

Vlăduţ scratches his cheek, his mouth skewed in thought. "If Lord Father is prince then why are we moving to Sibiu and not to the castle in Tîrgovişte?"

"There are many matters your father must attend to. There are treaties and alliances to forge. Every single Turkish soldier must be driven from the land. He must find and kill Basarab Laiotă. Be patient. A good ruler strategizes and plots his moves with care. We will move to Tîrgovişte when your father's reign is secure." I glance at Bernádett. A single tear rolls down her cheek, for the lover she left behind no doubt. I give her hand a comforting squeeze.

"You've waited a long time to be a princess, my lady."

Bernádett dabs at her watery eyes. "I can't believe it finally happened."

"God rewards the faithful." I take my sons' hands. "Join me in prayer."

## 57

# Vlad

**Spring 1464**
**Székesfehérvár, Hungary**

Vlad Dracula watched Matthias receive the Holy Crown. This coronation legalized his Hungarian reign. Despite his two-year detainment in Solomon's Tower, Dracula was glad for the young king. Though their relationship had begun with betrayal, Vlad now forgave Matthias's youthful mistakes. Procuring the Habsburg estates of the besieged Emperor Frederick had clouded Matthias's judgment. The lure of additional titles, lands, and wealth had suspended Matthias's moral duties to God. And his five-year armistice with the sultan had placed him in a complicated position.

During one of their many conversations Matthias showed Dracula the letters intercepted by his nobles, letters allegedly written by Dracula promising loyalty to Sultan Mehmed.

Dracula exposed them as forgeries. The awkward mis-conjugated Latin. The flowery obsequious tone. The forger had minimal Latin skills and even less understanding of Dracula's life purpose. Dracula would never kowtow, never promise loyalty to Sultan Mehmed. Ever.

King Matthias knew this. After all, it was he who ordered the forged letters written. But he would never admit it. Would never admit Dracula's arrest was a mistake. Never admitted that Dracula's imprisonment caused countless diplomatic problems. Never admitted that many rulers, advisors, and even the pope were displeased. A king never admits he was wrong.

Instead, King Matthias granted Dracula privileges and comforts of an esteemed visiting dignitary.

Dracula kept busy during his two-year stay at Visegrád. He spoke often with Niccolò Modrussa, the Vatican legate sent to write an account of the true events leading to his arrest. Dracula met with foreign emissaries, loyal boyars, wealthy courtiers, prominent nobles, and members of the Diet. He read. He wrote. He studied the *Book of the Şolomonari*. He planned his return to the Wallachian throne.

Two long years.

Now he sat shoulder-to-shoulder with the most influential men in Christendom and chatted about crowns and politics and hunting.

His gaze wandered the cathedral until alighting on the young blonde beauty he met earlier.

Margit Szilágy. His dear friend's youngest daughter. A coquettish and silly girl. Beside her, sat a dark-haired maiden. Ilona, Mihály Szilágy's middle daughter, he recalled. She appeared spirited and curious, observing everything around her as not to miss a single detail. Her face captivated him, although he did not understand why. No single feature in of itself was exceptional, yet as a whole it proved extraordinarily beautiful. She radiated intelligence and pluck, rare traits to which Vlad found himself drawn like a bee to a flower...or a wolf to the moon.

Hours later, after returning from his audience with King Matthias, Dracula sauntered down the receiving line, offered compliments and courtesies to each guest, and hid his impatience to speak to the maiden who had captured his attention.

"Lady Margit." Dracula bowed low. "It is an honor to see you on this celebrated day."

Lady Ilona lifted her head. Once again, Dracula was struck by her essence, sensed a fire raging within her.

Margit curtsied and began to babble. Dracula waited only for the introduction to her dark-haired sister.

"—and have you met my older sister, Ilona?"

Vlad bowed. Lady Ilona curtsied. Their eyes locked.

Her gaze did not waver, and its intensity unsettled him, her brown eyes luminous with a vivacity that bore into his soul. Ilona's fixed look pierced his public veneer, ripped the fabric of pretense and politeness, shred each piece, and left him feeling raw.

Dracula grinned. She would be a fierce and determined princess. This maiden had done what no other woman ever had. Entranced him beyond all measure.

## 58

## Ilona

**December 1476**
**Dracula's Mansion in Sibiu, Wallachia**

I fold Vlad's most recent letter and push it into my bodice close to my heart. Until the next one. Vlad finds comfort knowing his words lay on my breasts like kisses.

Wallachia, Făgăras, and Amlaş are secure. Vlad has only to ready Tîrgovişte castle for our arrival. One more week! I will be a proper princess. Sit on a throne. Learn to rule. Make a difference in people's lives. I can't help but smile. I will now wield more power than Aunt Erzsébet.

Messengers arrive each day. One tells me farmers saw Vlad's men burying treasure. A second confirms all the loyal boyars rally around him. Another reports that Basarab Laiotă gathers his men.

Most news is encouraging. Some, troubling. Like today's news about more skirmishes with Basarab Laiotă's rebel forces.

My hand rests against the dagger hidden in my pocket. "All is well?" I ask the captain when I see the guard doubled outside.

"Yes, my lady." He stands straighter. "Prince Vlad ordered extra guards as a precaution. Do not fret, Basarab Laiotă will be apprehended any day now."

Relieved, I thank him for his service and proceed to the great chamber where my new ladies-in-waiting and servants decorate for the Christmas Eve feast.

Twirling a spray of holly between my fingers, I look about the room. "Where's Bernádett?"

"She's in your chambers, my lady," says Gizella draped in greenery, "trying to match a button to Vlăduț's shirt."

"Well, at least, his didn't tear it this time." I tuck a sprig of holly in my bodice. "I'll be in my chambers."

It is with happy and naughty thoughts about Vlad, that I pull open my chamber door.

Bernádett spins around, eyes wide, jaw gaping.

"What are you doing?" I stare at the book clutched to her bosom.

"The *Book of the Şolomonari* belongs to my uncle."

My mouth goes dry. She knows. How is that possible? "Since when can you read?"

"Long ago my uncle drew a picture of the signs and symbols on the first page. This is their sacred book. Prince Vlad stole it." Her voice is low, tight with anger.

I step forward, my tone light and easy. "Give me the book." I hold out my hand.

"Vlad Țepeş is not worthy." Bernádett steps back. "He's not fit to unlock its ancient secrets."

"How dare you!" My composure snaps like a brittle twig.

"He corrupted you." She retreats, her back to the blazing hearth. "You surrendered to his vile ways with your wicked lovemaking and striving ambition. Do you think I never saw the bruises on your neck and shoulders? Or the chaffed skin around your wrists?"

I push down my fury with slow deep breaths. "He's my husband. I must submit to him."

"You fornicate like demons. It's vile and ungodly." Spittle flies from her lips. "Why do you think God took those two babes and left you only those conceived from pious intimacies?"

I gasp, stagger back. All this time...

Bernádett's lip quivers. "Did you know my mother was your father's mistress?"

"I..."

"You knew," she hisses. "I don't remember Lord Mihály, but Mother spoke fondly of him. She also knew Prince Vlad. She told me stories—horrible stories of his murdering everyone in her village—driving sharp sticks up their buttocks and out their mouths. They were innocent. Poor villagers and unlucky merchants whose only crime was living in a town that harbored his enemy."

"The cost of treason." Rage claws its way past my fragile self-control. "You know nothing about governing—the decisions, the sacrifices."

Bernádett's lip curls with contempt. "Dracula twists your mind."

"He did what every ruler does. He sacrificed a few to save many. Have you forgotten that everything Vlad does is to protect us from the sultan and his quest for world domination?"

Bernádett's head shakes back and forth like a woman possessed. "Dracula is evil. Satan made flesh. He must not have this sacred book, this book of life, when he brings only death." Her eyes flick to the hearth. "I made a vow to my uncle and Mother to burn the book if ever I found it."

I step forward, palms out. "I don't understand. How did—"

"On her deathbed Mother pleaded with your father to take me to Buda. She knew, because my uncle foresaw it, that my future would cross with Dracula's. Don't you see? I'm saving

Dracula from himself by protecting the Şolomonari's secrets."

"All this time you were searching for the book?" I step closer.

"Not always." Shame darkens her face. "I was so relieved when you were engaged to Luigi della Scala. But then you married Dracula and you changed. You believed his lies. Did anything for him. I didn't know what to do and then...then I met Claudius—"

"The bottler's apprentice?" It all made sense now.

Bernádett lifts her pointy chin. "I love him and he...he made me see how important it was to renew my search for the book. This book." Bernádett flings the *Book of the Şolomonari* into the fire.

I lunge at the hearth, fall to my knees. Vlad needs this book! His salvation depends on it! My fingertips brush the spine...

I grab the dagger from my skirt pocket, prod the book away from the flames, and snatch it like a hawk does a rabbit. Only the edges are singed.

I turn on Bernádett, the dagger clutched in my fist. "I can have you killed for this."

Bernádett backs away, her eyes darting to the door. "You'll tell Dracula to impale me, won't you?"

"No, I would never...Bernádett, please I—"

"Too bad he'll never make it back from Bucharest."

Her words punch my stomach, steal my breath. "What do you mean?" I rasp.

"Assassins," she whispers and runs for the door.

The world stops. The room crystalizes into a brilliant clarity. My naiveté falls like scales from my eyes. Rage erupts.

I drop the book, run after her, seize her arm, and wrench the traitorous bitch to the floor. "What assassins?" I straddle her, dig my fingers into her scalp, beat her head against the stone. "What assassins?"

"I don't know," she sobs.

"You traitor! All this time you served me, bathed me, comforted me, held my babes. Pretending all this time!" I smack her.

Blood drips from her nose.

"I never pretended to like Dracula," whispers Bernádett through clenched teeth.

She's right. She never did. She only stopped voicing her opinion after we became engaged. How foolish to keep her in my employ. How reckless to think her duty to me would overcome her hatred of Vlad. I smack her again. It felt good. Very good.

"You're just like him now." Bernádett glares at me through wet eyes. "You have no honor, no remorse."

"There is no honor in your treachery." I twist a clump of her hair in my hand until she winces. "There's no honor in your betrayal of everything Vlad has done for you and his people."

Bernádett spits in my face.

Rage takes over.

I lift the dagger over Bernádett's heart. Plunge it downward through her wool bodice and into her beating duplicitous heart. My wrist twists—like Vlad taught me.

Bernádett gasps, her eyes bulge, her body writhing under me.

"This is for my sons." I drive the dagger back into her. "This is for my dead daughter." I stab her again. "This is for Gizella." Blood spews from her breast, her limbs jerking. "This is for Vlad." I plunge again and again. "Go to hell."

Bernádett's body is still, her face bloodless, life's fluid pouring from her chest and puddling on the floor.

I rise, stand over her, my dress blood-soaked, the dagger dripping crimson in my hand, my heart battering against my chest. If this is the cost of bringing peace, prosperity, and freedom from Turkish domination it is a small price.

Bernádett's body is still warm when I send soldiers to alert Vlad of an assassin in his midst.

## 59

## January 1477
### Dracula's Manse in Sibiu, Wallachia

Gizella, wringing her hands, stands in the doorway. "Brother Constantin, a monk from Snagov monastery, is here to see you."

I leap from the chair. "A monk? Does he have word of Vlad? A letter?" A week has passed since I sent soldiers to Bucharest to warn Vlad. Since then, nothing. No messengers. No news. No gossip. I doubled the guards. Hide behind the mansion's high walls. And wait.

"He wouldn't tell me, my lady."

I rush from the room.

The monk is grim-faced, his hands folded in front of his protruding belly. I sit on the chair, smooth my skirt, and take Gizella's hand in mine as the other ladies-in-waiting gather behind me. "Please sit down, father, you've had a long journey." I indicate the chair opposite.

Brother Constantin sits on the edge of the seat, brings his clasped hands to his mouth, and closes his eyes. When he opens them, they are wet with tears. "Princess Ilona, I bring grievous news. Prince Vlad is dead."

My fingers wrap around the amulet at my neck. Blood pounds in my ears. Our blood vow...

The floor drops away. The room spins. Blackness swirling inward. And then I hear nothing but a tremendous roaring...

"My lady," says Gizella as many hands lift me from the floor. "My lady, can you hear me?"

The spinning roar slows. Stops. My vision clears. My feet touch the floor. I lift my head.

"Do you know the manner of his death?" I do not wipe away my tears.

Brother Constantin nods, his face contorted with grief. "There is some speculation."

"Tell me," I sit up straight, scrape my nails back and forth against my palm. "Leave nothing out."

Brother Constantin drags a handkerchief under his nose. "Two of our monks found his body in a marsh across the lake from the monastery."

"No." My stomach clenches. Bile burns my throat.

"Someone stabbed him in the back." The monk blew his nose. "Many believe Basarab Laiotă made a deal with the Turks. His allegiance to the sultan in exchange for paying the assassination fee, which I heard was so exorbitant it defied all logic."

"It would have to be. The Turks feared the Curse of Dracula." I shake off my ladies' comforting caresses and rise from the chair, wrap my arms around myself, and pace the room. "How did this happen? My husband is always vigilant."

"We believe the assassins—"

I spin around. "More than one?"

"That's the rumor. We think they might have posed as loyal serfs and somehow came into Prince Vlad's service. A steward, a groom, or a cook perhaps. They waited until he was alone to strike."

"Vlad is never alone," I snap. "Where was Rareş?"

"Rareş and ten Moldavian bodyguards, those sent by his cousin Stephen, were out of the room. They ran in as soon as they heard the commotion." Brother Constantin dabs at his sweaty brow with the cuff of his sleeve. "Rareş and the others were hacked to bits."

My knees buckle. I lean on the table, steady myself. "What else do you know about these assassins?"

"Only rumors." Brother Constantin shifts in his seat. "Supposedly, the chief bottler's assistant—"

"Claudius?"

"Yes, that one. He has family ties to Basarab Laiotă and provided some kind of insider information before leaving the king's service."

Bernádett's lover, Claudius. My god, treachery is everywhere. Vlad was right. No wonder Vlad forbade me to take Vlăduţ and Mircea to Buda during his campaign. My sons could have been kidnapped. Or worse. "Where is Mihnea?"

"Gone...disappeared." Brother Constantin shakes his head.

I sift through the possibilities. Mihnea may be in hiding. Buried alive like Vlad's brother. Kidnapped. He's old enough to be a real threat to Basarab Laiotă. And to my sons. Vlad would want me to find him.

Brother Constantin clears his throat, tugs at his tight collar. "There's something else. The Turks claim to have Prince Vlad's head."

"What?" I reel back, horror stabbing at me like a knife.

Brother Constantin jumps up. "It's a lie spread by Prince Vlad's enemies. They have someone's head." He helps me back to my chair.

My hands clench into fists, and I cross my wrists, pressing my arms to my chest, fold into my grief. "I will return to the monastery with you. Prince Vlad asked me to..."

I squeeze shut my eyes, search for the right words, "say a final goodbye before you entomb him in his crypt."

There is a long silence, an awkward stillness.

I open my eyes. "Is that a problem?"

Brother Constantin swallows, tugs at his collar again. "Prince Vlad rebuilt and improved the monastery in many unique ways, but he renounced his Orthodox religion, the faith of his people, for Catholicism. For you."

"What are you saying?" My voice stiffens.

"Prince Vlad cannot be interred in his desired location. We will need to find a more discreet resting place."

Will the insults to Vlad's character never cease? I slow my breaths and sit tall. "Prince Vlad was a paragon of Christianity. A warrior for Christ. An Orthodox in his heart and only Catholic on paper. Everything he did, he did for his people. I will go to Snagov with you, and then we will discuss a suitable location for such a valiant ruler and protector of Christendom."

Brother Constantin mops his brow. "I must caution you, my lady. It's too dangerous to travel through a country of murdering rebels."

I rise from the chair like a queen, fold my hands together. "Gizella, show Brother Constantin to the guest room. We leave for Snagov monastery before dawn." I have a blood oath to honor.

The next few hours are a whirlwind. I send my ladies back to their families. I write a letter to Matthias telling everything I know and beg for twenty-four-hour protection for Vlăduţ and Mircea. They are not safe in Sibiu. I kiss my sons goodbye and order a contingent of soldiers to ride nonstop to Buda castle. I pack a chest of items necessary for the ritual.

I rise before dawn, don a homespun dress, wool cloak, slip a hood over my head, and meet my traveling companions in the stable. The guards dress as farmers, their swords concealed under plain garments.

Night's blackness fades into a deep purple while we ride away on old mares without any emblems, barding, or decorative bridals.

It is a journey of a single sorrow and a thousand tears. I wrap my fingers around the amulet; draw strength from the blood covenant folded inside.

I lose track of time…of the distance traveled.

Father Constantin points ahead. "Not far now, my lady."

Familiar with the hidden path, Father Constantin guides us through a field of towering brown stalks, hoary with frost and glistening with frozen crystals. We make our way through this winter meadow of snow, ice, and barren saplings to a tiny dock where two weathered rowboats bob in the icy Snagov Lake. From here, I see the island monastery, its turrets rising above a leafless copse of trees.

I'm coming, my love, I mouth soundlessly as the guardsmen row across the frigid blue.

"It will be safer if you sit down, my lady," says Brother Constantin.

I shake my head. I must stand. One does not meet destiny sitting down.

The moment the boat knocks against the mooring, I leap out. Brother Constantin, seeing my impatience, hoists his heft over the side and onto the dock.

"Which way?" I ask.

"Follow me, my lady." He hurries up the path.

I stride behind, silently urging him to walk faster over the carpet of ice and mud and brown leaves.

We traipse around a snow-covered garden and pass the bell tower where three large dogs sprawl across the steps.

"This way, princess." Brother Constantin heads toward the chapel, an Orthodox cross etched into its tall oak door.

The chapel's beauty steals my breath. Walls, ceiling, arches, columns, everything is vibrant with painted saints, apostles, angels, fanciful creatures, and the holy family. Azure, cobalt, turquoise, indigo, pink, rose, red, purple, lavender, gold, yellow, and green; it is a divine fantasy of brilliant color. Rows upon rows of icons and portraits checker the walls. No wonder Vlad loved this monastery. It is a joyful artistic testament to God's love.

"Down here, my lady." Brother Constantin enters a small vestibule with a steep stone staircase.

"I'm here, my love," I whisper under my breath as we enter the small crypt under the church.

Brother Constantin lights the lanterns while the guards set the chest beside his coffin.

I walk around the plain coffin, my breath shallow and fast. All our hopes and dreams dead, confined in this wood box. "I need a few moments in private."

"We will wait in the sanctuary above." Brother Constantin shuffles away and the guards follow him out.

When the scraping of the monk's footsteps on the stone steps fades, I close the crypt door.

"My love." My hand flutters down on the coffin like a wounded bird. My heart pounds in my ears. Tears roll down my cheeks as I lift the lid.

My Vlad is covered by a thin shroud, which I peel back with trembling hands.

Breath leaves me. My knees buckle. I grab hold of the coffin, suck in the cold musty air with quick shallow gasps.

It is Vlad Dracula. And not him at all.

My Vlad is life and love and action. A warrior. Statesmen. Scholar. Husband. Father. Sovereign and servant to Wallachia. His wish for his people unrealized and unappreciated. The body in the coffin is a lost wish.

"I am here." I stroke his frozen gray cheek. "I will honor

our blood oath." I set a kiss on his bloodless cold lips, then gaze at the wood slat ceiling. "Forgive me, God Almighty, creator of heaven and earth, for performing this otherworldly ritual in your house. I made a blood oath to my husband, a warrior for Christ, and must honor it." I gulp the air. "You gave Solomon wisdom, great discernment and breadth of mind, like the sand on the seashore," I quote from I Kings. "You loved Solomon despite his hundreds of wives, wealth, and sins, therefore, I beg of you to look kindly on the ritual, which comes from ancient wisdom of your beloved Solomon himself." I stare at the chest on the floor and squeeze the amulet around my neck. "Give me strength."

The time has come.

I reach for the *Book of the Şolomonari* concealed beneath Vlad's formal burial clothes in the chest. I remove the ingredients. Myrrh for prayer. Rosemary for immortality. Sage for purification. Saffron for magic.

I unwrap the sacred woods. Cyprus bark for joining death and immortal spirits of the netherworld. Yew for imbuing the supernatural. A laurel twig for promoting peace, and resin from a tamarisk tree for bequeathing divine grace.

I lay these all out on a wooden table in the exact order Vlad had shown me. I return to the chest to retrieve the other ingredients. These are a mystery to me. Vlad refused to tell me what they were or how he procured them.

I work slowly, uncork the three flasks of liquid and unseal the four packets of colored powders. These ingredients hold the key to Vlad's salvation. Or so he read in the *Book of the Şolomonari.*

Vlad thieved for the ancient secrets written in this book. I murdered for it. His soul is worth the cost.

With a deep breath that does little to ease my worries, I open to the page in the *Book of the Şolomonari* marked with a red ribbon.

I measure ingredients. I infuse. I brush away tears during

the process. I rarify one mixture with fire, smudge the air with another. I recite the incantation. Draw a sign on Vlad's forehead with my finger. Draw another on his palms. I anoint his ears, nose, lips, forehead, eyes, hands, and soles of his feet. The rite complete, I collapse on the floor.

## 60

## February 1477
## Buda Castle, Hungary

After quarreling with the monks about the location of Dracula's crypt, after dressing my husband in the vestments of the Order of the Dragon, after setting his turquoise-inlayed crown and buckle beside him, after the funeral mass, after the monks reveal the location of his secret vault...only then do I depart for Buda.

By day we make good time. But it is the nights I yearn for. Vlad comes to me in my dreams, holds my hand, and takes me back into the past. Together we go into the Buda castle labyrinth where I relive our conversation, each touch, my handkerchief-covered first kiss. Together we ride into the forest where we watched the Şolomonari disappear into the mist. Together we descend into our cavern of fleshly delights where he spanks, teases, and torments me until I convulse with pleasure.

The dreams grow more vivid, each more real than the last. Vlad caresses my body with languid strokes, spreads my thighs, and takes me with such passion I wake in the throes of release. Even in death he brings me to bliss.

As much as I want to lock myself in my Buda chambers and sleep, I cannot. I must plan my sons' futures.

King Matthias insists Vlăduţ, Nicolae, and I make Buda castle our permanent residence. This diplomatic advantage pleases me. My sons are Dracula's heirs. Blood of his blood. Blood of the House of Drăculeşti. Blood of the House of Hunyadi. Blood of the House of Szilágy. My sons must continue Dracula's dynasty.

Matthias promises to finance Vlăduţ when it comes time to battle the usurper Basarab Laiotă. My sons must take their rightful place as princes of Wallachia, Făgăras, and Amlaş. Nothing else matters.

Ten days after arriving in Buda, Matthias summons me to his chambers.

"Mihnea was captured." King Matthias pushes a letter across the table. "The Turks demand I pay the ransom."

I look at the price and grimace. "That's rather excessive for a bastard."

Matthias gives me a hard look. "Mihnea has a claim to the throne despite what you may think."

I lift my chin. "The throne belongs to Vlăduţ."

"I agree, but it will be many years before Vlăduţ is ready," says Matthias as if I need reminding. "A good general does not send his best captains to the front lines." His mouth bends into a devious smirk.

I hear his unspoken plan. Let Mihnea wage war against Basarab Laiotă first. Let Mihnea deplete Basarab Laiotă's wealth and resources. If Mihnea dies, so be it. If he retakes the throne it will only ease Vlăduţ's path.

"Sovereignty is a bloody business." I foresee battles between brothers.

Matthias pushes the ransom letter aside. "I'll arrange for

Mihnea's release. We need the boy. Now, I insist you join the festivities this evening in honor of my new bride."

"I look forward to meeting Queen Beatrice."

I have no desire to engage in idle chitchat or dance with wine-addled courtiers. I attend the party for one reason only, to build alliances that will strengthen my sons' futures.

Matthias's seventeen-year-old bride is plump of cheek and breast, and though she is plain looking she carries herself with the haughty air of a noble beauty. Matthias, grown stout for his thirty-one years, appears well pleased with the fresh-faced youth of Beatrice of Naples.

"She's an excessively proper young woman," I remark to Aunt Erzsébet while watching Beatrice dance.

Aunt Erzsébet nods. "The girl will bring feminine grace and womanly virtues to his court."

Confused, I look at Aunt Erzsébet, who only flaps her bejeweled hand as if discounting her own considerable presence in Matthias's court. Despite having the body and soul of a woman, my aunt thinks like a man.

"Her dowry is worth over two-hundred-thousand gold pieces," adds Zsazsa standing beside us. "I've heard her education is exceptional, far exceeding that of most women."

"She brought her own library," says Aunt Orsulya.

"Then it is a good match," I say. "She and Matthias will always have something to talk about."

"Indeed, Queen Beatrice has rekindled his love of books." Aunt Erzsébet, an unenthusiastic reader but her son's most enthusiastic admirer, smiles proudly. "Matthias plans to have the grandest library in the world. He's already sent scholars to Rome and Venice to acquire new books."

Talk of Bibliotheca Corviniana reminds me of the *Book of the Şolomonari* locked in my cabinet. The book's secrets are too dangerous to be read without a reverent understanding of its power. The problem is, I cannot return it because Vlad never told me where he found it. Bibliotheca Corviniana presents the solution to my problem.

Much later, Aunt Erzsébet sidles next to me. "After John's death I found events like this difficult. Watching the happy dancing couples brought back many good memories. They fade eventually, but there are still times when it seems like yesterday." Aunt Erzsébet sighs. "See that maiden's yellow dress? I wore one like it when I met John. It had red embroidered flowers with tiny yellow centers." Her voice is faraway, her eyes staring into the past, her fingers twisting the vesuvianite ring. "Silly isn't it, remembering such details."

"Your ring," I gesture to it, "did Uncle John give it to you?"

Aunt Erzsébet drops her hands and does something I never saw her do before. She blanches. All color drains from her face. "Yes, he gave it to me when…well, that's not important." She avoids looking at me by pretending interest in the couples parading across the dance floor.

I bite my lip to keep from smiling. Finally. I have discovered Aunt Erzsébet's weakness. The mysterious event connected with her vesuvianite ring. I tuck this bit of insight away for future use.

Aunt Erzsébet's gaze returns to me, her face composed once again. "Our husbands were commanding men. Their strong spirit stays with us. I still hear John's voice on occasion. Memory is powerful. Sometimes I wish I did not hear his advice." Aunt Erzsébet emits a sound between a chuckle and a grunt.

I shift from foot to foot, grief tightening my throat. "I don't know how much longer I can be here."

"You're in mourning, no one will think less of you for leaving early," says Aunt Erzsébet.

"Good, then I bid you good night." I return to my room, but I do not remain there. I throw a thick fur-lined cloak over my shoulders and slide the *Book of the Şolomonari* under my arm. The winter winds blow cold and the castle is drafty, I will be one of many dressed this way as I walk through the castle.

Bibliotheca Corviniana is much different since I was last here. Long cloths drape the tables and shelves. Scaffolding lines the walls. Matthias's renovation is well underway.

I am alone, the copyists, scribes, and illuminators have left for the night. I wander about in the blue half-light, the moon's glow as somber as my deed. In the back of the library where drape-veiled shelves abut the walls, I tug back the velvet to find manuscripts bound with gold, leather, and silk. Those with silver studs and enameled clasps bear Matthias's coat of arms. Beneath the shelves, wooden chests hide the common and poor-quality manuscripts.

In the furthest corner, where neither moonbeam nor sunlight reach, I draw open the drape. Here, a thick veil of dust covers the manuscripts. Below, the trunks are shrouded in darkness. I lift one lid; inhale its musty odors as I dig beneath layers of old tattered stacks. Most are written in Latin and Greek, their authorship unfamiliar, the titles without merit.

I hide the *Book of the Şolomonari* at the bottom. No one will find it. I'm sure of it. After closing the lid, I push it behind another trunk.

I am dusting a cobweb from my skirt when I see it; a red ribbon peeking from between the pages of a nondescript manuscript. I smile, remembering the red ribbon I wore in my hair when Vlad and I explored the labyrinth. I pull the book from the shelf to discover its author and title. It has none.

The first page is blank. The second, third, and fourth as well. A blank book?

The fifth page is written in Romanian and takes me a moment to translate.

*Eleven-year-old Vlad grimaced as his mother fawned over his little brother.*

My mouth goes dry as I translate the next sentence.

"*Radu is seven-years-old, Lady Mother, how will he learn a warrior's courage if you fuss over a scratch on his cheek?*'"

My heart quickens when I recognize the handwriting. It is Vlad's. I finger the ribbon's length. My ribbon. He kept my ribbon. I blink back hot tears and flip through the pages. Vlad wrote this. All of it.

I kiss the cover and hug the book tight to my breast. "How clever of you to leave your memoir anonymous, although I suppose everyone will assume Niccolò Modrussa wrote it," I whisper as though Vlad hears me. The papal legate wrote down Vlad's every word the summer he stayed in Solomon's tower in Visegrád.

Trembling with anticipation, I return to my chambers with Vlad's journal clutched to my bosom.

I sit down, turn the first page, and do not stop reading. The sun slips over the horizon by the time I turn the last page.

My dearest Vlad spent more time imprisoned than free. His father betrayed him. Radu betrayed him. As did cousin Stephen, his boyars, his mistress, even Matthias. So much betrayal and heartache. Vlad loved Romania. Adored his family. Valued his people. Esteemed all that is righteous and honorable. And yet he was maligned and condemned.

The following night I return the book, place a soft kiss on the cover before hiding it behind another. Vlad's memoirs and the *Book of the Şolomonari* must never be found. Not until wisdom triumphs over ignorance.

MY NIGHTS ARE DREAM-FILLED. I hear Vlad laugh, see the crease across his chin, watch him rub the bridge of his nose and tap his lips with steepled fingers while thinking.

My days are busy discussing politics with envoys, talking

over imperial edicts with Aunt Erzsébet, listening to my sons' recount their lessons, and organizing events.

I am returning to my chambers after planning a welcome feast for a Saxon noble when a messenger hands me a letter. It is from Snagov monastery. Asking for donations, I suspect.

Once in my room I send the maidservant on an unnecessary errand. I like reading these letters in private, even if they are just solicitations. I settle into the chair, break the seal with a knife, and unfold the thick paper.

*Dearest Lady Ilona,*

*It is with utmost despair and sincerest apology that I convey the most grievous news concerning Prince Vlad Dracula's tomb. But before doing so, I am compelled to relate the extraordinary events prior to that which I am loath to share. A storm, most wretched with howling wind that felled many mighty trees and demolished our barn and storehouse, descended upon our island monastery. Rain, sharp as needles, drove sideways into the monastery, pelting the earth until we were knee deep in mud. Thunder shook the floor beneath our feet and lightning split a tree in two. Another bolt struck the chapel, causing stones and mortar to crash to the ground. The monks awoke to all this devastation the next morning. Two days passed while we made repairs before we were able to resume those small tasks such as lighting the candles in the crypts and polishing the holy vessels of our divine vocation. On the third day after the tempest, Brother Luke, as is his responsibility, entered the crypt where Vlad Dracula's coffin is interred. At first, Brother Luke noticed nothing amiss save the door was ajar. Fearing wind or water damage, Brother Luke, torch in hand, entered the vault to determine the cause of the breached door. To his great astonishment, he discovered the lid of Dracula's coffin on the floor.*

*Thinking some violent movement of the ground during the storm knocked it off, he stooped over to pick it up. Yet he did not because—my lady, may God and his angels have mercy upon us—the coffin was empty! Neither Dracula's body nor any of the objects interred with him remained. I know not when or by what nefarious means this horror was accomplished. There are not words enough to convey the depth of our sorrow and we beg your forgiveness. Perhaps it is a small consolation to know the monks pray daily for Prince Vlad Dracula's soul.*

*In God's love,*

*Brother Constantin*

THE LETTER SLIPS from my fingers and flutters to the ground.

"Ilona, *iubirea mea*," breathes a familiar voice.

My mind is whirling, so I know my mind hears the impossible. Grief is a trickster bent on deceiving my ears. The voice is only the murmur of fond memory, the hum of deep longing, the song of my sorrow.

"Ilona." It is a whisper now, clear and distinct behind me.

I do not turn around, for more peculiar than the imagined voice is the fragrance of forests, leather, rosemary, and spices. The scent of my husband.

No. I must be mad with heartache. And yet...

If it is Vlad every fragment of my Christian beliefs is torn asunder and shredded to ribbons. The orthodox God replaced by the heretical Divine. If I acknowledge this specter there can be no going back. Frozen with shock I stare ahead, too overwhelmed to look behind me.

"*Iubirea mea*." The voice, Vlad's voice, calls to me again.

This time the summons suffuses my soul, warms my heart, and makes clear every doubt in my mind. I turn, fearless and joyful, to confront the man I know and love so well.

# AUTHOR'S NOTE

Vlad Dracula possessed the mind of a scholar, the body of warrior, and the spirit of a philosopher. He received the finest education available during those harsh times and, like many of his contemporaries, used every tactic possible to maintain his position and power.

There is much speculation about the location of Vlad Dracula's grave, which is not unexpected considering records of his death and burial are contradictory and vague. What is surprising, however, is that Ilona's tomb has never been found either.

Rulers and generals, then and now, often write their memoirs. They share their secrets of success, lament failures, and manipulate the truth. In fact, it would be more curious if Dracula did not write his memoirs.

In the years following King Matthias's death in April 1490, Bibliotheca Corviniana was looted and plundered. His bastard son, John, made off with many illuminated manuscripts before fleeing Hungary. Wladislas, the next King of Hungary, paid scant attention to the library, thereby allowing nobles to swipe manuscripts without a librarian to guard the precious volumes. Louis II was the next ruler to raid the library. When Sultan Solyman invaded Buda in 1526 he commandeered most of the remaining books. Any leftover manuscripts were destroyed from rodents and neglect.

Was Vlad Dracula's journal among them?

Need another decadent and delicious story by Autumn Bardot?

There's more!

Never miss a sneak peek, giveaway, or discount of upcoming novels, and get an Advanced Review Copy of historical fiction by signing up for my newsletter at:
**www.autumnbardot.com**

**Historical Fiction**
**Available summer 2019: *Dragon Lady*.**

"Prostitution required only the violation of my body. Piracy requires my soul. The first enslaved me. The second set me free." Against all odds, a prostitute becomes the most powerful pirate chieftain in the South China Seas. Sold into slavery by her parents, Xianggu works on a floating brothel for ten years before a midnight pirate raid changes her life. Determined to rise above her lowly status, the fearless young woman embarks on a journey requiring beauty, brains, and brawn. Red Flag boss, Zheng Yi, is captivated by the spirited Xianggu and soon makes her his wife. This begins her adventure into the violent world of sea banditry. But Xianggu must do more than learn to wield a sword, sail a ship, and swim across a bay. She must become indispensable to Zheng Yi or risk losing everything, even her life. Amid the famines, feuds, and fighting, Xianggu must battle ancient prejudices and jealous men. In 19th century China, when men made and enforced the rules, the Dragon Lady lived by her own.

### Historical fiction coming fall 2019.
### *The Emperor's Assassin.*

A young herbalist is forced into a world of decadence and corruption when Nero commands her to become his personal poisoner. The story chronicles the life of Locusta of Gaul, a shadowy figure whose poisonous deeds remain only conjectures.

Locusta is not only a survivor, she is a complex and brave woman who embraces her cunning, sexuality, and herbal skills when fate sweeps her into a world of Roman depravity, scandal, and murder. During a time when defying an emperor results in death and treason lurks behind every corner, Locusta must embrace her profession or die. But sometimes love has a different agenda.

### Historical erotica available January 2020: *Confessions of a Sheba Queen.*

A temptress. A jinni. A queen. A determined young woman pursues revenge, lust, and wealth but instead finds friendship, love, and purpose.

Connect with Autumn and visit her at:

www.AutumnBardot.com

Facebook

Instagram

Twitter

Goodreads

Hankering for some erotic fiction?

*Legends of Lust, Erotic Myths from around the World is* fourteen romantic and erotic tales of Vikings, goddesses, shape shifters, jinn, and fae that are sure to take your love of myths to a whole new level!

Start reading on www.autumnbardot.com